TSAR

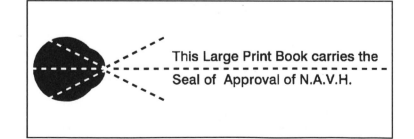

TSAR

A THRILLER

TED BELL

THORNDIKE PRESS

A part of Gale, Cengage Learning

GALE
CENGAGE Learning

Detroit • New York • San Francisco • New Haven, Conn • Waterville, Maine • London

GALE
CENGAGE Learning™

Thorndike Press® Large Print Thriller.
The text of this Large Print edition is unabridged.
Other aspects of the book may vary from the original edition.
Set in 16 pt. Plantin.
Printed on permanent paper.

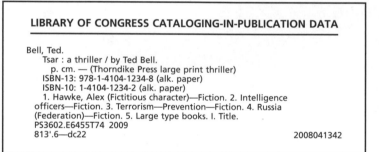

LIBRARY OF CONGRESS CATALOGING-IN-PUBLICATION DATA

Bell, Ted.
   Tsar : a thriller / by Ted Bell.
     p. cm. — (Thorndike Press large print thriller)
   ISBN-13: 978-1-4104-1234-8 (alk. paper)
   ISBN-10: 1-4104-1234-2 (alk. paper)
    1. Hawke, Alex (Fictitious character)—Fiction. 2. Intelligence
officers—Fiction. 3. Terrorism—Prevention—Fiction. 4. Russia
(Federation)—Fiction. 5. Large type books. I. Title.
   PS3602.E6455T74 2009
   813'.6—dc22   2008041342

Published in 2009 by arrangement with Atria, an imprint of Simon &
Schuster, Inc.

Printed in the United States of America
1 2 3 4 5 6 7 12 11 10 09 08

For Page Lee Hufty,
with undying love and eternal gratitude

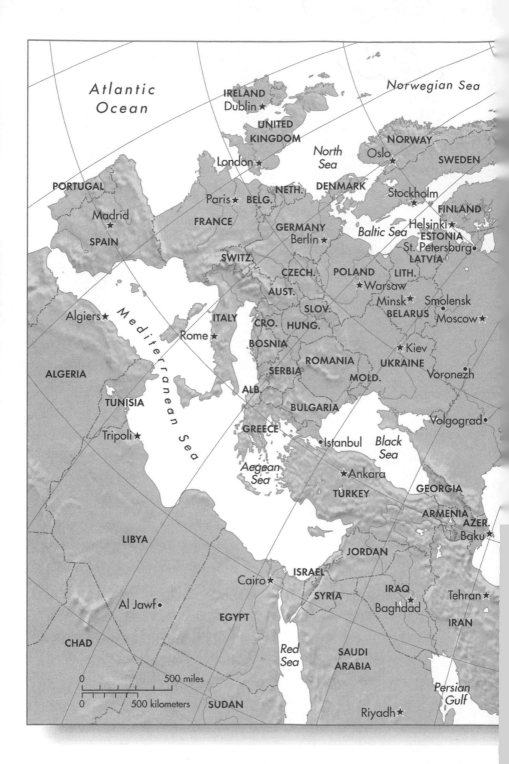

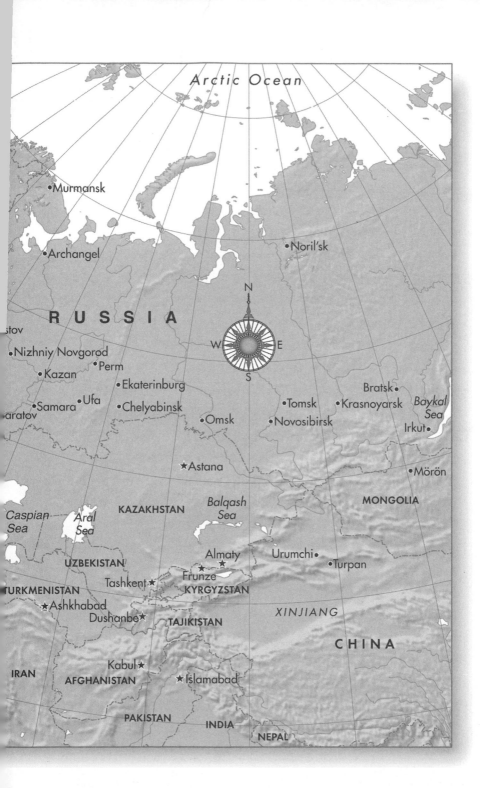

"I cannot forecast to you
the action of Russia.
It is a riddle wrapped in a mystery
inside an enigma."

— *Winston Churchill, 1939*

PROLOGUE

October 1962

The end of the world was in plain sight. Missiles sprouted in the cane fields of Cuba, American and Soviet battleships squared off in the South Atlantic. America's young president, John Fitzgerald Kennedy, had had himself one hell of a week.

The Kremlin's angry salvos continued night and day, as events spun rapidly out of control. Bellicose communiqués volleyed and thundered between Moscow and Washington; frayed nerves snapped and sizzled like live wires at either end. Diplomacy was long past the tipping point, and the old, tried-and-true Cold War rules of engagement no longer applied.

There were no rules, none at all, not now. Not since Russian premier Nikita Khrushchev had started declaring "We will bury you!" to Western ambassadors and banging his shoe on the table at the UN. And certainly not since Castro's imported Russian ICBMs

11

had been discovered ninety miles from Miami.

The once rock-solid fortress of Camelot, the cherished, peaceful realm of the handsome young king and his beautiful queen, Jacqueline, had begun to crumble and crack. And through that ever-widening fissure, Jack Kennedy knew, lay a doorway straight to hell.

Between them, the two major combatants had more than fifteen thousand nuclear warheads aimed at each other's throat. On the borders of Western Europe stood ninety Soviet divisions, ready to roll. America's Army, Navy, and Strategic Air Command bomber squadrons had gone, for the first time in history, to DEFCON 2, a heartbeat away from all-out war. And that's where things had stood all week.

Two helpless giants, afraid to breathe.

Until now.

On this rainy, late October afternoon in 1962, Jack Kennedy was well aware that global nuclear annihilation was no longer the stuff of nightmares; it was right around the corner.

It was closer than Christmas.

At the nightmare's vortex stood the embattled White House. Everyone who worked at 1600 Pennsylvania Avenue was struggling to function for one more hour, one more day, in an atmosphere of impending doom. On people's desks, the faces of cherished children, pets, and loved ones, many framed in crayon-colored Popsicle sticks, never let them forget for an instant what they might, at any moment, lose forever.

The U.S. response time to a Cuba-based incoming Soviet missile attack was only thirty-five minutes. That gave a few lucky White House staffers and high-ranking generals seven minutes to scramble into helicopters bound for the "Rock," a top-secret underground bunker carved inside a Maryland mountain.

Those remaining behind would just have to grab their pictures, shut their eyes, and dive under their desks, like the schoolkids in those pitiful Civil Defense ads on TV. The Desk against the Bomb. It was a sick joke.

Jack Kennedy ducked into a darkened West Wing alcove and popped two Percodans. His Addison's was acting up, his nerves were shot, and his back was killing him. But his brother Bobby was waiting for him in his last remaining sanctuary, the Oval Office, and he headed for the stairs.

Kennedy had just emerged from the Situation Room after yet another superheated briefing with his Joint Chiefs. The hawkish Pentagon brass wanted immediate preemptive nuclear strikes, deep within the heart of Russia. Kennedy wouldn't budge. His Cuban naval blockade, he insisted, was America's best hope of calling Khrushchev's bluff and averting all-out war.

Behind the closed doors of the Oval Office, Jack Kennedy paced before the crackling fire, his public face gone, his private one a rictus of worry and pain.

"You heard about this goddamn Redstick business, Jack?" Bobby Kennedy asked his older brother.

"Hell, it's all they want to talk about down there. Now that they've finally got the stick to beat me with, they are hell-bent on using it."

"Tell me, Jack."

"At the Russian convoy's current speed, the Pentagon calculates Soviet ships will arrive at our outer defensive perimeter in less than seventy-two hours. But based on all this new information we've been getting from British Naval Intelligence, the scales may have tipped dangerously in favor of Russia's submarine hunter-killers."

"Why?"

"The Russkies have some new kind of undersea acoustic technology called SOFAR, an advanced sonar buoy code-named Redstick. Apparently, they can pick up our sub's screw signatures from a thousand miles away. Jesus, Bobby, if it's true, it means our blockade is full of holes. Worthless, just like the Chiefs have been telling me for days."

Bobby, his hands shoved deep into his pockets, his shoulders slumping with fatigue and anxiety, stood staring through the window at the sodden Rose Garden. He wasn't sure how much more bad news his brother could take. He put a smile on his face and turned toward Jack.

"Look. The Brits are on it. All we can do at the moment is being done."

"Any word from them? Christ, we've been waiting to hear something from that sub of theirs since dawn. Timely information from these people is as rare as rocking-horse shit."

"Naval Intelligence London called Defense ten minutes ago. Their sub *Dreadnought* is steaming at flank speed, en route to pick up one of their top field agents in Scotland. A man named Hawke. Sub's ETA at Scarp Island in the Hebrides is oh-six-hundred GMT. Hawke will be inserted inside the Soviets' Arctic Redstick base six hours later. If their man gets in and out alive, we'll know something definitive about Redstick's range parameters, acoustic sensitivity, communication capabilities, and —"

"Fuck the acoustic sensitivity! I want to know how many of these damn things they've got and where the hell they're located! If they're anywhere near our theater of operations, I want to know how fast we can take them out."

"The Brits say we'll have that intelligence in twelve hours."

"Twelve? Bobby, goddamn it, I need this

information *now.* If they've deployed these fucking Redsticks in the South Atlantic, it affects every single defensive operation Admiral Dennison's submarine forces are conducting down there."

"Apparently, Hawke is the best they've got, Jack. If anything can be done, he can do it."

"Well, I hope to God they're right," Jack said, collapsing into his favorite wooden rocker, the one with the cane seat and yellow canvas covering the wooden back.

He rocked as he stared into the fire, desperately trying to come to grips with the fact that he was suddenly entrusting the fate of the whole damn world to some goddamn Englishman he'd never even heard of.

"Hawke?" Jack Kennedy said, rubbing his reddened eyes and staring up at Bobby.

"Who the living hell is Hawke?"

He had a rifle slung on his back and a single bullet burning a hole in his pocket.

His name was Hawke.

He was a hard-hearted warrior in a Cold War suddenly gone piping hot. Killing time before a mission pickup, he was stalking a giant red stag across the rain-swept moors of Scarp Island. The Monarch of Shalloch had eluded him for years. But Hawke's trigger finger was itching so severely he thought this might be the day man and beast would have their final reckoning.

16

Marching along the seaside cliff, head high, Hawke himself was like a stag in a state of high alert. The year was 1962, and he was twenty-seven years old, already an old man in Naval Intelligence. After many long months patrolling these very waters aboard a Royal Navy destroyer, searching for Russian submarines, he'd personally felt the menace and reach of Soviet power. He was always aching to strike back, and it looked as if he might finally have a sporting chance to spill some bright red Russian blood.

He'd arrived on the godforsaken island of Scarp two days ahead of his scheduled submarine pickup, travel arrangements courtesy of the Royal Navy. His mission, Operation Redstick, was so highly classified he wouldn't be briefed until he was aboard *Dreadnought* and headed north of the Arctic Circle. There, on a Norwegian island called Svalbard, was some kind of secret Russian listening post. That's all he knew.

He could guess the rest. It would be his job, he imagined, to find out what the hell the post was all about and then destroy it. Getting out alive would not be mentioned in his brief. But that would be the tricky bit, all right, always was.

Sod it all. He wasn't dead yet, and he still had a few hours left until his pickup. The Monarch, a great red stag, was out there somewhere on the moors or the cliff below.

The single bullet in Hawke's pocket had its name engraved on it. He began a careful descent of the cliff face. It was bitterly cold. A fog was rolling in from the sea. Visibility: not good.

Suddenly, amid the cries of gulls and terns, an odd sound made him look up. Bloody hell, it sounded like the crack of a high-powered rifle!

Another stalker tracking the Monarch of Shalloch? Impossible. This miserable island was inhabited only by sheep, crofters, and farmers. They would hardly be out stalking on a god-awful day like —

Christ! The bastard fired again. And this time, there was no mistaking his target. Hawke ducked behind a rocky outcropping and waited, forcing his heart rate to slow to normal. Another round whistled just above his head. And another.

He caught a glint of sunlight up above, probably reflected off the shooter's binoculars. The man was climbing. Hawke's own position was dangerously exposed. He looked around frantically for cover. Should the man climb even a few feet higher, he'd be completely unprotected. That thicket of trees on the ledge below now looked very good.

Hawke bolted from the now worthless protection of rock and leaped into space. He landed on the ledge on his feet, went into a tuck, and rolled inside the trees. A hundred feet below, the cold and fog-bound sea crashed against ageless rocks.

Five more shots rang out, rounds ripping into the thicket of birch above his head, shredding leaves and branches, debris raining down. Firing blindly now, the shooter knew he was the one exposed for the moment.

Hawke removed the single red-tipped cartridge from his pocket, inserted it into the breech, and shot the bolt.

He took a deep breath and held it, slowing his mind and body down. He was a trained sniper. He knew how to do this. He knew the distance to the target, about 190 yards, the angle of incidence, approximately 37 degrees, humidity 100 percent, wind three to six miles per hour from his left at 45 degrees. One bullet, one shot. You got the kill, or you did not.

Stags, of course, could not shoot back if you missed.

Hawke tucked the stock deep into his shoulder and welded his cheek to it. He put his eye to the scope and set his aim, bisecting the target's form with the crosshairs. His finger closed, adding precisely a pound and a half's worth of pressure to the trigger, not an ounce more. Keep it light . . . deep breath now . . . release it halfway . . . wait for it.

The crosshairs bisected the target's face. That's precisely where he aimed to shoot him. Right in the face. Into his eyes. Shoot him in a part of the skull that would cause irrevocable, instantaneous death.

He fired.

The round cooked off; his single bullet found its mark.

His stalker lay facedown, a pool of dark blood forming under what remained of his head. He was dressed for the hunt, in a well-used oiled coat and twills. Hawke looked at his boots and saw they were identical to his own, custom-made at Lobb's of St. James. An Englishman? He fished inside the dead chap's trouser pockets. A few quid, an American Zippo lighter, a book of matches from the Savoy Grill with a London phone number scrawled inside in a feminine hand.

Inside the old Barbour jacket pockets was nothing but ammunition and a tourist map of the Outer Hebrides, recently purchased. He pulled off the boots and used his hunting knife to pry off the heels. Inside the left boot heel, a hollowed out space had been created professionally.

After opening the small oilskin packet stuffed inside, Hawke found a thin leather billfold bearing the familiar sword-and-shield pin of the KGB. He knew its meaning well enough: the shield to defend the glorious Revolution, the sword to smite its foes. Inside the wallet were papers in Cyrillic, clearly issued by the Committee for State Security, popularly known as the KGB.

Also inside the wallet, a not unflattering photograph of Hawke himself taken recently at an outdoor café in Paris. The woman at the table with him was a pretty American actress from Louisiana. His beloved Kitty. Moments after this picture had been taken, he'd asked her to marry him.

Was this just an isolated assassination attempt, based on his past sins? Or had the KGB penetrated Operation Redstick? If the latter, the mission was clearly compromised. The Russians on that frozen Arctic island would be waiting for him. Losing the cherished element of surprise always made things a bit spicier.

He stood there, looking at the dead Russian, an idea forming in his head. Whitehall could immediately put out a coded signal, on a channel the Russians regularly monitored.

"*SSN HMS Dreadnought* arrived on station 0600 for pickup," the false signal would read. "Two corpses found at site: British field agent and KGB assassin both apparently killed during struggle. Mission compromised, operation aborted per Naval Command Whitehall."

Worth a shot, at any rate.

There was a collapsible spade inside the stalking pack on his back. Hawke slipped out of the canvas shoulder straps, removed the shovel from the pack, and, his spirits lightened considerably, found himself whistling his favorite tune, "A Nightingale Sang in

21

Berkeley Square" as he plunged his spade again and again into the icy ground.

Sometimes a man just had to bury his past and bloody well get on with it.

■ ■ ■ ■

PART ONE:
BLUE DAYS

■ ■ ■ ■

1

Bermuda, present day

War and peace. In Alexander Hawke's experience, life usually boiled down to one or the other. Like his namesake late father, a hero much decorated for his daring Cold War exploits against the Soviets, Hawke greatly favored peace but was notoriously adept at war. Whenever and wherever in the world his rather exotic skill set was required, Alex Hawke gladly sallied forth. Cloak donned, dagger to hand, he would jubilantly enter and reenter the eternal fray.

He was thirty-three years old. A good age, by his accounts, not too young and not too old. A fine balance of youth and experience, if one could be so bold.

Alex Hawke, let it first be said, was a creature of radiant violence. Attack came naturally to him; the man was all fire. Shortly after his squalling birth, his very English father had declared to Kitty, his equally American mother, "He seems to me a boy

25

born with a heart ready for any fate. I only wonder what ballast will balance all that bloody sail."

He was normally a cool, rather detached character, but Alex Hawke's simmering blood could roil to a rapid boil at very short notice. Oddly enough, his true nature was not readily apparent to the casual observer. Someone who chanced to meet him, say, on an evening's stroll through Berkeley Square would find him an amiable, even jolly chap. He might even be whistling a chirrupy tune about nightingales or some such. There was an easy grace about the man, a cheery nonchalance, a faint look of amusement uncorrupted by self-satisfaction about the eyes.

But it was Hawke's "What the hell" grin, a look so freighted with charm that no woman, and even few men, could resist, that made him who he was.

Hawke was noticeable. A big man with a heroic head, he stood well north of six feet and worked hard at a strict exercise regimen to keep himself extremely fit. His face was finely modeled, its character deeply etched by the myriad wonders and doubts of his inner experience.

His glacial blue eyes were brilliant, and the play of his expression had a flashing range, from the merriment and charm with which he charged his daily conversation to a profound earnestness. His demeanor quickly

26

could assume a tragic and powerful look, which could make even a trivial topic suddenly assume new and enlightening importance.

He had a full head of rather untamable jet-black hair, a high, clear brow, and a straight, imperious nose. Below it was a strong chin and a well-sculpted mouth with just a hint of come-hither cruelty at the corners.

Picture a hale fellow well met whom men wanted to stand a drink and whom women much preferred horizontal.

He'd been dozing on a pristine Bermuda beach for the better part of an hour. It was a hot day, a day that was shot blue all through. The fluttering eyelids and the thin smile on Hawke's salt-parched lips belied the rather exotic dream he was having. Suddenly, some noise from above, perhaps the dolphinlike clicking of a long-tailed petrel, startled him from his reverie. He cracked one eye, then the other, smiling at the fleeting memory of sexual bliss still imprinted on the back of his mind.

Erotic images, fleshy nymphs of pink and creamy white, fled quickly as he raised his head and peered alertly at the brightness of the real world through two fiercely narrowed blue eyes. Just inside the reef line, a white sail shivered and flipped to leeward. As he watched the graceful little Bermuda sloop, the sail turned to windward again, and from across the water he distinctly heard a sound he loved, the ruffle and snap of canvas.

No question about this time and place in his life, he thought, gazing at the gently lapping surf: *my blue heaven.*

Here on this sunlit mid-Atlantic isle, peace abounded. These, finally, were the "blue days" he had longed for. His most recent "red" period, a rather dodgy affair involving a madman named Papa Top and armies of Hezbollah *jihadistas* deep in the Amazon, was mercifully fading from memory. Every new blue day pushed those fearful memories deeper into the depths of his consciousness, and for that he was truly grateful.

He rolled over easily onto his back. The sugary sand, like pinkish talc, was warm beneath his bare skin. He must have drifted off after his most recent swim. *Hmm.* He linked his hands behind his still damp head and breathed deeply, the fresh salt air filling his lungs.

The sun was still high in the azure Bermuda sky.

He lifted his arm to gaze lazily at his dive watch. It was just after two o'clock in the afternoon. A smile flitted across his lips as he contemplated the remainder of the day's schedule. He had nothing on this evening save a quiet dinner with his closest friend, Ambrose Congreve, and Congreve's fiancée,

Diana Mars, at eight. He licked the dried salt from his lips, closed his eyes, and let the sun take his naked body.

His refuge was a small cove of crystalline turquoise water. Wavelets slid up and over dappled pinkish sand before retreating to regroup and charge once more. This tiny bay, perhaps a hundred yards across at its mouth, was invisible from the coast road. The South Road, as it was called, had been carved into the jagged coral and limestone centuries earlier and extended all the way along the coast to Somerset and the Royal Naval Dockyard.

Fringed with flourishing green mangrove and sea-grape, Hawke's little crescent of paradise was indistinguishable from countless coves just like it stretching east and west along the southern coast of Bermuda. The only access was from the sea. After months of visiting the cove undisturbed, he'd begun to think of the spot as his own. He'd even nicknamed it "Bloody Bay" because he was usually so bloody exhausted when he arrived there after a 3-mile swim.

Hawke had chosen Bermuda carefully. He saw it as an ideal spot to nurse his wounds and heal his battered psyche. Situated in the mid-Atlantic, roughly equidistant between his twin capitals of London and Washington, Bermuda was quaintly civilized, featured balmy weather and a happy-go-lucky population, and it was somewhere few of his acquaintances, friend or foe, would ever think to look for him.

In the year before, his bout of nasty scrapes in the Amazon jungles had included skirmishes with various tropical fevers that had nearly taken his life. But after six idyllic months of marinating in this tropic sea and air, he concluded that he'd never felt better in his life. Even with a modest daily intake of Mr. Gosling's elixir, called by the natives black rum, he had somehow gotten his six-foot-plus frame down to his fighting weight of 180. He now had a deep tan and a flat belly, and he felt just fine. In his early thirties, he felt twenty if a day.

Hawke had taken refuge in a small, somewhat dilapidated beach cottage. The old house, originally a sugar mill, was perched, some might say precariously, above the sea a few miles west of his current location. He had gotten into the very healthy habit of swimming to this isolated beach every day. Three miles twice daily was not excessive and not a bad addition to his normal workout routine, which included a few hundred situps and pullups, not to mention serious weight training.

His privacy thus ensured, his habit at his private beach was to shed his swimsuit once he'd arrived. He'd made a ritual of stripping it off and hanging it on a nearby mangrove branch. Then a few hours sunning *au naturel,* as our French cousins would have it. He was normally a modest man, but the luxuriant feeling of cool air and sunlight on parts not normally exposed was too delightful to be denied. He'd gotten so accustomed to this new regime that the merest idea of wearing trunks here would seem superfluous, ridiculous even. And — what?

He stared with disbelieving eyes.

What the bloody hell was *that?*

2

A small rectangular patch of blue had caught his eye. It lay on the sand, a few yards to his right. Raising his torso and supporting himself on his elbows, he eyed the offending item. Detritus washed in from the sea? No, clearly not. It seemed that while he'd slept, serene in his *sanctum sanctorum,* some invidious invader had arrived and deposited a blue towel on his shore.

The thing had been scrupulously arranged on the beach by the silent marauder, at right angles to the surf, with four pink conch shells at the corners to hold it in place. There was, too, in the middle of the dark blue towel, a fanciful K richly embroidered in gleaming gold thread. Above the initial was a symbol he thought he recognized, a two-headed eagle. A rich man's beach rag.

Bloody hell. No sight of the owner. Where had he got to, this cheeky Mr. K? Off swimming, Hawke supposed. Why, of all places, should he drop anchor here? Surely, the sight of another man — a nude man, for God's sake — sleeping peacefully here on the sand would be enough to encourage an intruder, this K whoever the hell he may be, to look elsewhere for solitude?

Apparently not.

At that moment, a woman appeared from the sea. Not just a woman but perhaps the most sublimely beautiful creature Hawke had ever seen. She emerged dripping wet. She was tall, with long straight legs, skin tanned a pale shade of café au lait. She was not quite naked. She wore a small patch of white material at the nexus of her thighs and, over her deeply full and perfect pink-tipped breasts, nothing at all.

She wore a pale blue dive mask pushed back above her high forehead, and damp gold tresses fell to her bronzed shoulders. He had never witnessed such raw animal beauty; her presence as she drew near seemed to give him vertigo.

She paused in mid-stride, staring down at him for a moment in frank appraisal. Her full red lips pursed in a smile he couldn't quite read. Amusement at his predicament?

Hawke cast his eyes warily at the mangrove branch some ten yards away. His faded red swim trunks hung from a bare branch among the round, thick green leaves. Following his gaze, the woman smiled.

"I shouldn't bother about the bathing suit,"

33

she said, her wide-set green eyes dazzling in the sun.

"And why should I not?"

"That horse has already left the barn."

Hawke looked at her for a long moment, suppressing a smile, before he spoke.

"What, if I may be so bold, the bloody hell are you doing on my beach?"

"*Your* beach?"

"Quite."

"What does it look like I'm doing?"

She was carrying a clear plastic drawstring bag containing what looked to be small pink conch shells and other objects. Hawke also noticed a line looped around her waist, strung with a few small fish. His eyes had been far too busy with her extraordinary body to register the spear gun in her right hand.

"Look here," Hawke said, "there are countless coves just like this one along this coast. Surely, you could have picked —"

"The shells here are unique," she said, holding up the bag so it caught the sun. "Pink Chinese, they're called."

"No kidding," Hawke said. "Do they come in red as well?"

"Red Chinese? Aren't you the clever boy?" she said, laughing despite a failed attempt at a straight face.

For the first time, he heard the Slavic overtones in her otherwise perfect English. Russian? Yes, he thought, suddenly remembering the double-headed eagle above the monogram, the ancient symbol of Imperial Russia.

She continued to stare down at his naked body, and Hawke shifted uncomfortably under her unblinking gaze. The intensity of her stare was causing an all too familiar stir, both within and without. He thought of covering himself with his hands but realized that at this late juncture, he would only appear more ridiculous than he already did. Still, he wished she'd stop looking at him. He felt like a bloody specimen pinned to the board.

"You have an extraordinarily beautiful body," she said, as if stating a scientific fact.

"Do I, indeed?"

"Light is attracted to it in interesting ways."

"What on earth is that supposed to mean?" Hawke said, frowning. But she'd spun on her heel in the sand and turned away.

She strode lightly across the sand to the blue towel and folded herself onto it with an economy of motion that suggested a ballet dancer or acrobat. Crossing her long legs yoga-style before her, she opened the tote bag and withdrew a pack of Marlboro cigarettes. Then a slender gold lighter appeared in her hand. An old Dunhill, Hawke thought, adding *rich girl* to his meager knowledge base. She flicked it and lit up, expelling a thin stream of smoke.

"Delicious. Want one?" she asked, looking at him out of the corner of her eye.

He did, badly. "You must have missed the 'No Smoking' sign I've posted out there in the surf."

No response to that. She plucked one of the violently pink shells from her bag, dropped it onto the sand beside her, and began sketching it in a small spiral notebook. She began whistling softly as she drew and soon seemed to have forgotten all about him.

Hawke, who felt that her skimpy white triangle of pelvic cloth gave her an unfair advantage, rolled over onto his stomach and rested his head on his forearm, facing the girl. In truth, he would have loved a cigarette. Anything to calm his now disturbed mental state. He found he could not take his eyes off her. She was leaning forward now, puffing away, elbows on her knees, her full, coral-tipped breasts jutting forward, rising and swaying slightly with each inhale and exhale of the cigarette.

Watching her body move to adjust the shell or flick an ash, he felt his heart miss a beat, then continue, trip-hammering inside his rib-cage. It seemed to ratchet, and each thud only wound him tighter.

She smoked her cigarette, not bothering with him anymore, staring pensively out to sea every few moments, then plucking her pencil from the sand once more, resuming her sketch. Hawke, transfixed, was faintly aware that she seemed to be speaking again.

"I come here every day," she said casually over her shoulder. "Usually very early morning for the light. Today I am late, because . . . well, never mind why. Just because. You?"

"I'm the afternoon shift."

"Ah. Who are you?"

"An Englishman."

"Obviously. Tourist?"

"Part-time resident."

"Where do you live?"

"I've a small place. On the point by Hungry Bay."

"Really? I didn't think anything lived out there but those nasty spider monkeys twittering in the wild banana trees."

"Just one small house still standing on the point. Teakettle Cottage. You know it?"

"The old mill. Yes. I thought that ruin blew away three hurricanes ago."

"No, no. It survived," Hawke said, feeling inexplicably defensive about his modest digs.

"Squatter's rights, I suppose. You're lucky the police don't rout you out. Bums and hoboes aren't good for Bermuda's tourist image."

Hawke let that one go. She was staring at him openly again, her eyes hungry and bright. He avoided those riveting emerald searchlights only by looking out to sea, scanning the horizon, looking for God knows what.

"You've got an awful lot of scars for a beach bum. What do you do?"

"Alligator wrestler? Wildcat wrangler?"

The girl, unsmiling, said, "If you're so damned uncomfortable, just go and get your swim trunks. I assure you I won't watch."

"Most kind." Hawke stayed put.

"What's your name?" she suddenly demanded.

"Hawke."

"Hawke. I like that name. Short and to the point."

"What's yours?"

"Korsakova."

"Like the famous Russian composer Rimsky-Korsakov."

"We're better known for conquering Siberia."

"What's your first name?"

"Anastasia. But I am called Asia."

"Asia. Very continental."

"I'm sure that's an amusing joke in your circles, Mr. Hawke."

"We try."

"Hmm. Well, here's Hoodoo, my chauffeur. Right on time."

She pulled a tiny white bikini top from her magic bag and slipped herself into it, one pale and quivering breast at a time. Hawke, unable to stop himself from missing a second of this wondrous performance, found his mouth had gone dry and his breathing was shallow and rapid. Her rosy nipples were hard under the thin fabric, more erotic now that they were hidden.

Hawke again felt the stirring below, suddenly acutely aware of his missing bathing trunks. He quickly turned his thoughts to a humiliating cricket match from long ago, Eton and Malvern at Lord's, a match he'd lost spectacularly at age twelve. That painful memory had successfully obliterated ill-timed desire in the past, and he prayed it would not fail him now.

Seemingly unaware of his agonizing predicament, she quickly gathered her things and leaped to her feet as a small center-console Zodiac nosed into the cove. At the helm was an elegant black man, lean and fit, with snow-white hair. Hoodoo was dressed in crisp whites, a short-sleeved shirt, and Bermuda shorts with traditional knee socks. He smiled and waved at the beautiful blond girl as he ran the bow up onto the sand. There were two big outboards on the stern. Must be four strokes, Hawke thought. They were so quiet he hadn't even heard the small boat's approach.

Hoodoo hopped out of the inflatable and stood with the painter in his hand, waiting for his passenger. He looked, it occurred to Hawke, like a young Harry Belafonte whose hair had gone prematurely white.

Asia Korsakova paused, looked down at

Hawke carefully, and said, "Good eyes, too. An amazing blue. Like frozen pools of Arctic rain."

Hearing no response from him, she smiled and said, "Very nice to have met you, Mr. Hawke. Sorry to have disturbed you."

"Yes. Lovely to meet you, too, Asia," was all Hawke could muster as he turned and lifted himself to say good-bye.

"No, no, don't get up, for God's sake, don't do that!" She laughed over her shoulder.

Hawke smiled and watched her take Hoodoo's hand, step gracefully into the bobbing Zodiac, and perch on the wooden thwart seat at the stern. Hawke saw the name *Tsar* stenciled on the curve of the bow and assumed this was a tender to a much larger yacht.

"Good-bye," Hawke called out as the small boat swung round, turned toward the open sea, and accelerated out of the cove.

Whether she'd heard him or not, he wasn't sure. But Anastasia Korsakova did not turn back to look at him, nor did she acknowledge his farewell. Having deeply resented her intrusion, was he now so sorry to see her go? He'd always been amazed at the way the face of a beautiful woman fits into a man's mind and stays there, though he could never tell you why.

His eyes followed the little white Zodiac until even its wake had disappeared beyond the rocks.

He stood up, brushed the sand from his naked body, and fetched his faded swimsuit. After donning it, he walked quickly into the clear blue water until it was knee high and then dove, his arms pulling powerfully for the first line of coral reefs and, beyond that, his little home on the hill above the sea.

Mark Twain had said it best about Bermuda, Hawke thought as he swam.

Near the end of his life, Twain had written from Bermuda to an elderly friend, "You go to heaven if you want to, I'd druther stay here."

Maybe this wasn't heaven, but by God, it was close.

3

Moscow

The Russian president's helicopter flared up
for a landing on the roof of the brand new
GRU complex. GRU (the acronym is for the
Main Intelligence Directorate, or Glavonoye
Razvedyvatelnoye Upravlenie) was a source
of some amusement to President Vladimir
Rostov. The frequency with which each new
regime changed the names and acronyms of
various institutions was a holdover from the
old Chekist days: secrets within secrets.

Every breathing soul in Moscow knew this
building for exactly what it was: KGB headquarters.

Vladimir Vladimirovich Rostov was a lean,
spare man, a head or more taller than most
Russians, with a dour demeanor and a long,
pointed nose like that of a Shakespearean
clown. He walked with an odd stoop, like
some faux act of courtesy, simultaneously
genteel and insinuating, a walk much paro-
died behind his back in the hallways of the

Kremlin.

His moniker, the Grey Cardinal, spoke volumes.

At this moment, gazing down at the gleaming grey streets of Moscow from the sleet-streaked window of his helicopter, he looked grey and tired. He was within a nose of entering his eighth decade. Although it would be political suicide to admit it, he was feeling every year in his bones as he arrived back in the capital at the end of a long journey. He was returning from naval maneuvers on the Barents Sea.

The endless flight to Moscow, aboard a Tu-160 strategic bomber, had been cold, rough, and uncomfortable. Still, he was happy, all things considered. He'd managed to enjoy two exhilarating days at sea observing military exercises. Russia's reborn Northern Navy had been surprisingly successful in the long-awaited war games. Indeed, the Russian Navy, he would soon report to the GRU, was nearly back to full strength after a decade-long hiatus.

From the bridge of the *Peter the Great,* a nuclear cruiser, the president had stood in freezing rain observing night launches of his newest Sukhoi fighters, taking off from the nearby aircraft carrier. Then, at dawn the next morning, had come the true reason for his visit. A new intercontinental ballistic missile was to be launched from the *Ekaterinburg,*

Russia's latest nuclear submarine.

The missile, a sea-based version of the Topol-M called Bulava, was Russia's most powerful offensive weapon to date, at least three years ahead of anything in the American arsenal. It carried ten independently targeted nuclear warheads and had a range of 8,000 kilometers.

The Bulava launch, to the great relief of all present, had been spectacularly successful. It was believed the Russians now had a weapon fully capable of penetrating America's missile defense systems.

At dinner in the fleet admiral's cabin aboard his flagship that evening, the Bulava Program officers had described how the initial velocity of the new missile would, in fact, make all of America's missile defense systems obsolete. This was a quantum leap forward, and this was the news President Rostov would be carrying home happily to Moscow.

All had gone exceedingly well, Rostov thought, settling back against the helicopter's comfortable rear seat cushion. His report at that morning's top-secret meeting with Count Ivan Korsakov and members of "the Twelve" would be positive, full of good news. This was a good thing, Rostov knew. Count Korsakov was the most powerful man in the Kremlin, and he had little tolerance for bad news. Rostov had learned early in their relationship that for the count, order was the ultimate priority.

On that most memorable day, pulling him aside in a darkened Kremlin hallway, Korsakov had whispered into his ear that Putin would soon be gone far, far away. And that then he, Vladimir Rostov, would become the second-most-powerful man in all Russia.

"Second-most?" the Grey Cardinal had said with his trademark shy grin.

"Yes. You will be president. But we all know who really rules Russia, don't we, Volodya?" Count Korsakov had laughed, placing a paternal hand on his shoulder.

"Of course, Excellency."

Korsakov — the Dark Rider, as he was known — secretly ruled Russia with an iron fist. But since he had no official title or position inside the Kremlin, only a handful of people at the highest echelons knew that Korsakov was the real power behind the throne.

As the president's army MI8 helo touched down on the rain-swept rooftop, he saw his defense minister, Sergei Ivanov, striding out to meet him. A light December rain was turning to snow, and the rotor's downdraft was whipping the man's greatcoat about his slender frame. Nevertheless, Ivanov wore a huge smile. But it was pride in his new HQ, not the sight of the presidential chopper, that gladdened his heart.

Sergei's headquarters, built at a cost of

some 9.5 billion rubles, was the new home of the Russian Main Intelligence Directorate, the GRU. In an exuberant burst of construction, it had been built in just three and a half years, a miracle by Moscow standards. Thus, the minister's smile was justifiable.

The two men shook hands and hurried through the rain to the glassed-in arrival portico.

"Sorry I'm late," Rostov said to his old KGB comrade.

"Not at all, Mr. President," Sergei said. "Still time for us to have a quick look around the facility before the Korsakov meeting. I promise not to bore you."

Overlooking the old Khodynka airfield on the Khoroshevskiy Highway, the GRU's new headquarters stood on the site of an old KGB building long laughingly referred to as "the aquarium." It had been an eyesore, a decrepit reminder of the old Russia. This glass and steel structure was huge, some 670,000 square feet, containing the latest in everything. Defense Minister Sergei Ivanov had seen to that. This was, after all, the New Russia!

Inside the building were a plethora of high-cost secrets and state-of-the-art communications technology. Nevertheless, a large portion of the funds budgeted had been expended toward the construction of the wall that surrounded the building. On their way down to the Situation Room, Sergei assured the president that his new wall could withstand the assault of any tank on earth.

"I'll have to ask our tank commanders about that," Rostov said. Long experience had made him skeptical of Russian military claims.

But during the brief tour, Rostov found himself deeply impressed with the new Situation Center. As was his habit, he chose not to show it.

He casually asked one of the nearby officers, a young colonel, exactly what situations the Situation Center had been designed for.

"Why, practically any situation at all, Mr. President," the man replied, beaming proudly.

"So, did you follow the American Senate hearings on arms appropriations on C-SPAN last night?" Rostov asked, matching the underling's toothy smile tooth for tooth. "That was a situation worth following!"

"Well, not a lot, sir," the man said, fumbling for words. "Some situations are —"

A general stepped forward to cover the younger man's embarrassment. "That's more the job of the SVR, Mr. President."

SVR was the External Intelligence Service. Of course, Rostov knew it well. When Rostov had been head of the KGB, he had been personally responsible for that service's complete overhaul.

"Really?" Rostov said, eyeing the general

with some amusement, "The SVR's job, is it? Isn't that fascinating? One learns something every day."

Embarrassed eyes were averted as Rostov smiled his shy, enigmatic smile, nodded briefly to everyone in the room, and took his leave. Korsakov was waiting upstairs.

"The man's a fool," Sergei Ivanov said in the elevator. "My apologies, sir."

"That ridiculous little general? Yes. Somebody's son or nephew, isn't he?"

"He is. Putin's nephew."

"Get rid of him, Sergei. Energetika."

Energetika was a maximum-security prison on a desolate island off the Kronstadt naval base at St. Petersburg. The facility was unique in the history of Russian prisons. It had been deliberately built atop a massive radioactive-waste site. Prisoners who entered those walls had a death sentence on their heads whether they knew it or not.

Rostov's predecessor, the steely-eyed prime minister who'd overstayed his welcome, was a guest there even now. Rostov wondered briefly if his old comrade Putin had any hair left at all now.

The elevator came to a stop, and they stepped off.

"We've come a long way, Sergei Ivanovich. Eight years ago, we had more important things to do, even in the military sphere, than build fancy administrative buildings. But the

GRU is the eyes and ears of the Russian Army, the entire Russian state to a significant degree. Its workers deserve such modern conditions."

It was true. After the collapse of the Soviet Union in 1991, Soviet intelligence services had embarked on a decade of serious decline. The much-feared KGB, where Rostov had spent his former life, had been an institution in free fall. A great many Soviet spies had defected and sold their secrets to Western intelligence agencies. Communism was dead. MI-6, the formidable British intelligence service, had simply declared its mission accomplished, packed up, and headed home.

Better dead than red, the Brits and Americans used to say.

That era was clearly over.

The Dark Rider, Count Ivan Korsakov, had appeared to save Mother Russia.

With Rostov at his side, Korsakov would now restore Russia to her rightful place in the world.

On top.

4

"Good morning, gentlemen," Count Ivan Ivanovich Korsakov, KGB code-named Dark Rider, said from behind his crimson curtain.

His bottom-of-the-barrel voice, amplified, had a disembodied quality that added to the anxiety of everyone within earshot. He could see them, but they could not see him. Few people, beyond his closest confidants in the Kremlin, were ever privileged to gaze upon Korsakov's countenance. He moved and worked in the shadows.

Never interviewed by the media, never photographed, he was rich beyond measure. The most powerful man in Russia was a very private man.

But everyone in the New Russia and, to some extent, nearly everyone on the planet felt the emanations of that vastly powerful intellect. In the dark, secret chambers at the heart of the Kremlin, Count Korsakov reigned as a virtual Tsar. Inside those thick, red brick walls, erected in the fifteenth century, it was even whispered that one day Korsakov might lose the "virtual" part of that title.

President Rostov, and his *siloviki,* the twelve most powerful men in Russia, filed into Korsakov's private conference room. This splendid gallery, with its huge gilded chandeliers, had been allocated to the count by presidential fiat. It was for Korsakov's personal use whenever matters of state security needed to be discussed at the new GRU headquarters.

The gilt-framed pictures adorning the paneled walls depicted the count's great passion, airships. From an engraving of the first hot-air balloon ever to fly, the one that soared above Paris in 1783, to oil paintings of the great Nazi zeppelins, they were all there. One huge painting, Korsakov's favorite, depicted the German ZR-1 on its infamous night raid over London, its gleaming silver hull glowing red from fires raging in the streets below.

The room was dominated by a table Rostov himself had ordered built from his own design. It was long and could easily accommodate up to twenty-five people on all three sides. It was the shape that was so unusual. The table was a great equilateral triangle, fashioned in gleaming French-polished cherry wood. At the triangle's point, of course, stood the count's large leather armchair, now occupied by Rostov. It was the president's idea of a small joke: there could be only one head at this table.

Behind Rostov's chair hung the very same red velvet curtain made famous during Stalin's reign of terror. At the Kremlin during certain kinds of gatherings, Stalin would sit behind this very curtain, listening carefully to conversations, words of which could often come back to haunt those who uttered them. At the end of the room opposite Stalin's red curtain hung a beautifully carved and gilded two-headed eagle, the ancient symbol of Imperial Russia.

Now, behind the old worn curtain sat Count Korsakov. Like Stalin before him, he was the wizard who pulled the strings of true power.

The Twelve seated themselves along the three sides of the brilliantly polished table. Place cards identified their seating assignments, and the solid gold flatware and elegant red china permanently "borrowed" from the palace of Peterhof meant breakfast would be served. At that moment, a troupe of waiters, resplendent in white jackets with golden epaulets, appeared and began serving.

Rostov entered only when they were all seated, taking his place at the "point." He smiled as a servant seated him, warmly at some, coolly at a few, pointedly ignoring others completely. The tension increased dramatically when one of the Twelve who'd been ignored accidentally elbowed his goblet, spilling water across the table. A waiter quickly mopped up the mess, but Rostov's icy stare sent the man even lower in his chair.

Beside each golden water goblet on the table was a small gift, presumably from the count. Rostov picked up his present and examined it: a small gold cloisonné snuffbox bearing the image of Ivan the Terrible. Rostov got the joke. This was clearly to be a very special occasion. It was even Fabergé, he saw, turning it over in his hand.

"Good morning, comrades," the familiar disembodied voice boomed from hidden speakers. It sounded as if a subwoofer somewhere needed adjusting. But the count's tone was unmistakable. Heads will roll today, Rostov thought, smiling to himself, heads will roll.

"Good morning, Excellency!" the Twelve replied, nearly in unison and perhaps a bit stridently.

Of the thirteen men assembled at the table, only the Russian president was utterly silent. He smiled indulgently at the others, a smile of almost paternal amusement. The good news he carried allowed him to seem relaxed and in good fettle. The others at the table all exhibited a greyish pallor and seemed unable to control their darting eyes, nervous tics, and trembling limbs. This was despite the fact that many of them were wearing both the Hero of the Soviet Union and the Hero of Russia stars on their uniforms. Such was the enormous power of the one known within the Kremlin walls as the Dark Rider.

"Everyone enjoy the tour, I trust?" Korsakov said.

Heads bobbed and a number of *Da, da, da*'s could be heard. The president's head was one of the few not to bob. He'd learned a trick early on, a way of not automatically agreeing with everything Korsakov said. He planted his right elbow squarely on the table and made a fist of his right hand, placing it firmly under his chin and keeping it there for the duration of any meeting. No mindlessly bobbing head for the president of Russia!

"Let us begin, comrades," Korsakov said. "We welcome President Rostov home from the Barents Sea, and we anxiously await his report on the sea trials of our new Bulava missile systems. But our first order of business will be to clean up a little untidiness. At a Kremlin meeting one year ago today, I gave this group two very simple things to remember. I insisted that you pay your taxes. To the last ruble. And I insisted that you engage in no political activity that could in any way be construed as harmful to our beloved president. Does everyone here recall that?"

An uncomfortable silence descended upon the room. Even the waiters were aware of the tension and stepped away from the table. The president's two security officers, a pair of bulky Ukrainians who'd remained by the door, now moved along one wall.

"Apparently, not everyone remembers. I would like for General Ivan Alexandrovich Serov please to stand."

The general, old, bald, and gone to fat, managed to get to his feet, knocking over his water goblet again as he did so. His face had gone a deathly shade of pale, and his right hand, holding the snuffbox he'd been inspecting, trembled uncontrollably.

"Thank you, General. Now you, Alexei Nemerov. Stand up, please."

Nemerov, a thin, waxy figure with wispy blond hair, stood, his eyes blazing behind his round steel-rimmed spectacles. He realized he'd been deliberately seated next to the general, and they now stood side by side. Both were visibly shaken, one with fear, the other with rage.

"Excellency, there has been some mistake," Nemerov said, glaring at the red curtain as if his eyes could pierce it, as if his hands could reach the man behind it, strangle the life out of him before he could —

Korsakov's voice was low and full of menace. "There certainly has been a mistake, Alexei! Both of you seem to have forgotten why you have risen to such exalted stations in our glorious New Russia. Sitting atop your billions, lounging in your villas at Cap d'Antibes. You are here today only because I trusted you. And you will be gone today because I no longer do."

Rostov's two bodyguards, who had entered the room unnoticed, now edged along the wall until they stood directly behind the two traitors. Each took a step forward, silent and unseen by their intended victims. The other eleven averted their eyes from the bloody drama sure to come.

Serov and Nemerov staggered against the table. Both felt the sudden press of cold steel at the bases of their skulls, and both closed their eyes, waiting for the inevitable.

"Where chaos reigns, order retreats," Korsakov said. "Let order reign once more."

It was a signal. The two gunmen fired simultaneously, the hollow-point Parabellum rounds spattering bits of skull and a fine mist of pinkish-grey brain matter into the air above the table, gobs of cerebral tissue spattering the shocked faces of the men seated directly across the table from the victims.

Before the two dead men could collapse to the floor, the president's bodyguards had grabbed each corpse under the arms and quickly pulled them away from the table, dragging them toward the door now being opened by one of the waiters.

"Close the door, please," Korsakov said when the bodies had been removed and the waiters had removed their unsightly broken china and cleaned up a bit of the mess. The bloody napkins used by the men most affected by the carnage were replaced with crisp white linen.

"And let's continue. Please, gentlemen, enjoy your breakfast. I have a few more comments to make before the president gives us a report on the Barents Sea naval exercises. Anyone have any questions? No? Good. Let me tell you what this meeting is really all about. I promise you will find it most interesting."

Here, Korsakov paused, giving the Twelve, now the Ten, a chance to compose themselves. When he saw that they were following Rostov's lead and had begun to sip their short glasses of "little water," what Russians called their beloved vodka, and push around the eggs and pickles and sausages on their plates, he continued.

"First, regarding our own internal issues, particularly the recent Chechen atrocities, I would say that we must learn to look at all problems all-sidedly, seeing the reverse as well as the obverse side of things. In given conditions, a bad thing can lead to good results, and a good thing can lead to bad results. The massive loss of civilian life at Novgorod was regrettable, but we shall turn it to our advantage, believe me.

"The world is once more in chaos, gentlemen. That's because it has no bipolar symmetry. Since the catastrophic collapse of the Soviet Union, there has been only one superpower, the United States of America. There is no longer any global counterbalance to enforce a sense of symmetric order on our planet. The Europeans try and predictably fail miserably. The Chinese would gladly try, but their nuclear arsenal is woefully inadequate, at least as of the moment. Everyone agree?"

There was murmured assent, everyone still too much in a state of shock over the recent violence to respond normally.

"Only two global powers have any realistic chance of challenging the United States, two governments capable of bringing back balance, restoring order and political symmetry: our own and, at some point in the future, the Chinese. Personally, I would much prefer our own humble motherland to take the lead on this battlefield."

With laughter and applause, relaxation returned to the body language of the Ten. Although the smell of cordite and the coppery scent of fresh blood still hung in the air, the two dead colleagues were already fading from the collective memory.

"Good, good. So let me propose a notion to remedy this crisis, shall I? This morning, I tell you that our immediate goal is to stop the American encroachment on post-Soviet territories. To do that, I suggest that we reclaim the lost republics of our former Soviet Union. Not all at once, too provocative, but rather one bite at a time. We will begin perhaps with little Estonia, such a thorn in our side. A great deal of the groundwork there has already been done. At a subsequent meeting, I will inform you of the actual timing and strategy. Once the West has digested that and thinks we're done, we will take them all back! Either by force or by subterfuge, but we will take them back.

"When we have accomplished the reintegration of our beloved motherland, we will look beyond those new boundaries, east and west. Because I tell you, gentlemen, the only way to protect our borders is to expand them!

"Returning our beloved Russia to her rightful place as the dominant world power will require nothing less than a new revolution! It will not be easy. As Chairman Mao once said, 'A revolution is no dinner party.' But we will prevail, gentlemen, we will prevail!"

Rostov got to his feet first, clapping his hands loudly. The other soon followed, leaping out of their chairs and applauding vigorously. This went on for at least five minutes, until Count Korsakov spoke again.

"Thank you all. I appreciate your sense of duty and love of country. But to achieve this glorious rebirth and revolution, we will need to keep the West from interfering. Keep their noses out of our nest. We will need a *ruse de guerre,* a trick, a distraction that prevents any counterattack by our enemies when our tanks roll. Any thoughts?"

General Arkady Gerimosov, who had perhaps drunk more "little water" than his comrades, spoke first.

"We could distract them by taking out New York, Chicago, and Los Angeles, Excellency? A most persuasive *ruse de guerre, non, mes amis?*"

The laughter in the room was explosive, but not everyone thought it was funny. Some of them privately thought it was a seriously good idea. Korsakov was not amused.

"A most entertaining idea, General Gerimosov, but, as Napoleon once said, 'There are but two powers in the world, the sword and the mind. In the long run, the sword is always beaten by the mind.' And on that note, there being no further business until the president's presentation later on, this meeting is adjourned."

"Volodya?" Korsakov said, speaking privately to the president via an earbud in Rostov's ear.

"Excellency?"

"I desire a private word with you. I wonder if you might excuse yourself for a few minutes and join me in my office?"

"Indeed. I'm on my way."

Rostov put his napkin to his lips, smiled at his colleagues, and slipped behind the curtain to see the wizard.

"Yes, Excellency," Rostov said to the silhouetted figure sitting in the shadows. He took his usual chair, crossed his legs, and lit a cigarette.

"There is a man who needs watching, Volodya."

"Who and where, Excellency?" Rostov replied.

"An Englishman named Hawke. I have some history with his family. He recently moved from London to Bermuda. He has somehow become involved with my daughter, Anastasia. A romantic liaison, perhaps. Perhaps not. He would appear to be a private citizen, extraordinarily wealthy. But I've reason to believe he's MI-6. Or perhaps just a freelance operative for hire."

"He needs watching or killing?"

"Both. For now, just watch. Contact my private security force on Bermuda. A Mr. Samuel Coale on Nonsuch Island. The old American NASA downrange tracking base. He'll know what to do. When it's time for Hawke to go, I will inform you. Then I will want you to contact Mr. Strelnikov. Paddy Strelnikov. An American gun of mine. He's the only one I would send up against this Englishman."

"He's good, is he, this Brit?"

"Perhaps the best. He has caused our comrades in Havana and Beijing no end of trouble. Also, I am worried about my darling Anastasia. My daughter has been . . . unhappy since the untimely death of her husband, Vanya. She seems quite taken with this Hawke. It is troubling. I don't want him in our nest."

"Perhaps you should tell your daughter to steer clear of this man, Excellency. She is, after all, the soul of obedience."

"Perhaps. But for a time, maybe, he will make her happy. And besides, who knows what she might learn from this Englishman in the meantime, eh, Volodya?"

Rostov nodded.

"Where is Paddy Strelnikov now, Excellency?"

"On assignment in America. Taking care of business."

5

Badlands, North Dakota

The road ahead looked like a frozen snake. Black and glistening in his headlights, slithering out there, disappearing into the distant snow-white hills. Paddy Strelnikov had his high beams on, but still, mostly all he could see was swirling snow. Wet stuff, soft blobs of it hitting his windshield. *Splat.* The wipers were working okay, but he still couldn't see shit.

He found the stalk on the left side of the wheel and put the dims back on. Yeah. That was better, less snow and more road.

Strelnikov didn't know from driving out in the middle of nowhere at night in the middle of a freaking blizzard. He was a Russian emigrant from Brooklyn, f'crissakes, where they had normal highways. The BQE, the Long Island Expressway, hell, even the Santa Monica Freeway out in L.A., et cetera, those he could handle. This road? North Dakota? Forget about it, brother. This was freaking Mars.

He glanced at his chunky gold watch, saw what time it was, and accelerated, fishtailing a little. He watched the red needle climb past eighty, ninety. He hoped to hell this automobile had traction control. He thought they had a switch for that on these new cars, but he hadn't been able to find one. He wasn't exactly sure what traction control was or even where he'd heard about it. TV commercial, probably. Whatever it was, it sounded good to him. When it had first started snowing hard, he'd pulled into a rest stop and looked for the switch.

Good luck. There were a whole lot of knobs and switches on the dash, way too many, in fact, but not one of them said anything about traction control. It was no wonder Detroit was going down the toilet. Nobody had a clue how to work the damn cars anymore. Somehow, a few years back, some genius in Motown had decided everybody in America wanted dashboards to look like the cockpits of a 747. Now, they all did, and nobody had a clue what button did what anymore.

He'd looked around inside the glove box for some kind of a manual, but of course there was none. Just his rental contract and a folded map of North Dakota, which he did not need, and his .38 snub-nose, which he *hoped* he would not need. He really did not have time to dick around with this car anymore so he'd pulled back out onto the I-94 highway and kept on heading west, hoping for the best.

Maybe traction control was even standard on this thing, automatic, he told himself now, speeding up a little. But about an hour ago, he'd almost skidded into a ditch. Twice. The road conditions were so bad back there it had been like trying to drive a friggin' schoolbus across a frozen lake.

The car, a black Mustang coupe rented at the Bismarck airport Hertz counter, had a good heater, at least, once you finally found the knob that turned it on. He'd come across it only by accident, looking for the traction-control thingy, just like he'd finally found the button that turned the radio on. At least a previous renter had punched in some pretty good radio stations. Must have been some fuckin' electronics engineer or jet pilot or something who'd done that. Whatever happened to two knobs, over and out?

There was an all-night talk show out of Chicago he'd been listening to. Pretty good reception, and the show was good, too, called *The Midnight Hour* with your host, Greg Noack. Tonight's topic was capital punishment, of course, because tonight was the night old Stumpy was going to ride the needle.

Everybody in the country, not just Chicago, was talking about Charles Edward Stump, a.k.a. Stumpy the Baby Snuffer. Yeah, talking about Stumpy's impending execution, et cetera. This case had gotten media attention worldwide, not just the tabloids, either.

Mr. Stump was, in fact, the reason Fyodor Strelnikov, known since childhood as Paddy, was driving through the Badlands of North Dakota on this most miserable night in December. The execution was scheduled to take place at midnight tonight, which was, he saw, looking at his watch, exactly two hours and six minutes from now. Stumpy's *sayonara* party was going down at Little Miss, prison slang for the Little Missouri State Penitentiary just outside the town of Medora, North Dakota.

Distance to the joint from here was approximately sixty-seven miles.

Paddy snugged the pedal a little closer to the metal. He had time to do what he had to do, but he didn't want to cut it too close. Get in, make his delivery, and get the hell out of this friggin' state. You had to figure the joint would be mobbed, all the protesters and media crawling all over the place. He stuck the needle on 100 miles per hour.

"The real question is, is Charles Stump insane?" a caller said on the radio.

"Insane?" Greg Noack said. "Anybody who kills eight newborn infants in their incubators while their mothers are sleeping in the maternity ward down the hall is completely

66

off his nut, man!"

"That's my point exactly, Greg. Stumpy's not guilty by reason of insanity. Can't right-wing geniuses like you and Rush Limbaugh understand that!"

And on and on like that the calls went. The armies of bleeding hearts were out in force on the airwaves tonight. Apparently, in addition to the media forces gathered for the last two days, there were three or four hundred people standing in the freezing cold outside the prison gates at Little Miss. They were lighting candles, good luck in this weather, protesting the death penalty, et cetera, claiming Stumpy was emotionally distraught at the time of the murders, he'd been abused by his insane mother, blah-blah.

Like that made it okay, like Stumpy shouldn't stretch hemp because *he was a victim, too.* Right. We're all victims now. Hitler was a fricking victim. His mommy was mean to him when he pee-peed in his pants. Here you got a guy, at this moment probably the most despised human being on the planet, and still, the governor was, even at this late hour, considering a stay. A *stay?* Politics. Enough said. The trial jury, at least, had had the balls unanimously to put Stumpy down as a stone baby killer.

But Paddy Strelnikov knew that Stump's train went a lot farther than that.

A *whole* lot farther.

Strelnikov had made Stumpy his personal hobby when the powers that be in Moscow had given him this current assignment a couple of months ago. Before writing up his report, he'd read all the trial transcripts, bought a few drinks for people here and there, interviewed nurses on duty that night, the K-9 guy who'd found the little bodies in their shallow graves, the arresting detectives, the ME, the whole nine yards.

Then he'd gone to have a little chitchat with Mrs. Stump in the Lorraine, Illinois, loony bin where she'd been doing crossword puzzles since 1993. Oh, the stories that little ninety-two-pound, white-haired, wack-job chick could tell.

According to Mom, who was wearing an attractive housecoat with sleeves that wrapped all the way around and fastened with heavy buckles at the small of her back, little Charlie, when he was just a tyke, had amused himself by putting insects, goldfish, rodents, and then abducted kitty cats inside an old microwave he kept in the basement. Zapped them at full power. Then he'd graduated to higher life forms.

Nurse Stumpy, her golden boy, had been abusing and killing infants and children for years, his mom told Paddy, with a gleam in those weirdly protruding blue eyes, and then, what he'd do, Stumpy began calling the victims' families around Christmastime, taunting them by implying that their babies were still alive. And how did she know all this? Because she was upstairs, listening in on the other line, that's how. This was the Stump family's idea of holiday entertainment, their special holiday greeting card.

And that's the final report he'd made, the report he'd sent to his boss, who'd told his boss, who'd told his boss, et cetera, and that's how come he was out here in the middle of friggin' nowheresville making sure everything was copacetic in connection with this particular execution. There were to be no loose ends, et cetera, in the case of Charles Edward Stump.

The Wiz, as he privately called his boss, didn't like loose ends. And the Wiz ruled his world. Paddy, he was just muscle for hire. He knew that. Accepted it. He was a gun, that's all. But by God, he was a good one. He was a fuckin' Howitzer.

Strelnikov saw the fluorescent green exit sign for Medora coming up and moved over to the right lane. He'd take a little-used two-lane state road from here the rest of the way to Little Miss. He reached over and shut off the radio. He couldn't stand to hear those people defend that moron anymore. Even now, just thinking about it, Paddy was shaking his head at the stupidity that seemed to run in the Stump family.

For instance, it takes a real numbskull to

get the death penalty in a state that doesn't even *have* the death penalty.

Charles Edward Stump had been convicted on eight counts of first-degree murder. Stumpy, who was twenty-seven years old at the time of the killings, had been a male nurse at the Fargo General Hospital, working in the maternity ward. Hello? Background check? So, one dark night three years ago, nobody knows why, Nurse Stump had gone into the incubation ward and suffocated all of the newbies, one after another, with a pillow.

Lights out, kiddies!

Then, according to the transcripts Strelnikov read, he had gathered up all of his little victims into a pair of pillowcases, walked out of the hospital, and got into his car. He drove south from Watford City, where the hospital was located, and transported the dead babies just across the Little Missouri River. He parked on a dirt road outside Grassy Butte and buried them in a mass grave in a deeply wooded area just inside Theodore Roosevelt National Park.

An autopsy later revealed two of the babies had been buried alive.

If Stumpy had had even half a brain in his head, he might have noticed the word *national* in Theodore Roosevelt National Park. National meant it was a *federal* crime. And now it was the feds who were going to tuck

Stumpy onto his cozy little gurney and put him to sleep permanently tonight.

Blue lights flashing in Strelnikov's rearview mirror snapped him back to reality.

"Great," he muttered, slowing down and pulling over to stop on the shoulder. Hell, he was only doing a hundred. Somebody on Mars had a problem with that? He reached over and popped the glove compartment, his fingers closing around the little snub-nose. He shoved it under his right thigh, the grip sticking out where he could get it if it came to that.

A second later, the cop was standing outside his window, shining a flashlight in his face. He wound the window down, cold air and snow blowing in, and said, "How you doing, officer?"

The cop bent down, shining the light in Paddy's eyes. Then he directed it into the backseat, where something shiny had caught his eye.

"What the hell is that?"

"An alligator case."

"What's in it?"

"What's in it?"

"That's what I said."

"Hairbrushes. Soap. Perfume bottles, et cetera. For my lady's bath. I'm a salesman. I sell these things."

The cop looked at him a second. Paddy was used to it. He knew he didn't look like a

traveling salesman. He looked like a professional wrestler in a shiny navy-blue suit two
sizes too small.

"Driver's license and registration, sir."

"Yeah, well, hold on a sec." He reached
inside his breast pocket and pulled out his
driver's license. The license wasn't in his wallet, no, it was wrapped inside five crispy one-
hundred-dollar bills with a rubber band
around it, just in case of a situation like this
one. He handed it to the cop, who played his
flashlight on it.

"What's this?"

"That would be my driver's license, officer.
Wrapped inside five hundred spanking-new
U.S. dollars."

"Sir, you —"

"Officer, look, I'm in kind of a hurry here,
and I'd appreciate it if you'd just give me my
license back and take the rest as a small token
of my undying gratitude."

"Look, pal, I —"

"Okay, okay, I gotcha."

Strelnikov stuck his hand back inside his
pocket and pulled out a neatly packed wad of
cash.

"Five thousand dollars. That's my final offer," Paddy said, giving the guy his killer
smile, the one he'd learned on the streets of
Brighton Beach and Coney, use it just before
you punch some scumbag's lights out.
"Christmas is right around the corner, you

know, officer. Five large could come in very handy."

He could tell from the look on the cop's face which way this thing was going to go. Due south.

"Okay, sir, I'm going to ask you to step out of the vehicle. Now. Keep your hands up where I can see them."

"Look, you're making a fatal mistake here, officer."

"Out of the car, sir," the trooper said, backing away with his hand on his holster. "Now!"

The honest cop didn't see the ugly little snub-nose appear just above the windowsill. Maybe he'd missed that word, *fatal.* Too bad, it was a key word.

Pop pop, went the .38. Two of the best, smack dab in the middle of the trooper's noggin.

"Buh-bye," Paddy said, looking out the window at the dead man splayed in the red snow as he accelerated away, the Mustang fishtailing wildly on the icy shoulder of the highway.

Hey. Shit happens.

All you can do is try, right?

6

Bermuda

Teakettle Cottage perched on a narrow coral precipice some fifty feet above the turquoise sea. It was a study in simplicity. The cottage was perfectly suited to Hawke's needs. In addition to satisfying his desire for peace, the precariously situated house provided a sense of "living rough." Hawke's more romantic instincts, which he would never admit to possessing, equated roughness with reality.

He had discussed this rather arcane notion over cocktails one rainy evening with the brainiest man he knew, the famous criminalist Chief Inspector Ambrose Congreve of Scotland Yard.

Congreve had said that Hawke's very human instinct, he suspected, equated the sheer discomfort and occasional violence of living directly on the sea with some guarantee of authenticity. Living always on the very edge of things the way Hawke did, with the attendant lack of safety, provided Hawke, Congreve believed, with a measure of truth.

That, Hawke had informed his friend, was laying it on a bit thick. But while Hawke much preferred to swim on life's surface, Congreve tended to dive deep. It's what had made their lifelong friendship such a lasting and successful one. In the cloak-and-dagger world they inhabited, they needed each other.

Hawke's modest limestone house was partially hidden in a grove of ancient *lignum vitae,* kapok, and fragrant cedar trees. Coconut palms lined a sandy lane that finally arrived at the house after winding through a mature banana grove. The layout of the house proper was an exercise in minimalism: a broad coquina-shell terrace that overlooked the Atlantic fanned out from a rounded, barnlike main room open to the elements.

A crooked white-bricked watchtower on the seaward side of the domed house formed the teakettle's "spout."

The large whitewashed living room, with its well-worn Spanish-tile floors, was furnished with old planter's chairs and cast-off furniture donated or simply left behind by various residents over the years.

The massive carved monkey-wood bar standing in one corner had been donated by Douglas Fairbanks Jr., who'd lived in the house on and off for many seasons. At one end of the bar stood an ancient but still operable shortwave radio. The old set was rumored to have been used by Admiral Sir Morgan Wheelock, commandant of the Royal Navy Air Station Bermuda during World War II. From Teakettle's terrace, he'd monitored the comings and goings of U-boat and German merchant marine traffic just offshore.

Rumor also had it that Teakettle was once a safe house for briefing British spies en route to assignments in various Caribbean stations. Having heard that rumor, Hawke delighted all the more in his tiny home, his little den of spies.

The battered mahogany canasta table where Hawke took all of his indoor meals was allegedly a gift of Errol Flynn. Flynn sought refuge in the cottage for a few months in 1937, during a particularly stormy period in his marriage to Lili Damita. Leafing through the faded guest book one rainy night, Hawke saw an entry in Flynn's own hand, saying he'd found Teakettle "a perfectly ghastly house, no hot water, pictures of snakes plastered all over the bedroom wall."

There was plenty of hot water now, and Flynn's snake pictures were mercifully long gone. There were only two pictures in Hawke's bedroom now: an old black-and-white of his late parents seated in the stern of a gondola on their honeymoon in Venice and a picture of his late wife, Victoria, taken when she was a child. In the photograph, she was sitting on an upper limb of an old oak tree on a levee beside the Mississippi River.

On a table in the bedroom's corner was an old Victrola, a Cole Porter disc still sitting on the turntable, next to it a Royal typewriter. Hawke had seen Hemingway's name scrawled in the guest book. Papa had apparently stayed at Teakettle a few times, too. He'd visited the island during a fishing tournament, staying on as a guest of Flynn, working like mad to finish his book *Islands in the Stream.* Hawke could imagine him over there in the corner, shirtless and sweating in Bermuda shorts, sipping Cinzano from the bottle and banging away on the Royal.

Hawke took great comfort in his strange little house. Oddly enough, considering his substantial real estate holdings, it offered him a sense of abiding peace he'd not found elsewhere. In addition to his small room, there were three other bedrooms. Hawke had chosen the smallest for two reasons. It had three large windows, framed with vivid purple bougainvillea, that opened directly onto the sea. And the most intriguing thing of all was that it had a secret door, one that concealed an escape hatch.

At the back of his cedar-lined closet, a door-sized panel slid upward to reveal a serpentine staircase of hand-hewn coral. The narrow steps curved down to the most perfect fresh saltwater pool you could imagine, a fairly large deep-water lagoon, sheltered within rock walls but with a sizable opening to the sea. The deep blue pool was edged with jade where it washed over the rocks. He'd had a wooden dock built and kept his pretty little masthead sloop tied there, the *Gin Fizz.*

Hawke had indulged himself with one expensive eccentricity. Knowing his bedroom was some twenty feet directly above the surface of the lagoon, he'd had a three-foot-diameter hole cut in the floor and installed a gleaming brass fireman's pole in the center of it. This system allowed him to slip naked from bed of a morning, still half asleep, grab the pole, and slide into the water below without even opening his eyes until he was three feet below the surface.

It was a lovely way to wake up.

He'd paddle around for ten minutes or so in the pool of sea-blue water, swim out into the open Atlantic, and commence his five-point daily regimen.

The newly devised fitness program was straightforward enough.

First, a 500-yard open-water swim, breaststroke or sidestroke, to be completed in less than twelve minutes, thirty seconds. A minimum of eighty pushups, four sets of twenty in two minutes. He would do the last set with one arm. Next, a minimum of eighty situps in two minutes. A minimum of eight dead-hang pullups. And finally, a 1.5-mile run along the beach to be accomplished in less than eleven minutes, thirty seconds. This run was always completed wearing combat assault boots, namely his old Oakleys from the Royal Navy.

Hawke was first and foremost a warrior, and he placed his emphasis on strength and speed but with no premium on bulking up. Bulk just makes you slow, especially when running in soft sand in combat boots.

He prized speed above all else. Speed through the water, speed over the ground, and speed of thought in rapidly evolving combat situations. He'd long ago lost his awe for the heavily muscled body-building types. They always looked ferocious but were never a match for a fast, highly trained martial artist. Reggae god Jimmy Cliff had said it best, as far as Hawke was concerned.

De harder dey come, de harder dey fall.
One and all.

Morning routine done, Hawke would climb the winding steps back to his room, pull on a pair of faded khaki shorts and a T-shirt, and join dear old Pelham for some marvelous breakfast or other. This was the kind of simple, idyllic life he'd long dreamed of. And now that dream seemed to be coming true.

The old mill house had been electrified during the war years, but at night, Hawke preferred candles in wall sconces, oil lanterns, and the kerosene Tonga torches ringing the open terrace. On cold, rainy nights, Pelham got a roaring fire going. The fireplace had a lovely mantel of old Bermuda cedar inlaid with polished pink conchs. Atop the mantel was a model of *Sea Venture* that Pelham had found in Hamilton. The English vessel, en route to rescue Jamestown settlers, had suffered an unfortunate encounter with Bermuda's reefs, and thus *Sea Venture* had provided Bermuda with its first European settlers.

Hawke had tried to persuade the feisty octogenarian to stay put at Hawke's London house in Belgravia, but Pelham, the family retainer who'd practically raised Hawke from boyhood, wasn't having any of it. So here they both reigned in squalid splendor, two happy bachelors in paradise. The fact that a half-century separated their birthdays mattered not a whit. They'd always enjoyed each other's company and were long accustomed to each other's idiosyncrasies.

It was six p.m. Hawke's dinner invitation at Shadowlands was called for eight sharp. The lovebirds, Ambrose and Diana, had only just arrived from England a few days earlier. Hawke was looking forward to a quiet evening spent in the company of two dear friends.

Outside, soft dusk cooled the waning day. Hawke stood at his steamy bathroom mirror, shaving. He'd been ignoring his beard for some few days and was sure his friend Congreve would not approve should he darken Lady Mars's door unshaven. No doubt, Am-

80

brose would cast a stern eye on his hair as well. His unruly black locks threatened to brush his shoulders. If it got much longer, he'd let Pelham have a whack at it with his kitchen shears.

In the dense banana grove beyond his opened window, the tinkle and zing of nocturnal insects kept him company while he shaved. Another thing he liked about this island: the simple music of everyday life. The birds, the bees, the Bermudians. Every passerby you met seemed to be either singing or whistling some tune or other all day long. Bermudians were happy people. Hawke was happy, too.

"But I say," Hawke suddenly sang out loud, simultaneously lifting his voice and his chin, scraping the straight razor's blade upward along his throat, "dat de women of today, smarter than de man in every way . . ."

He put his straight razor down on the sink and stared at himself in the mirror.

Where on earth had that strangled lyric come from? He had a terrible singing voice and seldom used it. At his school in England, there had been two choral groups: the headmaster had named them the Agonies and the Ecstasies. Hawke had been a proud member of the former group. Couldn't sing a note. He smiled, picked up his blade, and continued shaving, picking up the tune with gusto.

"Dat's right, de woman is smarter, dat's

81

right, de woman is smarter . . ."

Someone was knocking at his bathroom door. Pelham, come to complain about the noise, no doubt.

"Begging your pardon, sir," came the voice outside.

"What is it?"

He was still warbling the old calypso tune when Pelham rapped again on the loo's louvered door.

"Yes?" Hawke said, cracking the door an inch with his bare foot.

"Telephone for you, sir."

"Who is it?"

"A young lady, I believe."

"Did she give her name?"

"No, m'lord, she did not."

"What on earth does she want?"

"I couldn't really say, sir. Something about a painting, sir."

"Painting? We don't need any painting."

"Yes, sir. She'll pay a fee, but not more than a hundred Bermuda dollars an hour."

Hawke uttered something unprintable and splashed hot water on his face. Grabbing a towel from the door hook, he wrapped it round his waist and strode down the short hallway that led to the great room. A vintage Bakelite black telephone, the only phone in the house, sat where it always had, at one end of the monkey bar.

Pelham had followed him down the hall and

now moved quickly behind the bar. He got busy with a jug of Mr. Gosling's rum and ice, slicing a juicy lime within an inch of its life, preparing the evening restorative.

Hawke glanced at Pelham with a thin smile. Both men knew it was a bit too early for sundowners, and both also knew this mixology business was only Pelham's sly ruse for the most blatant form of eavesdropping.

"Hello? Who's this?" Hawke demanded, snatching up the receiver.

"Is this Hawke?"

"That depends. Who is this?"

"Anastasia Korsakova. We met earlier today, you may recall. I was just telling your . . . friend that I'm interested in painting you. I pay my models well, but I won't be bullied."

"What on earth are you talking about?"

"You. I want to paint you."

"Paint me? Good Lord. To what end?"

"I'm an artist, Mr. Hawke. I'm having a one-woman show at the Royal Academy in London come spring. I'm doing a series of male figures. Life-size."

"Why are you picking on me?"

"There is no need to be rude. I think you'd make a good subject, that's all. And based on your rather quaint . . . lodging, I assumed you might be a man who'd find the money attractive. Surely you've done some modeling in your time, Mr. Hawke. A hundred an hour is not easily come by on this island."

Modeling? Hawke stifled the urge to laugh out loud and said, "Miss Korsakova, I'm terribly flattered by your offer. But I'm afraid I must refuse."

"Why?"

"Why? Well, any number of reasons. I'm a very busy man, for one. I imagine this painting business would require a good deal of sitting around. And I don't at all like sitting around."

"Your schedule didn't seem too full this afternoon. Sleeping on the beach."

"That was a catnap."

"Look, I could paint you reclining, if you'd like. You could even sleep on the divan, for all I care. Wouldn't bother me."

"May I ask where you got my number?"

"Friends."

"Friends of mine?"

"Hardly. I would scarcely imagine we travel in the same social circles, Mr. Hawke. No, friends of mine found the number of your cottage for me."

"You have friends who know my number?"

"I have friends who know everything."

"Well, look here, it's been lovely chatting with you, Miss Korsakova, but I'm afraid I'm late for a dinner engagement."

"Will you consider my offer, Mr. Hawke? I'm really most anxious to get started on you."

Hawke held the phone away from his ear a

moment and accepted a frosted silver cup with a sprig of mint from Pelham. It was really a bit early, but what the hell. He took a sip. Delicious. A fleeting image of a nude goddess emerging dripping from the sea appeared suddenly before his eyes as he put the phone back to his ear.

Get started on me?

"Sorry," Hawke murmured, sipping. "Rum delivery man at the door."

"Well?" Korsakova asked, impatience frosting the word.

"I'll sleep on it."

"Do that. I call you first thing in the morning."

The line went dead.

"Bloody hell," Hawke murmured to Pelham. "She wants to paint my picture."

"So I inferred, sir."

"Ridiculous. Absolute rubbish."

"Are you going to do it?"

"Are you completely mad?"

Pelham's bushy white eyebrows went straight up.

"Really, m'lord. One hundred smackers an hour is nothing to sniff one's nose at. Pretty good gravy, in my view, sir."

Hawke laughed aloud, threw his head back, and took another healthy swig of Pelham's delicious concoction before padding off toward his bedroom to strap on the black tie and his Royal Navy dress uniform. It was

Saturday night. Congreve had told him they still dressed for dinner at Shadowlands. A quaint practice, but, to Hawke, anyway, an agreeable one.

The muffled strains of the calypso song soon resumed from down the hall, his lordship singing at the top of his lungs, "Smarter than de man in every way!"

"Trouble in paradise." Pelham sighed to himself, wiping clean the varnished bar and smiling at his reflection.

"Trouble in paradise," echoed Sniper, Hawke's pet parrot, who'd just flown from his perch and alighted on Pelham's shoulder. Hawke had cared for the bird, a black hyacinth macaw, since childhood. Despite her name, her color was a glossy ultramarine blue. She was almost eighty years old, had a very sharp tongue, and would probably live to see one hundred.

"Oh, hush up," Pelham said, and slipped the bird a few crackers from the bowl on the bar.

"Thanks for nothing, buster," Sniper squawked.

"Do sod off, won't you?" Pelham replied.

7

Medora, North Dakota

Paddy Strelnikov waltzed into the warden's office at Little Miss Penitentiary at eleven o'clock. Sleet was rattling against the window-panes. Stumpy's midnight date with destiny, in a little more than an hour, was going to happen right down the hall. Hell, he'd seen them getting ready, coming up the stairs to the warden's office.

The door at the end was open, and you could see inside to the pale green tile walls of the death chamber. Bright lights, like an operating room. Medical equipment. There was a lot of activity, and Paddy, catching a glimpse of the gurney, was curious about all of it. But he was on a mission.

It had taken Strelnikov ten minutes just to negotiate the Mustang through the mob scene of press and protesters at the gate. Then another twenty or so to get through the check points at Wing Block D, the maximum-security building at the rear of the Little Miss complex.

It was a long three-story building made entirely of concrete block with a guard tower rising at either end. In addition to the warden's office, D Block was home to Death Row. Sixty-one inmates were awaiting execution, including some of the most notorious pedophiles, sexual sadists, and serial killers west of the Mississippi.

Little Miss had replaced Terre Haute Correctional Facility in Indiana as the federal government's new special confinement unit for inmates serving federal death sentences. A couple of botched lethal injections (needles passing right through veins and injecting the sodium chlorate into the muscle) had led to public protests and the shutting down of the Indiana facility. Powerful lobbyists in Washington had made sure the new federal correctional complex ended up in North Dakota.

No one was ever quite sure who'd hired all of these expensive lobbyists, but no one much cared, either. In Washington, someone was always pulling the strings. Often, the true maestro went unseen and unnoticed. Like back in Russia.

Overhead, searchlights and TV lights lit the snowy skies like a Hollywood premiere. Lots of excitement when you pan-fry a guy as world-famous as Charles Edward Stump, when he walks that lonely last mile.

The warden, named Warren Garmadge, a

short, wide toad of a man in a double-wide paisley tie, stood right up when the deputies escorted Paddy Strelnikov into his flag-bedecked office. He stuck out his meaty hand, a big smile on his face. He seemed to be having a good time, being on TV a lot recently. Interviews and all, CNN, Fox, all the biggies. Also, he saw the beautiful alligator carrying case in Paddy's hand and figured it had his name on it.

He stuck his hand out, and Strelnikov shook it.

"Mr. Strelnikov, welcome to Little Missouri Prison. I'm honored you made time in your busy schedule to pay us a visit," the warden said, showing off his white Chiclet-capped chompers. Guy was a real pol, you could tell that by the firm, slightly moist grip of his fat little hand.

"Exciting time to be here, Warden Garmadge," Paddy said, taking one of the two red leather chairs facing the warden's desk. He put the case on the floor beside him, casual like, no big deal. Make the guy wait for it.

"Everything's going according to schedule, you'll be glad to know," Garmadge said, plopping down in his big executive swivel chair.

"A lot can happen in an hour," Paddy said, lighting up a big Cuban stogie he'd been saving for this meeting. He had another sticking out of his breast pocket with his hankie, but he made a point of not offering it to the warden. What he did, he crossed his legs at the knee, lifting the material of his grey silk trousers so that it draped nice, and smiled, expelling a stream of fragrant smoke at the warden.

"So. We're all right? We're a go?" Paddy said.

"Yeah. Don't worry. The governor has given me every assurance that there will be no last-minute surprises. As you know, the governor and I had a meeting of the minds on that subject one month ago."

Paddy laughed. "Yeah, an expensive meeting, from our point of view. What'd we finally do for hizzoner the governor? Two-fifty large? Two-seventy-five?"

"I believe that was the number."

"Which one?"

"The latter."

"Yeah, the latter, that's right." When shitbirds like this guy used phrases like *the latter*, it made him want to punch their friggin' lights out. Paddy looked casually around the office, one wall covered with photos of the warden with a lot of people nobody he knew had ever heard of. Local pols, police officials, et cetera. Martians.

"You ever witness an execution, Mr. Strelnikov?" Garmadge asked him.

"You mean other than the ones where I was personally pulling the trigger?"

The warden shifted in his chair, laughed uncomfortably, and said, "Yes, I mean a . . . court-ordered execution."

"Just one. Allen Lee Davis back in 1999. You familiar with that one?"

"Old Sparky, down there in Starke, Florida."

"Yeah. Starke was the only weenie roast I ever saw up close and personal. Soon as they flipped the switch, smoke and flames started to spurt out from Allen Lee's head, must have been flames a foot long or more. Like blue lightning coming out from under the little metal yarmulke on his head. Burned his eyebrows and eyelashes right off. It was some shit to see, I'll tell you. They shut the power down, then cranked it two more times before he finally fried. Must have taken him twenty minutes to check out, stick a fork in him, boys, he's done."

Garmadge was impressed, you could see it.

"Well, we pretty much got that all figured out now here at Little Miss. What happened down in Starke was, see, the saline-soaked sponge inside that little metal skullcap is meant to increase the flow of electricity to the head. In that case, the sponge was synthetic, which generated the problem. Starke uses only all-natural sponge now, and that solved that issue pretty much."

"Gone green, huh, warden? All-natural sponges?"

He smiled. "Lethal injection is much more humane, as you'll see down the hall in a few minutes," the warden said, glancing up at the clock, eager to move on.

"Humane, huh? I don't know if that's a good thing or a bad thing, warden, some of these animals you got sitting on Death Row don't deserve humane."

"Well, there is that," he said, coughing into his fist.

Strelnikov got to his feet.

"Anyway, I won't be sticking around for Stumpy's send-off, warden. I'm only here to make a delivery from my employers and your benefactors."

Paddy reached down and picked up the alligator case. Then he walked around the desk and placed it right in front of Warden Garmadge.

"Our organization is very grateful for your help over the years and especially your work with the governor in expediting tonight's main event, warden. The management asked me to personally show their appreciation with this little memento."

"Beautiful hide, absolutely gorgeous." He was feeling up that case as if he had a raging hard-on under the desk.

"Isn't it?" Paddy said. "Genuine alligator. Go ahead, open her up, warden."

"This is for me? What the heck . . ."

The guy's fingers were trembling as he

twisted the gold-plated clasp on the top and finally pulled the case open. The case was lined in black velvet. The object resting inside caught the light and sent silvery shimmers across the walls and ceiling. Garmadge sat back and stared.

"Omigod."

"Yeah. Something else, ain't it? Here, let me remove it and place it on the desk for you."

"What is it?"

"It's a computer, warden. The Zeta. The Platinum Edition, by the way."

"You're kidding me. Looks like a sculpture of a brain or something."

"That's the idea. It's our most popular design. You've seen the ads. 'Zeta, the last word in computers.' Get it?"

"No."

"Zeta's the last word in the Greek alphabet, I understand, but what the fuck. Some marketing bullshit. Kids have nicknamed it the Wizard or the Wiz, for short. See, the cord pulls out of the base of the brain stem. Let me plug it in for you, and I'll show you how it works."

"Where's the keyboard?" the warden asked.

"Wherever you want it," Paddy said. "Watch."

Strelnikov found an outlet and plugged in the silvery machine. A small hidden lamp in the frontal lobe projected a virtual keypad onto the warden's desktop.

"Holy smoke," the guy said, tapping his fingers on the nonexistent keyboard.

"Hit enter," Paddy said. "And there you go, you see the screen? It's a holographic image. See? Kinda floats in the air above the brain."

The Zeta machine was a piece of work, all right. From the supernaturally brilliant mind of Paddy's ultimate employer, a very reclusive Russian multibillionaire who didn't even have a name. Less expensive editions of the Wiz (with hardware made of mirror-polished aluminum, not platinum) would retail for about sixty bucks worldwide. Whole countries were already back-ordered for millions of these machines. India alone had ordered 10 million units at a discount price of fifty bucks. You didn't have to be a mathematical genius to figure the margins, how much that did for the company's bottom line.

"It's engraved," Paddy said. "Right here. 'To Warden Warren Garmadge, with everlasting gratitude.' "

"The most fantastic-looking thing I've ever seen," the warden said, stroking the sculpted brain's polished surface.

"Yeah, well, the *quesos grandes* I work for can be very generous when people see things their way. In your case, it's keeping these wild animals caged up. And taking a personal interest in Mr. Stump's going-away party. Nice meeting you, warden. I'm going to take off now. Sorry to miss the big bang tonight."

"Will you give your employer my deepest thanks when you see him?"

"See him?" Paddy laughed. "Nobody sees the big man. Nobody even knows his name."

"Why not?"

"He's the guy behind the curtain, warden. Like in that old movie, *The Wizard of Oz*? The boss of our operation? He's the friggin' Wizard himself."

Paddy drove slowly through the crowd gathered outside the prison gates. It seemed to have grown larger during the short time he'd been inside. The snow had let up some, now it was just cold, and hundreds of people were holding candles aloft, chanting some fruitcake-brotherly-love-a-weem-away song he couldn't hear the words to because he had the windows up and the radio on.

WKKO Chicago was still on the air, and the airy-fairy tree huggers and Stumpy supporters were still calling in, some of them wailing in despair as the final minutes approached. He looked into the rearview mirror and carefully peeled off his walrus mustache and the bushy eyebrows. He left the white wig atop his bald head, thinking it wasn't half so bad-looking as most of his wigs.

The show's host, the hyperkinetic night owl Greg Noack, was going back and forth to a WKKO reporter he had standing with the crowd at the gate, and now Paddy could hear the song. It was "We Shall Overcome," which Paddy thought was a slightly weird choice, since Stumpy was pure white trailer trash, not even a poor black dude who needed to overcome anything. But who could tell anymore what was correct or incorrect with these fruitcakes. In a country where "Merry Christmas" had replaced the F word as a big no-no, who could figure?

And Paddy wasn't even a Baptist, f'crissakes. He was Russian Orthodox!

Then Noack broke in all excited and said there was breaking news coming out of Bismarck, and they were going live to their man Willis Lowry, standing with the press corps just outside the governor's office on the capitol steps.

Lowry said, "In an amazing turn of events, Channel Five News has just learned that the governor has issued a last-minute stay of execution for Charles Edward Stump. Everyone here at the capitol is stunned at the news, because as late as eight o'clock this evening, the governor's office was insisting there was no chance of a pardon. But now we've learned that —"

"Fuck me," Strelnikov said, and turned off the radio. He reached over and grabbed his cell phone from the seat beside him. Flipping it open, he speed-dialed a number in New York.

"You watching TV? You believe this shit?" he asked Ruko, the guy who answered. "The asshole governor just pardoned the Stump. Hello?"

"Tell me you made the warden's delivery," the voice at the other end said.

"Done."

"Good. Do what you gotta do, Beef."

Because of his size and muscular build, all the boys in the old neighborhood had nicknamed him All-Beef Paddy. Pretty funny, right? Not.

The line went dead.

Paddy looked in his rearview. He could still see the prison back there, searchlights lighting up the sky. He pulled over onto the shoulder and set the emergency brake.

From his inside pocket, Strelnikov withdrew a small black radio transmitter. A tiny green light was illuminated. Paddy pushed one button, and the light turned red. Then he pushed a second button and held it down for three seconds. A signal went from his black box to a company Comsat satellite orbiting high above central North America.

The whole world lit up behind him, and a second or two later, the shockwave of the massive explosion rocked his rented Mustang nearly off its wheels.

Wing Block D, the toady warden, and all of the other illustrious doomed inhabitants no longer existed. It had been reduced to a pile of rubble by eight extraordinarily powerful ounces of Hexagon-based explosives carefully molded inside the hard drive of the Wizard computer Paddy had recently placed on Warden Garmadge's desk.

"Pop goes the weasel," Strelnikov said to himself, smiling.

Hexagon was another of the Wiz's inventions, discovered when he was experimenting with the molecular structures of nonnuclear explosives. It was bright blue, had the consistency of putty, and one ounce packed a wallop one thousand times that of nitroglycerine. By sheer accident, the man had discovered the most powerful nonnuclear explosive on the planet.

To prevent discovery of the Hexagon bomb hidden inside every Zeta machine, the case arrived from the factory permanently sealed. Should hardware problems arise, the machines were simply replaced free of charge. Should someone try to force the computers open, the presence of air would immediately reduce the Hexagon inside to an inert powder.

Genius.

He pulled back out onto the highway and accelerated rapidly up the snaky black road. He had a plane to catch. He was going to L.A. and from there to some godforsaken burg in Alaska to get briefed on his next assignment. Something to do with fish, he'd heard. But first, and he'd put money on it, he'd be paying a little surprise visit to the governor of North Dakota. Sometime in the next hour, his cellphone would ring, and he'd be headed for the governor's mansion. Can you say dead governor?

Fishing? In Alaska? What did he know from fishing? He was from Brooklyn, f'crissakes! But hey, a job was a job, right? Maybe he'd learn something.

Paddy smiled and turned the radio back on, looking for an oldies station. Life was pretty good, he had to admit. Yeah, his job kept him on the road a lot, but it was never, ever boring.

You kill three, four, maybe five hundred people over the course of a long and illustrious career, you think, well, it's maybe going to get boring at some point, right? You say, you know, how many times can I do this and keep it interesting? It has to get old eventually, right?

It doesn't.

It's all about creativity, baby.

Bottom line? You have to find a new way through the woods every time out.

Name of the game.

8

Bermuda

Hawke gunned his motorcycle up the final hill before turning into a shady lane that wound its way down to Lady Diana Mars's oceanfront property.

As part of his new program to simplify his life radically, Hawke had allowed himself only one toy on Bermuda, but it was perfection. The jet-black Norton Commando motorcycle, model 16H, had been built in 1949. The old bike had won the Isle of Man Race that year and had come fifth in the world championship. It was his favorite mode of transport and a perfect way to get around on the island's narrow and sometimes traffic-clogged roads.

The roads could be dangerous. Native Bermudians, teenagers mostly, had affected a riding style of casual nonchalance. They sat sideways on the seat, like a woman riding side-saddle, and guided their bikes with one hand. They took insane chances on roads built for horses and carriages, overtaking on blind curves, racing wildly through traffic. Hawke himself had narrowly escaped disaster at their hands many times. The Wild Onions, he called them privately, rebels without a clue.

After crossing the narrow swing bridge, originally built to take the old Bermuda train over to St. George's Island, he downshifted rapidly, delighting in the harsh *blat-blat* of the Norton's exhaust. Royal poinciana trees on either side of the lane formed a tunnellike arch overhead, and the soft but fecund smell of dark earth and night-blooming flowers was almost overpowering in his flared nostrils.

The massive iron gates of the Mars estate were coming up quickly on his right, and he braked sharply.

He'd not visited Diana's house yet and was exceedingly curious to see it. Vincent Astor had erected the legendary estate, called Shadowlands, in 1930. It was allegedly enormous, the house proper stretching out along a long, heavily wooded spit of parkland that ran parallel to the old, narrow-gauge railway tracks. In its heyday, Hawke had read, the house had boasted a large saltwater aquarium and Astor's own private railway, a toylike train called the Scarlet Runner that ran around the property.

He leaned into the bike, accelerated hard, and crested the hill. As both wheels left the ground, Hawke got his first good look at Shadowlands. It was spread out along the coast, moon shadows turning the succession of white buildings magical shades of softest blue and white.

The house was not one building; it was more a cluster of connected houses, all white with white roofs. The complex included every possible style of "Bermuda roof." He saw hipped roofs, fancy Dutch-influenced gable ends, raised parapets, shed roofs, and steep, smooth butteries. Various chimneys and towers completed the look. An architectural marvel, he had to admit.

Hawke smiled as he roared up to a covered portico, which he had to assume was the main entrance. He shut down his machine and climbed off, brushing the road dust from his white officer's dinner jacket. He'd worn his Royal Navy Blue No. 2 regalia for the occasion, the Navy's evening dress for formal dinners. It demanded a white waistcoat, miniature medals, and the three gold bands at the sleeves signifying his rank of commander.

Removing his helmet and straightening his thin, double-ended black satin tie, he took in Shadowlands with a sense of pure delight. This "house" Ambrose had invited him to looked more like a small fairy-tale village set along a cliff overlooking the sea.

Ambrose Congreve was suddenly standing

at the opened door, bathed in buttery yellow light from inside the house. He was resplendent in beautifully tailored black evening clothes and shod in gleaming patent-leather pumps. He was still using his gold-headed ebony cane, Hawke was sorry to see, but the smile on his face and the angle of the well-used pipe jutting from one corner of his mouth told Hawke all was well with his oldest and dearest friend.

Hawke removed the key from his still-ticking machine and turned the bike over to a smiling young Bermudian in a starched white house jacket who promised not to run off with it. Hawke watched the young man wheeling it away and then turned to the legendary Scotland Yard detective.

"Hullo, old warrior," he said to his friend. "Still using the swagger stick, I see."

It was his leg. Ambrose had been tortured by a pair of Arab fiends in the Amazon jungle many moons earlier. They'd systematically broken most of the bones in his right foot, knee, and lower leg. Doctors at London's King Edward VII Hospital who'd performed the knee replacement had originally thought he'd not regain use of the leg. But, not surprisingly, the tough old Scotland Yard copper had prevailed. After months of anguished therapy, with Diana's love and encouragement at every painful step, he'd left the hospital for good. He'd walked out with a cane, but he'd walked out.

Hawke stuck out his hand, but Ambrose ignored it, stepping forward to embrace him. They stood that way for a moment, arms wound tightly around each other, neither saying anything, just two men exceedingly happy to see each other once more. Hawke, who was not normally given to leaky displays, had to use every ounce of his will to keep the tears that filled his eyes from spilling over.

"Alex," Congreve said finally, clapping him smartly on the shoulder and stepping back to take his measure. "God, it's good to see you looking so fit."

"And you," Hawke managed to croak as they entered the house side by side. "Where is everybody?"

"Diana will be down in a moment. She's upstairs gilding the lilies. Let's go out on the terrace, shall we, and have something lethal. What would you like, Alex?"

"Rum, please. Gosling's if they've got it."

Hawke followed Congreve through the main house, moving slowly down a long vaulted and torchlit hallway that led to the white marble terrace and the moonlit sea beyond. There seemed to be chaps in white jackets everywhere, all with shiny brass buttons and highly polished black shoes. Congreve had certainly landed himself in cushy surroundings, up a notch or two from his quaint cottage in Hampstead Heath.

"They've got it. You're quite sure you don't want a Dark and Stormy?" Ambrose asked.

"Never heard of it."

"Really? Local favorite, practically the national drink of Bermuda. Rum, dark, of course, and ginger beer."

Hawke nodded.

"Desmond," Ambrose said to the lovely old fellow hovering nearby, "a pair of Dark and Stormys when you've got a moment . . . not too much ice. Ah, here we are! Lovely night for it, wouldn't you say?"

The two men had arrived at the carved limestone balustrade surrounding a lower portion of the terrace, a curved patio directly on the sea. There was no wind tonight, Hawke noticed, and not a ripple on the ocean, all the way to the horizon. The light of the full moon on the glassy water was electric, producing an almost neon blue that was startlingly beautiful. A fishing boat lay at anchor, so still it might have been welded to the sea.

Desmond arrived with a silver tray, and each man took one of the icy sterling tumblers.

"Well," Hawke said, taking a swallow of the potion, "let me raise a toast, then." He lifted his drink and said, "To health. And to peace."

"Peace and health," Congreve said, lifting his own goblet. "Long may they wave."

"Are you happy?" Hawke asked his friend,

pretending to stare out to sea.

"I am," Congreve said, his eyes shining. "Very."

Hawke smiled. "Good. Then let's get down to cases, shall we, Ambrose? Tell me, how does it look?"

"How does what look?"

"Come on. The bling-bling."

"The *bling-bling?*" Congreve said, regarding Hawke as if he'd lost his mind. "What on earth are you talking about?"

"The rock, the ice, the D flawless. Remember?"

"The *ring,* do you mean, for heaven's sake? My mother's diamond?"

"Yes, of course, the ring, Constable. The diamond engagement ring. Was she floored? KO'd in the very first round, I'll wager."

"Still upright, I'm afraid. I haven't given the thing to her yet."

"Not given it to her? Really? Based on our last dinner conversation at Black's in London, I should have thought the presentation was imminent. That's why you two were coming out to the balmy mid-oceanic isles. Seal the deal or do the deed or whatever."

"Hmm."

"So. Where does the thing stand now? Are you engaged or not?"

"Bit difficult to say, really, isn't it?"

"Not at all. You proposed to the woman. She accepted. I was there at Brixden House the night you dropped a knee, remember? That orchestral proposal? Berlioz?"

"Ah, yes. That's correct. But there have been . . . complications. Things have arisen since then."

"What kind of complications?"

"Well, I mean to say, difficulties."

"Difficulties with what?"

"Communication, apparently."

"Communication?"

"Hmm."

"What about it?"

"It seems we don't."

"Don't communicate?"

"Precisely. Don't communicate my deepest feelings."

"You're a man. You don't have any deep feelings."

"I keep saying that."

"She loves you."

"I know. And I her."

"Well? Give her the bloody ring, and get on with it! Is there anything on earth more symbolic of one's deepest feelings? I mean, a diamond is forever. Isn't that what they say?"

"I suppose you're right."

"Of course I'm right. You brought the rock along to Bermuda, one hopes. Ideal setting to bestow precious stones upon females feeling insecure about a chap's deepest feelings, much less his honorable intentions."

"Yes, yes, of course I've brought it. It's

upstairs in my shaving kit, awaiting the ideal moment. Perhaps on a sail in the moonlight. Something along those lines."

"In your shaving kit? You're kidding."

"No, no. It's safe as houses. I've got an old can of *mousse a raser* with a false bottom. It's in the bottom of the can."

"I suppose that's all right if you trust the staff. I'd hide it someplace more original were I you. When do you intend actually to bend the final knee, then, old fossil? Full moon tonight, you know. How those facets will sparkle. I could excuse myself early and —"

"Alex, please. These things take time. Planning. I alone will know when the moment is right. Now, then, what are you up to? You certainly look tan and fit. No hint of the dreaded *accidie* about you."

"*Accidie?* Is that more of your bloody French lingo?"

"Boredom, Alex, in any language. You show no signs of it, dear boy. What accounts for that? Keeping busy, are you, you and Pelham in that cozy little cottage of yours? Bermuda's own odd couple, I must say."

"Pelham and I? We're not odd at all. A trifle eccentric, perhaps, rough and ready, but hardly odd."

"So, what do you two hardy boys do with yourselves all day? To keep you both from going barking mad?"

"Pelham has his needlework in the evening.

He's taken up fishing, too, uses a monofilament hand line and reels them in by the bucketload. Many's the evening he fries up something he's hooked in our little lagoon. Rockfish à la Pelham with a Gosling's Black Seal rum sauce. Bloody marvelous should you ever be lucky enough to receive a coveted invitation to Teakettle Cottage."

"Diana and I would be delighted. What else?"

"Bit of Scrabble or Whist on rainy nights, the two of us. I'm reading a lot. I finished *Tom Sawyer,* and now I'm on to *Huckleberry Finn.* Bloody marvelous, Mark Twain, I never realized. Did you know Twain adored Bermuda? Came here scores of times."

"I need hardly remind you your dear mother was born on the Mississippi, Alex. Small wonder you find Mr. Clemens's marvelous books so appealing."

"I suppose you're right. I do get a sense of her in those pages of his."

"So, in a nutshell, you're reading Twain by the fireside while Pelham lurks about down by the lagoon, harrying the finny denizens of the deep. That about it?"

"What else? We've a small stable on the property, and I ride on the beach most mornings. Good strong black horse named Narcissus, loves to run. Swimming a good deal helps, I suppose. Six miles a day. Which reminds me. I must tell you about the most

remarkable woman I met this afternoon and
—"

Lady Diana Mars appeared at Hawke's elbow, all gossamer and glittering stones at the neckline and sparkling in her swept-up auburn hair. She was a beautiful woman with a fine mind and a generous spirit, and Congreve was damned lucky to have found her, especially so late in his life. Alex, along with everyone else, had put the renowned detective down for a lifelong bachelor. Diana had changed all that.

"Alex, you darling boy," she said, going up on tiptoes to kiss his cheek. "It's so very good to see you."

"And you," Hawke said. "You look lovely, Diana, absolutely radiant. And Shadowlands is wonderful."

"I'll give you the grand tour later if you'd like. We can even take the Scarlet Runner around the grounds. They've gotten the steam engine up and running again, apparently. But right now, I've got to go to the kitchen and see about dinner."

"Just us three," Hawke said. "What a treat."

Ambrose and Diana looked at each other.

Diana said, "Well, yes, Alex, it was just the three of us until about an hour ago. We've a surprise guest for dinner. Ambrose hasn't told you?" She looked at her man again, and Congreve frowned.

"Sorry, dearest, hadn't got round to it yet,"

Ambrose said, expelling a fragrant cloud of Peterson's Irish Blend.

"Coward," Diana said to her beloved, taking Ambrose's hand and squeezing it.

"Well, who is this mystery guest?" Hawke asked, looking at the two of them, who were looking at each other. "Don't tell me the monarch heard I was coming and arrived unexpectedly on your doorstep."

"No, no, not Her Majesty the Queen, I'm sorry to say. But someone equally formidable. Tell him, dear, don't keep the poor boy hanging."

Ambrose looked at Hawke like a brain surgeon steeling himself to deliver a less than ideal diagnosis.

"Sir David Trulove rang me up earlier today, Alex. He just arrived in Bermuda late last evening. I offered to put him up, but he's staying with some dear old friends who live here on the island, Dick and Jeanne Pearman. They've a lovely place over in Paget called Callithea. They've put Sir David in their guest house, Bellini."

"C is here? On Bermuda? Why?"

C was the chief of MI-6, the British Intelligence Service. As far as Hawke knew, his idea of an extended vacation was a leisurely stroll to the corner concessionaire for a pack of his favorite smokes, Morland's, a blend of Turkish and Balkan tobaccos with three gold bands on the filter.

"Well, good question. He's been out inspecting the Royal Navy Dockyards all day. Lord knows why. Nothing but curio shops and a few restaurants out there now. At any rate, he called here rather early this morning looking for you. Sounded as if you yourself might be in a spot of *eau chaud* with the old boy."

"*Eau chaud?*"

"Sorry. Hot water."

"Just because one *can* speak French doesn't mean one should."

Congreve sighed and gave Hawke a narrow look.

"At any rate, he feels you dropped off his radar without much warning. I told him of our dinner plans with you tonight, and it would have been rude not to include him."

Hawke was astounded. "What on earth would he be doing in Bermuda, Ambrose? C, of all people. He doesn't take holidays, as far as I know. He barely takes food and water."

"You'll have to ask him, I'm afraid," Ambrose said, getting his pipe going again.

"Oh, come on, Constable. Spill it. You must have some inkling. What does your gut tell you?"

"My gut? I wouldn't trust my subconscious if it were only just around the corner."

Hawke had known Ambrose Congreve for far too long not to suspect he was holding something back. He could feel the beginnings

112

of tension surging into his neck and shoulders, and the feeling was not altogether unpleasant. Of course, he could be leaping to conclusions. C, the chief of British Intelligence, might well take a few days' island time. He worked like a dog, round the clock, but the head of MI-6 was certainly entitled to some vacation now and then.

But he would not be calling around looking for Alex Hawke if something spicy wasn't up. Would he?

Diana squeezed Alex's hand and moved away. Hawke watched her floating across the moonlit terrace toward the house and thought she'd never looked lovelier. Congreve was a lucky man.

"Dinner will be served in one hour. I'm off for the kitchen," Diana said, smiling back at the two men, "Sir David's just arrived, Alex. I put him in the library. He said he had to make a few urgent calls, but he wanted a word with you before dinner. I have a feeling you're in for quite a session."

"So much for peace," Hawke said to Ambrose after Diana had left them alone. "That's what I bloody came here for, isn't it? A little peace?"

"Qui desiderat pacem, praeparet bellum!"

"I'm sorry. What did you say, Constable?"

" 'Let he who desires peace prepare for war.' Flavius Vegetius Renatus. Roman military strategist, fourth century."

"Ah. I thought that might have been Flavius. Sounds like something the old bugger might say."

Congreve was not amused.

"Vastly overrated, peace, I daresay," Ambrose said, looking at his friend with narrowed eyes.

"Well, that's a fairly bellicose comment, coming from one who fancies nothing so much as burrowing about in his garden amongst his bloody dahlias."

"I have hidden depths, Alex. Even from you."

Hawke took a long swig of his rum. "Ah, well, no matter. Easy come, easy go."

"Another Dark and Stormy?"

Alex shook his head. "You know what this is all about, don't you, Ambrose? Why C is here on the island?"

"Hmm," Congreve said, and he meant it.

"Spill it."

"Russians."

"Russians?"

"Remember the hungry Russian bear, Alex? Remember the Cold War?"

"Vaguely. That was my father's war, not mine."

"Well, it's back with a vengeance. Only this time around, it's not cold. It's hot as hell."

9

Gulf of Alaska

The skipper of the *Kishin Maru,* a giant commercial fishing trawler sailing out of Shiogama, Japan, had been on the bridge for the duration of the sudden and appalling storm. The blow had appeared out of the clear blue, with nothing on radar or weather sat to indicate its approach or severity. Only a sharp drop of the mercury minutes before the storm hit had alerted the crew to what was in store for them.

The waves were mountainous, now thirty feet or more and building. Winds, now out of the northeast, were clocking at more than fifty knots. And the barometer was at 29.5 and still dropping.

The skipper's trawler, normally in use as a pirate longliner, was now seining in the Gulf of Alaska for Alaskan pollock. Noboru knew he was inside the two hundred mile limit imposed by the Americans because of over-exploitation, but at the moment that was the least of his problems. The sudden blow had caught him unawares and he was scrambling to secure his vessel.

Captain Noboru Sakashita's trawler, owned by the giant Japanese fishing conglomerate Nippon Suisan, was accustomed to navigating dangerous waters. Indeed, it was company policy to push the edge of the envelope, as the Americans said.

Noboru's company was run by a madman named Typhoon Tommy Kurasawa, a man who liked to live, and work, dangerously. He had one rule for his commercial skippers: Do whatever it takes to fill your holds. The ships in his fleet were all "pirates." They carried no markings, to ensure that they could fish without restriction. These fishing pirates all flew "flags of convenience" to hide their owners' identities. FOCs were sold by many countries with no questions asked.

Typhoon Tommy hated the Americans. But he loathed the Russians more. Russians shot first and asked questions later.

Just six months earlier, Noboru's FOC trawler had been fired on by a Russian Border Coast Guard patrol vessel. The Japanese captain, under corporate orders, had been fishing the banks off Kaigarajima Island, part of the disputed Russian-controlled northern territories. It was there, in a place called the Kuril Islands, that the shooting took place.

116

When Noboru, under orders, had sailed outside the authorized area, the Russians had immediately fired flares in an attempt to get him to stop. He slowed his vessel, radioing Nippon headquarters for further instructions. Meanwhile, the Russians had launched dinghies loaded with armed men in an attempt to board him. That's when he'd further ignored their orders and tried to escape. The border patrolmen in the small boats had opened up with machine-gun fire.

Three of Noboru's crewmen had been killed instantly. Three others who had been wounded had fallen into the water and were taken captive aboard the Russian patrol boat. Later, the Russians claimed the illegal Japanese trawler had rammed their patrol boat and refused to stop despite repeated orders to do so. The Russian ambassador to Japan had taken this case to Tokyo, and there had been a very public trial. Protesters from Greenpeace had hounded the captain mercilessly every day outside the courthouse.

Noboru was lucky just to avoid the loss of his commercial license and even jail.

"Sir!" the radioman shouted above the noise of the wind. "We have an emergency distress beacon. Repeating SOS signal. Very close by, sir."

Noboru stepped away from the helm and held out his hand for his binoculars.

"How close is the EPIRB?"

"Half a mile off our starboard bow, sir. You may be able to see him shortly."

The captain stood at the rain-streaked windows and scanned the horizon as much as the shifting waves allowed. The emergency position-indicating radio beacon used a five-watt radio transmitter and GPS to indicate the precise location of a mariner in distress. It was odd, Noboru thought, that he'd heard no radio messages of a vessel in distress prior to the EPIRB broadcast. Whatever boat this raft had come from, she'd gone down in an awful hurry.

A minute later, he saw the life raft sliding down the face of a huge wave. It looked like a small red mushroom bobbing on the storm-tossed sea. By its size, he judged it to be an emergency offshore raft, two-man. Self-righting, with the bright red canopy top providing high visibility and protection from hypothermia. Probably from a small yacht and not a commercial vessel. That might account for the lack of a radio distress call prior to abandoning ship.

Yachtsmen tended to panic in an emergency.

"All back one-third," the captain said.

The big trawler, already under just enough power to give her steerage in the huge waves, slowed even further as the crew made preparations to take the raft aboard.

■ ■ ■ ■

The two Russians sealed inside the enclosed circular life raft were ready to rip each other's throat out. If they hadn't both been so violently seasick, it's possible they might have succeeded. The waves were tossing them around inside like a pair of dice in a cup. It was impossible to remain in any one place for more than a split second.

The stench of commingled vomit was contributing mightily to their extreme irritation with each other. Because of the sloshing puke, it was even harder to keep from sliding around inside, slamming into each other every time the raft crested a wave and started screaming down the other side.

"What is this fucking storm?" Paddy Strelnikov shouted at his companion. "I didn't volunteer for any fucking typhoon duty!"

"Look, you think I did?" Leonid Kapitsa said. He was ex-merchant marine, a burly Russian émigré, maybe forty. He was probably KGB, secret police, just off the fucking boat, as far as Paddy was concerned. All muscle, no brain. Just the kind of guy you want with you when your life is coming to a speedy conclusion. The guy's English was pathetic, so they were screaming at each other in Russian. In the old KGB days, field agents were trained in languages. Not anymore, obviously.

"It was flat calm when they launched us. Why didn't they tell us it was going to get this rough?" Paddy shouted hoarsely.

"The storm came up fast. I don't know. Maybe they didn't know about it, either."

"My ass. These big yachts have weather radar and shit. They know what's going on. They knew we would —"

"They said we'd be floating out here for no more than an hour before the beacon got us picked up. It's been three hours now. And they didn't say anything about Hurricane Katrina showing up."

"You were supposed to turn on that EPIRB thing as soon as the yacht was out of sight."

"Yeah, well, I was too busy puking my guts out to remember."

"Look, you're the merchant marine guy. You're not supposed to get sick. You're supposed to know what you're doing out here. That's the only reason I agreed to have you along."

"Wait — I hear something. You hear that?"

Paddy did. Japanese voices, shouting somewhere above them, muffled but very close. The wind was still howling, but suddenly the raft wasn't bucking and yawing around so much anymore. It felt as if they were being lifted straight up out of the sea. Yeah, he could hear the gears grinding on a winch somewhere.

"Finally," Paddy said. He tried to wipe his face clean but only smeared stuff in his eyes and made it worse.

"I'm going to be sick again," Kapitsa said, and suddenly was.

"Ah, fuck," Paddy said, trying to steer clear of the latest volley of projectile vomit to head his way.

It was warm and dry in the captain's cabin just aft of the bridge. Paddy and Kapitsa sat on the only two chairs, wrapped in wool blankets and drinking steaming-hot green tea. At Paddy's feet was a waterproof sea bag he'd had in the raft, a yellow duffel that contained some equipment and his personal items. Kapitsa had a bag, too, slightly larger.

Now that he'd had a hot shower, Paddy's teeth had stopped chattering, and he felt halfway human again. The Japanese sailors had given them crew clothes, denims and T-shirts and wool sweaters that almost fit. The Japanese captain, who spoke pretty good English, sat at his desk. He had some papers he was filling out and was asking a lot of questions. Since it would never matter what he said, Paddy was having fun with the guy, making stuff up, whatever popped into his brain.

"You are Russian?" the captain asked.

"He is," Paddy said, indicating Kapitsa and

sipping his hot tea. "I'm a Russian-American. Third generation."

"Your name?"

"First name? Beef. B like in boy, e-e-f," Paddy said, carefully enunciating each letter, dead serious.

"What city you from in America, Mr. Beef?" the guy said, writing that down and then holding his pencil ready.

"Me? Orlando," Paddy said, saying the first town that popped into his head. "You know, Mickey Mouse? Goofy?"

The captain smiled and nodded, getting it all on paper.

"You know why Mickey got so pissed at Minnie, right?"

"Mickey pissed at Minnie?" the captain said, writing it down.

"Yeah. He said she was fuckin' goofy."

"Ah, yes," the skipper said, looking now at Leo. "And what about him?"

"Him? Forget about him. He's from frickin' Siberia. Just put Siberia, that'll be good enough. Every Russian postman knows where it is."

"Last names?"

"Stalin and Lenin."

"You joking?"

"No, no. Those are two very common names in Russia."

"What happened to your boat? We did not hear a distress call."

"Yeah, well, it happened pretty fast."

"You were only two aboard?"

"Nah. There were some other guys. They didn't get off in time. Tragic."

"So. No other survivors?"

"Nope. Just us."

"What was name of your vessel?"

"*Lady Marmalade.*"

"How you spell that?" He was actually writing all this shit down. Guy didn't have a fricking clue.

"L-A-D-Y M-A-R-M-A-L-A-D-E."

"How big?"

"Maybe a hundred feet. Maybe two hundred. Hard to say. I'm not into boats. And Orlando's not a real yachty town, you know what I'm saying, Captain? Middle of the state, only a couple of dipshit lakes in the orange groves."

"What happened to yacht? Fire? Explosion?"

"Beats the shit out of me. I think we just got knocked over by a big-ass wave. She rolled upside down and didn't come back up for air."

"You very lucky to get off."

"You think so? You weren't inside that frickin' life raft, Cap."

"Okay. You get some sleep now, Mr. Beef. I will radio news of your rescue to my company."

"That won't be necessary, Cap," Paddy

said, pulling the little snub-nose out from under his blanket. "We don't want to be rescued quite yet."

"What you — what you want?" the captain said, his eyes suddenly gone saucer wide.

At Paddy's nod, Leo Kapitsa got out of his chair and went over to lock the captain's cabin door. Then he went around behind the captain, standing behind his chair. He placed both hands on the captain's head, cupping his temples. Then he began to apply pressure, gentle at first, then increasing it in tiny increments, just enough to make the pain excruciatingly unbearable.

"What do we want?" Paddy said. "We want to take care of business and go home, that's what we want. But first we want you to get on the horn and order a lifeboat lowered."

"Lifeboat?"

"Here's the deal, Skipper. Your boss Tommy Kurasawa fucked with the wrong Russians back there in the Kuril Islands. Could you stand up for me a second? Help him up, Leo. Gently, gently."

Kapitsa lifted the captain straight up out of his chair by the head. The guy looked as if he was going to have kittens.

"We brought you a little something," Paddy said. "Take a look."

Paddy had unzipped the sea bag and taken out a large metal disc about four inches thick and twelve inches across. It was a dull grey color and had a digital display panel blinking red on one side. Paddy stood up, took the disc over, and placed it on the seat of the captain's chair. Thing was heavier than it looked. Must have weighed twenty-five pounds, including five pounds of the explosive sky-blue putty known to terror cognoscenti as Hexagon.

"Sit him back down," Paddy said, and Leo let go of the guy's head, letting him drop two feet onto the top of the disc. Paddy pointed the gun at the captain's nose and spoke softly.

"Pick up that phone to the bridge and order the lifeboat ready, Cap. We're going to be running along now."

"You leave ship on lifeboat?"

"Exactly," Paddy said, reaching between the captain's trembling legs to key a code into the disc's arming mechanism. "Here's the thing. This object you're now sitting on? Now that I've enabled the system, it's extremely pressure-sensitive. That's why Mr. Lenin has his hand on top of your head. You lift your ass up even a fraction of an inch off the pressure plate? Boom. There's enough explosive packed inside that thing to break this boat in half. So you want to be very, very careful, okay?"

"Bomb?"

"Bomb, exactly. It's set to go off at some point in the very near future. But it'll go off sooner if you raise your ass. Got that? Okay.

Pick up the phone. Call the bridge and tell them about preparing the lifeboat. Mr. Lenin-san here is an expert seaman, so you don't have to worry about us getting away safely, okay?"

"Can't get up?" Noboru said. "Leave chair?"

"Wouldn't advise it. Absolutely not."

"What I do?"

"If you're a good boy and don't move, after we're safely away from your boat, I'll turn the bomb off with this remote thingy. Then you can get up. Otherwise . . . well, I can't vouch for your personal safety."

The captain, whose natural skin color was a greyish yellow, had gone more over to the grey side.

"Pick up the phone and call the bridge," Paddy said, "and don't try anything funny. I speak perfect Japanese." He gave him a quick burst, asking the captain in Japanese where he kept the good sake locked up.

While Paddy and the captain were talking, Leo had gotten two Russian submachine guns out of his bag. The subguns were Bizon 2s. The Bizon was new, designed by Mikhail Kalashnikov's son, Victor. Pretty straight-forward weapon with a folding stock, standard black AK-74M pistol grip, and, at the muzzle, a small conical flash suppressor with teardrop ports. The magazine, aluminum, held sixty-four rounds.

Leo hefted the gun. Short and light, it was only twenty-six inches long. He looked at the subgun's selector switch and moved it to what he called the "group therapy" position. Full auto. He didn't anticipate much excitement with the Japanese fishermen up on deck, but you never knew. He put the weapon on the captain's desk, pulled the portable sat phone from his bag, and handed it to Paddy.

When the guy on board the Russian mega-yacht *Belarus* answered his call, Paddy told him they had pretty much wrapped things up here and were ready to leave the *Kishin Maru*. They would be boarding the lifeboat within the next five minutes. He would call again once they were at sea, but Kapitsa had advised that they'd be able to arrive at their prearranged GPS coordinates for a pickup in one hour.

"Sit tight, Cap," Paddy said to the captain as he went toward the door followed by the big Russian.

"Head," the captain said in a strangled voice. He was clutching the arms of his chair, his knuckles showing white with the strain.

"Head?" Paddy said. "Fuck's wrong with his head?"

"He means the bathroom," Leo told him, going out into the companionway with his Bizon submachine gun out in front of him. "He's gotta go."

"Bad idea, Cap. Seriously bad idea. I'd try

127

and hold it if I were you, think about something else."

Paddy took one last look at the captain sitting there on the pressure-sensitive plate bomb and then went out and pulled the door closed behind him.

Nice touch, he thought to himself, the pressure-plate idea. He'd have to remember to send corporate an appreciative note about that.

10

Bermuda

Hawke entered the book-lined library and saw C sitting quietly by the fireside. The room was an octagonal tower, bookcases on all sides rising two stories tall, with a clerestory window at the top. Sir David Trulove had a small volume of poetry lying open in his lap and had removed his gold-rimmed glasses. He was pinching the bridge of his nose and seemed lost in thought. A wine-red-shaded table lamp cast him in shadow.

The former admiral, one of nature's immutable forces, was a great hero of the Falklands War. Tonight he seemed subdued. It was out of character and gave Hawke pause.

"Good evening, sir," Hawke said, as mildly as possible. "Nice surprise, finding you here on Bermuda."

"Ah. The reclusive Lord Hawke," Sir David Trulove said, closing the book and looking up at him with an unreadable expression. He placed the slender volume on an end table beside the telephone and got to his feet, extending his hand. The older man was a good inch taller than Hawke, exceedingly fit, with a full head of white hair, furious white eyebrows, and a long hawklike nose. *Noble* was the word that came to mind.

Tonight, in perfectly cut evening clothes, with his lined sailor's face and clear blue eyes, hard as marbles, he looked like some Hollywood movie director's vision of a very elegant English spy. He was elegant, all right, but with a backbone of forged Sheffield steel.

"Do you read Yeats at all, Alex?" Trulove said, glancing down at the splayed book on the table.

"No, sir. Most poetry eludes me, sorry to say."

"You really shouldn't give up on it. I can't abide much poetry myself, but Yeats is sublime. The only truly heroic poet we have, I suppose. Well. Surprised to see me here, are you?"

"A bit. Mind if we sit?"

"Not at all. Would you be comfortable sitting over there?"

Alex nodded and took the other fireside chair. The old worn leather felt good, and he collapsed into its embrace. He was conscious of C's unwavering eyes and stared back at the older man. Neither looked away. It was a game they played, one that, so far, neither had lost.

"Having a splash of whiskey myself. Join me?" C said, his eyes drifting past the decanters on the sideboard and up toward the shelves of books rising to the octagonal skylight above. A narrow railed parapet ran around the room at the second-story level, looking hardly substantial enough to support a bird, much less a human being with a stack of books in his hands.

"No, thank you, sir."

"Alex, I hate to disturb what is no doubt a pleasant interlude in your life. God knows, after your last assignment, you've certainly earned your respite. But I'm afraid we must speak about a situation that may require your involvement."

He looked at Hawke, making him wait a beat. Both men knew perfectly well the precise three-word phrase forthcoming from the lips of the head of British Intelligence. He did not disappoint.

"Something's come up."

"Ah." Hawke tried not to betray the pulse-quickening feeling that always accompanied hearing those three magic words from his superior.

"Are you fully recovered from your maladies? Jungle fevers gone? No recurrence?" His hard eyes regarded Hawke attentively. Hawke had very nearly died of an assortment of tropical diseases, including malaria, in the Amazon recently. There were some in C's in-

131

ner circle at the old firm who believed Hawke might never fully recover.

"Clean bill, sir. Never felt better, to be honest."

"Good. I've made an appointment for you tomorrow morning with a friend of mine here on Bermuda. At St. Brendan's Hospital. Chap named Nigel Prestwick. Internist. Quite a good man. Used to be my personal physician in London before he came out."

"I'd be happy to see him, sir," Hawke said, trying to hide his irritation. He'd yet to meet the doctor who knew his body better than he did, but it was obvious C was taking no chances. Hawke was secretly pleased. This level of concern boded well for an interesting assignment.

"I very much doubt that. Your feelings about physicians are no secret. Nonetheless, your appointment is at nine sharp. No food or drink after midnight. After your physical, I'd like you to meet me out at the old Naval Dockyards. You'll find a car and driver waiting outside the hospital. I'm looking at some real estate out there, and I would value your opinion."

"Real estate, sir?"

"Yes. Let's skip the chase and cut to the *denouement,* shall we?" C said, leaning forward and putting his hands on his knees.

"Fine with me."

"It's the Russians."

"Back to the good old Cold War, are we?"

"Not yet. A lukewarm peace, perhaps. But it won't last. There's a distinct chill in the air."

"A new turn for the worse?"

"You remember when Mother Russia was the sworn enemy of democracy and freedom?"

"I do."

"She's swearing again. Like a bloody sailor."

"I'd really no idea."

"Good heavens, Alex, have you read a newspaper lately? Turned on your television?"

"Don't have a telly. And my reading pretty much centers around a pair of chaps named Huck Finn and Nigger Jim at the moment. I did hear something about critics of President Vladimir Rostov, journalists, getting bumped off at a rather alarming rate, but I'm afraid that's about it."

Sir David rose to his feet, clasped his hands behind his back, and began pacing back and forth in front of the hearth as if he were stalking the poop deck while enemy mastheads climbed the far horizon.

"These recent political assassinations are the tip of the iceberg. Our relations with the Russians have just about bottomed out. Last summer, Russia signed a billion-dollar arms deal with Hugo Chavez, the charming Venezuelan chap you had a run-in with recently. Chavez wasted no time in fantasizing aloud

133

about using Venezuela's new weapons to sink one of our aircraft carriers, the HMS *Invincible,* which is in the Caribbean at this time. Last week, the Russians delivered highly sophisticated SA-15 antiaircraft missiles to Iran. We know why, too. To defend Iran's nuclear sites, a clear threat to the balance of power."

"The new Russia's sounding a lot like the old Russia."

"If that's not enough, the Sovs — excuse me, the Russians — are building a bloody billion-dollar Bushehr reactor for Iran, which will produce enough spent plutonium to produce sixty bombs minimum."

"These are not our friends."

"How much do you know about the Grey Cardinal and the Twelve?"

"Sorry? Grey Cardinal?"

"Kremlinese for Rostov. Tells you a bit about how he's regarded."

"Don't know a great deal, sir. Ex-KGB. Strong, silent type. Cold as ice. Impossible to read."

"Hardly. He's a passionate, emotional man who is extraordinarily good at concealing his true feelings."

"A good poker player."

"As a matter of fact, yes, he loves the game."

"I hope you're not going to ask me to lure him into a few hands of five-card stud. Cards are hardly my strong suit, sir."

A brief smile crossed C's lips.

"Vladimir Rostov is not a democrat. Nor is he a Tsar like Alexander II, a schizophrenic paranoid like that pockmarked dwarf Stalin, or a religious nationalist like Dostoyevsky. But Alex, he is a little of all of these. And that is just what the Russians want in a leader right now. He is *nashe,* even though he frequently drinks Diet Coke instead of vodka."

"Nashe?"

"Russian word for 'ours.' Symbolic for the new Russian pride in all things Russian. A reaction against the groveling, humiliating embrace of Western culture during the nineties, guilty embarrassment at being caught at a McDonald's wolfing down a Big Mac, slurping Pepsi instead of quaffing vodka like a true Russian. Listening to the Dixie Chicks on the radio."

"I would also imagine it is quite refreshing not to have your brave leader stumbling around the Kremlin knocking over the samovars."

C smiled. "I miss Yeltsin, actually. Look here, I have our abbreviated Rostov dossier, which you can read at your leisure. But let me give you a quick sketch as a basis for our immediate discussion. Vladimir Vladimirovich Rostov, known popularly as Volodya, was born into a poor working-class family in 1935. Both parents were survivors of Hitler's brutal nine-hundred-day siege of Leningrad. His two brothers were killed by the Nazis and his father grievously wounded in the defense of the city. These were prime motivators in his decision to enter the intelligence game."

"So, he hates the Germans. That could be useful."

Trulove nodded, happy to note that Hawke was already thinking ahead. He said, "At age fifteen, Rostov saw a film, *The Sword and the Shield,* which glorified a Soviet spy's exploits inside Germany during the war. He tried to join the KGB at age sixteen. Just marched into the local headquarters and asked to sign up. They turned him down, obviously, and told him to get a university degree, study law and languages. He did, and they recruited him upon graduation from Leningrad State University."

"He finds espionage romantic," Hawke said, rubbing his chin.

"What?"

"I've seen that film you mentioned. Very romantic portrayal of the fearless Soviet double agent, alone, deep inside the Reich, stealing secret documents to sabotage German operations. In other words, accomplishing single-handedly what whole armies could not."

C took a sip of his whiskey.

"I wonder, do you find it romantic, Alex?

Espionage? The black arts of derring-do?"

"Not even slightly."

C's eyes registered approval, and he continued, "Tall, thin, and delicate in appearance, our little Volodya, at age ten, fell prey to neighborhood bullies. He began a lifelong study of *sambo,* a Soviet combination of judo and wrestling. He was deadly serious about it. Still is, actually. He earned black belts in both *sambo* and judo and nearly made the Olympic team. A year after earning his international law degree and joining the KGB, he became judo champion of Leningrad. I mention all this only because I think it provides a vital clue to his true personality."

"Yes?"

"His boyhood judo coach is still alive. One of our chaps in St. Petersburg had a chat with him recently. Let me read you a bit from his dossier: 'Volodya could throw with equal skill in both directions, right and left. His opponents, expecting a throw from the right, would not see the left one coming. So, he was pretty tough to beat because he was constantly tricking them.' "

"I see what you mean."

"Rostov's inherent inscrutability and judo were perfectly matched. He's got an innate ability to read his opponent's moves while concealing his own intentions."

"It's not a sport to him. It's a philosophy."

"Exactly."

"It's fascinating, sir," Hawke said. "I'm most anxious to learn where all this leads."

"To Moscow, Alex."

"And once there?"

"You'll know more tomorrow. For now, let me just tell you why I'm here on Bermuda. I intend to establish a new top-secret section of MI-6. For want of a better name, I've decided to call it Red Banner. Its sole reason for being will be vigorous counter-intelligence operations against the newly reconstituted Russian Cheka."

"Cheka?"

"Chekists were the Bolshevik version of the KGB. A word formed from the Russian acronym for Lenin's Extraordinary Commission, or secret police. It's run by a group of men inside the Kremlin I may have mentioned earlier. They're called the Twelve. In Russian, it's the *siloviki*. Translation, the all-powerful."

"Their role?"

"We think it's possible they pull all the strings. That the Grey Cardinal serves at their pleasure and acts at their direction."

"So Rostov's a disappointment, is he? We had rather high hopes for him at one point."

"There's some very unpleasant news coming out of Moscow, Alex. Our highest priority is to protect the young states of Eastern Europe. The Kremlin has already tried to force the collapse of democratically elected governments in Estonia and Georgia. And punished other independent neighbors by cutting energy deliveries."

"To what end? They're all sovereign states now."

"We think all this strong-arming is only a prelude. There's a strong possibility she may try to take them all back. Restore her old Soviet borders by force. And once she's digested her eastern neighbors, she's going take a hard look at the rest of Europe. Western Europe's at Russia's mercy, even now. The Kremlin can shut off the flow of energy to our European allies any time it damn well wants to."

"Christ."

"You could say that. That's why this urgent need to revitalize our intelligence operations vis-à-vis the Russians. And we need to do it *now.*"

"And our new counter-Chekist branch will be based where?"

"Right here. On Bermuda. We're going to the Dockyards in the morning after your appointment in Samara with Nigel Prestwick. Find some office space for you."

"For me?"

"You're to head up this new special division, Alex. I've thought long and hard on this, and I'm convinced you're the ideal chap to take this on. You've put together quite an outstanding record these last years, you know."

"I'm honored. Thank you, sir. Of course, I —"

"Alex, you can have some time to think this over. But time is short. I need you to be brutally honest. Do you have any qualms? Reservations?"

"My Russian is nonexistent, for one."

"But your comrade-in-arms Chief Inspector Congreve is fluent. And you'll be surrounded with other fluent personnel from the firm."

"Ambrose knows about this — Red Banner?"

"He's part of your team. Already signed on. Two other young fellows from the MI-6 Russian division have come over as well. Benjamin Griswold and Fife Symington. First-rate lads, both of them."

"I see. Well —"

"Listen, Alex. I know this is all quite sudden. You don't need to respond tonight or even tomorrow. But if your answer is affirmative, the sooner I know, the better, so I might get on to the next candidate. It's early days, but we're at a critical moment in a new duel with these twenty-first-century Chekists."

"Pistols at dawn?"

"Not quite. But we do need to move with alacrity. Something's very much up, as I said, and I doubt it will be an extended olive branch. One year ago, I would have put the number of Russian covert operatives working inside Britain at fewer than one hundred. In the last month alone, I've seen estimates that put that number at well more than a thousand."

"Astounding. Any correlation with what our American cousins are seeing?"

"The same, if not worse. Your friend Brick Kelly at CIA is just as concerned as we are. The Kremlin is sitting atop a deeply entrenched criminal enterprise with unlimited wealth and natural resources as yet untapped. The Russian economy is suddenly booming right along with the price of oil. As I say, they could bring Europe to its knees in less than an hour by simply turning off the oil and gas taps. They won't do that unless pushed, of course. They like the cash flow too much. So, what the devil is going on with the big Russian bear? That, Alex, is what Red Banner is going to find out."

"I understand. One question, if I may, sir. Why base this new operation in Bermuda, of all places?"

C smiled. "For one thing, it's almost equidistant from London and Washington. But more important is secrecy. I can't run this thing out of 85 Vauxhall Cross. Think about it, Alex. The Russians have invaded London. Not only the obscenely wealthy oligarchs buying up Mayfair palaces but the newly reborn KGB, as well. The bloody Russian spooks and tycoons are everywhere you look. Dysfunctional, amoral, and nothing is out of bounds."

"I'd heard the Russian *mafiya* are buying up casinos and completely taking over London's prostitution rings. White slavery run out of Eastern Europe and the Gulf States. Londonistan, I hear they're calling it these days."

"I'm afraid so, Alex. In the nineties, we were dealing with a kleptocracy, a government in chaos run by competing thieves. These billionaire bandits have stolen Russia blind. Literally, in a few short years, stolen an entire country in what amounts to the greatest theft in history. Now the country is in the hands of the secret police. Putin was first to put former KGB cronies in every possible position of power. The New Russia is the world's first true police state, ground up. Now, rich beyond measure because of soaring oil revenues, they're looking around for new worlds to plunder."

"I'm still not sure I understand your choice of Bermuda for Red Banner, sir."

"Again, geography. Is there a more isolated, a more pristinely British spot on earth than this tranquil little pastel archipelago? Any Russian setting foot on this island to poke about in our nest will stand out like a sore thumb."

Hawke was about to mention the exquisitely beautiful sore thumb he'd met on the beach earlier that afternoon, but at that moment, Lady Diana Mars poked her lovely head inside the library door and said, "Gentlemen, dinner is served."

"After you, comrade," C said to Hawke with a smile.

"Spasiba," Hawke said, thanking him and virtually exhausting his Russian vocabulary.

He'd have to learn some bloody good Russian swear words so he could let Ambrose have it for leading him by the nose into this little trap C had laid for him.

11

New York City

Sleigh bells ring, are you list'nin'? Paddy still got that old tingle. Christmas in New York, you couldn't beat it with a stick. Something in the air, that's what they said, and they were right. Fuckin' magic, that's what it was. He was leaning on the rail on the Fifty-third Street side, overlooking the skating rink at Rockefeller Center. He still got a kick out of it, just as he did when he was a snot-nosed kid living at the wrong end of Neptune Avenue in Brighton Beach. Coming into the city with his dad had been a big deal, especially at Christmastime.

A light snow was falling, like movie snow, it was so fine and sparkly, and it was getting dark fast, making that huge tree glimmer and shine. He squinted his eyes, making the tree go all hazy the way he used to do as a kid. How about that, huh? Beautiful thing to see, even at his age.

Even the skaters were still fun to watch.

The babes in their little pleated skating skirts were the best ones. You couldn't put on an outfit like that and step out onto the ice unless you could skate like an angel. Then you had the guys. Something about a guy lifting one leg and skating along like a friggin' swan just didn't sit right with him, never had.

Like guys who took tub baths instead of showers, tough to trust. The really good guy skaters had to be fairies, right? And the really bad ones, like this gangsta character who just took a header and slid butt-first into the wall, should not have been on the ice for any reason whatsoever.

"Hey, Spazmo! Yeah, I'm talking to you, the great one! Nice move, man, look like Wayne friggin' Gretzky out there!"

He laughed and looked at his watch. The office Christmas party started at six, and here it was now already quarter past. After the endless flight from Fairbanks friggin' Alaska, he'd gone straight to his room at the Waldorf and gotten a few hours' sleep, leaving a wake-up call with the operator for four-thirty.

He'd stopped in at P.J.'s for a couple of pops and lost track of the time. But yeah, he was pumped about the party. It would be the first official event at the new corporate offices at the top of the Empire State Building. Somebody said they were having Gladys Knight, but that could have just been the water cooler talking.

He wasn't sure what time the big boss would show up for this wing-ding, but that was something he definitely didn't want to miss. Most employees never got the chance to see the man himself. The Queso Grande, the honcho, the muckety-muck, the man behind the curtain. Yeah, tonight was going to be very special. There was even a crazy rumor about the way the old man was going to arrive tonight. He had no idea how, but he was pretty sure the boss man wasn't going to be stepping off a Fifth Avenue bus.

Better get a move on. He turned away from the skaters and started walking quickly east along the beautifully decorated mall toward Fifth Avenue. Christmas shopping was going full-bore now, and he had to be careful about knocking anybody down who got in his way. People, when they saw his size, normally got out of the way fast. But in a crowd like this, it was tough to move fast without seriously injuring anybody.

Paddy hung a right on Fifth and started walking south down to Thirty-fourth Street. The crowds were amazing, especially the lines across the street forming outside the Saks windows. Something was also going on farther along the avenue, because they had these giant searchlights shooting straight up into the clouds. You could see the beams sweeping back and forth through the snow, lighting up the dark bellies of the low-lying clouds and flashing across the tall spires that lined the street of boyhood dreams.

It took him all of ten minutes to reach the Empire State. The searchlights, on flatbeds, were right outside the main entrance, aimed up at the tower. The tower at the top was always lit up with beautiful lights, sometimes red, white, and blue or red and green like now for Christmas. But the searchlights were crisscrossing the building, and it looked like some kind of Hollywood premiere or something. All kinds of TV trucks with big dish antennas out there, too. Something big was going on, all right.

Walking inside the three-story lobby, Paddy felt a touch of pride. After all, this was his office. Kind of.

He'd come a long way from the Brooklyn dockyards where he was just another punk longshoreman with a thirty-inch neck and a whole lot of attitude. He was now an important part of a multinational organization with a fancy corporate headquarters at one of the most famous buildings in the world. After September 11, 2001, it had become the tallest building in New York again.

He looked around the lobby, his lobby, taking it all in. Art deco, he thought they called it. Looked good to him. Glitzy, but old-fashioned glitz. He'd never been upstairs to the corporate offices before, so he went over to the fancy marble info desk and spoke to the nice little Jewish lady who looked as if she'd been behind that counter her whole life. Her nameplate said "MURIEL ESB." Esb? Esb didn't sound like any Jewish name he'd heard of, and then he realized maybe it was the initials of the building? Yeah.

"Welcome to the Empire State Building! How may I help you?"

"How you doing, Muriel?" Paddy asked her, showing her his employee ID card, "I'm looking for the TSAR Christmas party?"

"Oh! Aren't you the lucky one, Mr. Strelnikov? That's going to be something to see. Especially from up top where you'll be."

"Something to see? You mean Gladys Knight?" He could give a flying crap about Gladys Knight, but hey, it was Christmas, stick with the spirit.

Muriel smiled. "Didn't you see all the searchlights out there? And the TV cameras? It's not Santy Claus they're waiting for, you know."

"Yeah? Who they waiting for?"

"Your famous boss! He's supposed to arrive at seven o'clock. That's one half-hour from now, so you'd better get up there."

"What's he doing, flying in on Air Reindeer or something?"

"Something like that," she said, and they both laughed, and he asked her again where he was supposed to go.

"Your cocktail reception is on the very top

148

floor, where the 102nd Floor Observatory used to be. A lot of people aren't too happy about losing that observation deck, you know, Mr. Strelnikov. Even though we still have the one on the 86th floor, the 102nd was the best."

"Well, what are you going to do? That's progress for you. You take care of yourself, huh, Muriel? And Merry Christmas to you and all the other little Essbees."

The company had bought the whole top third of the Empire State two years ago, all the way from the 70th floor up to the 102nd floor. They'd spent a cool hundred mil or so gutting the place and outfitting it as befits the North American headquarters of Technology, Science, and Applied Research, Inc.

TSAR. Like the old Russian rulers. It was just more of the boss's sense of humor to call his huge company that. You had to hand it to the guy. For a bona fide genius and one of the top ten richest billionaires on the planet, the guy had a lot of style. But what he did that Paddy admired most, he took care of his people. All the way down to the little guys like Paddy himself. If you could call him a *little* guy, he thought, laughing at his own joke.

Paddy stepped into an empty elevator and hit the express button for the top floor. It shot up like a friggin' rocket, and he stepped out a couple of minutes later. It was like landing on another planet.

A marble-floored glass room now took up the whole top floor of the Empire State. The ceiling and walls, all glass and steel, had to be seventy-five feet above the heads of all of the people milling around drinking and schmoozing. He made his way over to the windows on the Fifth Avenue side. All around him were the tops of the towers of Manhattan and, overhead, the snow clouds lit up by the searchlights on the streets below. In the center of the room was a square glass elevator tower that went right through the ceiling and up to some kind of radio tower or something that rose another twenty stories or so above where he was standing.

There was a big covered platform about halfway up the tower and a lot of activity going on. He walked around a little, trying to see what the deal was, but it was impossible to see from down here.

"King Kong supposed to show up again tonight?" he asked the bartender at one of the many bars around the edges of the room. Most of them had lines, people waiting for a drink, but, for some reason, not this one.

The guy laughed and said, "You'd think, huh? No, just the world's richest man, is what they tell me."

"Gimme a vodka rocks, will you?"

"Vitamin V, coming right up."

"Thanks."

"You work for this guy?" the barkeep said,

filling a tumbler with the bar hooch and sliding it over.

"Yeah. Long time."

"You in sales? I'll tell you why. I'd like to get one of those new Zeta machines for my kid. You know, the little computer that looks like a brain? I tried every CompWorld in town, but they're all like back-ordered forever."

"I ain't in sales. Sorry."

"Hey, no problem. You want another?"

"With a name like Smirnoff, it's got to be good, right?"

Paddy shoved his glass over for a refill, and the guy said, "So, your boss must be pretty smart, huh? Invent the Zeta and all that shit. He's what, a Russian, right? What's his name again?"

"Only name I've ever heard is somebody calling him Tsar Ivan. Tonight's my first shot at actually seeing the guy up close and personal."

"Well, guess what?" the bartender said, backing away from the bar and looking straight up, "I think you're about to get your shot. Holy shit. Will you look at that?"

Paddy backed away from the bar and looked up, too. He was so startled and amazed at what he saw that he dropped his glass, and it shattered on the marble floor. In the roar of the crowd, he never heard it hit.

■ ■ ■ ■

What Paddy saw floating high above the glass ceiling was nothing less than a flying miracle. It was not an airplane. And it was not a blimp, exactly, though it moved like one. It had to be some new kind of airship. But it was like nothing he or anybody else had ever seen before. It was this four-hundred-foot-long zeppelinlike thing, its hull a gleaming silver. On its flank, forward, was the huge word *TSAR* illuminated in bright red. On her tail section, the great Russian red star, restored to respectability by President Putin before he'd mysteriously disappeared off the face of the map.

But the thing wasn't shaped like any blimp he'd ever seen before, either. For one thing, there was a big opening at the nose, huge, and then the thing tapered back to a much smaller section at the tail. It didn't look like a Goodyear blimp at all, not in the slightest.

It was a strange shape, weird, but it reminded him of something. The only thing Paddy could compare it to, what it actually looked like, was one huge flying jet engine. As if a giant jet engine had fallen off some giant jumbo jet's wing and was just flying along all by itself. There were triple rows of windows along the side, and you could see all of the people in there, looking down at the party below.

Yeah, that was it, an enormous silver jet engine, moving very slowly toward the big aerial at the very top of the Empire State Building.

He kept backing up, trying to see more of the thing, and he backed right into somebody, knocking him to the floor.

"Hey, jeez, I'm sorry," Paddy said, turning around and offering the guy a hand, pulling him to his feet. He was a little guy, and Paddy almost jerked him off his feet into the air.

He'd been wearing thick black glasses, and they were tilted sideways on his face. Paddy adjusted them for him and tried to brush whatever he'd been drinking off the front of his thick wool sportcoat. Bloody Mary, it looked like from the stalk of celery balanced on his shoulder. Not good.

"Never mind," the man said. "It's all right. It was an accident."

Paddy thought the little guy was pissed off, but maybe he wasn't, so Paddy stuck out his hand and said, "Paddy Strelnikov, nice to meet you."

"Dr. Sergei Shumayev," the guy said in a thick Russian accent, re-adjusting his coke bottle glasses.

"Hell of a deal, huh? That thing up there?"

"Yes. What exactly do you do for us, Mr. Strelnikov?"

"Me? I'm in the, uh, 'analytical department.' "

Shumayev smiled at the egregious euphemism. Every large Russian corporation created its own mini-KGB, usually known as the "analytical department." It was staffed with people good at collecting information, eavesdropping on rival companies, and stealing documents. They also performed other, less sanitary services, what the American thriller writers referred to as wet work.

"What's your specific role in the department, Mr. Strelnikov?"

"Well, special assignments. Security, mostly. My section deals with industrial espionage, stuff like that. Here in the U.S., I also provide personal security to some of our high-level executives when they're traveling here and abroad."

"Ah, very good. A bodyguard."

"Something like that, yeah."

"That's a very unusual ring you are wearing. Does it have some special significance to your job?"

Paddy laughed. He loved it when people noticed his ring. "No, sir. This ring here I bought in a pawn shop in Hoboken for fifty dollars. Nobody knew what it was. See the lightning bolt? And the letters TCB? Well, that stands for Taking Care of Business. It's the exact ring that Elvis Presley gave to everyone in his posse. Back in the sixties.

That was their motto, TCB, and I made it mine, too."

"Fascinating."

"How about you, Doc? What do you do?"

"Aeronautical engineering. That's my baby up there."

Both of them watched as huge dangling cables were thrown down from the front and sides of the hovering airship and made fast to the mooring mast. Floating there in the clouds, with the searchlights playing on it, Paddy thought it was the most beautiful man-made thing he'd ever seen.

"No kidding! Wow! You worked on that?"

"*Vortex 1* is its name. I designed it. With a great deal of technical help from our chairman, of course. It was entirely his vision. His original concept. I was lucky enough to be able to execute it for him."

"No offense, but how come you're not up there on the platform with all the other big shots meeting him?"

Now the little fellow really was pissed off. "Officially, I'm supposed to be, of course. It's just that I've lost my wife in the crowd. She went to the ladies' powder room twenty minutes ago, and I haven't seen her since. She'd kill me if I went up there without her."

Paddy winked and said, "I know what you mean. Women, huh? I could write a book myself. Hey, let me ask you, Doc, what is that big hole in the front of the airship for? It's wild-looking."

"It's called a plenum," Shumayev said. "It draws in atmospheric air through a spiral-vortex-generating cone, hence the name of the ship. The air is then accelerated through a BDP Tesla bladeless disc air pump system. This accelerated and pressurized air is then forced out through a central ring of slits located along the side of the craft. You follow?"

"Sort of."

"Think of a fish's gills."

"Gotcha. So, what makes it go?"

"All that pressurized, oxygenated, and velocitized air flowing in through the plenum forms vortices along the outside hull of the airship. This reduces friction and creates a slip effect as the craft travels through the air. So, the craft is first pulled into a frontal vacuum, into the vortex, as it were, and additionally squeezed through the air, compliments of the greater pressure exerted by the expelled air traveling aft along the hull of the craft. That's pretty much it."

"How do you steer it?"

"See those outboard pods with the blinking red lights? They're fitted with smaller electric-drive BDP propulsion systems. We mounted them at different locations around the hull to provide a high degree of directional control and afford vectored thrust stability in any weather conditions."

"Wow."

"In a word, yes. Wow. That mast tower up there was originally intended to be a dock for mooring airships back in the 1930s. However, after several futile attempts at mooring a zeppelin in the strong winds present up here at 1250 feet of altitude, the idea was scrapped. So, Mr. Strelnikov, you and I have the honor of witnessing a very historic moment."

"How many passengers will it carry?"

"Exactly one hundred. Just like the late Concorde aircraft. But our passengers will travel in a great deal more comfort and style, I promise you."

"How fast?"

"A bit slower than the Concorde," the little guy said with a smile. "She's capable of 150 miles per hour. Considerably faster than the new *Queen Mary 2,* I might add, if one's crossing the Atlantic as she's just done."

"I think I just found your wife," Paddy said, grabbing the little guy's elbow. A huge red-haired woman in a black sequined gown was plowing through the crowd and headed straight toward them, murder in her eyes. "Thanks for the info, Doc. I'll be seeing you around."

"No!" Shumayev whispered, "Please don't go. Just stay with me for a few minutes, all right? Until she calms down?"

You had to feel sorry for a guy who needed a bodyguard around his wife. He said, "Yeah, okay. But it's going to cost you, Dr. Shumayev."

"Anything. What can I do?"

"When all the excitement dies down, I'd like a guided tour of that thing. The *Vortex 1*. Could you arrange that?"

"Consider it my privilege, Mr. Strelnikov," he said as the lady arrived.

Mrs. Shumayev was one unhappy camper. She was opening her wide, red-painted mouth to let her hubby have it when the little guy interrupted.

"Dearest, this is my colleague, Mr. Strelnikov. I was just about to invite him to join us aboard *TSAR* for the demonstration flight out to Long Island tomorrow morning."

"Say what?" Paddy said.

"Where the hell have you been?" the irate woman said in Russian. "I step into the powder room for two seconds, and —"

Paddy Strelnikov gave her his best smile and said, "It's my fault, Madame Shumayev. I'm with security. I thought there was a threat situation here, and I removed your husband until we got it cleared up. So — hold on a sec." Paddy spoke into the sleeve of his jacket and cupped one ear, listening intently to a nonexistent earbud. "What's that? All clear? Good." He smiled. "All clear now, Doctor. It's safe for you and your wife to go up to the platform now."

"Thank you, Mr. Strelnikov," Shumayev

said. "Your concern for our safety is deeply appreciated."

"TCB," Paddy said, and headed back to the bar for another cocktail. "TCB."

12

Bermuda

"Lovely day for it, Cap," Hawke's driver said, looking back at his passenger with a huge white smile. He was a handsome young Bermudian police cadet officer named Stubbs Wooten. Attached to the British consul's office in Hamilton, Wooten had been assigned by C to fetch Hawke from St. Brendan's Hospital.

Now they were driving west out along the South Road in the direction of Somerset Village. They had passed the venerable resort at Elbow Beach and the lovely old Coral Beach Club, and were en route to what Bermudians called the West End. There, at the very tip of the island, stood the Royal Naval Dockyard.

Having risen early and endured the physical ordered by his superior, Hawke was now scheduled to meet C at the Dockyard at eleven o'clock. He had half an hour, which Stubbs assured him was plenty of time.

The ocean, periodically visible on their left,

was brilliant blue, and only a few white clouds drifted in over the island from the west. Their route took them past the Southampton Princess Hotel, a huge pink palace sitting atop a hill overlooking the Atlantic. Just beyond, Hawke could see the soaring white tower of the Gibb's Hill Lighthouse, built of cast iron in 1846 and providing comfort to seafarers ever since.

But Hawke wasn't interested in sightseeing at the moment. He was far more interested in the noisy black motorcycle some hundred yards behind him. He thought he was being followed.

"I wonder, Stubbs," Hawke said, craning around once more to look over his shoulder at a lone motorcyclist. "Did you see that chap on the bike back there in the parking lot at St. Brendan's Hospital?"

Stubbs studied the fellow in his rearview mirror.

"No, sir. But I did notice he's been following us quite a while. A Jamaican, I think. Rasta gang member, possibly. You think something's wrong, sir?"

"I think he was parked up in the trees by the emergency entrance. I'm fairly sure I saw him when I came out to meet you."

"Possible, sir. You want me to lose him?"

"When is the next turning off this road, Stubbs?"

"We got Tribe Road Number Three coming

161

up on the right. 'Bout half a mile now."

"Good. Turn into it, and stop the car. Let's see what this fellow does."

"You got it, Cap," Stubbs said, clearly enjoying this bit of drama. He loved his job, the important people visiting his island whom he got to meet, but it was seldom exciting.

Stubbs didn't signal his turn or even slow much, just suddenly braked and jerked his wheel hard right. The little sedan threatened to go up on two wheels as it negotiated the hard turn. As soon as they were safely around, Stubbs stood on the brakes and skidded to a stop on the side of the road.

As the dust settled around the car, Hawke kicked open his rear door and said, "Wait here, Stubbs. I'll see what he wants."

"Are you armed, sir?" Stubbs asked.

"Yes, why?"

"Because some of these Rastafarian gentlemen will be armed, sir. Watch out for him. He most likely has a knife. Maybe a gun."

The cyclist, caught short by Stubbs's sudden maneuver, almost lost it. But he stayed upright and managed the turn without a spill. He braked to a stop, eyes on the man standing in the road, hands in his pockets, smiling at him. Without a word, the biker splayed his long legs out on either side of the bike and stared insolently at the tall white man now coming across the road toward him.

"Morning," Hawke said, looking around as

if taking in the beautiful day. The biker was dressed like a typical Bermudian tough. Jeans, motorcycle boots, and an oversized jersey with Emperor Haile Selassie's image plastered on the front. Masses of gold chains around his neck. Chunky gold watch that looked real enough.

He was young, maybe twenty-five, Hawke thought, and had the build of a serious prize fighter. One who still worked out with the bag or in the ring on a regular basis. His nose was as flat as his face. Massive upper-body strength, lean with well-developed arms, quads, and lats, and riding a very expensive Triumph motorcycle. He was either dealing drugs or working for someone who paid him large sums to do the odd, violent favor.

"I said good morning," Hawke repeated, taking another step toward the bike.

The kid didn't reply, just leaned back on his seat and slowly removed his helmet, shaking his head as he did so. Dreadlocks suddenly exploded from under the black helmet and fell to his shoulders. He smiled for the first time, revealing a mouth full of golden teeth.

"You got a bad driver, mon. I serious. Him very dangerous."

"What's your name?"

"My name? Desmond. Don't try to lose me like that again, mon. It won't work. I stick to you like glue on glue."

"Now, why on earth would you want to do that, Desmond?" Hawke asked, his right hand gripping Desmond's handlebar and wrenching the front wheel hard left so that the bike was immobilized.

"Hands off de bike, mon!"

"Who's paying you to follow me?"

"I just out for a ride, mon. It's a beautiful mawnin', like you say. Why you get so all excited? Having a little fun, dat's all, huh? And take de hand off my bike before you lose it."

"Lose it?"

Desmond lifted the jersey so Hawke could see the cane knife stuck in a scabbard on his wide leather belt. A sawed-off machete, razor-sharp on both sides.

"Desmond, listen carefully. I want you to turn this bike around and go back to wherever you came from. Tell whomever you're working for that following me is a very bad idea. I'm a very private person. I'm here for a quiet holiday. Someone spoils my vacation, they will wish they hadn't. All right? We understand each other?"

Desmond spat in the dirt and looked up at Hawke with his reddened eyes blazing. He was seriously baked on marijuana, Hawke realized. But the thug didn't say anything, just showed his gold teeth once more and reached for the knife.

The Jamaican was vaguely aware of blurred

movement. Hawke had seized Desmond's wrist in a compromising position before his fingers ever reached the knife handle.

"I will break it, Desmond, I promise," Hawke said. "Right now, I'm applying pressure directly to the scaphoid, the small carpal bone at the base of the thumb. It's the one easiest to break, also with the most painful result."

"Shit, mon, you ain't going to break it."

"No? Who paid you to follow me?"

"Fuck you, mon."

"Your place or mine?"

The kid spat, barely missing Hawke's left foot.

"Last chance?"

Desmond glared, wincing at the pain, saying nothing.

"No more joy rides for a while, Desmond," Hawke said, smiling at the man as he deftly snapped his wrist, eliciting a howl of pain.

Hawke's hand blurred again, moving for the ignition switch atop the fuel tank. In an instant, Hawke had plucked the key from the ignition and flung it out into the scrub brush on the hill beside the road.

"What you — aw, fuck, mon, now I going to have to —"

"Desmond, you're no good at this. Surveillance is a highly sophisticated art form. Go back to dealing *ganja*. Street dealers have a much longer life expectancy than people stupid enough to get involved with me."

Hawke turned his back on him and crossed the dusty road. He climbed back into his car, and Stubbs turned it around and headed back to the South Road. Desmond remained on his bike, too proud to let Hawke see him searching for his keys.

"You see all those gold teeth, Cap?" Stubbs said, looking at Hawke in the rearview mirror, waiting to rejoin the flow of traffic on the South Road.

"Hard to miss."

"Disciples of Judah. That's their trademark, replace all their teeth with gold. A Rasta sect, immigrated from the Blue Mountains of Jamaica many years ago to work in the banana plantations. They went bad. Drugs, sir. Cocaine, marijuana, heroin, you name it, the Disciples deal it. The big boss is a man named Samuel Coale. Call him King Coale. He was extradited to the U.S. a few years ago under the Foreign Narcotics Kingpin Act. We heard he was back on island. That boy you just talking to?"

"Yes?"

"He say his name?"

"Desmond."

"I thought that was him. He's the favorite son. The son of King Coale. Calls himself the Prince of Darkness. You see his graffiti tags all over the place you visit Skanktown on St. David's Island."

"He's a fighter, is he? Boxer?"

"How'd you know that?"

"Sometimes you can tell."

"Yes. Fought under the name of Prince back in Jamaica. Fought his way to the top, won the Golden Gloves in the Caribbean, and then went to the Olympics on the Jamaican boxing team. He won the gold medal at Athens in 2004."

"All downhill from there, it looks like."

"Couldn't handle the success, sir. The fame went to his young head, swole it up."

"Where can I find his father, this King Coale?"

"Hard to say, Cap. These boys move around a lot. There's a rumor they have an offshore compound out on Nonsuch Island down by St. David's. Illegal because it's a wildlife sanctuary. But that's what I hear. Squatters' rights."

"How long to the Naval Dockyard?"

"We'll be there in twenty minutes, sir."

"Could you make that ten?"

"I'd be delighted to try, sir," Wooten said, as he pulled a red flasher out of the glove box and stuck it on the dashboard.

Hawke sat back in his seat and gazed out the window, lost in thoughts that led straight to Anastasia Korsakova's door. She had called him at some ungodly hour that morning. He'd stumbled half-asleep to the bar and reached blindly for the phone. He had a vague memory of agreeing to come to her house that afternoon at five. He felt peace slipping away from his grasp. What with C's proposal and the appearance of the lovely Miss Korsakova, the halcyon days of idle bliss seemed to be waning.

"Hallowed ground on your right, Cap," Stubbs Wooten said, interrupting Hawke's reverie ten minutes later.

They were approaching the Dockyard compound. The mostly empty early-nineteenth-century buildings and facilities had not seen use since the Cold War. They were still lovely, though. Especially the twin spires of the Dockyard Clocks in the distance.

During that era, the Cold War, the Royal Navy had conducted clandestine air and submarine surveillance operations to keep the Soviets from regarding the Atlantic as their ocean. At that time, Bermuda was a principal naval base in defending the United States from Soviet attack. The Royal Navy still maintained a minimal presence here. Although it was minor now, with C's new operation, the old Dockyard might soon become more fully operational.

Hawke looked to his right and saw the hallowed ground. A lovely old cemetery nestled in a gently sloping valley between the growths of tall Australian pine trees on either hilltop.

"Royal Navy?" Hawke asked.

"Yes, sir. First consecrated in 1812 when the Dockyard was still being built. See that big stone spire, grass grown up all around? Many men from the British Army and Royal Navy buried there, mostly died of the yellow fever. But some of the newer headstones there are the final resting place for the seamen who died on their ships off Bermuda in actions against German pocket battleships and U-boats."

"I had no idea," Hawke said as they passed through the narrow entrance gates. They rode in silence as they passed the abandoned docks to their right and the Dockyard Clock spires on their left.

"See that building on the high hilltop over there? That's where your meeting is, sir. The Commissioner's Building. Will you be needing me to wait?"

"I'd very much appreciate that, Stubbs. I've an appointment later this afternoon out at St. George's. If you could take me out there?"

"Pleasure's all mine, sir."

"Place called Powder Hill. Do you know it?"

Stubbs turned around in his seat. "That's a private island, sir. You have to go by boat. Very tight security. Don't let anyone near that place."

"They're expecting me."

"Ah, well, you're fine, then."

Hawke smiled as the car came to a stop,

popped the door open, and climbed out of the back. The structure itself was a lovely old three-story British Colonial building, somewhat the worse for wear, built on a hill overlooking the sea. It was just inside the fortress walls and surrounded on all sides by bastions with cannons still in place. A wide verandah graced the two topmost floors, with shuttered doors on all sides.

He could see Sir David waiting in the shade at the covered entrance. As Hawke got closer, he saw that C was wearing old white duck trousers with a Spanish flare, a striped Riviera sweater, straw shoes, and an ancient Mexican hat.

Hawke could hardly believe the vision the head of SIS presented. And there was a woman with him. Blonde and very goodlooking, in a simple linen shift of lime green that did little to hide her spectacular figure. It was certainly Pippa Guinness, he thought, squinting in the sunlight, one of C's closest aides at MI-6 in London. Although he could not have explained why, Hawke was both surprised and not surprised to see her. The bad-penny principle, he supposed.

"Sorry to be late, sir," Hawke said, shaking C's hand. "Spot of bother on the road."

"Spot of bother?" Sir David said.

"Minor irritation."

C's idea of tropical attire threw Hawke a bit. It was difficult to take a man in such costume seriously. Hawke was accustomed to seeing Sir David in a crisp foulard tie and a three-piece worsted number in either navy or dark grey from Huntsman of Savile Row.

C said, "You remember our Miss Guinness, don't you, Alex? Guinevere Guinness? You two were on special assignment together, as I recall. Florida, wasn't it?"

"Of course. How could I not remember Pippa, sir? She's unforgettable. How do you do, Miss Guinness? Lovely to see you again."

Hawke had been intimately involved with the woman during a previous mission that had taken them both to Key West. She was an intelligence analyst at MI-6, assigned to Hawke at a Caribbean security conference. They'd had an ill-advised fling and had not parted on the best of terms. He waited for her response with some curiosity. He imagined she felt hard done by and wouldn't blame her if she did.

"Hello, Alex," Pippa Guinness said, smiling as if she were actually happy to see him. A strange girl, indeed. The first time he'd seen her, she'd been one of the Garden Girls, working for the prime minister at Number 10 Downing Street. The last time he'd laid eyes on her, she was storming down the gangplank of his yacht *Blackhawke,* in tears.

"Anything serious? On the road, I mean?" C said, interrupting the awkward silence that followed their exchange.

171

"Young thug on a motorbike followed me from the hospital. I had a chat with him and convinced him it was unwise to continue."

"Followed you. I don't like the sound of that."

"I've got a name. I'll look into it."

"Do that. Let's get started, shall we? Miss Guinness and I think we've found just the spot."

"After you, sir."

C led the tour. "The first two floors are devoted to the Maritime Museum. Wonderful displays, you should see sometime, Alex. Bermuda war history. We've taken over the entire top floor with permission of the Bermuda government."

C led them down a corridor and up three flights of beautiful Bermuda cedar stairs. Having attained the top floor of the building, Hawke saw that the abundance of tall French doors, windows, and warm sunlight made it far more hospitable than the ground floors.

"Here we are," C said, a broad smile on his face. "What do you think, Alex? The new headquarters for our secret nest of spies?"

"Lovely views," Hawke said. It was true. The views were to the south, across the South Channel toward the entrance to Hamilton Harbor. Sailboats, fishing boats, and ferries plied their way over the smooth blue surface of the Great Sound.

"Yes. I thought our chaps could take this

end of the hall. Griswold and Symington, the two young MI-6 fellows I mentioned bringing over, will have their offices down there near yours. And I thought we'd put the Yanks down there at that end."

"The Yanks, sir?"

"Didn't I mention that? This is to be a joint operation with our friends at Langley. We could hardly afford to go it alone on our budgets, and since we've clearly a common interest, Director Brick Kelly at the CIA has agreed to a goodly portion of the funding. He's picking someone now, a top American field operative who would liaise with you on Red Banner. Kelly envisions a secret allied counterterrorist training camp here. He's even trying to get the Pentagon to recommission the Dockyard's old sub pens and base one of their Atlantic Fleet attack subs here. SSN 640, the former USS *Benjamin Franklin.*"

"I think it's all brilliant, sir," Pippa said, favoring C with her winning smile and then looking at Hawke. "Don't you agree, Alex?"

"Are you planning to spend some time here on Bermuda, Miss Guinness?" Hawke said, his voice cracking slightly despite straining for nonchalance. Before she could open her lovely mouth, C spoke for her.

"I've asked Miss Guinness to be administrative head of Red Banner, Alex. Reporting to you, of course, should you decide to accept this assignment."

"Ah. Yes. Quite."

C looked at him and smiled. "What *have* you decided, Alex?"

Hawke looked at Pippa, smiling up at him with a combination of mirth and mischief in her beautiful eyes. He was trapped, and she knew it. Still, the job C offered was an important one. The more he'd considered C's offer during a restless night, the more inclined he was to accept. Red Banner section would be a good way to serve his country perhaps more substantially than he had done previously. Perhaps even more rewarding than some of his last efforts on behalf of the service. He realized he'd already made up his mind. And it was too late to change it.

"Well, Alex?"

"I'd be honored, sir. I'm very flattered that you and the firm put such faith and trust in my abilities."

"Splendid!" C said, putting a hand on his shoulder. "A good decision, Alex. Well, it's nearly lunchtime. I think a bit of celebration is in order, don't you both agree? There's a lovely pub out here, just opposite the Maritime Museum. Called the Frog and Onion. Shall we all stroll over and have a tot of rum?"

"Oh, let's do!" Pippa said, gazing not at C but at Hawke.

"Of course we should," Hawke said with as much joviality as he could muster, wondering what in God's name he had just gotten himself into.

He would learn soon enough.

13

New York City

Paddy felt a slight heaviness in his heels and knew that the airship must be climbing. He glanced out the nearest window and saw that they were angling upward, the sunlit towers of the Manhattan skyline pivoting away as they left the midtown mooring behind and headed out toward Long Island. So, he'd missed the whole departure thing, too, throwing off the lines and the TV crews and media people on the platform waving good-bye, et cetera.

Hell, he was news. For the first time in his whole freaking life, he was *news.* And he'd missed it.

He was also completely lost. He'd begun the tour along with his new best pal, Dr. Shumayev, and a bunch of journalists, everybody oohing and aahing over the luxurious interior appointments aboard the corporate flagship. He'd been at the back of the group and had stopped to admire a beautiful model of the

Hindenburg, about six feet long, inside a glass case. This was on the B Deck, in the Atlantis reception lounge, where blonde babes in blue uniforms served coffee and Danish before the grand tour began.

Anyway, when he looked up, the group had left him alone, and he'd decided to just wander around on his own, see what he could see. It was cooler, actually, than tromping around like a bunch of ducks, listening to the ship's purser (what the hell was a purser, anyway?) explaining everything in a whole lot more detail than he really needed. Looking at one of the passenger suites, the purser had informed them that all linen aboard was Egyptian cotton with a thread count of more than 1,200! *Really, 1,200? Sign me the hell up!*

So he set off on his own, heading aft along a wide corridor lined to his right with almost floor-to-ceiling windows. It was called the Promenade. Every five feet was a comfy-looking leather chaise facing the outward-slanting windows, little round tables in between. Light was pouring in, and a couple of windows were slid open a foot or so, and there was a nice chilly breeze blowing through. The views of Long Island Sound were spectacular.

Nice place to hang for a couple of hours or the rest of your life. Paddy could imagine it when there were passengers aboard. The ship was already sold out for its maiden crossing to England, the purser had informed them. *Maiden voyage? As in, all virgins? Hey, I'm in.* He could see all the swells sitting here, sipping their tea and reading novels or whatever they did. Nice way to travel across the Atlantic, he thought, skimming along a few hundred feet above the waves at 150 miles an hour, listening to the latest beach book on your iPod.

Yeah, one day, he just might have to spring for a trip on this beauty.

He came to the end of the Promenade. A glass door slid open, and he was in some kind of reading and writing room. There were comfy armchairs scattered around and also little desks with old-fashioned blotters and inkwells and stationery with a big red T engraved at the top. *Tsar.* Great name for a great ship, he had to admit.

Next was a kind of foyer with a staircase and another hall branching off that must have connected to the other side of the ship. He peeked inside a leather-padded door marked "Odeon." It was a little jewel box of a movie theater with red velvet seats and two golden dolphins over the screen. He kept going straight and found the gym, typical exercise bikes and treadmills and shiny weight machines all along the windows. Personally, he didn't see the kind of people who would book a flight on this thing being all that interested in sweat. More interested in the wine-and-cheese buffet, he'd bet.

And finally, as far back as you could go, there was a shiny silver elevator door with bronze dolphins carved into it. What the hell, he'd already seen what was up front. He pushed the button, and the doors slid open. There were a total of five decks, two below him and two above him. He pushed the top button. *Going up, ladies' lingerie.*

"Private," the big guy in the black suit said when the doors slid open. "Didn't anybody tell you? No press allowed." He was holding a small Glock submachine gun loosely at his side. He had a single gold stripe on each sleeve of his jacket. Private army. Ex-Russian special forces, had to be.

"Sorry. I'm freaking lost here."

Paddy reached for the button, and the doors had started to close when the muscle man stuck his foot out and automatically opened them again.

"Hold on a second," the guy said. "You're not Paddy Strelnikov?"

"Dimitri Popov?"

He knew the guy, all right. Gone to high school with him in Brighton Beach. Then his family had moved him back to the Soviet Union. Last time he'd seen Dimitri, it was on TV. Barbara Walters was interviewing him in Athens after he'd won the gold in Olympic wrestling for the Russian Federation.

"All-Beef Paddy!" Popov said, "Yeah, how you doin', player? Come out here, talk to me. It was you went out and blew up that prison in the boondocks, right? That was some sick shit, huh? Sixty jerkoff cons on Death Row catching the train on the same night? I loved that! And you know what? I wasn't the only one to think so. You got friends in high places, my man."

"Yeah, well."

"Listen, I'm not supposed to do this, but you want a quick look-see around? This is some serious shit up here."

"What about your elevator?"

"I'll lock it. Got a remote right here. There. Game's locked, throw away the key, remember?" He dropped the remote back into his pocket.

"What's up here?"

"The man, baby. This whole deck is his private world."

"Ivan?"

"Count Ivan Korsakov, baby. Who else?"

"He's a count?"

"Fuck no. He's a god. Come on, there's a bar down this way. I'm on duty, but I can get you a Bloody Bull. You look like you could use a little eye opener."

"Jet lag."

"You know what cures that? Pussy. We got that up here, too. In spades."

Paddy drained the last of his second Bloody Bull and put the glass down on the mahogany bar. The bartender, a Ukrainian girl named Anna who was a dead ringer for Scarlett Johansson, whisked his glass away and said, "One more?"

Paddy shook his head and turned to Dimitri. "So, let me get this straight. You're saying you think I could get a job working for the man? I mean, directly?"

"Man, I know you could. I'm telling you, he just lost his closest security guy in that latest assassination attempt three months ago in Moscow. Driving out of Red Square. This guy was more than muscle, he was the man's last surviving brother. In real life, his real brother, is what I'm saying. Lifelong best asshole buddies. The brother took a stomach full of lead for the man. Now he's got nobody."

"What about me?"

"What about you?"

"I'm nobody. Backstreet borscht with a gun."

"Fuck that! Man, he *knows* you. He knows exactly who you are. That prison thing? Shit, I was in the screening room watching CNN with him the night you showed the world the true meaning of Death Row, man. You should have seen him light up. I'd be surprised if he doesn't carry your laminated picture around in his fuckin' wallet. And sinking that Japanese trawler up in Alaska? C'mon, Beef. You think he doesn't know who's out there getting his personal shit done for him every day? He knows *everything,* man."

"Taking care of business," Paddy said, twisting his ring around so he could see the lightning bolt. "TCB."

"Straight up. Yeah. And you know what else, I personally think you should have a little talk with him."

"What?"

"Talk to him. See if he likes you. Why the fuck not?"

"He's here?"

"Of course he's here. You think he checked into the Plaza? This is where he lives half the time. Look, I'm going to call him, all right? Tell him you're aboard, that we're old friends and shit. You down with that?"

"Dimitri, hold on a second. What about you? Why don't you take the job?"

"Are you kidding me? I live in a flying pussy palace, Beef! I ain't going anywhere. Ever. Don't move, I'll be right back."

"You going to call him?"

"Hell, yeah, I am."

He left. Paddy said to Anna, "I gotta tell you, the views from this thing are unbelievable." He was staring down at forests of swaying treetops just below. The Pine Barrens, he thought, and that must be the Peconic River over there. Yeah, that's what it was, all right. They were about sixty miles from the city. A leisurely voyage, and so damn *quiet!*

"I've got the best office in the world," Anna said with a shy smile.

"You sure do. Tell me something, Anna, at what altitude does the *Tsar* sail?"

"Oh, right now, I'd say we're cruising at about six hundred fifty feet. That's our normal altitude when the winds allow. The captain likes to fly so the passengers have a view."

"We'll keep to that all the way out to Montauk?"

"If the winds hold. Normally, we would climb higher if the currents were more favorable aloft. But we're not trying to get anywhere in a hurry today."

"How high can you go?"

"Maybe four thousand feet."

"Anybody ever tell you what a pretty smile you have?"

"Occasionally," she said, laughing.

"You live on this thing?"

"Of course. It's my castle in the sky."

14

Five minutes later, Dimitri was back, dead-pan, no expression on his face. He plopped down on the adjacent barstool and ordered another club soda from Anna, then swiveled around and looked at Strelnikov.

"So?" Paddy said. "What? You talk to him?"

"Yeah, I talked to him."

"And?"

"He'd like very much to talk to you."

"You're shitting me."

"Nope."

"When?"

"Like, uh, now."

"Now. Where? Here?"

"Of course not here. In private. I'll take you. Come on."

"Where are we going?"

"The music room."

"Oh. The music room. Why didn't I guess that?"

"He's composing a fucking symphony. You believe that? For the Moscow Symphony

184

Orchestra. But he's going to stop right in the middle of that and talk to you."

"Holy Jesus."

"Let's go."

They left the bar and turned right down a softly lit corridor hung with what Paddy was pretty sure were paintings he'd seen in books. Each one had its own little brass light on it. Pictures of lily pads, et cetera, little bridges in gardens. French guy, what was his name? Monet or Manet or one of those.

"You're lucky, Beef," Popov said. "He's in a good mood today."

"Why is that?"

"He got a call from Stockholm early this morning. He's going to get the Nobel Prize in physics this year."

"Holy shit. What'd he do?"

"He's an astrophysicist, you know, just one of his many hobbies. He discovered something called a black body, some kind of radiation that helps prove the big bang theory or something. Dark matter. What do I know? He thinks the real reason he got the prize is the Zeta machine. Making a computer all the Third World countries could afford. He says the Nobel committee loves that do-gooder shit over there. Look at Al Gore, Carter, f'crissakes."

"Is he psyched? You gotta be, I mean the Nobel Prize, c'mon, jeez mareeze."

"Yeah. He's pretty happy about it. Here we are."

Popov rapped lightly on another leather-padded door, this one unmarked. He then pushed it open and stuck his head inside.

"Let's go," Dimitri whispered, taking Paddy's elbow. "Don't say anything. We'll just take a seat over there, and he'll talk to you when he's ready."

Walking into that little room was like stepping back a couple of centuries. It was four white walls with gold moldings everywhere. There were four large paintings depicting fairy-tale musical scenes in heavy gold frames, one on each wall. In the near corner was a harp. There were two men in the room, and Paddy didn't know who was who. Over in one corner by the window was a tall, gaunt man dressed in a black military uniform. He was standing with his back to the room, hands clasped rigidly behind his back, staring out the window.

The far corner was a kind of triangular bay window, containing a baby grand piano. The floor beneath the piano was glass. The other man, who was playing the instrument, did not look up and seemed unaware that anyone had entered his sanctuary. This piano guy, Paddy figured, had to be the man himself.

Korsakov, who had long snow-white hair, didn't look at all like Paddy expected. He was seated very upright on the bench. He wore a dark red velvet robe of some kind with a hood draped behind his head. He was playing the piano with his left hand and scribbling furiously with his right in a large leather notebook. There was a light on the piano, shining on the keyboard and a silver bowl of fruit.

To the right of the piano, along a wall some fifteen feet away, were a small silk-covered sofa and two armchairs. The new arrivals sat down on the sofa beneath a painting of angels playing harps and listened.

Paddy didn't know dick about classical music, but the notes Korsakov was playing sounded beautiful, or whatever. After a few minutes, Popov leaned over so he could whisper in Paddy's ear.

"That piano he's playing?"

"Yeah?"

"That was the piano on the *Hindenburg*."

"The what?"

"The *Titanic* of the Skies. The giant Nazi zeppelin that blew up at Lakehurst, New Jersey, back in 1937. You never heard of that?"

"Maybe. So, what, the piano didn't burn up, too?"

"It wasn't onboard. It was back in Germany at the Bluthner factory undergoing a tune-up. Made of aluminum and covered with pigskin. Hitler bought it and had it in his office at the Reichstag. The Russian Army smuggled it out of Berlin after the war. The boss bought it especially for this room."

Paddy was suddenly aware that the music had stopped and that Count Ivan Korsakov was staring at them over the top of Hitler's pigskin piano. He stretched his delicate fingers above the keyboard and clicked them like castanets.

"Good morning, Mr. Strelnikov," he said good-naturedly, in English. "Welcome aboard. I trust you are enjoying yourself on our sky vessel."

Without waiting for an answer, he stood up and walked across the parquet floor, taking one of the armchairs. He was tall and thin but muscled at the shoulders, and under the red robe he was wearing some kind of dark green velvet jacket. Very fancy buttons and piping on the sleeves. A smoking jacket, Paddy thought they were called. There was a gold pin stuck into one of his lapels.

At the top of the pin was a lapis lazuli crown with three red rubies, reminding Paddy that he was in the presence of true Russian aristocracy.

"You would like some Russian tea, perhaps? We have Kousmichoff, I believe," Korsakov said.

"I'm good, sir," Paddy said, crossing his legs and trying to hide his nervousness.

He didn't know why he was nervous. The man was the opposite of what he'd expected, some beady-eyed businessman. But no.

Handsome as a king in a storybook. His white hair reached his shoulders in curls, and his eyes were a pale watery blue. They looked right through you, but they didn't seem to mean any harm on the way inside.

"Someday, you must tell me the saga of the *Kishin Maru*," Korsakov said, smiling at him. "I understand it got a little rough in the life raft. Unpleasant."

"You know about that?"

"Mr. Strelnikov, I only have a few minutes. I am having one of my very rare musical inspirations, and if I let it expire without jotting it down, it may vanish forever. So, let me just say that I am aware of your recent activities and very pleased with the results. I've read your file. I thank you for your bravery and dedication to my cause. Do you know what that cause is?"

Paddy stared at him blankly. He didn't have a freaking clue.

"My cause is simple. Order. I cherish order. Only with the cosmic forces aligned in order can the heroic human quest for the sublime flourish. You cannot compose a symphony, or a Declaration of Independence, or even design a simple airship, for that matter, in the midst of chaos. Today, more than ever in human history, I believe, order and chaos struggle for supremacy in our world. Do you follow?"

"I think I'm with you so far."

"We are not involved in a clash of civilizations but in a clash between civilization and barbarism. Chaos."

"Yes, sir."

"I abhor chaos in any form. I am determined that order shall prevail. When I see countries ignoring the sanctity of our oceans, as Japan has done, I send them a signal. When a psychopathic monster wantonly murders newborn babies, I send a signal. I mention just two that you obviously know about. I send countless signals like the two I've just mentioned. All around the world. You are one of my messengers. So, you see, Mr. Strelnikov, how important men like you are to me personally. You sound my clarion call, you are my heralds of order. Some might say I seek nothing less than a new world order to come."

"Well, thank you, sir. I guess I don't know what to say."

What the fuck is a herald?

"Say nothing. I suffered a grievous personal loss three months ago in Moscow. In less than a minute, Chechen assassins plunged my life into chaos. I understand Dimitri has informed you of this horror."

"Yes, sir."

"I travel a good deal. Frequently to places where local security leaves much to be desired. There are many threats against my life, and I cannot eliminate them all. I need someone, Mr. Strelnikov, someone like you,

190

to help restore order in my daily life. Do you understand?"

"I do."

"Would you be willing to accept the position? I am talking about your becoming my chief personal bodyguard. Possibly, after a certain period of time has elapsed and you have proven your strength and loyalty, I would consider you for a higher position. Perhaps as one of those who will help me implement my worldwide vision for a new order. Security is order. Order is peace."

"Well, I, uh . . ."

"Consider the humble atom, Mr. Strelnikov."

"The atom."

"Yes. The atom. A positively charged nucleus surrounded by whirling negatively charged electrons. Immutable, indivisible, perfect. That is my cherished cause. That men and nations behave in an orderly fashion, like the very stuff they're made of. Atoms. So. Yes or no? What is your answer?"

"I'm not sure I follow. Is this about the atoms thing?"

"Do you want the job, or do you not want the job?" he said, a razor's edge in his voice.

"Oh, yes. I certainly do want the job, sir. Sorry if I —"

Ivan Korsakov got to his feet and returned to his piano. He sat down on the bench, took up his notebook, and immediately began playing a piece of music that sounded as if the little angels in the picture hanging over Paddy's head had written it.

After a few minutes, the two men on the sofa quickly realized they no longer existed and rose without a word, headed for the door.

"You start immediately," Korsakov said, not looking up or interrupting his playing to speak. "Dimitri will find you suitable accommodations aboard this ship and provide the necessary paperwork and orientation for your new position."

"Thank you, sir," Paddy said, but it was doubtful the great man heard him.

Once they were outside, back in the corridor, Paddy whispered, "I gotta be honest, I know he's a genius and all, but sometimes he sounds like a goddamn nutball."

"He gets on these jags about atoms, yeah."

"Maybe it's just me. But didn't we split the atom? It was in *Life* magazine years ago, f'crissakes. So, how is it 'indivisible'? See what I'm saying?"

Popov looked at him as if he hadn't a clue, which he certainly did not, pounded him on the back, and said, "But hey, there you go! What did I tell you? You're in! Welcome to paradise, Beef. Let's go forward to the observation platform and get a view of the landing."

"We're landing?"

"Yeah. He's just completed a new mooring

tower on his estate at the tip of Montauk Point. He's building these towers everywhere he has a house or palace, which is practically everywhere. Bermuda, Scotland, a Swedish fjord, you name it. We're going to try this one out for the first time today. There's a big lunch on the lawn for the press, and then we're heading back to the city to drop them off. Tonight, at midnight, we turn around and sail for Miami."

"Miami?"

"You got it, comrade. We'll be there by the end of the week, depending on the prevailing winds."

"Who was the weird Nazi in the black uniform?"

"That would be my boss. General Nikolai Kuragin. Head of the Third Department, the secret police."

"The Russian secret police?"

"Hell no. Count Korsakov's private army, his personal secret police. Kuragin was there checking you out. That's why he stuck around when you spoke to the big guy."

"Checking me out why?"

"That whole bodyguard thing was just a little game they were playing. Kuragin was the one interviewing you, to see how you handled yourself. He's considering you for a job. Bigger than what you're used to. High-risk. So he wanted a firsthand peek at the new guy. Now that you've been given the official blessing, I'm sure he'll be wanting to talk to you out at Montauk."

"What kind of job are we talking?"

"Ramzan Baysarov. Ever heard of him?"

"No."

"Chechen rebel warlord. Not even thirty years old and yet the scourge of the Kremlin. General Kuragin put a ten-million-dollar bounty on his head after that attack that killed the count's brother. Ramzan's also one of the guys linked to the 2002 Moscow theater attack that killed one hundred seventy people, the 2004 subway attack that killed forty-one, and a double-suicide bombing at a Moscow rock concert that killed seventeen."

"Seriously pissed-off guy."

"Yeah. Yeltsin and Putin had him sent to a Siberian gulag for twenty-five years. Apparently, he didn't like his pillow mints or the room service and checked out early. He just gave a press interview to ABC. He says he won't quit killing Muscovites until everyone in Russia feels his pain."

"And?"

"A couple of our guys had a chat with the ABC reporter last night. That reporter may have felt a little pain himself. Anyway, we now know where Ramzan is hanging out these days. Miami."

"Miami."

"Right. And Friday night is his thirtieth birthday. His Chechen *Mafiya* buddies in

Miami are throwing a little bash in his honor. Big mansion on the water in Coconut Grove. Half the fuckin' Chechen rebel sympathizers in America are going to be there."

"What's my job?"

"Make sure Ramzan doesn't finish blowing out all his little candles."

"Miami, huh? Beats the shit out of Alaska."

"Beef, trust me. You're going to love your new job."

"One more question."

"Yeah?"

"If I do this guy Ramzan, do I get the ten mil?"

15

Bermuda

Stubbs came to a stop where the sandy lane dead-ended at the dock. They'd reached the easternmost tip of St. George's, taking Government Hill Road all the way to Cool Pond Road. It was nearly five o'clock, and the sun was still shimmering on Tobacco Bay. A few very large sport-fishing boats were moored on the bay, riding the gentle swells.

There was a freshly painted white post bearing a very discreet sign that read "Powder Hill — Private." It stood just beside the floating platform that led out to the dock itself. The dock looked like any of the others jutting out into this small and tranquil bay. Most had small sailboats or runabouts moored alongside.

"Now what?" Hawke said, leaning forward to peer through the windshield.

"Looks like a phone box there, sir. Under the sign."

"Right. Hang on, I'll go see."

Hawke got out of the car and instinctively looked around to see if he'd been followed. He'd asked Stubbs to keep an eye on the rearview mirror, but they'd seen nothing out of the ordinary on the journey from the West End. Still, it didn't hurt to double-check. The narrow lane that wound down to the bay was empty. Golden-toothed Rastafarians on motorbikes were nowhere to be seen. He walked down the slight incline to the dock.

Mounted on the post was a phone inside a waterproof box. Fastened to the outside cover was a laminated sign: "Restricted Property! Invited Guests Only. Trespassers Will Be Prosecuted. Beware of Dogs. Armed Guards."

Sounds chummy, Hawke thought to himself, and opened the box. Ah, well, as Pelham had so aptly put it, a hundred clams an hour was pretty good gravy.

Hawke lifted the receiver to his ear.

"Yes?" said a noncommittal Bermudian female voice on the other end.

"Yes. Alex Hawke here. I believe Miss Korsakova is expecting me."

"Ah, Mr. Hawke," said the voice, much friendlier now. "Miss Korsakova is definitely expecting you, sir. She's at Half Moon House. I'll send the launch over immediately. Should be there in less than ten minutes. A driver will meet you at this end."

"Thanks," Hawke said, and replaced the receiver. He walked back up the hill to where

Stubbs waited with the car.

"They're sending a boat. Thanks for your patience, Stubbs. You should go home, it's been a long day. I'll make arrangements to get picked up here after my appointment."

"Yes, sir. It's been my pleasure driving you, Mr. Hawke. If you need me again, here's my card."

Hawke pocketed the card. "Stubbs, what do you know about this Powder Hill? Anything useful?"

"Small private island, sir. Maybe twenty-five acres. Originally, it was an English fortress guarding the approach to the north coast. Then a failed banana plantation. It sat in ruins for years. They tried to make a tourist destination out of it back in the sixties, but it was too difficult to access. There's a very strong riptide running between the island and the mainland. One day, the tourist boat capsized, and two honeymooners drowned, and that was the end of that."

"Then what?"

"It just sat out there. In the early nineties, we heard there was some rich European buyer. All very hush-hush. Turned out he was Russian, one of those new billionaires getting their money offshore. He poured millions into the place, kept most of the fort and made a house out of it. Put in a landing strip, a hangar, and a big marina on the western side of the island where he moors his yacht. Also recently erected a big radio and TV tower. No one knows what that's all about. Some say he's in the media."

"That yacht's not called *Tsar* by any chance?" Hawke asked, remembering the name stenciled on the hull of the Zodiac that had come for Anastasia Korsakova.

"*Tsar,* that might be it. Have you seen her, sir?"

"Not yet, but I suppose I will. Here comes my ride. Thanks again, Stubbs. I'll be seeing you."

"Pleasure was all mine, Mr. Hawke," Stubbs said. He waved good-bye, then turned around and headed back up the hill.

Hawke walked to the end of the dock, reaching it just as the gleaming white launch reversed its engines and came to a stop. He recognized Hoodoo at the helm. There was another chap, definitely not Bermudian, wearing crisp whites as well, who leaped ashore with lines and made them fast to the cleats. He kept an eye on Hawke the whole time, and it was hard not to notice the 9mm SIG Sauer MG-110 machine gun slung across his shoulder.

"Good evening, sir," he said, straightening up. "Mr. Alex Hawke?"

"Indeed I am," Hawke said, smiling at the young man, Russian by the sound of him.

"May I trouble you for some identification, sir?"

"You must be bloody joking. I'm an invited guest."

"Sorry, sir. House rules. We've had some problems."

"All right, then," Hawke said, opening his wallet to reveal the Florida driver's license he sometimes used. The address listed belonged to Tactics International. It was a company he partly owned in Miami, run by his good friend and comrade-in-arms Stokely Jones. "Happy?"

"Would you mind turning around and putting your hands above your head?"

"Of course not. Would you care to see my Highland Fling? It's legendary."

The man ignored this and went over every inch of Hawke's body with a handheld metal detector.

"Nothing personal, sir. Sorry for the inconvenience. All right, if you'll step aboard, we'll shove off."

"Hello, Hoodoo, I'm Alex Hawke," he said, grabbing one of the gleaming brass handholds and offering his other hand to the helmsman.

"Sir. Nice to have you aboard. We've met before, you say?"

"Just in passing. You probably don't recognize me with my clothes on."

Hoodoo, puzzled, smiled and shoved the throttles forward. Stubbs had not overstated the ferocity of the riptide currents roaring through the channel. Powder Hill was a fortress with a very intimidating moat.

"We don't get many visitors here," Hoodoo said, smiling at him.

"I imagine not. Few people would have the temerity to drop in unexpectedly."

Hoodoo's smile was enigmatic as he put the wheel over and headed for what appeared to be a large boathouse on the distant shore.

Ten minutes of rough water later, they arrived at the Powder Hill dock. At the far end was a block house that was clearly a security office. On the narrow paved road above, there was a dark green Land Rover waiting, the Defender model, all kitted out in brush bars, searchlights, and a siren mounted on the bonnet. Two men sat up front, a driver in khakis and another fellow in mufti wearing a sweat-stained straw planter's hat.

Hawke bid farewell to Hoodoo, stepped ashore, and made his way up to the waiting vehicle.

"Mr. Hawke," the passenger said as Hawke climbed into the small rear seat, "Welcome to Powder Island. My name is Starbuck. I'm the general factotum around here, prune the bougainvillea, keep Miss Anastasia's place looking good. Miss Anastasia asked me to fetch you and bring you round to her house." He had a broad black face and a beaming white smile. Hawke liked him immediately.

"This is a working banana plantation, Starbuck?" Hawke asked. They'd been winding up a hill through a dense, well-kept grove.

"Very small operation, sir. But yes, we turn a tidy profit every year. This island is self-sufficient. We grow all of our own vegetables, catch our own fish."

Hawke smiled. A few minutes later, they emerged from the gloom of the grove. They were atop a hill with great views in all directions. In the distance was St. George's. To his right, Hawke could see the main house. It was an eighteenth-century British fort that had seen a lot of restoration. There were a few cars parked on the gravel. To the right was the marina, with a very large yacht, more than three hundred feet, moored at the outer wharf.

To his left, the road wound down to a small bay on the far side. There was a two-story house by the water, lovely colonial architecture, enshrouded in bougainvillea. That, he assumed, would be Anastasia Korsakova's studio.

Between the two descending roads was a wide meadow of manicured grass. In the middle of that stood a steel tower about a hundred feet tall.

"Starbuck, tell me about the tower. For broadcasting?"

"No, sir, Mr. Hawke. That tower is a mooring station."

"Mooring? For what?"

"An airship, sir."

"Good Lord, still?" Hawke said. Airships had played a huge role in Bermuda's early aviation history, but he had no idea any of them still were in operation.

"This is a new one, sir. Built by the owner of Powder Hill. Before that, the last famous ones we had here on Bermuda were the *Graf Zeppelin* and the *Hindenburg,* both of which stopped here to drop off mail on the way to the United States. The owner of Powder Hill is building a fleet of airships for transatlantic passenger travel. Here we are, sir."

The driver pulled to a stop in front of the house, and Hawke climbed out, saying goodbye to Starbuck, who promised to return for him in an hour or whenever he called security.

The lovely old house had a wide covered verandah that wrapped all the way around the second floor. Hawke looked up to see Asia Korsakova standing at the bougainvillea-covered rail, smiling down at him. Her dark blonde hair was pulled up on top of her head, and she was wearing a pale blue linen smock spattered with paint.

"Mr. Hawke," she said, "you did come after all."

"You had doubts?"

"I thought you'd lose your nerve."

"There's still time."

She laughed and motioned him inside. The

203

wide front door was open, a dark foyer inside lit with guttering candles in sconces on the wall.

"Come straight up the stairway. My studio's up here."

The studio was a large space, a square, high-ceilinged room filled with the typical artist's chaos — easels, brushes, paint pots, and very large canvases stacked against the walls everywhere. Paddle fans revolved slowly overhead. What remained of the day streamed through the opened French doors and the big skylight overhead with filtered shades of rosy, buttery light.

There was a large open-hearth fireplace with a Bermuda cedar mantel. Above it hung a marvelous portrait of an inordinately handsome man in a splendid dress military uniform, standing beside a magnificent white stallion in battle livery. Hawke moved to study the work more closely. The effect was stunning, a powerful subject and a deeply heroic treatment, beautifully painted.

Anastasia appeared from a small adjacent room, carrying a tall drink on a small silver tray. He took it, and it was delicious.

"Welcome to Half Moon House," she said. "I'm so glad you came."

"Cheers," Hawke said, raising his glass. "Lovely painting over the fireplace, by the way."

"Thank you."

"Your work?"

She nodded. "I've always reserved that spot for the man I love. That's my father."

"Handsome chap."

"Comes from inside, you know. Always."

She looked even more luminously beautiful than the picture of her that he'd been carrying in his mind ever since that afternoon on the beach.

"Please sit over there in that wicker chair. I want to take a few photographs while we still have this beautiful light."

It was a long wicker chaise with a huge fan-shaped back and great rolled arms. The entire thing was beaded with beautiful shells of every color. There were deep cushions covered in rose-colored silk. It looked like the throne of some Polynesian king. Hawke removed his navy linen jacket, dropped it to the floor, and lay back against the cushions. She leaned in with the camera and began clicking away, shooting close-ups of his face.

"So, you do portraits."

"Yes."

"Judging by the one, you're quite good."

"Some people think so."

"Are you famous?"

"Google me and find out."

"I don't have a computer."

"Are you so desperately poor, Mr. Hawke?"

"Why do you ask? Is it important?"

"No. I'm simply curious. Your accent is very

posh. Yet you live in this crumbling ruin. With your, what's the current expression, partner. He sounds a trifle old on the phone. Do you like older men, Mr. Hawke?"

Hawke laughed. "I like this one well enough. We've been together for years."

"Really? What's his name?"

"Pelham. Grenville is his surname. He's related to the famous writer somehow. A cousin once or twice removed. Wodehouse, you know, one of my literary heroes. A genius."

"I prefer *War and Peace.* Anything at all by Turgenev. Nabokov's *Pale Fire* is my favorite novel. But Pushkin, of course, is the grandfather of them all. You know Pushkin? Next to my father, Russia's greatest hero."

"Hmm. Well, I guess I must have missed those, I'm afraid. Have you read Wodehouse's *Pigs Have Wings,* by any chance? No? *Uncle Dynamite*? How about *Jeeves and the Feudal Spirit*? No? Marvelous books, bloody marvelous."

"Are you an art lover as well as a connoisseur of great literature?"

"Art? I suppose some of it's okay. I quite admire Jamie Wyeth's portrait of John F. Kennedy. And that fat pig painting he did. And Turner. I am rather keen on Turner's watercolors."

"A lover of the old masters, one would suppose."

"The old masters? Me? Hardly. I'm glad they're all dead. I wish more of them had died sooner."

She looked at him; he just stood there, looking back at her. For a moment, their eyes were locked, and he had the unmistakable sense that both of their hearts had seized up and that neither of them was breathing.

She suddenly moved toward him.

"Stand up, please, and take your shirt off."

Hawke did so.

"Turn to the right, so the sun hits you full on the face. Good. Stop slouching, and stand up straight. Now, look at me. Not your head, just your eyes. Perfect. God. Those eyes."

"My late mother thanks you."

"What do you do? To support yourself?"

"This and that. Freelance work."

"Freelance. That covers a lot of ground. Trousers off, please. And your knickers."

"You're joking, of course."

"Everything off, come on! I'm losing my light."

Hawke mumbled something and stripped off his remaining clothing.

It was an odd feeling, standing naked in front of a fully clothed woman like this. It was not completely unpleasant, bordering on the erotic. He felt a distinct stirring below and quickly turned his attention to the portrait over the fireplace. Her father was, Hawke noticed again, fully clothed. No nudes

207

of him around here, one only hoped.

"Happy?" he said.

"I will be happy, Mr. Hawke. Now, turn around so I can shoot your bum."

"Christ. I can't believe I'm doing this."

"Too late now."

"What are these pictures for? I thought this was to be an oil painting. This portrait or whatever."

"This is just reference. Stuff I can use to work on the portrait when you're not here in person."

"How reassuring. And what do you do with them, these naughty photographs, when you're finished?"

"Post them on the Internet if you'd like."

"You know, Miss Korsakova —"

"Asia."

"Asia. You know, Asia, I'm not at all sure I'm cut out for this sort of thing."

"On the contrary, you're perfectly cut out for it. Have you never looked in a mirror? All right, lost the light. You can get dressed now. We're done for the day."

"That's it?"

"We'll start roughing you in on canvas next time. Which do you prefer, check or cash?"

"Check would be fine."

She went to her desk and opened a checkbook. "Hawke with an e?"

"Yes."

She handed it to him. He noticed the check

was drawn on a very good private bank in Switzerland. Banque Pictet on the Rue des Acacias in Geneva. He knew it. He banked there himself.

"I'm going to paint you lying on that wicker chaise. It's beautiful, isn't it? I found it in Bali. It was in the royal palace. Perfect for you."

"This portrait, will it be life-size?"

"Yes, it will."

"A nude portrait?"

"Of course."

"My God."

"My exhibition will be at the National Portrait Gallery at Trafalgar Square next spring. And there'll you be, hanging amongst all my other beautiful men, in all your glory. Bigger than life!"

"Really?"

"Yes, really. Relax, Mr. Alex Hawke of Teakettle Cottage. Come springtime, all of London will be oohing and aahing over you. The gallery staff will have to provide linen handkerchiefs for the droolers."

Alex zipped up his trousers and looked at her. He'd never felt so ridiculous in his life.

"Ah. May I sit for a moment? I'm a bit dizzy for some strange reason."

"Listen, what are you so anxious about? You're going to be famous, you know."

Famous?" Hawke said, sitting, the blood freezing in his veins. He'd had a chilling premonition of C pausing before a portrait at the exhibition and saying, "Good Lord, Stevens, that can't be *Alex Hawke,* can it?"

"Yes, famous. Shall we say next Tuesday at one o'clock? The light will be good for two hours."

"Tuesday?" Hawke said absently. "Yes. I think Tuesday will be fine."

He couldn't help himself now.

He was already too far gone.

16

Miami

Friday night, Stokely Jones Jr. was on his way to a birthday party. He was arriving in style on Fancha's beautiful sixty-foot sport-fishing boat, *Fado.* Invited, not, but that was completely irrelevant. This soiree was strictly business. The birthday boy was a psychotic Chechen terrorist warlord with a price on his head, rumored to be a pretty big number. Apparently, this psycho, name of Ramzan Baysarov, had royally pissed off the Kremlin kingpins.

Kidnapping schoolchildren, blowing up Moscow apartment buildings, spraying bullets inside packed churches in Novgorod and kiddie matinee movie theaters, crap like that. No wonder the Kremlin was PO'd. So, Ramzan was wisely AMF out of Russia for the time being, keeping his head down, right here in sunny Miami.

He was in the country illegally, and federal marshals had been trying to find him for a month with no luck. Hard to believe, terrorists on the loose like that, but there you go. Good for business.

Tonight, according to Stoke's extremely highly paid informants, Ramzan was going to stick his psycho head up just long enough to wolf down some ice cream and birthday cake.

You had a large expatriate Russian community here in Miami now. And a whole lot of them were dirty, some of them mobbed up. Stoke's main clients, the Pentagon and Langley, were naturally very interested in seeing exactly who attended Ramzan's Friday night birthday bash. Hence Stoke's unannounced attendance.

Tactics International, Stoke's private intel-gathering operation, had recently been hired by a Pentagon guy named Harry Brock. Assignment: Help Harry covertly surveil Russian and Chechen *mafiya* types who'd caught the eye of Homeland Security. Word was, the Russian bad guys were planning some kind of terror event on U.S. soil. Stir up more trouble between the U.S. and Russia. Why? That was what Harry Brock wanted Stoke and Company to find out.

Stoke's little start-up had gotten a big shot in the arm with this one. Washington and Moscow at it again. And Russians had come to Miami in droves, buying up yachts and mansions, Bentleys and Bvlgari watches. Stoke had eventually heard about the party by asking all of his PIs about anything unusual on the Russian front. It seemed like a perfect opportunity to shoot lots of video of the attendees.

The skinny, according to Special Agent Harry Brock, was that U.S.-Russian relations, bad as they were recently, were about to get a whole lot worse. CIA intercepts indicated a bunch of U.S.-based Russian-American superpatriots with Kremlin ties were planning something big on the East Coast, just maybe right here in River City. These Kremlin bad boys didn't seem to have any problem getting expatriated *mafiya* types to do their dirty work, either, Harry told Stoke.

"You mean, like back when the CIA hired Bugsy Siegel and his boys to try and whack Castro?" Stoke had asked Harry. Harry didn't think that was very funny. He was sensitive that way.

Stoke stepped outside *Fado*'s main cabin and called to the man atop the tuna tower, three stories up in the chill night air. The salty air felt good. It was cool in Miami tonight, even for December. The good news was, despite the forecast, it wasn't raining. Rain would have put a real damper on their video surveillance plans.

"Come on up, man. See the world of the rich and famous," Sharkey Gonzales-Gonzales called down to him from his tiny helm station thirty feet above the deck. The big yacht was going dead slow, sliding up the wide residential canal at idle speed. Huge mansions on either side of the waterway. Megayachts moored at docks along the seawall. You could see why the Russians would be taken in by all this glitz. Miami in December beat the shit out of Moscow in June or any other damn month.

Sharkey, the one-armed Cuban fishing guide who was Stokely's sole employee, was running the boat from up top tonight. That's where Harry had mounted the sophisticated gear, digital video cameras like the ones the unmanned spy birds carried, no bigger than a deck of cards but equipped with night vision and audio dish intercept stuff. There was even a tiny video camera mounted at the very tip of one of the tall outriggers. Harry had set it up so you could swing it around just like that Skycam the NFL used.

All this state-of-the-art tech stuff was provided by Mr. Harry Brock of JCOS at the P House. That's Joint Chiefs of Staff at the Pentagon for anybody lucky enough to be living outside the Beltway.

Harry Brock was a spook, a Tactics client, but over the years, Stoke and his pal Alex Hawke had gotten to like the guy okay. He was a little too laid-back California for Stoke's New York tastes, but he could be funny sometimes. Besides, he was a true hard case who'd helped save Alex Hawke's life down in the Amazon a while back, so he had a lot of gold stars on his beanie.

"Coming right up," Stoke said, starting up the stainless-steel ladder of the jungle-gym tuna tower.

There were four of them aboard the white Viking sport-fishing boat belonging to Stoke's fiancée, the beauteous Fancha. The Viking was called the *Fado,* after the kind of music Fancha sang. Sad Portuguese ballads, and when she opened her mouth and sang them, man, the melodies stuck a knife in your heart. She'd come out of nowhere to become the hottest thing in Miami right now. That's why Stoke had had little trouble getting her the terrorist birthday party gig.

Since leaving the dock at Fancha's home on Key Biscayne, Stoke and Harry Brock had been huddled below in *Fado*'s main cabin. They'd been looking at the four monitors broadcasting and recording direct live feeds from four very high-tech cameras and sound equipment mounted on the tuna tower. The stationary cameras were working great, but the mobile Skycam was giving Harry fits. It was tough to swing the outrigger around steadily enough to get a decent picture.

Fancha, Stokely's main squeeze for these last few years, had inherited *Fado,* along with one of the more spectacular estates on Key Biscayne, Casa Que Canta, from her late husband. She was from the Cape Verde

Islands and was beginning to make a serious name for herself as a singer. She had a new album out, *Green Island Girl,* nominated for a Latin Grammy as Breakthrough Album of the Year. He was proud of her. Hell, maybe he even loved her.

"Shark, my little one-armed brother, how you doing up here?" Stoke said, arriving up at the small helm platform. It felt like a hundred feet in the air, the way it swayed up here under the big black man's weight. Tear Stokely Jones down, Hawke once said, and you could put up a very nice sports arena. Didn't seem to bother Shark any. He was steering the boat with his good right arm and aiming one of the cameras with his flipper. Luis Gonzales-Gonzales was a former charter skipper down in the Keys. He'd lost most of an arm to a big bull shark one day and decided the spy business was a lot safer than fishing.

"Hey, Stoke."

"Look at you up here, man!" Stoke said to the wiry little guy, "Busier 'n a long-tailed cat in a room full of rocking chairs. You cool? Everything all right?"

"I'm cool. I'm having a tough time navigating some of the narrow canals, but we're good to go, going to be at the man's dock right on time. How are my TV pictures looking down below?"

"Brock says okay, but your zooms are a little

216

shaky, and there could be sharper contrast. Maybe open up the apertures a squidge, he says. We're not getting much moonlight tonight. You know what? Don't worry about it. You drive the boat, Shark. I'll see what I can do about the cameras."

Stoke adjusted one of the camera's aperture controls and did a slow zoom in on somebody's patio and then back out to the wide shot. "How's that, Harry?" he said into the lip mike extending from one of the headsets all three men were wearing for the operation.

"Better. Yeah, open all four of them up," Harry replied in his headphones. "I'm recording sound now, doing a sound check, so watch what you two buttheads say about me up there."

Stoke laughed and said, "Guy who called you pencil-dick, shit-for-brains, total buttwipe a few seconds ago? You heard that? That was the Sharkman called you that, not me, boss."

Sharkey laughed. "How's the star doing? She ready?"

"Getting ready. Doing her hair and makeup down in the owner's stateroom."

"That's one gorgeous chick, man. Very, very special lady. You know that, right?"

"I kinda had that feeling already, but I appreciate the added input, Shark."

"Hold on!" Sharkey shouted suddenly.

Stoke reached out and grabbed hold of the

217

back of the helm seat. The wake of a passing boat plus his own massive weight atop the stainless-steel erector set made the tower sway sickeningly. He wasn't used to being up on the tuna tower, and he didn't much like it. He hated fishing, always had, and he hated tuna more than most fish. The ex-SEAL belonged under the surface, not rocking and rolling up on some Frisbee-sized platform. But his size was an asset in business.

Stoke, who was about the size of your average armoire, was a good guy to have around when you needed someone to, say, run through a solid brick wall or knock down a mature oak tree.

"That's the house up ahead, all lit up," Shark said, throttling back to neutral. The big boat instantly slowed to a crawl. "See it? Out on that point."

"See it? How can you miss it? Looks like a country club."

"Yeah. Russians have all the money now, seems like."

"Okay, Harry," Stoke said into his mike. "We've got the house in sight. Headed for the dock. Five minutes."

The huge, bloated house was situated on a point of land sticking out into the bay, with a wide apron of grass extending to the canal on two sides. It was one of the newer McMansions, all glass and steel, very *Miami Vice,* Stoke thought. The pool was a free-form infinity number and had little bridges and rocky grottos that meandered down to the seawall at the seaward end of the point.

There was a large terrace surrounding the pool, where tiki bars and catering tables had been set up. The party was scheduled to begin in less than half an hour, and the only people visible were waiters and sound technicians, setting up the speaker systems for Fancha's performance.

Stoke saw the small stage set up on the near side of the pool. Fancha's six-piece *fado* band had just arrived, tuning up, the amped-up sound of a guitar easily carrying all the way across the water. The neighbors weren't going to be getting much sleep tonight.

The dock was unoccupied, just the way it had been when Sharkey had scouted the location earlier that afternoon. The host, a Mr. Vladimir Lukov, didn't own a yacht, Sharkey had learned. Sharkey had been counting on them being early, the only guests to arrive by sea. At the very least, he hoped he'd be first and get the dock before anyone else. It looked as if he'd been right. Or maybe just lucky.

Shark maneuvered the big boat alongside the wooden dock, then used his bow and stern thrusters to crab the boat sideways toward the piling fenders. Two young guys appeared on the dock, ready to take *Fado*'s lines. Stoke saw another couple of guys in black, clearly security, making their way down the sloping lawn to the dock.

"I'll take the helm," Stoke said to Sharkey. "You go down and handle the lines."

Sharkey turned the wheel over to his boss, then scrambled below to heave the preset bow and stern lines to the boys waiting at either end of the dock.

"Here we go, Harry," Stoke said into the mike as they bumped up against the rubber fenders. "Roll tape."

"You got it. We're rolling. Perfect camera position, by the way, great angle from up there. We got the back of the house, the whole terrace, the pool, perfect. My compliments to the camera crew."

"Fancha ready?" Stoke asked.

"Our star's coming up on deck right now. Wait till you see her outfit, Stoke. Unbelievable."

Stoke shut the twin two-thousand-horsepower CAT diesel engines down, removed his headset, and stowed it in the compartment under the helm station. He'd be wearing a different commo system now. An invisible earbud and a tiny mike hidden inside the sleeve of his jacket would keep him in constant contact with Harry Brock aboard *Fado* as he moved through the party.

"Harry?" he said into his sleeve. "Radio check."

"Loud and clear," Harry said, and Stokely hurried down the ladder. It sounded like one of the badass security guys was already giving Sharkey a hard time. These weren't rent-a-cops trucked in for the birthday party. Stoke could tell just by the way they moved and carried themselves that these Russian boys were in the death business.

"You got a problem, chief?" Stoke asked the big blond Russian dressed head to toe in black combat fatigues. The guy was standing on the dock with his feet wide apart and his arms folded across his chest, giving Stoke what must have passed for the evil eye back in Mother Russia.

"*Nyet.* You got a problem. Your little one-armed bandit here says he doesn't have an invitation. This is a private function on private property. So, unless you show me an invitation, and your name appears on my list, you got two minutes to get this boat out of here."

"I'm sorry," Stoke said, stepping to the rail and smiling at the guy. "I'm sure we spoke on the phone. But I've forgotten your name. You work for Mr. Lukov, right? Chief of security? Boris, isn't it?" It was the first Russian name that popped into his head, but it didn't seem to faze the guy.

Stoke stuck his hand out, and the man instinctively took it. Stoke squeezed a second too long and caught the guy wincing. He was a seriously big guy, ex-military, no doubt about it. Had that unmistakable special-forces look about him.

"Who the fuck are you?" the man said, withdrawing his hand with some difficulty from Stoke's bone cruncher. Boris's black nylon windbreaker fell open, and Stoke saw a Mac-10 light machine gun hanging from a shoulder sling. Probably to keep the kids in line bobbing for apples or playing Pin the Tail on the Donkey later.

Stoke smiled at Boris again. "Levy, Sheldon Levy, Suncoast Artist Management. That ring a bell?"

No reply.

"We're providing tonight's entertainment."

"What entertainment? The birthday singer?"

"Exactly. The singer. And look, Boris, here she is now."

Fancha stepped out of the shadows of the boat's main salon as if out of a dream. Her bold brown eyes, slightly uptilted at the corners, were shining beneath a fringe of silken black hair. She climbed two steps in her shimmering sequined red dress and stood on the bridge deck next to Stokely. He'd never seen her look so beautiful. He looked at the Russian.

"This is —"

"Fancha," the security guy said, trying to keep his jaw off the deck. He looked as if he was going to dissolve into a puddle and just drip over the gunwales into the canal. He looked around at his buddies. "It's Fancha," Boris said, reverent, as if Madonna had suddenly popped out of a pumpkin.

Stoke looked at her and smiled. "Some dress, huh, Boris? Who's that designer you're wearing tonight, Fancha? Oscar? Lacroix? Zac Posen?"

"What a lovely house," Fancha said, ignoring Stoke and smiling at the drooling security guy. "Sorry I'm late, gentlemen. I hope my band hasn't been waiting too long for the sound check."

"Oh, no, not at all," the guy said. "They just got there. Here, I mean. Still setting up. I will escort you up there to the pool? I'm afraid the grass is a little wet still from the sprinklers, and it can be slippery. Please?"

"You're so kind."

Stoke rolled his eyes as Boris held out his hand to her. She took it and stepped lightly from the boat onto the dock, beaming at the good-looking Russian.

Stoke's fists clenched involuntarily. He knew this guy. Didn't really know him, of course, but knew his type, guessed who he was. One of the Kremlin's storm troopers in a previous life. The Black Berets, they were called. Riot police, which, in the new post-Democratic Russia, meant they had the legal right to beat the crap out of anybody whose skin color they didn't like. Namely, black. *Black* covered a lot of territory in Russia and included Chechens, Jews, and, of course, Africans and their cousins, African-Americans.

"And what's your name?" Fancha asked the guy, smiling up at this dickhead as if he was freakin' Dr. Zhivago.

"I am Yuri. Yuri Yurin."

"I'm Fancha, Yuri," she said. "Nice to meet you."

"Let me give you my card," Yuri said, pulling out a business card and handing it to her. Without even glancing at it, she handed it to her one-man entourage, Stokely, and started off across the grass, letting Yuri hold her by the damn arm the whole way.

Stoke turned the card over in his hand. It had a picture of a sleek offshore racing boat, a Magnum 60. Beneath was Yuri's name, Yuri Yurin, and his office address over on Miami Beach. Something called the Miami Yacht Group Ltd. So, Yuri only moonlighted as security. His day job was yacht salesman. Fish where the fish are, Stoke thought. Russians were buying most of the big yachts these days. Yuri was probably getting rich, too.

"That's pronounced 'Yurin' like in piss, right?" he called after the Russian, but he guessed Yurin hadn't heard him, because there was no reaction.

Fancha paused to look back at Stoke, still holding onto the guy. "Oh, Sheldon?"

"Yes, my Fancha?" Stoke said, bowing

slightly from the waist.

"My Fiji water?"

"We have Fiji at all the pool bars," Yuri said, the little shit.

"She has her own Fiji," Stokely told him, maybe a little too loudly. "Estate-bottled for her in Fiji personally by David and Jill Gilmour right at the spring on their property at Wakaya."

"Estate-bottled Fiji water?" Yuri said, finding it hard to believe there was some luxury item on the planet he'd not yet heard of.

"Of course."

"Sheldon? My water?"

"I'll be right there with it."

"Chilled, Sheldon?"

"Chilled to perfection, goddess."

17

Half an hour later, Fancha was onstage, in the middle of her first set, singing her little heart out. Stoke was busy invoking Rule One of fancy cocktail soirees: Circulate. He was cruising the crowd like a hungry shark, using his nom de guerre, Sheldon Levy, talking to anyone and everyone who looked interesting, just seeing what itch he could scratch here and there.

Aboard *Fado,* Harry's digital audio recorders were picking up everything he was hearing at the party, so Stoke didn't pay too much attention to most of these drunks. Still, some of what they were saying would no doubt prove useful to some intel wonk at Langley down the line. Harry also had rigged an online feed to VICAM. He could send video stills of anyone who caught his eye to D.C., right from *Fado,* and get instant rap-sheet feedback, should any of these distinguished gentlemen have a criminal record.

Stoke was hoping to bump into Ramzan

himself, but so far, the birthday boy hadn't shown for his own gig. Wanted to be fashionably late, Stoke guessed, an old Chechen custom, maybe. The Russians he did meet were mostly big and noisy. Most of them were noisy in slurred English. Vodka, Stoli, Imperia, all headed down wide-open hatches by the gallon at various bar tables situated under the palms around the property.

Not a drinker, he'd passed on the vodka in favor of Diet Coke, but he'd put away about a pound of Beluga caviar so far and felt he could probably go for another. There were mountains of the delicious stuff everywhere, so you didn't have to feel greedy spooning two tablespoons onto your toast points.

The women, he had to admit, were mostly beautiful. Lots of low-cut dresses, sequins, and major bling. A whole lot of very big blonde hair. You had a good cross-section of wives, trophy wives, girlfriends, and professionals. Some of them had to be imports from the Ukraine, some of them were clearly home-grown, and a few were right up there with South Florida's finest.

Sharkey deserved a lot of credit and maybe a raise for the idea of using Fancha's yacht as the surveil vehicle. Since the party was mostly on the back lawn around the pool, the docked boat was the only feasible way to cover this assignment. He had to laugh every time he looked out at *Fado,* thinking about the countless hours he'd spent staking out some dirtbag in Queens, munching doughnuts, freezing his tail off behind the wheel of some crummy Dodge Dart with a bad heater.

Down below in the cabin, positioned in front of his monitors and camera controls, Harry Brock was a busy boy. Every time a couple of guys or a group out on the lawn strayed anywhere near the boat, you'd see that portside outrigger come creeping around, dangling the little Skycam over their unsuspecting heads. He even had instant replay on the damn thing.

Harry had been right about the outrigger as a camera and boom mike. People were so deep into the cocktail hour now that nobody seemed to notice when the stray outrigger on the big sportfish did weird things, waving around over people's heads like a magic wand.

Stoke decided to make his way inside the palazzo. People were coming and going, and it wouldn't hurt to see what was going on indoors, beyond the camera's reach. The house, mobbed with people, was pretty much what you'd expect, a style Stoke called Early Boca. Twenty-foot ceilings. A lot of heavily gilded furniture and artwork that was supposed to look as if it had come from some Italian castle. Big curving stairway with a huge bad portrait of the owner's wife halfway up the curving wall. Chandeliers of melting icicles they'd maybe bought at Mickey's Magic Castle Gift Shoppe over in Orlando.

He pushed his way into the foyer (*fwa-yay,* as his buddy Chief Inspector Ambrose Congreve would say) and stepped through the double front doors at the home's grand entrance. There he paused to admire the steady stream of gleaming Bentleys, Rollers, Escalades, Rangers, and big black Hummers. None of them, of course, could hold a candle to his 1965 black raspberry GTO convertible, capable of a standing quarter-mile in less than eight seconds. Street legal.

The gleaming parade of pimped-up rides was coming through the ornate iron entrance gates and rolling to a stop under the portico where the valet boys waited. A bright red Ferrari Enzo rumbled up, and three valet guys converged on it as if somebody had just dropped a million-dollar bill on the pavement, which they probably had.

Stoke checked his watch. It was past nine o'clock, and Fancha was supposed to sing "Happy Birthday" at nine-thirty sharp, so a lot of people were eager to get back to the pool. Stoke thought half the guests had probably come because she was singing. Wouldn't surprise him if it was more than half. Girl was climbing the charts.

The woman he maybe loved was maybe, just maybe, on her way to stardom, and it made him proud to catch her name whispered around the room.

Have you heard that beautiful girl sing? Fancha? Go! Go out there! You've got to hear her!

Something was going on out on the front lawn. There was a white bakery truck, looked like, motor still running, pulled over on the grass, and the driver was standing outside surrounded by a few of the black-shirt boys. Pretty tense situation. Stoke decided he had time to go check it out.

"Fuck you doing, coming in the main gate?" one guy was screaming at the driver. "You didn't see the sign, 'Service Entrance,' around the side? Whaddya, blind, you dumb shit?"

The delivery guy, who looked like a big blond bear in white pajamas, wasn't backing down. He'd didn't look as if he'd back down from Mike Tyson, to tell the truth. He got up in the guy's face quick.

"Listen up, pal, like I said, I got the freaking birthday cake in the back there. It won't fit through the pantry door. So I'm bringing it around to bring it in the front door. Because it's *wider.* Okay? Just like your caterers in the kitchen told me to do. Awright with you, you skinny fuck?"

The driver's white outfit had the name "Happy" stitched over his breast pocket. It said "Happy's Bake Shoppe" on the side of the white truck. This Happy character was a big guy, seriously large, and the security guys were having some second thoughts about messing with his ass too much.

"Is there a problem?" Stoke asked, pushing his way past two of the black-shirted Russian muscle boys.

"There was one. Now we have another one. You. Who the hell are you?"

Russians so full of attitude lately, you notice that? Still pissed about that Cold War thing, Stoke figured. And now that they were rich, well, you know how that goes. He smiled at the guy, stuck out his hand.

"Sheldon Levy. Suncoast Artist Management. I'm coordinating this evening's entertainment for your employer, Mr. Lukov. I hate to interrupt this little scuffle, but the lovely Fancha is scheduled to sing 'Happy Birthday' to the guest of honor in fifteen minutes. I'm afraid if we don't get that cake through the door and out to the stage, all of our timing will go down the tubes. I don't think Mr. Lukov would be very happy about that, do you gentlemen agree?"

Happy the Baker smiled at Stokely. "Finally, someone around here who makes some freaking sense."

"Can I offer you a hand with the cake?" Stoke asked Happy.

"Nah, we'll help him," a black shirt said. "C'mon, guys, gimme a hand here with this freaking cake, all right?"

As the security team opened up the van and

unloaded the huge white and pink cake, Stoke went over and offered Happy his hand. Something about the guy looked very familiar.

"Sheldon Levy," he said.

"I'm Happy," the baker said, pumping his hand. If he'd expected Stoke's hand to be small and breakable, he was sorely disappointed.

"Yeah? You're Happy, huh? Good thing your momma didn't name you Gay, right?" Stoke laughed. The guy didn't seem to get it.

"Have we met before?" Stoke said. He was sure he'd either met this guy or seen his picture fairly recently.

"The Steiner wedding?" Happy said. "Maybe that was it."

"I missed that one. Didn't make the cut, I guess. No, somewhere else, must be. C'mon out back, Happy, I'll introduce you to Fancha."

"You know Fancha?"

"Know her? I'm her manager. C'mon, we'll make sure they don't drop your cake going through the house. Cake like that, what does that beauty go for, Happy?"

"Twenty-five."

"Hundred?"

"Thousand."

"For a cake? You got Celine Dion in there? Well, it's a work of art. I'm sure it will be a huge surprise for the guest of honor."

"Oh, you're right about that, Mr. Levy. A huge surprise."

Happy looked happy as he saw his masterpiece being paraded through the crowded house above everyone's head and lofted out toward the stage overlooking the deep end of the pool.

Fancha was just finishing up one of the hit songs from *Green Island Girl,* one that might go gold called "*A Minha Vida,*" when the cake arrived onstage with her.

She looked at the six-foot-high frosted monstrosity and said softly into the mike, "Isn't that beautiful? A symbol of one life lived. You know the word *fado* itself means fate, destiny, and — oh, here's the birthday boy himself! Let's give him a big round of applause, shall we?"

A thin, clean-shaven man, with dark, deep-set eyes beneath fierce black brows, stepped up to the microphone. It was Ramzan, all right, although in the pictures in his dossier, he'd had a luxuriant beard. He was swaying a little bit and had a kind of goofy grin plastered on his face for a fierce Chechen warlord. Miami got to people, Stoke thought, that's all there was to it. Ramzan looked out at the crowd and spoke, sounding like that Ali G guy in that *Borat* movie, but that was just Stoke's opinion.

"I want to thank my dear friend Vlad for having this wonderful excitement party. And all of you coming. I am very happy we can take time out from our struggle and come together in such a joyful party time."

That was the wonderful excitement speech, and then Fancha took the mike off the stand. The crowd got quiet fast as she sang the opening lyrics with the voice of an unreachable angel. Behind her, they were lighting the candles on the cake, waiters standing on stepladders. The candles lit up like sparklers, and the crowd cheered as Fancha lit up the whole night with her voice.

"Happy birthday to you . . . happy birthday . . ."

Stoke smiled at her and then looked around at Happy standing a few feet behind him. He had a funny look on his face. A little nervous, maybe. Nervous? About what? His cake was a hit.

A big surprise.

Stoke raised his sleeve to his lips and whispered, "Harry?"

"Yeah?"

"You getting this?"

"You bet."

"Zoom in on the baker in the white suit. Big gorilla. A few feet behind me. Wait, he's moving away. You got him?"

"Yeah, I got him. Let me get a close-up."

"Does he look familiar to —"

"Oh, shit."

"What?"

"Stoke! Get the hell out of there! Now! Grab Fancha and run . . ."

"What? What is it?"

A big surprise.

"That's the Omnibomber! The guy the FBI thinks blew up that prison a few weeks ago. Little Miss. The Death Row Bomber. I saw the prison security-camera shots just yesterday. It's him, all right."

"Oh, shit. The cake."

"Yeah, the cake. Gotta be. Come on, Stoke. You gotta move. Get out now, Stoke! I mean it. Those candles, those are probably fuses or somebody's got a remote detonator, one or the other. Go! Go!"

Stoke looked around. Fancha was still singing her birthday song, her eyes on Ramzan, making it just for him. The baker was gone, melted into the crowd and probably headed for his truck. He looked at the candles, spewing fiery sparks. They'd burned almost all the way down to the icing on the cake. Time to go.

He stepped up onto the stage, right behind Fancha, swept her up into his arms, and leaned into the microphone. Fancha was squirming, trying to finish her song, looking at him as if he'd lost his mind.

Stoke said, "Isn't she fabulous, ladies and gentlemen? The lovely Fancha! We'll be taking a short break while the guest of honor blows out all those candles, but don't worry, folks, she'll be back for an encore!"

With that, Stoke stepped off the stage, Fancha twisting in his arms, and started pushing his way through the crowd headed toward the dock. He could see Sharkey on the bow, already heaving the bow line ashore, and Stoke heard the muffled roar of *Fado*'s big diesels coming to life.

He saw Harry at the top of the tower, screaming at him to hurry, hurry, and the crowd finally had thinned to the point where he could break into a full-tilt run across the sloping lawn toward the dock.

Sharkey was on the stern, heaving the line, and the big Viking's props were churning now. She was beginning to edge away from the dock.

Two of the black shirts saw him coming and stepped in front of him. Stoke just ran right through them, flinging them to either side, and they sprawled to the ground. He had maybe twenty yards to reach the dock. The distance between the boat and the dock was opening up fast. Three feet, four . . . he sprinted that last bit, took a running jump off the dock, and leaped across the widening gap, landing hard on the deck in the aft cockpit. He managed to keep his balance and hold tightly to Fancha at the same time.

"Are you crazy? Put me down!" Fancha shouted in his ear, pounding on his shoulders with her fists.

There was a lot of shouting and confusion back on the lawn as Harry leaned on the throttles and the big yacht jumped up on plane and roared away from the dock.

"Go!" Stoke yelled up at Brock, "Hit it! Get us out of here!"

Stoke was in a crouch, moving with Fancha toward the door to the main salon, when the whole world was rocked on its side. The night sky lit with a white flash and then an intense blossoming orange glow that was blinding. Stoke, still cradling Fancha in his arms, dropped to the deck as the shockwave of the massive explosion slammed the big yacht, rolling her over onto her side, nearly broaching her completely. Stoke and Fancha slid down the deck, crashing against the gunwale. He protected her as best he could, but both of them were stunned.

Fado righted herself, rolling violently. At the top of the tower, Harry, clinging desperately to the wildly careening helm station, managed to hold on and speed away from the scene of horrible death and destruction behind them. *Fado* — intact, it seemed — roared out into the blackness of the empty bay. Stoke lifted his head and looked back at her wildly foaming white wake. In the distance, he could see the point of land protruding into the bay. No lights on, either around the pool or what was left of the house. No one moving, small fires blazing everywhere.

Where the pool had been, nothing but a large black hole. The whole backside of the house was gone, and you could look into the interior rooms of the Russian's flaming mansion as if it was some kind of oversized, burnt-out dollhouse.

He looked down at Fancha, her head in his lap, staring up at him with those great big beautiful wide-open eyes.

"You okay, sugar? You hurt anywhere?"

"I thought you'd lost your mind, Stoke, grabbing me off that stage."

"I was just trying *not* to lose you."

"Oh, baby. I never saw somebody move so fast. I didn't know anybody could run like that."

"You watch me run to you next time you call my name."

She reached up and brushed his cheek with the back of her hand.

"Stokely Jones Jr., I don't know how to —"

"Shh. You thank me later. I've got to go see if Harry and Sharkey are okay, jump on the horn, tell my clients in D.C. what just happened to Comrade Ramzan."

"Love you, baby."

"Love you more."

Stoke shrugged out of his jacket, folded it, and put it beneath Fancha's head. Then he started climbing the stainless ladder to the top of the tower, moving fast.

Harry Brock was up there, staring at something in the sky through his binoculars.

"Holy shit. Will you look at that?"

"What?"

"Over there. To the west, just coming up over the *Miami Herald* building. Some kind of fuckin' UFO or something."

Stoke looked at the thing. "Damn."

"What the hell is that thing, Stoke?"

"Some kind of new airship, I guess. Doesn't look like any blimp I ever saw. Military, maybe, looking for go-fast drug boats coming up from the Keys."

It was massive, whatever the hell it was. Stoke stared at the great silver ship floating over the Miami skyline toward him, a giant round opening where the nose should be. Weird-looking. Scary-looking, almost.

Make that definitely scary-looking.

18

Bermuda

Hawke, arriving at Shadowlands, found Ambrose Congreve standing at the front door, dressed to the nines, but adamantly refusing to get into the automobile Hawke had shown up in.

"Some car, isn't it?" Hawke said, grinning. "Absolutely ripping."

"I simply won't ride into town in that contraption, Alex," Congreve said. "I won't."

"Why not?"

"Why not? Look at it. It's a deathtrap, for one thing. No doors, no roof. It's utterly ridiculous."

"It has a delightful roof. A daffodil surrey roof of fringed canvas, I'll grant you, and the fringe is a bit outré, but a roof all the same."

Congreve disdainfully tapped one of the tiny moon-shaped wheel covers with the tip of his walking stick, making a hollow, tinny sound. He looked at Hawke and did not bother to disguise his sigh of frustration.

"Frankly, Alex, I find it astounding that you can transit this island in such a conveyance and keep a straight face. This . . . car, if one can call it such, looks as if it formerly belonged to a circus clown."

"Mind your tongue, Constable. And get in the damn thing. C is waiting, and we're already late."

"Yes, and this is quite a serious meeting he's invited us to. We're taking on the dreaded Russians again, Alex. If Sir David happens to be standing outside the club when we arrive, he'll think he's invited the bloody Ringling Brothers to help him save Western civilization."

Hawke tried not to laugh out loud.

Because of traffic congestion on the small island, every residence on Bermuda was allotted only one vehicle per household. Hawke was driving the car that had come along with his cottage. This tiny vehicle by the noble Italian design house of Pininfarina, was a 1958 Fiat 600 Jolly, and he'd somehow acquired it when he signed his lease for Teakettle Cottage.

It was an odd duck, to be honest, bright sunshine yellow, with seats made, improbably enough, of wicker.

But Hawke thought it quite sporting, and certainly Pelham enjoyed squiring the Jolly around town on his market runs each week. Besides, Congreve was right, there were few places on earth where a man could drive such an outrageous automobile and maintain a straight face. But Bermuda was one of those places.

Congreve sighed one of his immense sighs and settled his rather large person into the wicker armchair bolted after a fashion to the floor. He was shocked to discover that even the dashboard was wicker. He looked at Hawke with dismay. He felt as if he were riding in a ladies' sewing basket.

He put his smart straw hat firmly on his head and prepared for the worst.

"Not even an airbag?" Congreve said, running his fingers along the wicker dash.

"Oh, I daresay it's got one now," Hawke said, engaging first gear. "On the passenger side at any rate."

"Go, go, go," the detective said, searching in vain for a seatbelt. "Let's get this Mad Hatter's wild ride over with."

Hawke laughed, popped the clutch, and started off along the gently winding drive that traversed the shaded narrow length of Lady Mars's Shadowlands estate. They drove the first few minutes in silence, the famous detective somehow maintaining an immutable scowl despite his deceptively innocent baby blue eyes and rakish mustache.

"Looking rather gay for our luncheon with C," Hawke said finally, glancing over at his friend's natty attire. Congreve was wearing lime-green Bermuda shorts with navy-blue knee socks, a Navy blazer, a pink shirt, and a pink and white madras bow tie. Tortoiseshell sunglasses completed the look. On his head was a straw boater.

"*Gay?* Really, Alex, you do push me to the brink."

"As in festive, Ambrose. It was meant as a simple compliment. Shorts are a bit nancy for my taste, but what do I know?"

"*De gustibus non est disputandum.*"

"Exactly."

Hawke turned left out of Shadowlands' bougainvillea-covered stone portals and onto the South Road. They were heading east past the Spittal Pond Nature Reserve on their left. It was another perfect day in paradise, Hawke thought, brightly colored birds darting about flowering woods and tropical gardens on either side of the road. When he came to Trimingham Road, he whipped the little yellow buggy around to the right, coming to the first of two roundabouts that would lead him to the town of Hamilton proper.

Two cruise ships were moored along Front Street, and the charming old town was crowded with automobile traffic, motor scooters, and pedestrians. He looked at his watch. They were already ten minutes late, and C did not like to be kept waiting. He'd sounded very serious when he'd called, wanting Hawke and Ambrose to join him at the

Royal Bermuda Yacht Club at noon sharp. He wanted to discuss the status of Red Banner and hear their thoughts on getting the thing up and running.

"Ah! Hold on to your hat, Constable!" Hawke had spied a fleeting opening between an enormous cement truck and a taxi and inserted the little Jolly between them, just catching the green light by so doing.

"I say!" Ambrose said, giving him a stern look.

"Sorry. Look, here we are, and you're still intact."

"Shaken to the core by that last maneuver."

Hawke smiled as he put the wheel hard over, and the little Jolly sailed into port. He pulled into the yacht club's car park, finding a spot beneath a large ficus shade tree, and they climbed out. The club was at the end of a short street, situated at Albuoy's Point, right on the harbor. The RBYC was a large, distinguished building, painted what Hawke could only describe as an odd Bermudian shade of plum. Like many things here, it would certainly look strange in London, but somehow it worked on the island.

They passed through the entrance where stood a beautiful old binnacle atop a compass rose in inlaid marble. A portrait of the queen hung to the left of the door leading to the small paneled bar where C had asked Hawke to meet him. It was a charming room of highly varnished Bermuda cedar, filled with ancient silver regatta trophies and faded yacht burgees from decades past. An elderly barman smiled at them as they entered.

C was waiting at a corner table beneath a window overlooking the club docks beyond. He stood up when the two men entered.

"Alex, Ambrose, hullo! Please order a drink, won't you both?"

He didn't seem at all aware of the fact that they were fifteen minutes late. Or, if he was, he was certainly nonchalant about it. Bermuda was good medicine for Sir David Trulove. Hell, it was good for all of them, Alex thought.

The beautiful little bar was empty. Still, Hawke thought it a strangely public place for discussing the establishment of a top-secret British counterintelligence operation.

"Don't worry, Alex," C said, seeming to read his mind. "We're not lunching here. My dear old friend Dick Pearman, whose guest house I'm using, has generously offered the use of his yacht *Mohican* for that purpose. She's just out there at the docks. Lunch will be served aboard."

"Pearman?" Congreve said. "Is he Bermudian?"

"Sixteenth generation. Why?"

"Had Dick and Jeanne for tea last week. Lovely couple. Did you know he's the All-England croquet champion, Sir David?"

Hawke smiled at all this benign gentility and turned his attention to the faded yacht burgees hanging round the room. He'd once invited Ambrose to a croquet match at Hawkesmoor and Congreve, who loved only golf, had replied, "Croquet? Do you think I'm a barbarian?"

Congreve and Hawke got their drinks and followed C outside into the bright sunshine, headed toward the club docks.

When the three men were comfortably seated at the semicircular banquette on *Mohican's* lovely stern, C looked at both of them while stirring his soup. Luncheon had been served, chilled cucumber soup and a lovely piece of Scottish salmon.

Trulove said, "First, I'm extremely grateful to both of you for agreeing to this scheme. I predict Red Banner will one day prove critical in our dealings with this former foe, now reinvigorated."

"Alex and I are deeply gratified by your confidence in us," Ambrose said.

"Indeed, sir," Hawke said. "I've been reading the dossiers Miss Guinness provided. I think your assessment of a renewed Russian threat to her neighbors is well founded. We'd both appreciate some sense of how you see Red Banner coming together to combat it."

"Yes," C said, forming a temple with his fingertips and resting his prominent chin on it. This was, of course, his subject, the one true love of his life, and he warmed to it quickly and with enthusiasm.

"First things first, lads. Let's touch on the status of our adversary for a moment. Russia is, of course, our old enemy, and from all appearances, she still regards us as such. It will no doubt come as a shock to you to learn that the firm's recent intelligence indicates Russia is again contemplating some future war with the United States and NATO. We know this because we have intercepted her new military doctrine, replacing the one published in 2000. Doctrines, as you both well know, let military commanders know what they should be preparing for."

"Old habits die hard," Hawke said.

"Yes. Russia clearly still sees herself and her former client states as under siege by the U.S. and NATO and a target for domination by the West. This is the result of seven decades of Communist insecurity and paranoia regarding the West. When East European nations began joining NATO and the European Union, well, this got the Russians extremely peeved. They liked their old borders. My guess is they'd like to have them back."

"Understandable," Hawke said. "Were I in their shoes, I might feel exactly the same way."

"Fair enough. At any rate, the Kremlin fired off all manner of nastygrams and sent them westward. They were not happy about losing the Cold War, Alex, and they are still clearly nervous about aggression from Western Europe, especially Germany and France, both of which have invaded Russia in the past two centuries."

"Germany, I understand," Hawke said with a wry smile, "but France?"

"The French recently invaded Oman at the behest of the Chinese, as you should remember, Alex."

"I can understand Russia's residual anger at having lost the Cold War," Congreve said, "but this level of paranoia is perplexing, if not downright ludicrous."

"It is, indeed, from a Western perspective. But it's our job to understand what makes this new Rostov regime tick, and that will be a big part of Red Banner's mission."

"Sir David," Alex said, leaning forward, "how do you envision Red Banner from an organizational point of view?"

"Ah, that will be your primary responsibility, Alex. I myself see Red Banner, or RB, as a straightforward OPINTEL organization. Operations, supported by intelligence. Basically, here on Bermuda, a real-time watch floor and support organization. One that will provide instant information and support during covert operations vis-à-vis the Russians."

"Similar structure to America's NSA for SIGINT support to OPS?" Alex said, slipping easily into the jargon he so abhorred but felt obligated to use in these situations.

Sir David smiled. "Exactly. We want to create a highly compartmental group within MI-6, outside of SIS, but you'll be using all of their intelligence sources, as well as additional people from our other intel organizations. Players normally associated with a compartmented cell will include ops, intel, comms, logistics, and specialized assistance from respective areas depending on specific mission."

"Sounds good, sir," Hawke said. "And how do you see the U.S. component's involvement?"

"I've set up a meeting in Washington for you to discuss that issue precisely. It's next week, Friday, to be exact. I've arranged military transport for you to and from Washington. But briefly, I see the CIA component as supplementing and integrating within Red Banner. You might well decide to incorporate special operations from other coalition military organizations, Joint Special Operation Command, et cetera. Field intelligence units you've worked with previously, Alex, Centra Spike, Torn Victor, and Grey Fox."

"Good," Alex said, warming to the task. He was certainly not going to want for resources.

"Jolly good, every bit of it," Congreve said. "But tell me, Sir David, what will be Red Banner's primary focus?"

"It could well change, of course, depending on events. But if you ask me for an answer today, I would say this. Terrorism has changed how we look at military threats forever. Thus, we won't be concerning ourselves with, say, disarmament infringements, Russian warhead counts. No, we'll be looking at threats to our food and water supplies. Nuclear reactors. Harbor attacks and biological outbreaks, electronic attacks and EMP. And, of course, the Butterfly Effect."

"A new one on me, sir," Hawke said.

Congreve looked at Sir David. "May I?"

"Please, Ambrose."

"The Butterfly Effect, Alex, is a phrase that encapsulates the more technical notion of sensitive dependence on initial conditions in theory. Small variations of the initial condition of a nonlinear dynamical system, say, may produce huge variations in the longterm behavior of the system. Do you follow me?"

Hawke smiled at Ambrose's typical pyrotechnic display of scientific erudition and said, "A ball placed at the crest of a hill might roll into any of several valleys depending on slight differences in initial position. Right?"

Trulove chuckled and said, "Well said, Alex. I guessed I had the right chaps for the job, and I was right."

Hawke said, "Sir, as for Red Banner's counterterrorism operations, I presume our intel analysis will include work from the cybercafé, cut-outs, and runners. We'll no doubt get hints and sniffs from various cooperating U.S. organizations as well, their homeland defense, immigration, and so on. Correct?"

"Right. Over time, we'll be piecing the puzzles together using multi-intel disciplines such as imagery, UAV, communications intercepts, field agents, and the like. Your American partners will be using all of your favorite three-letter organizations, CIA, DIA, NGA, and NSA."

"So," Ambrose said, pushing his plate away and getting his pipe going, "it would seem the bad old days are back. Global ideological confrontation, proxy wars, arms races, and, last but not least, mutually assured destruction."

"Cold War Two," Hawke said, eyeing both men.

"One could almost wish, Alex," C said, returning Hawke's gaze. "What we had in the first Cold War was a certain cozy equilibrium based on mutual fear of mutual destruction. In those days, one party was afraid to take that extra step without first consulting the other. It was indeed a fragile peace and certainly a frightening one. But looking at those years from today's vantage point, I'd say it was reliable enough. And I would also add that today, the peace between East and West is not looking nearly so reliable. The New Russia. That's the new threat and we seem to have arrived at the *hora decima.*"

"Hora decima?" Hawke asked.

"The eleventh hour," Ambrose translated.

Sir David raised his glass. "To Red Banner, then. Long may it wave."

"To Red Banner," Hawke and Congreve rejoined, glasses high.

In the dark weeks to come, the three men would look back on this meeting as a wistful dream, when their sunny optimism was matched only by their unimaginable naiveté.

19

Moscow

Twenty-five miles west of Red Square and you will find a beautiful country estate dotted with pine and white birch trees, called Novo Ogarevo. The grounds of this bucolic dacha included stables, a recently restored Orthodox church, a well-tended vegetable plot, and, nearby, a helipad. The original house was built in the late nineteenth century for a son of Tsar Alexander II. The helipad was fairly new. So was the security cordon.

This large manor house was now the official state dacha and residence of one Vladimir Vladimirovich Rostov, his wife of many years, Natalia, and their grown son.

President Putin had had the house renovated and begun using it as his personal residence in 2001. Rostov followed after Putin was arrested and sent to Energetika Prison near St. Petersburg. He now spent a good deal of his time here in the country. It was where he was most comfortable and happiest. His unseen neighbors were wealthy Russians who had constructed opulent, if often tasteless, dachas. None of them had ever met their famous new neighbor, and none of them ever would.

As one might imagine, there was not a great deal of neighborly socializing at Novo Ogarevo. Visitors were usually members of the president's inner circle, a small group of ten who had his full confidence, nearly all of whom he'd known for years, two of whom, the closest, were ex-KGB. There were also figures of national importance, such as visiting governors from the Federation, and the occasional head of a foreign state who came to call. Visitors came and went at all hours of the day and night. Mostly night, when the president worked into to the wee hours, sipping tea laced with vodka.

Like many Russians who enjoyed their national drink, Vladimir Rostov was not a morning person. Many days, he didn't even roll out of bed until the crack of eleven. Even on those days when he was driven to his office in the Kremlin, he seldom left the dacha before noon.

Today, the president was working at home. There were certain visitors he preferred to receive at Novo Ogarevo, beyond the gaze of his office courtiers. Rostov was a born spy, a man who'd spent his entire career operating in the shadows. One would expect such a man to be possessed of a suspicious mind. Before ascending to the pinnacle of Russian power, he had been chief of the KGB, at one time the most feared secret police service on earth.

At eleven-fifteen on this particular December morning, the president of the Russian Federation padded downstairs in his heavy woolen robe. Despite his hangover, he was in a particularly good mood on this cold and drizzly day. The president began each working day at home with a vigorous workout in the compound's small indoor pool. For a man getting on in years, he was in fairly good shape. Once he'd swum his accustomed number of laps (the butterfly stroke was his favorite), he'd adjourn to the small breakfast room. And there, VVR, as his staff privately called him, would sit down to enjoy his mid-morning meal.

"Good morning," he said to the wait staff as he took his place at the table. He smiled as they replied in kind. There were three newspapers arrayed beside his place setting. *Pravda*, the *New York Times*, and the London *Times*. He was smiling as he pulled up his chair, they noticed. Only one guest was expected today. That meant a light day ahead for all of them. It made everyone in the kitchen happy, which in turn made everyone in the household staff happy on this grey, rainy day.

Raising a teacup to his lips, the president heard an odd sound, discordant on a peaceful Thursday morning in the country. Glancing up from the lead article in *Pravda,* Vladimir Rostov was surprised to see a long black limousine, considerably longer than his own heavily armored Mercedes Pullman, approaching the house at a high rate of speed.

He knew who was riding in the rear. It was Nikolai Kuragin, now a member of his innermost circle, formerly a KGB general who had served under Rostov in the bad old days when they shared an office at Moscow's Lubyanka Prison, better known as the Gateway to Hell. Nikolai was one of a few men the president had known most of his life. The ten men, known as the *siloviki,* always maintained a tight orbit around their president. Proximity to power was the defining political imperative inside the Kremlin walls.

Since Vladimir Putin's arrest and imprisonment at Energetika, a plot in which they were all equally complicit, they had constituted Rostov's Soviet-style politburo. Together, this small cadre was the executive and policymaking committee responsible for restoring Russia to world prominence and moving the motherland forward into a glorious new age.

The limo was going far too fast for the narrow drive. And General Kuragin was an hour early. What the hell? Rostov stood, irritation plain in his cold blue eyes, left the table, and went upstairs to dress.

Ten minutes later, the president sat behind the desk in his private day office, listening to Kuragin's fascinating tale of recent events in Miami. He was absentmindedly drumming his fingertips on the desktop, a habit he'd formed early in his life and one of the few he'd never been able to break. It was nerves, he knew, nerves and repressed energy. There was so much to do in Russia, so many vast acres of lost ground that needed covering.

"And Ramzan is confirmed dead?" the president asked the smartly uniformed man in the chair opposite. Nikolai wore custom-tailored black uniforms that gave him the look of a Nazi SS *Obergruppenführer,* which Rostov knew was a resemblance he cultivated. Even to the close-cropped grey hair dyed an unconvincing blond.

Kuragin was not pretty to look at above the neck — or below it, for that matter. He was a tall skeleton of a man with dark eyes sunk deep in shadows above a long thin nose. His flesh, a pale greyish yellow, hung from his bones. His smile was thin and often cruel.

It was his lovely mind Rostov cherished. He knew everything, he remembered everything, past and present, as if he lived in a room full of clocks and calendars. Kuragin kept the working details, the vast minutia of the president's official life, in perfect working order. He was indispensable and so prized above all.

"Vaporized, my dear Volodya. I have the pictures from Miami party here, jpegs downloaded at KGB Lubyanka not an hour ago. You may recognize some of our old foes."

Nikolai passed a sealed red folder across the desk. Rostov took it, broke the seal, and extracted two dozen or so glossy eight-by-ten color prints. Without a word, he began to scrutinize each photograph, staring with fierce intensity at the faces of the hated Chechen leadership as he had done for years, waiting for the pop of recognition.

He found the face he was looking for, and doors within doors of his memory were opened as if by magic.

Rostov found himself looking at a picture of Ramzan's decapitated head lying upside down against a blackened palm tree. He angrily threw the photo onto the pile.

"I wanted this Chechen pig arrested, Nikolai, not eliminated. As you well know, it was my intention to speak privately with this scum in the basement at Lubyanka."

"Yes, sir. This is indeed most unfortunate. We had tracked him to Miami and were hours away from making that arrest. But someone else got to him first. He had many enemies here in Moscow."

"Do we know who?"

"We are working on it."

"Has Patrushev seen those photographs?

Or Korsakov?"

Nikolai allowed a wan smile at this small joke. General Nikolai Patrushev, director of the KGB since 1999, was Kuragin's immediate superior. But Nikolai's lifelong allegiance was to two men only: his old comrade seated behind the desk and Count Ivan Korsakov, a man whom Nikolai believed Rostov might one day order him to eliminate. If the president were to maintain his grip on power within the long halls of the Kremlin, he could not long tolerate rivals as strong as Korsakov.

The count, a national hero, was growing in power every day. Rostov was clearly aware of it yet never mentioned it. Nikolai believed it was only a matter of time before the two men came to a crossroads. Only one of them would walk away. The general was shrewd enough to keep his powder dry for the moment, playing both sides against the middle.

"I thought perhaps you should see them first." Kuragin smiled, showing his yellowed teeth. "It's the reason I'm a bit early. I have a meeting with Count Korsakov and Patrushev at two o'clock."

"Good. Where was this party?" Rostov said, examining a print.

"Miami. The residence of Lukov, a man we've been watching for the last month. A birthday party for Ramzan. One of my Miami field officers, Yuri Yurin, was looking into reports of Ramzan's possible presence at this event. Genady Sokolov and Yurin managed to get inside the house, posing as hired security, and shot these photographs surreptitiously."

Rostov threw a photo across the desk and said, "Here is Ramzan arriving. Find out who was driving his limousine. Talk to him. If he knows anything, talk to him some more. I want to know who was sheltering him in Miami."

"Yes, sir."

"These pictures are remarkable. I want a name to go with every face at this party."

"By Monday."

"This woman on the stage. She's beautiful."

"An entertainer. Singer. You'll see her in the next shot. A large black man grabbing her and leaping off the stage. Just before the explosion."

"The bomb was probably in the cake. This *hornye* had foreknowledge of the explosive device's existence. How did he know? Was it his? Get his name first."

Nikolai strongly disapproved of the derogatory slang the president had just used but nodded in the affirmative and said, "Notice also the big man in white. He has a name, 'Happy,' embroidered over his left breast. Perhaps he is in league with the black man? This one delivered the cake, and then, and now here, you see him quickly moving away, pushing through the crowd surrounding the stage. Our agents in Miami are looking for him now."

"Who do we have in Florida now?"

"Nikita Duntov and Grigori Putov and their crew. I pulled them out of Havana last night."

"Using what cover?"

"A couple of movie producers from Hollywood. Korsakov's new production company, called Miramar."

"Perfect. This man Happy, he won't be happy long," Rostov said, now staring at the last few photographs. "This yacht intrigues me, too. Moored at the dock, one man on deck with binoculars, another at the top of this fishing tower. Hand me that magnifying glass."

Kuragin and Rostov examined the picture closely.

"The *Fado.* See the name on the stern? That's what she's called. Come take a look, Nikolai. Up here, the man at the top of this superstructure. What is he doing? Some kind of equipment, not for fishing, I don't believe."

"Cameras?"

"Yes, exactly, surveillance cameras. It appears others besides ourselves were interested in Ramzan that night. The *hornye* and the singer leaped aboard this boat seconds before the explosion, and here, the boat leaves the dock just in time to avoid the blast. I want

261

them all taken care of, understand?"

"*Fado*. I'll get everything I can on it and call you first thing in the morning, sir. Is there anything else? I'm afraid I must get back to the office if I'm to meet with our friend at two."

"There is always something else, Nikolai. But for now, I'm going to finish my breakfast and enjoy a quiet afternoon worrying about our country. Thank you for bringing this to my attention. I want to know who killed Ramzan."

"The enemy of my enemy is my friend," Nikolai said with a smile.

"Friends till death."

They both laughed.

20

Bermuda

Warring thunderheads muscled one another about out over the aquamarine Atlantic. The western skies were lead-blue and getting blacker. Seabirds mewled and swooped overhead. Bermuda Weather Service had forecast gale-force winds later in the day, with moderate to heavy chop in Hamilton Sound. Seas were expected to be running six to ten feet offshore, increasing to twelve to fifteen later in the day.

An exciting day to be offshore, Hawke thought, missing his pretty little twenty-six-foot sloop, *Gin Fizz.*

Wind never bothered him much at sea. As an old sailor once put it, the pessimist complains about the wind; the optimist expects it to change; the realist adjusts his sails. "Reef in a blow" was one of Hawke's favorite life mottos, and so far, it had served him well. Today he would put it to the test.

The approaching storm front was moving

east-northeast, approaching Bermuda at twelve miles an hour. The temperature had fallen at least ten degrees since he'd left Teakettle on his motorcycle. He was wearing only his scuffed boat shoes with no socks, old khaki trousers, a grey Royal Navy T-shirt, and a faded blue wind cheater. Aboard the Norton on the coast road, it was cold as hell.

Eyeing the approaching squall line, he estimated perhaps an hour before the full force of the oncoming storm made landfall. He twisted the handlebar grip and leaned into the lefthand turn. Traffic was light, police presence was invisible or nonexistent, and if it continued, he could arrive at his destination on time and dry as a bone.

Hawke, pushing his treasured Norton motorcycle hard, was racing east along Harrington Sound Road. To his left now, there were whitecaps frothing in the small inlet locally known as Shark's Hole. The little bay was swollen like a blister, bulging. As he leaned into a turn, the first drops of rain stung his face and hands like angry bees. Then, just as suddenly, the rain stopped, and the sun returned, warm on his face and turning the world green and gold again.

This road would lead to the causeway, round the north side of the airport, and from there out to the tip of St. George's and his destination, Powder Hill. It was Tuesday. He had a one o'clock appointment with Asia

Korsakova. He had no idea why he was going. Perhaps to tell her he'd changed his mind about the portrait. That was one of the reasons he told himself he was going. There were many others better left alone.

Suddenly, he was aware of another motorcycle hard on his tail. He darted a look over his shoulder and saw the rider accelerating, closing the gap. He had long, matted dreadlocks whipping around from beneath his black helmet. Hawke thought he caught a glint of gold chain at the fellow's neck. One of King Coale's riders, the Disciples of Judah? Entirely possible, he decided. The bike behind him was a red Benda BD 150. At 150 cc, it was the most powerful engine legal on Bermuda. But his machine, as the Jamaican would soon learn, was no match for the ancient Commando.

Hawke grinned and slowed his bike, allowing the Rastaman's Benda to close within a few yards. He looked back at the rider and saw him smile, the sun catching the trademark gold teeth that filled his mouth. Hawke smiled back, then opened the throttle on the Norton. The acceleration was explosive, and he surged ahead, reaching the next turning along Harrington Sound flat out, probably doing eighty miles an hour. He braked, caught the apex perfectly, and accelerated again, quickly winding it up to ninety.

Rounding a wide bend, he came up suddenly behind a slow-moving taxi, filled with tourists headed for the airport. He swung out and around without slowing, passing the Toyota van and rapidly coming upon the turn for Blue Hole. The airport and his intended route to the east end of St. George's were to his right.

Rather than bear right, however, Hawke swung left, racing up the improbably named Fractious Street. A few hundred yards later, he veered into the small petrol station looming up on his right. He braked hard, tires squealing, and tucked in behind a large commercial van topping off at the pump. He waited for his tail to appear.

"Lost him," Hawke said to himself five minutes later, having seen no sign of the Disciple. He was almost disappointed. He wanted to know what these fellows wanted to know. When he had the time, he intended to find out. Find this King Coale and have a little *tête à tête.*

He backtracked and was soon racing across the narrow two-lane causeway and bridge that spanned Castle Harbour. At the opposite end of the bridge lay the island of St. George's and Bermuda's airport. A big Delta 757 was on final at the field, roaring just above his head as he negotiated the roundabout that would spin him off toward the easternmost tip of St. George's.

■ ■ ■ ■

Hoodoo smiled as Hawke stepped aboard the launch. There was none of the security business this time, no pat-downs, wands, or metal detectors at the shore station; there was only a friendly greeting and a tip of the hat from the launch man who had been waiting at the dock when Hawke arrived.

"How do you do on this lovely day, sir?" Hoodoo said, leaning on the throttles and getting quickly up on plane. Across the water, Powder Hill seemed to hover, sunlit, a brilliant parrot-green isle against a backdrop of deep purple skies.

"Well, and you?" Hawke replied.

"Can't complain, sir."

"Hoodoo, isn't it?"

"It is, Mr. Hawke. Pleasure to see you again."

"And you," he said, extending his hand. The man took it, and his handshake was strong and dry.

"Storm on its way, sir. Bad one, I'm afraid."

Hawke nodded and said, "I'm curious, Hoodoo, and perhaps you can help me."

"I'll try, sir."

"What do you know about the Disciples of Judah? I only ask because they seem to have taken an unhealthy interest in me. Following me about all over the damned island."

267

Hoodoo looked at him a beat too long and said, "Jamaicans. Bad magic. Bermudians hate the Jamaicans, but what can you do, sir? We all brothers, right?"

"Ever hear of a Jamaican chap named Coale? King Coale?"

"Don't recall that name. I steer clear of that bunch. I urge you to do the same."

Hawke thanked him and kept his thoughts to himself for the rest of the short voyage to the island of Powder Hill. As the island grew larger, the knots in his stomach tightened. He knew he was on a fool's errand, but by God, he was nothing if not a willing fool.

The feelings Hawke had for Anastasia Korsakova were about as unambiguous as a grizzly bear in a brightly lit kitchen.

21

Hawke arrived at Half Moon House, said good-bye to Starbuck, the estate caretaker, and watched the green Range Rover disappear up the muddy lane that wound into the banana grove. The little crescent bay beside her pretty stone house was riffled with whitecaps. Unlike on his last visit, the artist-in-residence was not waiting for him up on the verandah. He ducked under the portico, entered the cool darkness, and tiptoed up the wooden staircase. He paused on the landing a moment, waiting for his heart to cease its pounding.

Hawke had been deeply in love only once. He had married a beautiful woman whose name was Victoria Sweet, only to have her die in his arms on the steps of the wedding chapel. She had haunted his dreams for years but, thank God, no longer. He was alone. The depression had faded over time, leaving only sad remnants. There was not even a ghost left now to drift with through the remaining years. He could stretch out his arms as far as they could reach into the night without fear that they might brush a silken shoulder. He —

He decided the hell with it and entered Asia's studio. He found her with her back to him, perched on a blue wooden stool before an easel. She was using a broad brush to cover a large canvas with white gesso.

She was all in white, a low peasant blouse pulled down around her shoulders and a long white cotton skirt that fell to her ankles. Below a hem embroidered with coquina shells, her tanned feet perched on a rung like a pair of small brown birds.

"Asia," he said from the doorway.

In that split second before she replied, he noticed that the hair on his forearms was standing on end, ionized by the waves of heavily charged particles swimming through the airy room; he saw that there was a wide verandah beyond all four sides of the high-ceilinged room, and a paddle fan spun lazily above, French doors were flung open all around, and the tall louvered shutters, banging about in the freshening breeze, gave out to the surrounding banana groves, whipping to and fro in the fresh breeze like a vast undulating mass of torn green flags.

Blades of sunlight slashed through the gathering storm clouds, filling the room with shining golden light. She glanced at him briefly over her shoulder and returned to her easel. But in that instant, her eyes had spoken. *I see you. You have registered. Anything is possible.*

"Mr. Hawke. So you came after all."

"I wasn't expected?"

She swiveled on the stool to face him, rearranging her skirt so that now her twin brown knees were visible.

"Frankly, no. I didn't think you'd show."

"I need the money, remember."

She smiled. "Fancy a drink?"

"How did you guess? What have you got?"

"Rum."

"Love some."

She nodded, put her brush down, and walked over to a small sideboard that served as a drinks table. Her hair was pinned up on top of her head, stray gold ringlets on her forehead and a single one coiling beside her pink cheek.

"No ice," Hawke said. "Neat."

She poured out two fingers of Black Seal into a crystal tumbler and handed him the short glass.

He put it to his lips and drank the rum at a draught, then held out the glass.

"Another?" she asked.

"Hmm. One for the road."

"Leaving so soon?"

"I meant it metaphorically."

She laughed as she poured the dark rum

271

and looked at him with fresh eyes. "Are you funny as well as insanely good-looking, Mr. Hawke?"

"I've no idea."

"What a terrible waste you are, Alex Hawke," she said after a long moment. "If you had two nickels to rub together and weren't so . . . otherwise inclined, you could have every woman on this island."

"I don't want every woman on this island."

She looked away, gazing out at a lone bird, unnaturally white, winging away over the tumult of green banana trees, fleeing the approaching storm. "I'm going out there for a cigarette. Be ready when I come back."

"Ready?"

"On the chaise. Naked."

"Ah."

She slipped off the stool without another word and went outside. Hawke stood where he was, watched her standing at the rail, a white silhouette against the darkening skies, her back to him, smoking, the wind whipping the thin skirt around so that it clung to the shape of her clearly naked hips and buttocks, downpour threatening, heat lightning blooming inside the boiling clouds, the rumble of distant thunder drawing near. From a garden somewhere, the perfume of gardenias came floating in with the sweet breath of approaching rain.

He sipped his rum and noticed that the iron

railing, peeking through the bougainvillea, was filigreed with rust.

Hawke was standing just as she'd left him when she returned.

"Something wrong?" she asked, taking a deep pull on her cigarette and expelling a cloud of blue smoke.

"No."

"What is it, then? We'll only have this beautiful light for a short while."

"Role reversal."

"What?"

"You do it."

"Do what?"

"Exactly what you told me. Naked. On the chaise."

"*Me?* You must be joking. Really. Or quite mad."

"Yes, you. Do it. Now."

She walked over to a chest of drawers and angrily stubbed out her cigarette in the large ashtray on top.

"Listen, Mr. Hawke, I don't know who the hell you are or who you think I am. I am a professional artist. I don't derive any erotic pleasure from my subjects. I try only to paint the truth of them. Now, if you —"

"So, I'm a subject, is that it?"

"Of course. What did you think? That I had some other —"

"Asia. Don't talk. Just do what I say. The blouse first."

She looked at him, hands balled into fists, eyes ablaze.

For a moment, he thought she might rush him, strike him, rake her fingernails across his cheek, pound his chest. But she didn't. Rather, the anger fled, and she gave him a smile, skeptical, tolerant, languidly amused. She slowly lowered her head and began to unbutton the row of tiny pearl buttons down the front of her blouse. There were a lot of buttons, and Hawke saw that her slender fingers were trembling.

"You are full of surprises, aren't you, Mr. Hawke?" she said, fumbling with the buttons.

"You have no idea."

"I was fairly certain you went the other way."

"You mean there's another way?"

She laughed, her eyes afire. She was beyond caring which way he went, she realized. Far beyond.

Hawke, his own eyes never leaving her, went over to the stool. He picked it up and placed it beside the Balinese chaise. He sat on the edge of the stool and took a sip of the rum, feeling it burn down into his gut. She finished with the buttons and stood with her hands on her hips, the cotton blouse agape.

"What are you waiting for?" he said. "Take it off, Asia."

She pulled the blouse off and dropped it to the floor, suddenly looking up at him with a glance akin to defiance but edging closer to something deeper in the heart. She was wearing no brassiere. Her breasts were full and alabaster pale against the mocha brown of her deeply tanned stomach, arms, and shoulders. The rosy nipples were hard, erect in the damp coolness of the room. Pointing at him.

He looked at her for a long time, passion beating inside him like a second heart.

"Now the skirt."

She lowered her head again, reaching behind her with both hands to unbutton the skirt. She let it fall to the floor, where it puddled around her feet. She stepped out of it and kicked it away with one foot. Her finely muscled legs were long and lean and brown. There was a thatch of curly gold between her smooth thighs.

He tore his eyes from her body and said softly, "Look at me, Anastasia."

She complied, holding his steady gaze. Then she cupped her right hand beneath her left breast, holding it as if in offering, closing her eyes, caressing herself, running a finger over one protruding nipple, then pinching it, kneading it roughly between her thumb and forefinger.

Her mouth was open now, but he could see her nostrils flare as she inhaled through her nose. Her left hand was drifting downward over her belly.

"I want to . . ." she said in a small voice.

"Yes," he said.

She reached between her legs. Two fingers disappeared into the already glistening flesh between her now parted brown thighs. Her head fell forward again, and she swayed slightly, a low moan escaping her lips. Hawke watched her, deeply moved by the very sight of her. Stirred, he felt himself growing harder and straining with the need for her but wanting to prolong the intensity of this moment, preserve desire, stay perched on the knife's edge of it forever.

A savage bolt of lightning struck in the banana grove, very close to the house. For an instant, the room filled with blinding white light. Even the crackling air around them smelled singed, burnt. Hawke felt a slight ache in his heart, caused, he thought, by the bolt. A deafening thunderclap came a second later. The wind had roared up to gale force, and with it came the rain at last, a drenching downpour, hard and slanting almost sideways. The louvered French doors were banging wildly on their hinges. Hawke reached out and stroked her cheek.

"Stay there, please. Don't move."

"I'm cold."

"I'll close the doors."

He went around the room and locked the shutters one by one. On the west side, it was difficult to get them closed, the howling wind was now so strong. When it was done, he went back to her, standing close, crowding against her, his face smiling down at her.

He crooked one finger beneath her chin, lifted it, and kissed her upturned lips, parting them with his tongue. She turned her face away, her breathing shallow and quick.

"You are so beautiful," he said. "Just as you are. Just at this very moment. Unforgettably beautiful."

"Alex."

She retreated a step and pulled the tortoise-shell comb from her hair. Tresses fell to her shoulders in a tangle of dark golden curls. She looked at him, seized the thin grey cotton of his shirt in one fist, and yanked it away from his chest, the old shirt ripping away easily, now discarded, and then her hands were at his belt buckle, not trembling now but furious, whipping the leather strap away and ripping his trousers open, pulling them down with her as she fell back against the chaise and sat there before him, looking up with wide eyes at the upright declaration of love or lust or whatever the hell he so obviously had in mind. It no longer mattered to either of them. They were simply locked together, trapped inside the same storm.

She leaned forward and touched her lips to the tip of him, then took a deep breath and touched him lightly with her darting tongue, first tracing a small circle, then lapping at the length of him, licking him, no longer lady-like, just greedy and hungry and thirsty, her lips moving over the taut veins, marveling at the steely flesh so soft and yet so hard. She pushed her head forward, flattening her face against him, and felt his hands at the back of her head, his strong fingers entwining themselves in her hair, guiding her movements.

"Asia," he murmured, and she heard him from her submerged depths, heard, too, the raindrops beating hard against the roof and shutters as the storm finally broke wide open overhead, heard fierce winds screeching around the eaves, a tumult of thunder crashing somewhere above, not far above, and she lay back against the ruby silk cushions, hooked one long leg over the arm of the chaise, and waited for him.

"You certainly could have fooled me, Mr. Hawke," she said, laughing, catching her breath, and beckoning him toward her with a curling index finger.

Skin on skin, he moved on her, his weight suddenly upon the length of her, a hardness probing first outside, rubbing against the drenched lips, then pushing deep inside her as she cried out and raised her hips, realigning them, and then he was within her, fully, searching for more and more of her, as if there were no limit to this seeking.

A groan rumbled from the back of his throat, and then his hands were beneath her, clenched, gripping, cradling, willing her to come with him to the next level, too strong to wait, too gentle to force her, his mouth finding hers, crushing her lips, and then his head thrown back in abandonment and surprise as he felt her nearing and then reaching the moment, both of them crying out as the shutters at the foot of the bed were suddenly ripped open by the tearing wind, and the hard slanting rain came down upon them like a waterfall.

"Oh, God, Alex."

He looked down at her lovely face, quizzically, and saw her smile, breathless and panting, and heard something resembling laughter bubbling up from inside her, as she shook her head from side to side, her face full of delight and wonder, blinking the streaming raindrops from her eyes.

"We're getting drenched, you know," Hawke said, his face buried in her hair, his lips pressed against her ear.

"Don't worry, darling, this can't last forever."

"It can't?" Alex Hawke said, raising his head and smiling down at her, wanting her again already.

22

Miami

Fast Eddie Falco, the septuagenarian security guy at Stoke's condo, One Tequesta Point, jerked his head up like a startled chicken. He dropped a worn paperback book into his lap and stared at the vision before him. One of his residents, the human mountain known as Stokely Jones, had just emerged from the north elevator looking like a presenter on that MTV awards show.

"Hiya, Stoke," Eddie said, eyeballing his friend from head to toe and wolf-whistling through his remaining teeth.

"Good evening, Edward," Stoke said, pausing to toss his GTO keys into the air and catch them behind his back. "How good do I look? Tell the truth."

Stoke turned around to let Eddie get a good look at him. He was sporting a white satin dinner jacket over a black ruffled shirt with a sky-blue silk bow tie and matching cummerbund, patent leather shoes on his feet, size 14 EE.

"How do you look?" Eddie said, rubbing his grizzled chin. "I'll tell you how you look. You look like you're going to a goddamn rap-star coronation or something. Who's getting crowned tonight? Scruff Daddy? P. Diddly? One of those characters? Hell's his name, Boob Job? That Poop Dog fella? Those guys change their names so often I don't know how they ever get any damn mail."

Stoke laughed out loud. *Poop Dog? Boob Job?*

Eddie went back to his book. He was sitting in his highly customized golf cart with a stone-cold stogie jammed between his teeth, reading one of his treasured paperback mystery novels. He was in his reserved parking place, which happened to be right next to where Stokely parked his metallic black-raspberry 1965 GTO convertible.

Stokely's GTO could, according to its owner, do the standing quarter-mile in less than eight seconds, NHRA certified. Eddie was mildly impressed. God knew the damn thing was loud enough to make a deaf man's ears bleed. He braced himself, waiting for his pal Stoke to crank up the big mill any second now.

Eddie much preferred his own vehicle, a vintage machine built in the early sixties by Harley-Davidson, back in the glory days when Harley had the wild-assed notion of building golf carts. Totally custom job, and Fast Eddie had poured his heart and soul into his baby, one of a kind, a classic. Only one Stoke had ever seen with an actual Rolls-Royce grille on the front. Sure, it was unusual transportation for security work but right at home among the high rollers on the little island of Brickell Key.

"Poop Dog?" Stoke said again with a grin, headed for his car, twirling the keys around his finger. "Is that what you said? *Poop Dog?*"

"Whatever," Eddie said, not even looking up from his novel. "You know who I'm talkin' about, I forget what the hell his name is."

"*Snoop* Dogg happens to be the cat's name," Stoke said, unlocking the driver's-side door. "And no, it ain't him."

"So, who's getting crowned?"

"Fancha. She's the opening act at the opening night of a new joint over on the beach. Elmo's."

"Club El Morocco. S'posed to be very upscale according to an article in the *Herald* this morning. Russian money, I hear. Hold on to your wallet."

Stoke climbed in behind the wheel. The big V8 roared to life as he turned the key and simultaneously hit the switch that lowered the ragtop.

"What are you reading?" he asked Eddie over the low rumble of the 541-cubic-inch engine, leaning out his window. He liked to let his baby warm up for a minute or two, get her juices flowing.

"What?" Eddie cried, cupping his hand behind his ear. The acoustics inside One Tequesta's garage did wonders for a 600-horsepower engine.

"What book are you reading?" Stoke shouted.

"*Bright Orange for the Shroud,*" he said, holding it up.

"Again? We already read that."

Stoke and Eddie were the founding members of a two-man book club, the John D. MacDonald Men's Reading Society. They confined themselves to the twenty-one greatest works of literature ever written, namely the Travis McGee novels by the master himself. Sometime ago, they'd even driven the GTO up to Lauderdale on a kind of pilgrimage. They'd had lunch at Pier 66 and then visited the holy shrine, slip F-18 at Bahia Mar, home to McGee's houseboat, the *Busted Flush.*

Stoke backed out of his spot and stopped opposite Fast Eddie's cart. "We read *Bright Orange* last week, Eddie. Remember?"

"Yeah, yeah. Well, I'm reading it again. I like it."

"I'm already halfway through *Darker Than Amber,*" Stoke said, putting the Hurst four-speed shifter into neutral and blipping the throttle, giving Eddie a blast of pure mechanical adrenaline. "You better catch up."

"Don't you worry about me, pal," Eddie said, face already buried back in the book with a babe in a black bikini on the cover. "I happen to be an Evelyn Wood graduate."

Stoke was about to pop the clutch and burn a little rubber when something occurred to him. He hit the brakes.

"Hey, listen up a second, Eddie. I just thought of something. Serious."

Eddie put the book down and said, "Now what?"

"Might want to keep your eyes open tonight. I got a bunch of weird hang-ups on my machine today. Heavy breather, thinks I'm a chick maybe, I dunno. I'm listed in the book as S. Jones."

"A stalker? Stalking *you?* Poor bastard."

"All I'm saying is, you see anybody doesn't look right poking around tonight, don't hesitate to call your PD buddy at Miami Dade, okay? Seriously. Anybody come asking for me, call my cell."

"Those Russians that blew up half of Coconut Grove the other night? Something to do with that, maybe, you think?"

"Maybe."

Eddie knew Stoke's company, Tactics, was involved in some very weird government stuff, he just didn't know what or how weird.

"I'll hold down the fort. Don't worry about

me," Eddie said, going back to his book as Stoke pulled out of the garage, "Give my regards to high society."

Stoke laughed and accelerated down the curving palm-lined drive. He'd head over to the Hibiscus Apartments on Clematis and pick up Sharkey. Then he and Luis would blast over the causeway to South Beach. Fancha had gotten him a reserved table right down front, but he was pretty sure there'd be a howling mob outside the velvet rope. After all, tonight, Elmo's and his baby were the two hottest tickets in the hottest town in the hottest hemisphere on the planet.

Waltzing into Club El Morocco, already fashionably shortened by the locals to "Elmo's," Stoke felt as if some time machine had whisked him back to Manhattan in the thirties. Everyone in South Beach seemed time-warped tonight. You had surfer dudes in top hats and tails and glam queens in old black-and-white-movie-star dresses; but it was the décor that knocked Stoke out. Descending the wide marble staircase with his pal Sharkey in tow, he half expected the smiling ghost of Clark Gable or Jimmy Cagney to pass them on their way up.

Below them, the curving walls of the oval room were blue and white zebra-striped. There were life-size snow-white palm trees all around the room, the fringed white fronds moving idly in the air-conditioned breezes. At the far end of the main lounge, he could see the large bandstand. There were about fifteen cocktail tables around a blue-mirrored dance floor, dancers circulating in the semi-darkness. From below came the smell of cigarettes and the sound of clinking glasses. Against the bar, a group of celebs was being photographed, flashes going off every other second.

A fifteen-piece swing band, dressed in white tie and tails, was in full swing on the bandstand. There were blue and white zebra-striped banquettes around the room, already full of rich folks who'd come early or somehow gotten seated at the most expensive tables. One small round table remained, just below the bandstand, and it looked empty.

"C'mon, Shark," Stoke said. "Our table awaits."

They made their way downstairs and through the crowded room, Stoke running interference for the little Cuban guy.

"Great table," Sharkey said, pulling out his chair, looking around at the sparkling crowd, hands touching jeweled hands over white tables dotted here and there with famous faces. "Let's order us a bottle of pink champagne, boss."

"Do it," Stoke said. "Just get me a Diet Coke."

The waiter brought their drinks just as an

announcer in a white-sequined tuxedo came out and introduced — ladies and gentlemen, one word was all it took to get the crowd's attention — *Fancha!*

The now empty stage went dark except for a single spot creating a white circle of wavering light floating across the sequined curtains. The piano tinkled a few notes, and a lovely disembodied voice floated out over the room. Everybody seated under the drooping white palms suddenly went dead quiet.

Fancha stepped through the curtain and into the light to a sudden burst of loud applause. Fancha, wearing a midnight-blue gown, sang "Maria Lisboa." It was the slowest, saddest, most beautiful song Stoke had ever heard her sing, and when she was finished and stood quietly with her head bowed, letting the adulation wash over her, he got to his feet, putting his hands together for his woman, and he didn't even see that everyone else was on his or her feet, too, applauding his baby in a standing O.

A few minutes later, during a lull in the show, a waiter bent and whispered into Stoke's ear, something about two gentlemen who wanted him to join their table for a cocktail.

"What?" Stoke said, looking at the white card on the silver tray. It had a big black M on it. Somebody named Putov, an executive producer, it said.

"Mr. Putov," the waiter said, indicating the banquette with his eyes. "Miramar Pictures, Hollywood. You are Mr. Levy, no? Suncoast Artist Management?"

"Is that who they said? Sheldon Levy?" Stoke smiled at Luis. His cover was holding.

"Yes, sir, they said, 'Please take this to Mr. Levy at the front table.' "

Stoke looked across at the banquette, smiled at the two guys. "Ever heard of Miramar Pictures?" he asked Shark out of the corner of his mouth.

Luis had some kind of weird Hollywood fixation, always reading movie magazines, *Variety,* and *Billboard,* left them lying around the office, drove Stoke crazy. Come in Stoke's office, asking him if he knew how much *Spider-Man 4* had grossed over the weekend, Stoke sitting there reading about his beloved Jets going into the tank halfway through the season, have to throw Shark's skinny ass out of his office and close the door.

Shark said, "You kidding me? Miramar? They're huge, man. Ever hear of Julia Roberts? Ever hear of Angelina Jolie? Ever heard of Penelope Cruz? Salma Hayek? Halle —"

"Yeah, yeah. Halle Berry I *have* heard of, believe me. What the hell these show-business types want with us?'

"Not *us,* boss. Gotta be Fancha, man. Let me paint you a picture, baby. They know you two are an item, maybe, got to be what it is. They think you're her manager or something. They want an introduction to the next Beyoncé, baby, that's all they want, using us to get to her."

Stoke hadn't seen the wiry little guy so excited since he'd been in a swimming race with a giant mako down in the Dry Tortugas a couple of years ago.

"What do you think, Shark? Should we go over there?"

"Ah, hell, no. What does Fancha need with the two biggest producers in Hollywood, boss?"

"You're right. Let's go see what they have to say."

Five minutes later, they were sitting with Mr. Grigori Putov, who didn't seem to speak much English, and the other guy, Nikita, "call me Nick," last name unpronounceable, who spoke a lot of English. Grigori, bulked up and handsome, wearing a shiny black suit and a massive gold Rolex, just smiled and drank vodka rocks and smoked cigarettes. Nick, on the other hand, now, he was a total piece of work.

He was a crazy-looking little bird, two small eyes pinched closed together on either side of a beaky nose. He had a topknot of wild crackly yellow hair and a shiny green silk suit, which made him look a little bit like a parrot that had just been dragged backward through a hedge. His eyes were blazing behind little gold-rimmed glasses perched on the end of his nose.

They were both kind of pale, too, for Hollywood types, Stoke thought, but maybe pale was in these days. What did he know from Hollywood?

"Let me get this straight, Nick," Stoke said. "A two-picture deal. Now, what does that mean, exactly?"

"It means money, Mr. Levy. May I call you Sheldon?"

"Why not, Nick?"

"Twice as much as a one-picture deal, Shel. Your girl Fancha is going to be a big star, let me tell you that right now. She's definitely got the chops for it."

Nick talked fast, as if he was trying to jam all the words he could into the shortest possible amount of time.

"Sounds good to me," Sharkey said, all lit up. He loved this Hollywood crap, that much was obvious. "Are we talking net or gross points here?"

"Who is this guy again, Shel?" Nick asked Stoke, still smiling.

"Luis is my attorney," Stoke said.

Nick nodded and said, "So, we should contact Mr. Gonzales-Gonzales directly regarding taking a meeting with Fancha?"

"Have I met you guys somewhere?" Stoke said, not able to shake the feeling that he had.

"It's possible. But let's talk about Fancha's back end."

"Talk about what?" Stoke said, not liking the sound of that.

"He means distribution of profits at the back end of the picture," Sharkey said. "By the way, I just want to make sure we're going to be above the line, right, guys?"

Nick smiled.

"Of course, Luis. Now, what Mr. Putov here would like to suggest is that we schedule a screen test at our offices here in Miami. We are about to go into preproduction on a project Mr. Putov, as executive producer, has just green-lighted, a picture called *Storm Front*. Romantic action adventure. Think *Key Largo* meets *Perfect Storm*, right? Bogie, Bacall, and a fuckin' hurricane. The male lead has committed. I can't give you his name, but think George Clooney. We're looking for the female lead. Mr. Putov and I think your Fancha is perfect for the part."

"Wait a minute," Stoke said, smiling at Nick. "You guys are Russian. You were at that birthday party."

"I beg your pardon, Shel?" Nick said.

"Yeah, that's it. You remember. The big blast in Coconut Grove last Friday night. You gotta remember that party. I saw you getting out of a yellow Hummer right before the cake went off."

"Ah, of course. Mr. Ramzan's last birthday. Yes, I was there, now that I recall. He was an investor in *Storm Front*. A great tragedy. He will be badly missed."

"Really? Well, how about that? I give you my card that night, Nick? I'm wondering how you know my name."

"No, no. I saw you with Fancha and asked who you were. Yuri Yurin, one of the host's personal security guys, he gave me your card."

"Security guys that night out looking for work now, I imagine," Stoke said. "Thing like that happens to your boss. That was one serious breach of security."

"Whoo! You can say that again, boss!" Sharkey said.

Nikita and Putov just looked at him.

"Let's get back to the back end, Nick," Sharkey said, all business. "We'll want full participation in the soundtrack album, of course."

"Yeah," Stoke said. "We'll want that, all right. That and a whole lot more."

"Tell you what," Nick said. "I like you, Shel. I've got some skin in this deal myself, and I think we can do business. The owner of Miramar Pictures is going to be here in Miami in a day or two. I'd like you and Fancha to join us aboard his private aircraft for a luncheon cruise down to the Keys. Does that sound doable?"

"What about me?" Shark asked.

"Of course! We can't do business without the attorney, can we?"

Nick's cell phone rang, and he whisked it out of his inside pocket. It was one of those diamond-studded Vertu phones, natch. And Nick was one of those guys who wanted everyone in on his private conversations.

Nick said, "You're talking to him. Hello? Maury? How are you, babe? Good, good. I'm in Miami, back in L.A. Monday. No, I can't do lunch Tuesday, Tuesday is no good. When? How about never? Is never good for you, Maury?"

He smiled at them, slipped the phone back inside the pocket of his shiny green silk suit, and took a sip of his martini, like a bird dipping his large beak into a very small birdbath.

"Old friend?" Stoke said.

"Naah, just some putz from RKO. A nobody."

When he smiled, he looked just like the damn cuckoo bird on a box of Cocoa Puffs.

23

Washington, D.C.

Arriving from Bermuda aboard the British military transport flight, Alex Hawke found his prearranged D.C. taxi waiting in the rain at Andrews Air Force Base. His first stop was the Chevy Chase Club, where he'd drop off his luggage. The venerable club was located in the heart of a Maryland suburb just outside the D.C. line. It was a fine old place, full of sporting art and graceful period furniture. Pulling up under the portico of the genteel main clubhouse always put him in mind of arriving at some sleepy Southern plantation.

Bradley House, a two-story stone residence reached by covered walkway, had become Hawke's home away from home ever since he'd sold his house in Georgetown.

Hawke had told the cabby to wait under the portico while he went inside to leave his bag. Five minutes later, he returned and asked to be taken directly to Old Town Alexandria's city marina on the Potomac.

Hawke paid the taxi driver and walked through light rain down to the docks. He quickly located *Miss Christin,* a typical tourist day cruiser, boxy and double-decked. Fifteen minutes before she sailed, most of the passengers, families and groups of noisy schoolchildren, seemed to be aboard. On this cold and rainy mid-December day, most had chosen to sit inside the enclosed lower deck.

Hawke boarded the vessel as instructed by C and climbed the aft stairs to the rain-swept upper deck. Not a soul up there. Despite the weather, he was looking forward to the downriver trip. He'd never seen much of the Virginia and Maryland countryside, really, and certainly not from the river. Nor had he ever visited General Washington's home at Mount Vernon. He took a bench seat near the starboard rail and settled in for the peaceful river journey.

"If I was a bad guy, you'd be dead now, Cap."

That Southern California drawl could belong to only one person: Harry Brock. Hawke hadn't even heard his approach.

He turned and saw his old friend. Harry was wearing a trench coat with the collar up and a black watch cap pulled down low and wet with rain. Harry stuck his hand out, and Hawke shook it with real affection. A year or so earlier, Hawke had been imprisoned by

Hezbollah forces down in the Amazon, and this man had risked his life to save his bacon.

"Agent Brock, reporting for duty, sir," Harry said with a mock salute. Hawke was taken aback and took no pains not to show it.

"You? You're my Red Banner guy?" He'd had no idea whom the Americans would choose as his Red Banner counterpart, but still, Brock was a surprise choice.

Brock was bit of a rogue, charming at times, tough as nails, a classic Yank piss artist, habitually dodging an army of red-faced superiors whilst building castles of imminent success in the air.

"You?" Hawke said again, as Brock slid in beside him.

"Looks like you lucked out. Anyway, you're stuck with me again, boss."

"I can't believe I didn't make you. Which stairway did you come up? The one forward?"

"That one at the stern. Must be my clever disguise."

Hawke looked him up and down, noticing his brilliantly shined shoes. If twenty years in the Marine Corps had taught Harry anything, it was how brilliantly one could shine his shoes.

"Christ, Harry, you mean to tell me the Joint Chiefs trust the two of us to run this damn thing all by ourselves? I assumed they'd send me some goddamn four-star. Some flinty-eyed general looking over my shoulder, always pointing out the errors of my foolish ways."

"Nope, you got me to point those out for you. By the way, I'm not working for the Joint Chiefs anymore. I'm back at Langley. I guess the sixth floor didn't know what the hell else to do with me, so they gave me to you."

"Well, by God, I'm glad they did something right for a change!" Hawke said. "Come on Harry, let's go below and stroll out on the bow. I want to watch the approach to Mount Vernon. The general is a great hero of mine. I'm very much looking forward to seeing his old homestead."

"You've never been?"

"No. C'mon."

They walked quickly forward to the prow and descended a staircase leading to the chained-off bow. One of the ferry crewmen, apparently recognizing Harry, opened the chain and let the two men move forward to the "Crew Only" section.

"Why the star treatment, Harry?" Hawke asked.

"I'm kind of a regular."

Moments later, they saw the beautiful old colonial house high on the hillside loom up out of the mist and rain.

"Lovely," Hawke said. "Just the way I've always imagined it."

"Did you know Washington was the architect?"

"I did not."

"Designed the whole damn thing himself. Not as elegant as Jefferson's Monticello, maybe, but I like it better."

"Me, too. What's in the bag, Harry?"

Brock held up the large dark green plastic shopping bag he was carrying. "This? Top-secret spy shit. I'll show you later."

The two men climbed a steep footpath that led up the hill through the old Virginia woods. Far above them to the right, Hawke could see the red rooftop and the white cupola of Washington's home. The dirt path was strewn with rocks, slippery with mud, and fairly hard going. Hawke noticed that none of the other passengers aboard the *Miss Christin* had chosen this difficult route to the top.

"Are you sure we're going the right way?" Hawke asked after a few minutes' climbing. "The house seems to be the other way."

"Trust me, okay? I'm a professional."

They eventually came to a tiny open area in the woods, paved with mossy stone. A small brick structure with black wrought-iron gates stood against a thick backdrop of barren winter trees.

"What's this?" Hawke asked.

"Washington's Tomb. Not very grand, is it?"

"Grandeur wasn't his style, from what I've read."

"First time I came here, I was nine years old, and this place was completely overgrown with ivy. Nobody around, just an old guy standing at that gate there, gazing inside, tears running down his cheeks. I asked him why he was crying. Said his name was Timonium. Said he was descended from slaves Washington freed in his will. He said this was the grave of his true father."

Now, instead of weeds and overgrown ivy, the area was manicured and well kept. There was even a small security booth off to one side of the tomb. An elderly black man in uniform was standing inside. He waved at Brock and stepped out to greet him, raising a small black umbrella over his head.

"Mr. Brock, a pleasure to see you as always, sir."

Harry shook his hand and said, "Come say hello to my friend Alex Hawke. He's from England. Came all this way to pay his respects to the general. First-time visitor."

"Pleased to have you with us, sir," the old black man said with a shy smile.

"Pleased to meet you as well. What's your name, sir?" Hawke asked.

"Timonium, sir. And welcome to Mount Vernon. Let me open up the general's vault for you, Mr. Brock. I know you're most anxious to pay your respects."

Timonium had a big brass ring of keys, and he used one large black one to open the heavy gates. Hawke saw a simple white marble sarcophagus in the middle of the small dark vault and felt a sharp chill run up his spine as he gazed at the final resting place of perhaps the greatest leader of men who'd ever lived.

"Let's go inside," Harry said quietly.

Hawke followed him into the dark tomb. There were two crypts inside. The plain white one to the left was the resting place of Martha Washington. The adjacent one, with a carved eagle crest, belonged to the general. Hawke felt another shiver up his spine and knew it wasn't the damp and cold.

"I'll only be a moment," Harry said. "You can stay if you like."

Harry bent to one knee beside the white marble crypt and opened the bag he'd brought along. Inside was a beautiful wreath of fresh olive branches. He placed the wreath atop Washington's sarcophagus. Timonium stood watch just outside the gate, his umbrella folded, his head bowed in reverence.

Harry whispered a few inaudible words, his right hand reverently placed on the marble. Hawke found himself so moved by the sight that he, too, lowered his head. Placing his hand on the cold white marble, he found his own words of thankfulness come quite easily to mind. He was, after all, American on his mother's side, and here lay an American hero for all time.

Harry rose to his feet and moved to the front of the crypt, peering into the gloom. There in the shadows, Hawke saw a leather courier's portfolio resting against the base of the tomb's rear wall. Hawke finally understood why Brock had brought him here. The Yanks were using Washington's Tomb as a dead drop.

"Thank you for that, Harry," Hawke said, visibly moved, as they walked out into the misty rain.

A few feet outside the vault was an old iron bench, placed there for quiet meditation. Hawke and Harry Brock sat there now, quietly watching Timonium lock up Washington's Tomb before heading back to his station.

"Your orders?" Hawke asked, looking at the courier's pouch resting on Harry's knees.

"Yours and mine, Alex. There's a fat Langley envelope in here for you, too. From the director, no less."

"If you know what's in it, tell me now, Harry. I'll read the rest later on the plane."

"Bottom line, we're likely to be going to war with Russia again. Not now but soon. I'm sure you know most of this. We're both going to have to scramble to rebuild our espionage network operations, and fast. Back to levels we had at the height of the Cold

War. Lot of spade work ahead, old buddy."

"Time to invoke your old 'Moscow Rules' again, eh, Harry?" Hawke asked with a smile, knowing how much Harry Brock loved rules of any kind.

The list of famous Cold War CIA survival stratagems had been developed by American clandestine operatives trying to stay alive for one more day in an extraordinarily hostile environment. The most famous of the rules, "Float like a butterfly, sting like a bee," had been borrowed from Muhammad Ali.

"Fuck the Moscow Rules. There are no rules in Moscow. Not anymore. The only rule that will work now is, 'We win, they lose. Period.' "

"Yeah. But to win, you've got to have boots on the ground. You don't, and neither do we, partner."

"No shit. For twenty-five years, they've chained our spies like dogs to a stake, and now that the damn house has been robbed, we get yelled at for not protecting them. Jimmy Carter, in his infinite wisdom, decided the best way to gather international intelligence was to use spy satellites, since, after all, you could see a license plate from two hundred miles up. Very helpful if you've been attacked by a license plate. But we're being attacked by humans, and you can't find humans with satellites. You have to use other humans."

"Like us, Harry. We've got to find out fast who's still usable on the ground," Hawke said, thinking the thing through. He hadn't been to Moscow in years. All of his former contacts there were surely long gone. It would not be easy.

Harry said, "CIA thinks the notorious gang of Twelve may be secretly planning a coup to overthrow President Rostov. Too doveish, I figure. Once he's gone, they move troops and tanks into the old Eastern European republics."

"That's hard intel? What's the psychology of these damn people?"

"Inferiority complex. That's the trigger. These old Soviets, they see the U.S. running around the world playing planetary police, telling everyone what to do. And frankly, they don't like it. They're personally tired of being pushed around. Witness their reaction to us putting missiles into Poland and Czechoslovakia. On the flip side, they see our president as seriously distracted all around the planet, and they want to strike while the iron is cold."

"Back to square one." Hawke sighed.

"I'm afraid so, buddy."

Hawke leaned back against the cold iron bench and stared into the wintry sky.

"God, democracy is a fragile damn thing," Hawke said after a few long minutes had passed. "I don't know how the hell anybody in Washington and London ever thought it could take root in Russia, of all places."

"Cockeyed optimists, Alex, that's all we are."

"There was a moment there, though, when it actually had a chance," Hawke said. "Before the bloody criminal class starved and bled it to death, there was a tiny window of opportunity. But Russia had no infrastructure to support something as tricky as democracy. You know the history, Harry?"

"Not all of it."

"After Yeltsin emerged victorious from the August 1991 Putsch, only one man stood between him and absolute rule of the Soviet empire."

"Gorbachev."

"Right.

"And since Gorbachev had assumed his position legally, in accordance with the Soviet Constitution, there was only one way for old Boris to get rid of him. So, early that December, Yeltsin flew to a Belarussian hunting resort known as Belovezhskaya Pushcha. There he met with three other men, two of them leaders of the two other big Slavic republics — Ukraine's Leonid Kravchuk and Belarus's Stanislav Shushkevich. Together, on December 8, these three guys had a few cocktails and decided to simply abolish the Soviet Union."

"Christ."

"Right. Abolish it for good. Declare independence. That decision, just nine months after a nationwide referendum where seventy-six percent of Soviet citizens voted to keep the union intact, was both unconstitutional and antidemocratic. Basically, it was all over for Russian democracy right then and there. *Poof,* up in bloody smoke."

"Who was the other guy?"

"What other guy?" Hawke said.

"You said Yeltsin met with three men at the hunting lodge. You only named two. Who was the third?"

"Ah. The Third Man. I have no idea. That's what C wants us to find out. He's certainly a member of the Twelve. Maybe even the head honcho. The secret power behind the Kremlin's throne. We'll see."

"What's next?" Harry asked.

"We've got briefings all day tomorrow out at Langley. Brick Kelly wants to understand exactly how Red Banner and the CIA will function together. Then we'll head back to Bermuda tomorrow night and meet with C first thing next morning. You're flying Hawke Air, Harry."

Brock nodded. "What's on C's agenda?"

"A series of fairly intensive organizational meetings are going on right now. A skeleton staff there is already getting Red Banner up and running. C is remaining in Bermuda until we return. We'll get our first assignment from him."

"Moscow?"

"That would be my bet," Hawke said. "Slip ourselves into Moscow and try to find this Third Man."

"C have any idea who this third bird might be?"

"Only, as I said, that he's probably the power behind the throne. The one who's pulling all the strings inside the Kremlin. The man behind the Iron Curtain, one might say."

"Like that fat little bastard in *The Wizard of Oz*."

"Precisely. Our job is to put a serious damper on this Third Man's plans for global conquest."

"Tall order."

"Right, Harry, it's up to us. C, like everyone else in our service, is concerned that the West is desperately weak at this moment in history. America is tied down in a no-win war and has an unstable southern border, and Britain is preoccupied with a restive Muslim population, among other things. It's his view that if the allies are not especially vigilant at this moment in time, we may soon see the Iron Curtain descending over Europe yet again."

"And so Red Banner?"

"And so Red Banner, Harry. Let's get out of here. I'm cold as hell."

Hawke marched up the steps leading to his hero's home, feeling his blood quickening. He welcomed the familiar feeling of focus and suppressed excitement that preceded every important mission. After months of recuperation and hard training he knew he was as fit as he'd ever been.

He had no excuses.

He was ready to go.

It was good to know that the fight was well and truly joined.

24

Bermuda

Everyone was drunk. Or, at least, it certainly seemed that way to Diana Mars. She scanned the colorful crowd scattered over the lawn, looking for Ambrose. Had he left her? Or had she left him? She wasn't at all sure, but his absence was irritating all the same. Perhaps another drink was called for. After all, she'd had only one or two Pimm's cups. Or was it three? No matter. Everyone seemed to be having a jolly good time. The party, a spur-of-the-moment garden affair at the Darlings' quaint place on Harbour Road, was winding down.

It was nearly six o'clock on a drowsy Sunday afternoon, and the Darlings clearly wanted everyone to go home.

"No more Pimm's?" she asked the barman, cocking one well-arched eyebrow. "You cannot be serious." Diana rarely drank to excess, such was her horror of losing her *soigné* air, losing a touch of bloom or a ray of admiration. But this party was a trial.

They'd run out of hooch, for one thing. And the hors d'oeuvres platters were long gone. She settled for a tall club soda and wandered off to find her true love.

Lady Mars made her way through the twitter of golf chatter (it was always golf at these charming affairs, wasn't it? or bridge, grandchildren, or needlepoint?), hearing the lovely tinkle of ice in good crystal as she passed, moving across the sloping green lawn up toward the gabled and russet-painted house, moving through small islands of people, all dressed in various shades of pastel linen, the men in monogrammed velvet slippers with no socks, the chattering classes up to their usual boozy bonhomie.

There was a fresh whiff of scandal on the island, just in time for Christmas. The very married American chairman of one of the big offshore insurance companies was running off with the very young wife of the pastor at St. Mark's. Apparently, this torrid affair had been going on for years, right under Tippi Mordren's nose! In the vestryman's wardrobe!

Quel horreur!

Island gossip is so different from big-city gossip, she thought, pausing at the pantry door. Even the juiciest bon-bons (frequently with a nut or even a fruit at the center!) have a predictably evanescent arc. The tittle-tattle flares up suddenly and self-extinguishes, far more rapidly than elsewhere, poor things, for on a small island like Bermuda, the sly whispers simply have nowhere left to go. Even the hottest rumor burns itself out with a hiss at the shoreline.

She found herself in the empty pantry, pouring warm white wine from a large economy-sized jug into her water glass. These hot afternoons made one thirsty. And she was feeling most disagreeable, to be brutally honest. Put out with Ambrose for some reason she couldn't put her finger on. Poor dear. Every time he opened his mouth, she snapped at him. She loathed the hurt look in his innocent-baby eyes, but she couldn't stop herself.

Where is that damn ring? she thought, stamping her foot in a rare display of anger, realizing she'd just put her quite ringless finger right on the problem at last. She knew he had the ring. She'd heard it rattling around in his can of shaving cream when she was straightening up his bathroom one morning. So, why on earth hadn't he given it to her?

Wandering with her wineglass through the house, a warren of rooms, she finally found Ambrose in a small, low-ceilinged sitting room, a kind of den, she supposed, nautical regalia all round. Ambrose was seated in one corner, deep in conversation with Sir David

Trulove, predictably, as the two of them had been conspiring all afternoon. Talking about some top-secret project, the details of which Ambrose would not even share with her. This wrinkle, fairly new in their relationship, was troublesome. But she had decided not to let it bother her. He could have his secrets. She could have hers. *Tra-la-la.*

It wasn't as if he and she were formally engaged, after all. They'd been in Bermuda for weeks, and not once had the subject even come up. The question remained unpopped after almost a month. Why, she'd no sooner —

"Diana!" Ambrose said, leaping to his feet as she entered the otherwise empty room. "There you are, darling! We were just speaking of you." Steadying himself with his cane, he crossed the room to kiss her cheek.

"I very much doubt that," she said, smiling at him. "Here in this . . . den of spies, I rather doubt I'm topic A. Oh, hullo, David. I didn't realize you were here."

"Diana," C said, getting to his feet. "Sorry to keep the old boy from you all this time. Terribly rude, I'm afraid."

"Not at all," Diana said. "I've been having a splendid time wandering about by myself. I adore garden parties. Doesn't everyone?"

Ambrose could see she was peeved and said, "You were bored. I'm terribly sorry, darling."

"I could murder a gin and tonic right now.

Lot of heavy furniture out on the lawn, darling," she said, sipping her wine, "not that you'd have noticed, mind."

"What's that you said, dear?" C asked. Collapsing back into his deep chair, he pulled a pencil-thin cheroot from his gunmetal cigar case and lit it with a match. He let the smoke dribble out between his lips and inhaled the thick stream up his nostrils. "Something about heavy furniture?"

"Diana's code name for boring people," Congreve said.

C smiled. "You know Harold Nicolson's comment about boring people? 'Only one person in a thousand is a bore, and he is interesting because he's one in a thousand.' "

"Marvelous!" Diana giggled. "But, idiocy all the same."

"Listen, Diana," Ambrose said, looking around the room in a conspiratorial fashion. "Sir David and I are planning a little clandestine excursion this evening. We thought you might like to join us."

"Where to?" she said. At the moment, her idea of an excursion was climbing up into bed, popping a baby-blue Ambien, and getting a good night's sleep.

"We're going to take the boat for a moonlit sail around Nonsuch Island. Not that there's any moonlight tonight, thank heavens."

"Nonsuch? That dismal rock? Whatever for, dear?" she said.

"Surveillance. On that island, according to Alex Hawke, resides a well-entrenched Rastafarian criminal gang. Call themselves the Disciples of Judah. A Jamaican drug lord named King Coale runs the operation. He's been sending his chaps around, bothering Alex. Sir David and I want to find out why. And put an early end to the practice."

"Yes," C said, a serious expression furrowing his high brow. "For obvious reasons, I'm not at all comfortable having Alex Hawke's current movements a subject of interest to a criminal enterprise. Ambrose and I are going to snoop around a bit tonight and see what we can learn. It's been a while since I've been out in the field, as it were."

Diana saw the excitement at the prospect of adventure in his eyes. Who could blame him, trapped behind that desk at MI-6 year after year?

Diana plopped down into a soft tomato-red sofa and sipped her wine. "Which boat are you taking? *Rumrunner*? She's by far the fastest thing in the boathouse."

"No, no, dearest. It's stealth we're after tonight, not speed. We want to sail around the island, unobserved. We thought we'd take *Swagman*."

The white yawl, a Hinckley Bermuda 40, was Diana's own, a cherished gift bequeathed to her by her late father. She'd spent many childhood summers racing *Swagman* in

Bermuda Harbour and round-the-island races. Not a few trophies at the RBYC bore her name.

"Ambrose, there's a lot of shoal around that island, 'skinny water,' as Papa used to call the shallows. Are you two sure you can navigate safely at night?"

C spoke up. "That was why we hoped you'd consider joining us, Diana. No one knows those waters as well as you do. If things get interesting, we may need you at the helm to get us out of there in a hurry."

Suddenly, seeing herself in this heroic role, it seemed to her the most marvelous idea she'd ever heard of. She leaped to her feet, splashing a bit of wine onto the tiled floor.

"What are we waiting for, then, lads?" she said with a gay laugh. "The tide's right, and the wind's up. Let us away, hearties!"

An hour later, *Swagman* and her jolly crew of three were ghosting along across the wide mouth to Castle Harbour. The light breeze out of the west was on their port beam, and *Swagman* was heeling slightly, making a good seven knots through calm seas. Diana was at the helm, nursing a mug of hot coffee, her third. She needed a clear head about her. It would be up to her to get the big yawl somehow safely inside the submerged and treacherous coral reefs that guarded any approach to Nonsuch Island.

For many years, Nonsuch had been a strictly protected nature preserve. Many, many years before that, Diana and her older brothers had sailed to the island for picnics and exploration. Forts had been built, flags raised. They'd nicknamed it Mucky-Gucky Island. As they grew older, the children and their friends spent many happy hours out there, chasing pirates, cannibals, and all manner of imagined evildoers through the jungly interior.

Tiring of that, they'd whiled away the hours diving the many wrecks littering the bottom offshore.

Nonsuch, still nothing more than a squat, rocky hump on the horizon, was just one of many small islets that formed the visible tips of the Bermuda seamount. But, because it was surrounded by razor-sharp reefs, this area made for particularly dicey going. Congreve assumed it was the reason the Disciples of Judah had chosen the forbidding locale as their base of operations. It was hardly a welcoming sight.

Bermuda was, after all, the location that had given the infamous Bermuda Triangle its name. Below *Swagman*'s passing keel lay the wrecks of countless sailing ships and Spanish treasure fleets. Not to mention the silent hulks of freighters, rotting on the bottom, their hulls over the decades turned a putrid shade of green. Coral teeth had ripped great slashes in their sides. All had been dispatched to the bottom by the reefs, the sudden squalls, or the carnage of war.

The Jamaicans who inhabited the island now were squatters. It was clearly posted as a nature preserve. It was a mystery to everyone why the Bermuda police seemed to look the other way. Someone had gotten to someone, of that Congreve had no doubt. But why this interest in Alex Hawke? That was the question at the front of his mind.

"Mind your heads," Diana shouted forward. "I'm coming about!"

Ambrose and Sir David were both standing on the bow, taking turns peering at the dark silhouette of the island through a pair of high-powered binoculars Diana had brought up from below. The black hump had resolved itself somewhat, now resembling a giant comma, tapering down to the sea at either end. An old wooden dock extended out into a small cove at the center, the only sign of civilization so far.

"Dense vegetation up top," C said, "but I do see some lights winking deep in the interior. The light seems to be concentrated at the southern end. Some kind of settlement, all right. Have a look, Constable," he said, handing the famous Scotland Yard detective the glasses.

"Yes," Ambrose agreed. "And a couple of nondescript fishing boats moored at the long dock on the southern tip. There to provide transport to and from the mainland, one imagines. Let's move in a bit closer, don't you think?"

"Diana," Trulove called aft, "we'd like to get in a bit closer, my dear. Can you manage these reefs?"

"Say again," she called out.

C realized his mistake and made his way toward the stern, where they wouldn't have to shout. There might be guards posted on Nonsuch, and sound carried so clearly across open water, especially on a quiet, nearly windless night like tonight.

It was a dark night as well, no moon and few stars, but the woman at the helm knew these waters by heart, and C was not overly worried about navigation.

"All's well?" he asked, standing atop the cabin house.

"No worries, David," she said, as the former hero of the Falklands War stepped down into her cockpit. Diana kept one eye on the dimly lit fathometer mounted on the aft bulkhead of the low cabin house. She was on a starboard tack and still had a good twenty feet of water beneath her keel. "Do you want to circumnavigate the island, David? I think I could manage that, now that the tide is fully in."

"I don't think we'll need to, dear. We can see the layout of the island pretty well from here. I've been examining it through the glasses. There seems to be some kind of settlement in the interior, located out there near the southern end of the island. See the lights, winking through the trees?"

"Yes. Deep-water cove just to the west of there," Diana said, pointing toward it. "There are caves along in there, deep ones. Said to be pirate lairs back in the eighteenth century. I could get us in fairly close over there, if you wish."

"Yes, let's do that. What's the shoal situation around here? Do you need to tack, or could you just fall off the wind a few degrees?"

"I can fall off to port. There's a break in the reef right off my port bow there, known locally as the Devil's Arsehole, pardon my French. We can slip in and out of there fairly easily. You can use the dinghy on the stern davits. It's got a small outboard, but you should probably row. That motor's noisy."

"Fall off, then. And let's extinguish all our running lights, shall we, Diana? No need to alert anyone on shore to our presence. I'll shout a warning if Ambrose or I see any activity we don't like. I've got a sidearm, but I'd rather not use it. I just want to have a quick look around."

"Hard a'lee," Diana Mars said, and eased the tiller to starboard, falling off the wind ten degrees and heading straight toward the island's midsection.

Sir David made his way forward and rejoined his comrade at the bow.

"Anything interesting?" he said under his breath.

"Yes, as a matter of fact," Ambrose said, not removing the binoculars from his eyes. "A launch. Approaching at idle speed from the west. He's running without his navigation lights on, which is a bit odd."

"Forgot to turn them on?"

"Possible. Or, like us, he simply doesn't want to be noticed."

"Where's he headed?"

"He seems to be headed for that dock. I just picked him up a few minutes ago. But that seems to be his course."

"I've a thought, Ambrose. Diana says she can nip into a deep-water cove there on the lee shore. We're headed there now. What say we drop anchor inside, near the shoreline? You and I could row the dinghy ashore, then make our way along the coast on foot to the southern tip. See what we can see."

"Are you armed?"

"Of course."

"I think it's a splendid idea. Something about that pristine white launch piques my curiosity. It's all spit and polish. I can't imagine what business a vessel like that would have with the type of chaps who inhabit this rock."

"I agree. I'll go astern and tell her the plan."

It was rough going when they finally moored the dinghy and scrambled ashore. After shedding their jackets and shoes and tossing them into the dinghy, the two men sat on a fallen palm tree to roll up the legs of their trousers. Sir David had a pistol shoved into the waistband of his white trousers. It was an old Colt Python .357 Magnum revolver, the only weapon he'd owned since leaving the Navy.

"I'm ashamed to admit this to you, Ambrose," Trulove said, hefting the Colt in his right hand, "but this is the most fun I've had in bloody years."

"You should get out in the field more often, David," Ambrose said, grinning at the director of British intelligence.

"I may never go back," C said with a wry smile, getting to his feet. "Let's go, shall we?"

The vegetation grew right down to the water's edge, and swarming clouds of mosquitoes seemed to dog their every step. The slippery shoreline rocks and mangrove roots underfoot also made it difficult for the two men to work their way south along the island's perimeter. You had to hold on to the topmost branches of the mangroves to keep yourself from splashing into the sea, and Ambrose found himself wading through pools of water that rose above his knees.

So far, they'd seen or heard nothing that could be construed as threatening. No guards, although the sound of dogs barking could be heard coming from somewhere inside the dense interior. More than one dog? Yes. Guard dogs? Possibly. On this moonless night, the jungly place seemed forbidding and hostile. By day, sailing idly by, Nonsuch Island probably looked like an idyllic spot for a family picnic.

Finally, they reached the cove's southernmost point. The vegetation had retreated here, leaving a finger of white sandy beach protruding into the shallows. Ambrose looked back at *Swagman,* riding easily at anchor in the dark blue water of the cove. He saw Diana's silhouette, motionless; she appeared to be standing on the bow, watching their progress through binoculars.

From this sandy spit of land to their left, they could easily see the old wooden dock protruding into the water. A half-submerged shipwreck lay alongside the dock and looked as if it had been there for decades.

At the landward end of the pier, he saw what looked to be an abandoned village of small huts and shacks. No lights at all.

Deserted?

The white launch was now tied up alongside the crumbling pier. No one was aboard, as far as they could tell, though there was a small cuddy forward. Whoever had been at the helm had disappeared into the island's dark interior whilst they had been making their way along the coast.

"Let's go have a closer look at that launch, shall we?" C said, already moving quickly across the sugary soft sand.

"Wait for me," Ambrose said, quickening his pace. Running in soft sand had never held any great appeal for him. Running anywhere on any surface at all, to be honest, was not his idea of fun.

The village, or what was left of it, looked overgrown, nearly absorbed by the lush green jungle creeping in from all sides. It looked as if it had been uninhabited for aeons. The dock, too, was in a grave state of disrepair, with the odd missing plank, but it looked usable if you minded your step.

Making their way out along the rotted wooden structure, they glanced at the two fishing boats. Small, with inboard diesels, the kind typically used by one-man commercial operations, each with a little square pilothouse amidships and a mess of netting piled in the stern. One had the name *Santa Maria* painted on her flank, the other had the rather amusing name *Jaws II.*

The snappy twenty-six-foot launch was tied up near the end of the dock and looked completely out of place in this gloomy backwater. She had an inboard engine, a gleaming white hull, varnished mahogany trim, and beautifully polished brass handrails built waist high around the cockpit. Her name was in machined gold leaf on the stern. She was called *Powder Hill.*

Trulove said, "She's got cargo aboard, Ambrose. Let's take a look, shall we?"

Ambrose gazed down inside the deep hull. A white canvas tarp covered what appeared to be rectangular boxes, stacked high in the stern. Trulove and then Ambrose stepped aboard. The tarp was lashed down but came

323

away easily as the two men worked to see what secrets *Powder Hill* contained. Ambrose pulled back the canvas. There were six wooden cases, roughly five feet long by two feet wide, neatly stacked and lashed down with bungee cords.

There was some kind of lettering visible on the lid of the topmost boxes.

Neither man had brought a flashlight, but none was necessary. Congreve snapped open his gunmetal pipe lighter and held the flickering flame over the black type stenciled on the lid of the topmost case.

"Aha," Congreve said, and C knew from the sound of that single word that their trip to Nonsuch Island had not been in vain.

"You read Russian, Ambrose," C said excitedly. "What do we have here?"

"Weapons, I imagine, Sir David. These letters here, KBP, represent a Russian arms manufacturer of some renown. And here on the next line, you see the words 'Bizon PP-19.' A Russian-made submachine gun, if I'm not mistaken. Shall I open a box up and confirm? I've got a penknife that should do the trick."

"Yes, yes, by all means," C said, clearly excited by their discovery. "Let's see what we've got here."

Ambrose slid the blade of his knife under the lid to pry it open just enough to get his fingers under it. The small nails came away easily from the plywood case. He removed the lid and put it aside.

"Submachine guns, all right," C said, peering into the open box. "Now, what in the world do you suppose a ragtag bunch of dope fiends would need these nasty brutes for?"

At that moment, shots rang out in the interior. Distant and muffled but unmistakably gunfire. And the sound of someone crashing through the underbrush. Headed their way.

"Someone's coming. We've got to get off this dock," C said. "Quick, into the water with you."

"Into the water? Do you think I'm insane?"

Ambrose, who abhorred sea bathing, didn't relish the idea of slipping fully clothed into the blue-black water, but he didn't think they had time to make it back to shore using the dock. Another shot rang out, then a scream of agony, much closer now, and Congreve jumped in, feet first, fearing the worst.

It was surprisingly shallow, perhaps five feet of water, and he easily found the sandy bottom. He felt slithery things nipping about his ankles, but he preferred not to dwell on what they might be. He simply imagined himself to be somewhere else. In his Hampstead garden, with his dahlias, to be honest.

C remained on the dock, looking back at the overgrown village, his hand on the butt of his pistol. Ambrose could easily imagine what he was thinking. Admiral Sir David Trulove, ex-Royal Navy, was not one known for slipping away from a fight. The idea of a shoot-out with these druggy bastards was not without a certain appeal. Still, he knew himself to be seriously outmanned and undergunned.

"Come on, Sir David, get below!" Ambrose whispered loudly. "And for God's sake, don't dive. It's quite shallow!"

Trulove well knew they'd learn more from waiting and watching than from blasting away, so he sat down on the edge of the dock and withdrew his pistol from his waistband. Then, hoisting himself over the edge, he slipped easily into the water. Holding his gun aloft, he joined Ambrose under the dock.

"Shh!" he whispered. "They appear to be coming this way."

The two men crouched under the sagging wooden trestles, the water lapping at their chins. Even at high tide, there was about a foot of air remaining under the dock, enough for them to stand on the bottom with their heads barely above water, breathing easily.

"Quiet," C whispered. "Definitely coming this way."

Ambrose was glad Sir David had his trusty Colt. He'd just glimpsed a man covered in blood emerge from the brush, staggering right toward the dock. The poor fellow had one hand clutched at his midsection, as if he were trying to hold his guts in place.

The man stumbled once, then lurched out onto the dock. The boards sagged and creaked under his weight. He was close enough now that the two men hiding beneath the dock could hear his low groans of pain.

Then, when he was directly overhead, he moaned loudly and collapsed to the dock, facedown.

Ambrose, looking up through the cracks at the dark form above, felt a warm spatter in his eye. He wiped it and saw his fingers come away dark and sticky in the dim light.

Blood. The man was hemorrhaging badly from the head and groaning with the pain of his wounds. The blood, a lot of it, was darkening the water around Congreve. Blood in the water was not a good thing.

Was that a fin? Yes! It was definitely a fin he saw slicing through the water near shore. Yes, not one but two! Three!

"What's your name, old fellow?" C said, speaking as loudly as he dared. Between the cracks, they could see something of him. He had snow-white hair, matted with dark, gluey blood.

He murmured something unintelligible.

"Who shot you, old fellow?" C whispered.

"De guns, dat's de ting," the man croaked. "I tole dem de truth, but dey . . ."

Ambrose put a hand on Trulove's shoulder. "No time for this, Sir David. We've got to get out of here now!" Ambrose whispered, the fear in his voice palpable.

"We can't," C hissed. "The bastards who shot this one are coming through the trees. Hear them? They're likely armed to the teeth."

"But the blood! You know what blood in the water does to sharks! We have to get away from —"

Congreve froze. Something had just bumped into his thigh, hard. He looked down and saw one long, dark, hideous shape gliding away. And many more circling in the shallows just beyond the sagging dock beneath which he and Trulove crouched.

"Sharks," C said. "Good God, look at them all."

"Sir David," Ambrose said, his trembling voice barely above a whisper. "I don't tell many people this. You need to know, under the present circumstances, that I am ablutophobic. Severe case. I'm afraid this won't do at all."

"Abluto what?"

"From the Latin *ablutio,* 'washing,' and the Greek *phobos,* 'fear.' Pathologically afraid of bathing. In the sea, of course. Swimming. I do bathe at home. Frequently."

Trulove smiled and pried Congreve's fingers off his forearm.

"As long as we remain still, they shouldn't bother us," he reassured the inspector.

"Of course, they *shouldn't! Will* they, is the bloody question."

The deadly creatures had arrived en masse, just as Congreve had feared they would do. He stared at the menacing black shapes moving silently and swiftly just below the surface, tips of their dorsal fins slicing the water. They weren't ten feet away. The two men stared at each other; the dying man's blood was spattering the tops of their heads and splattering the water all around them. Ambrose eyed the Colt Python that C was holding just above the water. Better to die by his own hand than be torn to bits by frenzied sharks? Perhaps, yes.

There were excited shouts of Jamaican patois from ashore now, as gunmen emerged from the deserted village and raced toward the dock and their victim.

Ambrose looked at C, both of them realizing that there really was nothing for it. Thoroughly trapped beneath the dock, they watched in horror as at least a half-dozen sharks began closing in, swiftly moving in ever-narrowing circles.

"Bugger all. I'd rather get shot by those bastards up there than eaten alive," Ambrose hissed. He'd been absolutely terrified of sharks all his life. And now he was bloody *swimming* with them. He started to paddle away, but Trulove grabbed him and whispered fiercely in his ear.

"You *know* the bullets will kill you. With the sharks, we may have some ghost of a chance. Now, just remain perfectly still. I've got an idea."

"What? Bang them on the nose? That's a comfort."

"Hush up, will you, the crazy buggers are coming out onto the dock!"

26

Miami

"Who does this X-Men flying machine belong to, Stokely?" Fancha asked him nervously as they rode the moving stairs up toward the hovering airship. There was a gleaming stainless-steel escalator extending out of the stern to the roof of the *Miami Herald* building. Apparently, they were the last guests to arrive, since everybody else seemed to be already aboard.

"That's what I'm planning to find out on this trip," Stoke said. "TSAR is a major Russian technology and energy conglomerate that owns the world's third-largest oil company and this Miramar movie studio out in Hollywood, but who owns TSAR? Nobody seems to know."

Girl looked a little peaked. She hated flying in general, and she sure as hell wasn't thrilled about leaving the ground in something out of a damn comic book. But she was determined to go. A week had passed since their meeting at Elmo's with Putov and Nikita, the two movie producers. Fancha's phone had been ringing off the hook with calls from the studio about a possible movie deal, an action picture called *Storm Front.*

She'd agreed to a meeting with Miramar, and Nikita, a.k.a. Nick, had insisted they have it aboard the Russian spaceship. Some kind of flying press junket down to the Keys. They were going to love it, Nick said.

"C'mon, baby," Stoke said as they stepped inside the ship. "Let's go find Mr. Hollywood. See what he has to say for his bad self."

"I guess," she said, looking back as the stairs were retracted inside the fuselage.

"You do want this, don't you, honey? Be a star, all that."

"Baby, I want it so bad it hurts my heart."

"Well, let's go make it happen, girl. I wouldn't take you up in this thing if I didn't think it could fly."

The main solarium of the ship was officially called the Icarus Lounge. It was big and luxurious and could easily accommodate the hundred or so guests who'd been invited on the short cruise down to the Keys. The arched ceiling at the nose was mostly glass and steel, and the room was filled with sunny morning light. Normally, it would be a great place to read or relax, have a cocktail in one of the red-velvet upholstered armchairs or chaises. Today, it had been set up for a press conference they'd obviously missed.

Fancha left Stokely's side, wandered over to the nearest window, and looked down at blue Biscayne Bay. Up ahead, in the hazy distance, she could make out the outline of Key Largo.

Stoke noticed that there was an empty podium on the small stage. Next to it was a large model of another airship. It made the one they were flying in look like the entry-level model. It was sitting on a twelve-foot-long wooden table inside a glass case. It was all silver with gold trim. The word *Pushkin* stretched along its side.

Judging by the scale of the tiny model cars and little people on the ground holding the mooring lines, Stoke calculated the model airship to be at least five times bigger than *Tsar.* That would make *Pushkin* almost two thousand feet long. Behind the model, a flat-screen monitor was showing artists' renderings of the airship's luxurious interior. Staterooms, spas, movie theaters, the works.

"Sheldon, my man!" he heard somebody say, moving through the crowd with his hand in the air. Some little guy, Stoke couldn't see his face for a second, but he knew who it had to be. His second-in-command, Luis Gonzales-Gonzales.

"Shark bait!" Stoke said. "You made it."

"You think I'd miss this trip, Shel?" Sharkey said, holding out his fist for a pound.

"This thing is freaking awesome, man."

"You ready for this meeting, Shark? Fancha's right over there if you want to wish her luck."

"Luck is for losers, man. These guys won't know who ate them for breakfast. Sharkman O. Selznick at your service," the little Cuban said, tipping his hat.

Stoke laughed, assessing Shark's get-up.

"You look good, little brother. I like this style on you, son. It says, 'Gone Hollywood but got off the bus in Vegas to do some shopping first.'"

Luis was rocking what Stoke called his Frank Sinatra look, his straw hat cocked over one eye the way Frank used to do, with a pink blazer, white trousers, and his trademark white suede loafers. Kind of the ring-a-ding-ding outfit you might see on a Sinatra album cover from the fifties, with a TWA Super Constellation parked on the tarmac in the background.

Fancha saw Luis and came over to give him a peck on the cheek.

He said, "Do you guys believe this freaking batship? I've been all over this thing, man. Stem to stern, up and down. It's just unbelievable."

Stoke said, "You see our new pals from La-La Land?"

"Yeah. Nick is here, anyway. No sign of Putov. Nick was looking for you during the presentation. Dying to get with Fancha. He's got a little meeting room all set up for us in a private lounge all the way in the back on the promenade deck. He said we should meet him there about fifteen minutes after we shove off. They've got lunch coming in."

"Good, good," Stoke said, looking at the model in the glass case. "Hey, Shark, what's up with this model airship? *Pushkin*? Man, that big zeppelin is sick. Is it for real? I mean, they built it?"

"Damn right, it's real. It's being launched this week! Five times the size of this one. At least. Yeah, you missed the whole presentation, man. They had that guy from *American Idol,* Ryan Seacrest, up on the stage as emcee. It's their new passenger liner. Biggest airship ever built, more than nineteen hundred feet long. Going to be the new standard in transoceanic travel, the Seacrest guy said. New York to London, Paris, whatever. Carries seven hundred passengers. Five restaurants. Staterooms, suites, the whole deal. Very deluxe, seriously."

Suddenly, Fancha lurched and grabbed for Stoke's arm, a look of terror on her face. "Baby, is that an earthquake?" Stoke felt light in his shoes, as if his heels were going to come right up out of his loafers. But it wasn't any earthquake. He pulled her to him and gave her a hug.

"No, baby, we wouldn't feel any earthquakes up here. Look out the window. We're just lifting off, separating from the tower. Take it easy. Let's go over to the window, and maybe we can see your house down there, huh? Relax, baby, stay cool."

Stoke sipped his Diet Coke, listening to Nick schmooze Fancha. When they'd arrived at the meeting, Nick had said hello to Luis, nodded in Stoke's general direction, and then proceeded to ignore the two men for fifteen minutes or so. But he was all over Fancha, practically spoon-feeding her caviar and refilling her glass with champagne. That was lunch. Caviar and Cristal, a lot of both.

Nobody had any bubbly except Fancha. Luis, who was at the far end of the table taking notes on the meeting, was drinking Perrier. Stoke had told Sharkey that for this meeting, he should let Stoke do all the talking.

But it seemed as if Nick was doing all the talking.

He said he'd seen the local dramatic production Fancha had done for Univision. She had everything, all the tools in the actor's box. She could play sophisticated comedy, low comedy, straight drama, she could sing every possible kind of song, and she looked enchanting, the kind of face and body the camera would love. And *Storm Front* was sure to be a hit, with him, Nick, producing and

Ed Zwick directing. It was going to be a period picture, set in the 1930s, about a handsome rumrunner who falls for this babe singing in some joint in Key West during the worst hurricane on record. Romantic but with a lot of action. All of this in his Hollywood schmooze voice with the Russian accent on top.

He told Fancha she was going straight to the top; with her looks and her angel's voice, nothing could stop her. He said he was just glad he happened to be at the birthday party that night and heard her sing, because he wouldn't trust her Hollywood career to anyone but Miramar. He, Nick Duntov, would personally focus his full laser-beam attention on her alone, turn over all of his other clients to other producers at the firm.

"Nick, tell me something," Stoke said when it seemed as if he'd wrapped up the big schmooze. "How did you happen to be at the birthday party that night?"

"What?"

"No big deal, I'm just curious. Wasn't exactly a Hollywood crowd over there in the Grove, right? Just a bunch of mobbed-up Russians, from what I could tell. Gangsters and Chechen gang bangers."

"Mr. Levy, I don't want to be rude. But what the fuck would you know about Hollywood? Sun Coast Artist Management isn't exactly a player in that league."

337

"Did he just use the F word, Shel?" Sharkey said, looking up.

"I believe he did drop an F bomb." Fancha giggled.

Stoke said, "No, it isn't. I'm just a naturally curious individual. I'm just looking out for my girl."

"So am I. Look, we both have Fancha's best interests at heart, Mr. Levy. So, why don't we all try to get along, huh? Good idea? I have something here that will make you both happy."

He pulled an envelope out of his inside pocket, opened it, and slid a yellow check across the table. It was made out to Suncoast, payable to Fancha. It took a sec for the amount to register. It was made out for a quarter of a million dollars.

"What's this for?" Stoke said, looking at the name of the bank and the payee. It was a Swiss bank, small, private.

"Consider it a demonstration of my total belief in Fancha's career, Mr. Levy. I have booked a one-night engagement for her. That's her fee."

"One night? A quarter of a million dollars?" Stoke said. "Come on."

"Sheldon Levy, behave yourself," Fancha said. "Let's hear what the man has to say."

"Fancha, thank you. Let me tell you about this one very special and historic night. Are you both with me?"

"Hit it," Stoke said, leaning back in his chair. He glanced at Sharkey and rolled his eyes.

Nick paused a moment before he spoke, looking for some drama.

"Fancha, you missed this morning's presentation, but I assume you saw the model of the TSAR company's new passenger liner in the forward lounge? The *Pushkin*?"

"Yes, I did. Beautiful."

"I've been aboard her. Let me tell you, the *Pushkin* is the most luxurious passenger ship ever to sail the skies. Named in honor of the famed Russian poet. She will make her maiden voyage on December 15. She will sail from Miami on a transatlantic flight, arriving at Stockholm on December 17 in time for the Nobel Prize award ceremony that evening at the Stockholm Stadshuset. It may interest you both to know that the owner of this vessel himself is to be awarded a Nobel Prize for his work in astrophysics."

"She's going to sing at the Nobel Prize ceremony?" Stoke asked.

"No. She's going to sing onboard the *Pushkin* on her first night. There will be a gala dinner that night honoring the owner and all of the other Nobel laureates and nominees who will be joining us for the inaugural crossing. Many distinguished guests will be aboard, including the presidents of the United States and Russia and the premier of

China. Not to mention their royal highnesses the king and queen of Sweden."

"I'm going to sing for the president?" Fancha said.

"Yes, Fancha, you are. You're going to sing for the world before we're done. Does that sound interesting to you?"

Fancha looked at Stokely. "Two hundred and fifty thousand dollars? Baby, I'd do this gig for free!"

Nick smiled and pulled another envelope out of his pocket.

"What's next?" Stoke said.

"Yeah, what's next?" Sharkey echoed, getting into it.

"I have here a letter of intent saying that Fancha agrees to enter contract negotiations to star as the female lead in the upcoming Miramar production *Storm Front,* directed by Ed Zwick and also starring Denzel Washington and Brad Pitt. Executive produced by yours truly, Nikita Duntov. Accompanying the letter is a certified check from Miramar Pictures for two million dollars."

"Oh, baby," Fancha said, grabbing Stoke's hand. "Is this for real?"

"I don't know, Boo," Stoke said, looking hard at Nikita Duntov. "Is it real, Nick?"

"Take it to the bank and find out, Mr. Levy."

"You want to do this, baby?" Stoke said, looking at Fancha. She looked as if she was about to come out of her shoes.

"Do I want to do this, baby?" she said. "I've been wanting to do this since I was five years old!"

She jumped to her feet, grabbed Stoke's head, and crushed it to her bosom. Her cheeks were wet with tears.

"It's happening, just like I always imagined it. It's real, baby, can't you feel it? It's *real!*"

Stokely gently wiped away her tears, then held up his hand in front of Nikita's face.

"What's that wet stuff on my hand, Nick?"

"Teardrops?"

"Correct. Real tears, Nick. Remember the lady's tears, what they look like. Remember what's real and what isn't. Because if you forget, Nick, forget what's real, something bad is going to happen."

"Tears dry, Mr. Levy."

"Not these tears, Nick. Bet on it."

27

Bermuda

The midnight-blue Gulfstream IV was cruising at 45,000 feet. She'd slowed a bit for initial descent and was doing 400 kilometers per hour with a good tailwind due to the prevailing westerlies. She was less than an hour from her destination, Bermuda. The cabin lights were dimmed, and the two passengers were sound asleep. The attendant, a pretty young woman named Abigail Cromie, was making tea preparatory to landing, when a yellow light flashed in the forward galley. The captain wanted a word.

"Yes, Captain?" she said, poking her head inside the dark cockpit.

"I've got Diana Mars calling for his lordship," Captain Tanner Rose said, turning to look at her. The young Scotsman's usual smile was missing. Something was clearly wrong.

"He's sleeping, I'm afraid. He asked to be awakened a few moments before landing. I've just put the tea on."

"Well, you'd best wake him up, Abby. Lady Mars sounds desperate. She's calling from a sat phone aboard some sailing vessel. Tell him it's an urgent call."

"Right away, Captain."

Miss Cromie, a woman with ginger-colored hair and a well-tailored pale blue uniform, went aft to where Hawke was sleeping. His seat on the aircraft's port side was reclined to horizontal, and he was snoring lightly. Forward of him, on the starboard side, Harry Brock was snoring loudly.

"Telephone for you, m'lord," she whispered into his ear, simultaneously patting him firmly on the shoulder.

"What's that?" Hawke said, his eyes opening drowsily.

"Lady Diana Mars for you, sir. A sat-phone call from Bermuda. Captain says it's most urgent, I'm afraid."

"Oh," Hawke said, coming fully awake and bringing his seat upright. "Yes. All right, then, Abby, I'll take it."

There was a mounted telephone right beside Hawke's seat. Abby pressed the flashing button and handed the receiver to Hawke.

"Alex Hawke," he said.

"Thank God!" Diana said, her voice quavering.

"Diana, are you all right? What is it?"

"It's Ambrose, Alex. Ambrose and David

343

have gone missing. I'm afraid something terrible has happened. The two of them went ashore. Fifteen minutes later, I heard gunfire, and then —"

"Went ashore where?"

"Nonsuch Island. At the entrance to Castle Harbour. They decided to have a good look round. See what was going on with those damn Rastafarians, whatever they're called."

"Disciples of Judah. What happened, Diana?"

"They went ashore, as I said, whilst I remained aboard."

"Aboard what?"

"*Swagman.* You know, my father's old yawl. That's where I'm calling you from now. She's got a sat phone at the nav station, thank the good Lord."

"They went ashore, and then what happened?"

"I watched them make their way east along the coast. I was desperately worried about Ambrose stumbling around in the dark on his bad leg. He's only just got it working again, you know, after what that bastard did to him in the Amazon. Toward the southern end of the island, where we'd seen some lights in the interior, I lost track of them. They'd disappeared around the tip of the island, I imagine. There's a dock over there, and we'd seen a launch headed that way with no navigation lights. Then, about ten minutes

344

after I'd lost sight of them, I heard shooting."

"Were they armed?"

"Sir David had his handgun. That's it."

"How long ago was this?"

"Half an hour ago, maybe forty-five minutes. I can't stand it any longer, Alex, just sitting here. Should I go ashore and look for them?"

"No, Diana. Do not do that. Have you called the police?"

"Y-yes, of course, I did that first. I didn't want to bother you with this. I mean, it may very well turn out to be nothing, you know, but still, I —"

"Diana, calm down. It's going to be all right. Are the police coming?"

"I don't know. The chap I spoke to sounded . . . indifferent. They said they'd send the marine unit around to investigate, but they didn't sound any too urgent about it. It's been more than twenty minutes, and no sign of them."

Hawke looked at the digital map displayed on the small monitor beside his seat. It told him his location, air speed, and time to arrival and showed a real-time image of the plane's eastbound position approaching Bermuda.

"Diana, listen, I'm about half an hour out from Bermuda right now. This time of night, there's no other traffic, so I could be on the ground in less than twenty-five minutes. I'll tell the pilot to push it. Can you pick me up at the airport?"

"How would I do that?"

"You've got a dinghy, right?"

"Well, they took it ashore. But I could swim over and get it."

"Good girl. You say Castle Harbour. Can you see the airfield from where you are?"

"Barely. Nonsuch is way out at the harbor mouth. Next to Castle Island."

Hawke pressed a button and saw a Google Earth image of Bermuda. He quickly located Nonsuch Island.

"Outboard motor?" he asked.

"On the dinghy?"

"Yes."

"Right, a fifty-horsepower."

"Perfect. You'll see me land. My plane is a dark blue Gulfstream IV. I'll be coming in hot, right over *Swagman*'s masthead. I should be on the ground by the time your dinghy reaches the field. Just beach the dinghy wherever you can at the east end of the runway. Have you a flare pistol aboard, dear?"

"Yes."

"Take it with you. When you beach your dinghy, fire a parachute flare to mark your location. I'll come right to you. I've got someone with me, Diana. Fellow named Harry Brock. He and I can take care of this, all right? So don't worry. Ambrose and David are going to be fine."

346

"Oh, Alex, if anything happened to him, I just don't know what I would do. With his bad leg, he's so vulnerable, and . . . he means everything to —"

She was crying now, sobbing.

"Diana. Please listen to me. Ambrose is my best friend in the world. Sir David is my employer and the chief of the world's most formidable intelligence service. Believe me, I will not let anything happen to either one of them. I'll see you on the ground in twenty-five minutes, max."

"Please hurry, Alex. I'm so sorry to bother you. Good-bye."

Hawke quickly got up, pausing to rouse Harry Brock on his way forward to the cockpit. He quickly explained the situation to the captain and told him to forgo the performance parameters, firewall the throttles, and get him on the ground as rapidly as humanly possible. He held on to the back of the copilot's seat for a few seconds as the aircraft shot forward, then moved aft. He collected Brock, and they went to the aftmost part of the second cabin.

There was a head back there, with a full-length mirror on the aft bulkhead. The mirror, to Harry's surprise, swung open to reveal a tall gun safe with two wide drawers beneath, one for ammunition, the other containing camo clothing and other gear that one might use in an emergency like this one.

Hawke punched in a code, and the heavy safe door swung open.

"Guns," Harry Brock said with a grin, pulling an M349 light machine gun from the safe. "I like guns."

"Never leave home without one," Hawke said, grabbing an identical weapon.

The guns were called SAWs, which stood for squad automatic weapons. Hawke much preferred them in the field, because they could be used either as automatic rifles or machine guns. The gun had a regulator for selecting either normal (750 rounds per minute) or maximum (1,000 rounds per minute) rate of fire. Hawke pulled a few standard M16 magazines from the ammo drawer and inserted one of them into the mag well in the 5.56mm SAW.

Hawke also donned a black Nomex jumpsuit and urged Harry to do the same.

"Nomex," Harry said, holding one of the suits up. "I like black Nomex, too."

"Why?" Hawke asked.

"High CDI factor."

"CDI factor?"

"Chicks dig it."

"God help me," Hawke said, strapping on a Velcro thigh holster.

The jumpsuits had lightweight ceramic and Kevlar body armor sewn inside and were designed for jungle warfare. By the time the two men were dressed and fully armed with SAWs, assault knives, and SIG Sauer 9mm sidearms strapped to their thighs, the speeding plane was on final.

"Tea, gentlemen, before we land?" Abby asked as the two men in black returned to the main cabin and took their seats. Both were busy checking and rechecking their weapons.

Hawke caught the irony and smiled. "No, thank you, Abby. I'm afraid it might smear my war paint." He and Brock were now applying nighttime camo paint to their faces.

"Landing in two minutes," the captain announced. "Buckle up, please."

"How do I look?" Hawke asked, smiling up at Abigail. His face was now painted light green, dark green, and black.

Abby smiled. "Like a seriously confused zebra, sir."

Brock and Hawke laughed, fastening their seatbelts as Abby moved forward to her seat in the galley.

Looking out his window at the harbor spread out below, Hawke saw a pretty white yawl moored inside a small cove on the mid-sized island near the harbor mouth. A moment later, he saw the phosphorescent wake of Diana's tiny dinghy nearing the eastern end of the beach stretching along the perimeter of the Bermuda airfield.

A wee bit to the north lay another familiar

island, Powder Hill. He could almost make out Half Moon House, standing by a cove at the edge of the banana groves. Was Asia awake? Sitting before her easel in the small hours, smoking a cigarette and drinking gin while she painted his portrait? Was she sleeping on her big bed, the paddle fan revolving lazily overhead?

It was unusual, he knew, thinking like this. But it was the first time in a very long while that he'd been seriously interested in a woman. Since that first storm broke over Half Moon House, there'd been many blissful hours on the chaise and in her great four-poster bed. Her need was deep. As was his desire to fill it. Love? What the hell was that?

Harry was looking out his window as well.

"That's Diana Mars's yawl down there?" Harry asked, breaking his reverie.

"Yeah. *Swagman.*"

"Wooded area at the south end of the island," Harry Brock said. "And lights down there. No movement."

"Do you see the dock? The white launch tied up there looks very familiar."

"Everybody buckled in back there?" the pilot said over the intercom. "Touchdown in fifteen seconds."

"Drop your cocks and grab your socks," Harry Brock said, hands gripping the armrests of his seat. They were coming in extremely hot, just as Hawke had requested. It

350

was going to be an interesting landing.

Just as the rubber hit the runway, brakes screeching loudly because of the scalding approach, Hawke, craning his head around, saw Diana's bright orange flare arc into the black sky, ignite, and swing gently beneath its tiny parachute as it floated toward the beach. He knew exactly where to find her.

Diana ran into Hawke's open arms as soon as she saw him approach over the sand dune. There were two other men with him, one dressed like Alex in some kind of black camouflage, the other in a dark suit and tie.

"Thank God you've come, Alex," she said, clearly distraught. "I'm going out of my mind with worry."

"Diana, it's going to be all right. But we need to get moving. This is a friend of mine from Washington, Harry Brock. This other gentleman is my pilot, Captain Tanner Rose. Tanner's going to see that you get safely home."

"Home?"

"Yes. I want you to go there immediately. Captain Rose will stay with you. Don't do anything or go anywhere until you hear from me. Don't pick up the phone. Do you understand?"

"But, Alex, I want to —"

"There's nothing more you can do, Diana, believe me. Now, Mr. Brock and I are going over to that island. We will return shortly with your fiancé and Sir David. I'm afraid we've got to shove off. Tanner, take my car and see that Lady Mars gets home safely, will you? It's the little yellow Jolly in the lot, keys under the seat. Let's go, Harry."

Hawke opened the throttle, and the little inflatable got its rounded nose in the air and flew across the dark water. To the southeast, he could now see two larger islands silhouetted against a dim smattering of stars along the horizon. The one on the right, heavily fortified centuries ago, was called Castle Island. On the left was Nonsuch. He steered for the southern tip, where he'd seen the dock and the familiar white launch moored.

Presumably, Ambrose and Sir David had gone there, since Diana had last seen them headed in that direction.

It took them ten minutes. During that time, Hawke filled Brock in on what little he knew of the man called King Coale and his Rastafarian enclave on Nonsuch Island. The man was a big enough fish to have attracted the attention of the DEA and had done serious time in the U.S. prison system. Now he was back on Bermuda and had taken an unhealthy interest in Hawke's comings and goings. Tonight, Hawke planned to find out why.

"Red Banner to the rescue," Harry said cheerfully as they slowed, approaching the dock.

"Our first operation, and it damn well better be successful," Hawke said, slinging the SAW automatic weapon over his shoulder. "I can't imagine what those two were thinking, going ashore in the middle of the night."

"Looking for action, Alex. They don't see much anymore."

"I suppose that's about right, Harry."

In truth, he was far more worried about the two missing men than he'd let Diana see. Ambrose was a seasoned police officer. He'd risen from street copper through the ranks at the Yard and seen plenty of rough sledding in doing so. Sir David, on the other hand, was an old blue-water sailor. No one doubted his courage or intelligence, but he'd been piloting a desk for the last decade or so. Neither was a young man anymore, and Ambrose was still battling a crippling leg injury.

From what little he knew of the Disciples, they were a sketchy lot at best. Marijuana merchants being paid to keep an eye on him for some unknown reason.

At worst, they were a ragtag army of stoned killers.

There was no one in sight either on the shore or on the dock. Hawke disengaged the throttle and let the dinghy ghost up to the end of the old wooden pier. He looked closely at the island, his eyes roaming the dark fringe of vegetation reaching down to the white sandy beach. There was a village there, completely overgrown. It looked deserted, but a sniper could easily be waiting behind one of those vine-choked windows. He seemed to recall that this island had been home to a downrange NASA tracking station during the great manned-space-flight era.

He heard Harry slamming a mag into his SAW and looked up. They were three feet from the rotting wooden dock. There was a ladder descending into the water, and Brock tied the painter to it. The ladder looked barely strong enough to support their weight.

"You first, Harry," Hawke said quietly. "Don't forget to step up from the middle seat getting off. Balance."

"Jesus, you think I don't know that?"

"Just go, Harry."

Hawke checked his weapon one last time and followed him up the ladder a few moments later. The first thing he saw was Harry Brock, halfway down the dock already, crouched over the body of a man who appeared to be very dead.

Hawke sprinted toward Harry and heard a froth of angry splashing coming from the water beneath the boards.

"Dead?" Hawke asked, kneeling beside Brock.

"Yeah. Look at the water, Alex," Harry said.

Hawke did. It was a mess of sharks in a frenzy.

"Look at this," Brock said, pulling back the

dead man's trouser cuff. "One of these toothy bastards came right up out of the water and took off his whole goddamn foot."

28

The thrashing sharks were in a feeding frenzy, all that fresh blood in the water, flowing from the mutilated, nearly exsanguinated body above. The dead man was facedown, but Hawke already had a pretty good idea who it was. He knew that white launch well enough.

"Turn him over, Harry."

Harry got his hands under the corpse and gently rolled it onto its back. The body was almost completely bled out, and the grey face had been partly shot away, but Hawke recognized him instantly.

"His name is Hoodoo. That's his launch back there."

"Old pal of yours?"

"He works for a Russian here on Bermuda named Korsakov. Somehow, Korsakov's tied to this Jamaican lot. Let's go."

They quickly moved toward the deserted village of low concrete buildings, weapons at the ready, fanning out and looking for any hint of movement behind the black and empty windows. They'd decided to proceed with hand signals alone, and Harry now signaled Hawke that he'd enter the village first, clearing it with his SAW if necessary. Hawke indicated that he understood. Harry would clear; he would follow.

It wasn't necessary to clear. They proceeded into the island's jungle interior unopposed. It was tough going with the guns out front, their muzzles catching on the thick vines and undergrowth, but Hawke figured this was the way Congreve and Trulove must have traveled. The jungle gave way to a kind of path here, overgrown but clearly still well used as a route to and from the dock. Judging from the crumbling cement structures they'd seen, Hawke knew this was what was left of the old NASA tracking station, the buildings abandoned years ago. But these were pumping stations, maintenance sheds, and other secondary structures. The main building had to be somewhere deeper in the interior.

Brock went down on one knee, and his hand shot up, palm flat. Hawke froze, taking a knee as well, his SAW pulled tight into his shoulder. He could hear low voices ahead. The sweet smell of *ganja* hung in the still night air. After a few moments, he and Harry both pulled out the assault knives strapped just above their ankles and started moving again toward the sound of the voices.

There was a clearing and a small ravine

ahead, deep and wide enough to have a wooden suspension bridge strung across it. There were two men guarding the entrance to the bridge, although *guarding* may have been too strong a word. They sat on the ground, cross-legged, on either side of the narrow bridge opening, with what looked to be automatic weapons across their laps. They were passing a thickly rolled spliff back and forth between them, joking about something in hushed tones.

Hawke came up behind Harry and whispered into his ear, "I've got left, you take right. Go."

In an instant, moving swiftly and silently, they were on the two guards, wrestling them quickly to the ground. Hawke immediately went for his man's throat, drawing his razor-sharp blade from right to left, feeling the sudden warm gush as the man's jugular was sliced open. Harry's man suffered a similar fate. They left them there and crossed the wildly swaying rope bridge at a run, automatic weapons at the ready.

Moving through dark jungle on the ravine's opposite side, they felt the path start to climb. The vegetation was thinning out, there was starlight, and Hawke was sure they were nearing the Disciples' compound. It would only make sense that the primary tracking station would be situated on the island's highest ground.

"Lights," Harry whispered, and they came to a stop, crouching side by side at the edge of wide clearing, still hidden within the heavy foliage. "Up there on the hill."

A decrepit two-story concrete structure, almost completely hidden by heavy looping vines and overgrown banana trees, sat on the hillside. The windows were curtained, but pale light shone from within those on the upper floor. At the front, an arched entrance with the door ajar, light spilling out. On the roof, the rusted-out antennas and radar dishes of a bygone era, a space race the good guys won.

This building had once been used to monitor the trajectories of giant Atlas rockets roaring overhead just three minutes after they'd departed the launch pad at Cape Canaveral. How the mighty had fallen. Now this decaying ruin was the headquarters of old King Coale, and a not so merry old soul was he. At least, that's what Hawke would bet.

"Guy by the door," Harry whispered as they crouched in the bush. "Armed."

"Yeah."

"My gut," Harry said, "Ambrose and Trulove are inside that building."

"My gut, too, Harry. Sit tight. We've got to do this right the first time, or they could get hurt."

"Assuming they're still alive."

"We wouldn't be here if we didn't assume that."

Hawke felt an old twinge of irritation. Sometimes Harry talked too much. There was a negative cast to his personality that Hawke did not admire. Still, he was a good man in a fight, hard as hell to kill, and Hawke was glad he had him along tonight.

The man by the door was slouched in a chair, smoking a cigarette. A rifle dangled loosely from one hand. Hawke saw something familiar: the long dreadlocks hanging about the shoulders, the Selassie sweatshirt, and the heavy gold chains draped around the neck. And even in the low light, the gleam of gold at his mouth.

"I know this guy," Hawke said, studying the figure through a small monocular hung around his neck.

"Who is he?"

"Calls himself the Prince of Darkness. Name is Desmond Coale. He's the son of the man who's been invading my privacy, Samuel Coale. Coale's inside that building."

"Head shot," Harry said matter-of-factly. He'd affixed the silencer to his SAW and was putting his eye to the night-vision scope preparatory to putting a single round through Desmond's left ear.

"No," Hawke said, pulling the barrel down. "We'll use Desmond to get to the father. We'll split up, circle around through the woods to either side of the building, come at him from behind. On the count of thirty, make some kind of noise over on your side of the building, get him to come to you. I'll do the rest. Thirty seconds. On my mark. Ready, Harry?"

"Born ready."

"Remember, we want this character alive, Harry. Go."

They separated, Harry going left, Hawke right, each man moving quickly and silently through the dense vegetation that surrounded the old NASA building. Hawke saw movement behind the curtains in an upstairs window. Someone pulled the curtain aside and peered out into the darkness for a few moments, then disappeared. There was music, loud reggae, and some raucous laughter coming from that upstairs room. Hawke recognized the song playing. Jimmy Cliff's "The Harder They Come."

Hawke ran quickly from the cover of the woods to the side of the crumbling concrete building. He paused briefly, looking at his dive watch. In five seconds, Harry would somehow distract Desmond. He moved to the front of the building and peered around the corner. Desmond was still in his chair, head down, reading his newspaper in the yellow light of the doorway.

A second later, a muddy old soccer ball bounced from behind the other side of the building. It rolled to a stop maybe fifteen feet from young Coale's feet. He looked over at it, threw his paper to the ground, got up, and went over to see what the hell was going on.

"Who's dat fuckin' wit me?" he said loudly, still holding the rifle loosely at his side. Getting no reply, he went forward to pick up the ball.

That's when Hawke made his move. He was around the corner and up behind Desmond before the Rastaman had taken three steps toward the ball. As Desmond stood, Hawke snatched a great handful of thick, matted dreadlocks, yanked the man's head straight back, and lay the flat side of his serrated assault blade against his throat, just under the bobbing Adam's apple.

"Dat's me fuckin' wit you, Prince," Hawke whispered into the man's ear.

"Who?"

"My name is Hawke, remember me? My colleague and I have come here to kill you. Or collect our friends. Your call. Nod if you understand your two choices, Desmond."

The Jamaican made a strangled sound in his throat and said, "Dat's not me, mon. I ain't de Prince, mon, dat's Desmond, he's my bra'. My brother inside de house. I am called Clifford."

"You look a whole lot like Desmond to me."

"We *twins,* mon, I swear it's de troo't."

Hawke sensed it was. It was tough to lie convincingly with a knife at your throat.

"Say one word, Clifford, you make any sound at all, and you're dead. Understand me?"

Clifford managed to nod yes without slicing his own throat open. His brother had already told him this Hawke was a man to be taken seriously.

"Okay, Clifford, relax. We're all going inside now."

Hawke looked over his shoulder and saw Harry moving toward the open entrance with his weapon at the ready.

"Is your father inside? Upstairs?" Hawke whispered in Clifford's ear. "Nod, yes or no."

Getting a yes, Hawke said, "I believe the old man has company. Two Englishmen. Yes?"

He got another yes nod.

"Excellent. Let's go see how they're doing. You'd better start praying that no harm has come to them. You understand me?"

He turned the man around and marched him to the entrance, the two of them going inside the front door just behind Harry Brock.

They walked into a big square room filled with sofas and a blank large-screen TV on one wall. The room was empty except for the trash swept into the corners. So, apparently, was the smaller room beyond, which was dominated by a large snooker table, the felt long gone, probably used for meetings and dining. A naked bulb, dimly lit, dangled above the table. To the right, an open staircase led to the second floor.

"Where is everybody, Clifford? Whisper."

"Dey mostly off island, it bein' Saturday night. Drinkin' wit de Skanktown ho's at de Skibo Grill, mos' likely."

"Where's your father?"

"He upsteers. Wit de prisoners. Wit my bra'. Dey havin' a party up dere."

"Let's crash that party, shall we?"

They quickly mounted the stairs, Harry first with his SAW at the ready. There was a long hallway, hot, damp, and funky, leading to the rear of the building. The music was louder now, and also the sound of laughter was coming from the room Hawke had seen from the woods. The sweet stench of marijuana was almost overpowering. The heat inside the concrete building was intense, even hours after sundown.

"Okay," Hawke said. "Harry, you're through the door first, go in low, and show your weapon to get everyone's attention. I'll be right behind you with the Prince's lookalike. Got it?"

"Got it, boss," Harry said, smiling. He loved this stuff, lived for it. It was all over his face.

The peeling wooden hallway door was closed. From behind it came a confused roaring, laughter, and a breaking of glass. Hawke stood behind Harry, with Clifford still immobilized by his blade, and watched Harry's right foot strike the door halfway up, blowing it inward. Harry went in low and racked the slide on the SAW, letting everybody get a good peek down the barrel, not a sight recommended for the faint-hearted. The ragged men were stunned but remained sitting in rows of chairs three deep that formed a ring in the center of the floor.

Hawke followed Harry inside, took it all in at a glance. The temperature inside the unpainted concrete-block room had to be more than a hundred degrees Fahrenheit. The smells of copious sweat, coppery blood, and spilt rum hit him like a wall. There was a rooster trapped in the center of the circle, and the men seated all around were taking great delight in hurling empty rum bottles at the bird, the cock screeching and flapping about. The bird was bloodied, had been hit a few times, and the concrete floor was covered with smeared blood and broken glass. A pile of feathery corpses lay at the feet of one of the participants.

The men's golden smiles froze on their dark faces, and the effect was startling. Some of them still held half-empty rum bottles poised above their heads, but they lowered them as they saw the grim expression on Hawke's face. And the second semiautomatic weapon he held in his left hand.

Hawke pushed Clifford inside in front of

him and let everybody get a good look at him. Harry began patting down the party boys, looking for weapons.

"Anybody armed, Harry?" Hawke asked. "Aside from the rum bottles, I mean?"

"Clean so far," Harry said, moving around the circle, carefully checking each man for weapons.

"Which one of you hearty sportsmen is King Coale?" Hawke asked, although he'd already guessed Samuel Coale was the one in the flowing purple dashiki and the snow-white dreads that reached to his waist. He had a wide leather belt around his corpulent belly and an ugly machete dangling in a sheath. Behind him, on the wall, a huge Ethiopian flag and an old poster of Emperor Haile Selassie, fist raised, the Lion of Judah himself, reluctant father of the Rasta movement.

Old King Coale rose from his tatty throne, the only upholstered armchair of the lot. He kicked a few rooster corpses out of his way and took a step forward.

"Yahweh is Lord, and I am his king," he said, Rasta-style. "You come looking for your friends, Lord Hawke?"

"I have. Where are they?"

King Coale inclined his head left toward a closed door on the far wall.

Hawke pressed the muzzle of the SAW deep into King Coale's belly.

"You've got your Disciples following me all over this bloody island, Coale. Tell me why."

"Someone pay me good money, mon. Why else you do anything?"

"Who pays you?"

"I forget."

"Let me guess. Korsakov?"

"I tell you, he kills me."

"You don't tell me, I kill you," Hawke said, using the machine gun's muzzle to shove the man back into his armchair.

A loud shout of pain came from behind the peeling door. Hawke recognized the voice instantly. It was Ambrose Congreve.

"Harry, keep an eye on these gentlemen for a moment," Hawke said, turning away from Coale. He quickly crossed the room, twisted the knob, and shoved the door open. He craned his head around and peered inside. Then he glanced over his shoulder, looking at Brock.

He wasn't smiling.

"They're both alive," he said.

29

The two Englishmen were bound back-to-back, each sitting upright in a straight-backed wooden chair. At a cursory glance, both appeared to have been beaten about the head and face. A trickle of blood ran from Sir David's nose and mouth. Desmond, the Prince of Darkness, was standing before Ambrose with a length of iron rod in his hand. Ignoring Hawke's sudden appearance, he drew it back and struck Congreve against the shin of his wounded leg. The detective screamed out in agony, his body straining backward in his chair, his face a rictus of pain.

The explosive chatter of the SAW automatic weapon was deafening in the small room. All eyes swiveled toward Hawke, who had the ugly black weapon at his hip. He squeezed the trigger and fired another burst into the wall just beyond Desmond's head, showering him with chunks of plaster.

"What de fuck, mon?"

"Drop the rod, Prince," Hawke said evenly. "Now."

"You disrespected my family once. Once is all you get." He raised the bar again.

"Put the rod down. If you don't, I'll kill you where you stand."

Desmond turned and glared, somehow imagining he could force Hawke to look away.

"Drop it," Hawke said, "or die. Now."

"I'll drop de rod, mon. But you got to drop de gun. Then we see who de man is. Without de guns."

Desmond's eyes were blazing red, but whether it was rum or anger fueling his rage, Hawke was unsure. He could kill the man, shoot him now and be done with it. But something deeper, more primitive, in Hawke's brain stopped him from pulling the trigger. He wanted to hurt the man who'd hurt his friend. He wanted to hurt him with his bare hands. It was more than wanting, he realized, as he stared into those blood-red eyes.

It was *needing*.

Hawke had since early youth, not frequently but often enough, found himself drawn to the wild freedom of a fistfight: the taunting, the restraining of friends, the squaring up, the outrageousness of one's opponent. He found in fighting a thrilling unpredictability available to him nowhere else. Only when fists flew did he discover his spontaneous, decisive self — his truest self, he liked to think.

He smiled at Desmond and said, "You don't want to fight me, Prince. I'm way out of your league."

"Is dat so, mon? You mean 'cause you so old? Too old to fight like a man?"

"Just put the rod on the floor. Then I'll put my gun on the floor. Okay?"

"You got two guns, mon. De pistol, too."

Hawke put the SAW and the 9mm pistol on the cement floor, his eyes never leaving Desmond's. Then he pulled his assault knife out of its sheath and slid it across the floor.

"Harry?" Hawke called out.

"Right here, boss."

"I'm putting my weapons down in here. Keep yours at the ready until I'm done with this kid. Shoot anybody who moves in an unfriendly way."

"You got it."

"So," Desmond said, dropping the iron rod to the floor with a clang. "Maybe you do still got a little bitty fight left in you, old man."

"Harry," Hawke called again over his shoulder. "I'm going to need your help. Mr. Coale in here has challenged me to a duel. I have accepted. Will you get those fellows out there to clear a space and agree to referee?"

"You got it, boss. Let me just get rid of these fucking dead chickens, and I'll have a nice little ring set up."

"Untie my friends, Desmond," Hawke said, unzipping his jumpsuit and stepping out of it. Underneath, he wore only a faded Royal Navy T-shirt and a pair of boxer shorts, now suddenly wildly appropriate.

He motioned Desmond through the door and helped Ambrose and Sir David get to their feet. He was broken-hearted to see Congreve once more unable to stand on his own. Sir David got an arm around him and got him back into his chair. Ambrose had gone deathly white, and beads of perspiration broke out on his forehead. Sir David seemed sound enough and was rubbing his upper arms where the ropes had burned them.

"Are you all right, Constable?" Hawke asked his friend. "Tell me if you're not. I will pick up my gun, and Brock and I will get you to a hospital right now."

"I'll survive," Congreve said through gritted teeth. "But listen, Alex. You're not really going to fight this man, are you?" he whispered. "He claims to be an Olympic champion."

"Of course I'm going to fight the bastard. After what he did to you? It's an affair of honor, the Code Duello. Surely you remember that fine old tradition, Constable? Precious few left these days. Sir David, some water for the chief inspector would be helpful."

"Rum!" Congreve said in a hurry. "For

God's sake, rum! And then let's get on with it. I haven't seen a good fistfight in years!"

"Certainly," Trulove replied, handing Congreve a half-empty bottle of rum.

Hawke said, "You might also want to shove that nine-millimeter of mine inside your waistband for the time being, Sir David. And Ambrose, keep my SAW handy if you're up to it. Things might get spicy in there."

"Good idea," Trulove said, bending to snatch the weapons from the floor, handing Congreve the SAW.

Hawke left them and walked into the adjacent room. Desmond was posing in the center of the ring formed by the rows of wooden chairs and the Jamaicans who filled them, all of them now laughing riotously, clinking their rum bottles, smelling more blood. King Coale sat back regally in his tufted armchair, eager for the spectacle of his once famous son humiliating a white man.

Hawke stepped inside the ring, pulling his T-shirt over his head. He used it to wipe the green and black camo greasepaint from his face, then tossed the shirt aside. Desmond was dancing around on the broken and bloodied glass, stripped down to a pair of ratty track shorts.

It was close and unbearably hot inside the room. The two men in the ring were already drenched with sweat, though the fight had not even begun.

With the small crowd roaring support for their national hero, the two fighters squared up and began to circle each other. Desmond, a southpaw, quickly threw a few feints with his left to see if Hawke was paying attention. He definitely was. Hawke backed away, blinked his eyes rapidly, and tried to gather his wits. He'd boxed quite a bit in the Navy, with some success. But he'd never been in front of a lefty before.

Hawke was moving to his right. He immediately got tagged with a straight left hand to the jaw, followed instantaneously by a vicious right hook that connected, hard, rocking him back on his heels.

First blood. Hawke could taste it, the blood flooding his mouth. He remembered enough to swallow it quickly as he'd been taught, as something like tunnel vision and deafness descended on him. His anger at what this man had done to Ambrose had lifted itself and spiraled up into a kind of ecstasy. He was no great pugilist. But he was physically reckless, capable of unmitigated violence, he was strong, and he was motivated.

He had a chance.

Hawke smiled at his opponent, shaking it off, trying to rid himself of the carousel of cartoon canaries he saw circling inside his head.

"I've never been hit that hard before," Hawke said, and grinned. "This is going to be more interesting than I thought."

"I just gettin' warmed up, old mon."

"Your wrist seems to have healed nicely," Hawke said, trying to get his feet moving again. He'd been hoping the injured wrist might still be a problem for his opponent. Been counting on it.

"Dat was Clifford's wrist you broke, mon," Desmond said, jabbing hard. "Not mine."

"Called himself Desmond the day I broke his wrist on Tribe Road."

"Cliff always sayin' dat shit around town, mon. Sayin' he Desmond. Say he get more pussy when he call himself me."

Hawke kept his fists up beside his face in a defensive posture, still woozy from the tag, trying desperately to regain his composure. He knew he had to get back into the fight quickly. Because of Desmond's lightning speed and power, Hawke couldn't afford to get hit with another shot.

He moved left and right, stalling and thinking. The little camp boxing he'd done during the first Gulf War didn't seem to be helping him much now. But one piece of advice kept trying to come back to him. What the hell was it?

When you're facing a southpaw, Mr. Hawke, always lead with your right hand and throw a left hook behind it.

Yeah, that was it.

Hawke stepped into the man and threw the

two prescribed punches, using everything he had. He saw immediately that he'd loosened a few of those shiny gold teeth in Desmond's mouth. But Desmond shook it off and grinned.

The Jamaicans jumped to their feet, cheering their boy on with curses and shouts, hoots and hollers.

Desmond kept dancing, wiping the blood from his mouth with the back of his fist. "Is that it? Is that all you got, old mon? C'mon. Show me something. Show me what you got, white mon."

Hawke realized that he'd just given this kid his two best shots and that they'd barely fazed him.

The fight was on.

Hawke circled Desmond. The Jamaican stood his ground, watching and waiting, a huge grin on his glistening black face. Hawke was bobbing and weaving. Desmond began to throw some brutal right jabs. One of them connected, catching Hawke over his left eye. The blow opened a cut that began to bleed instantly, filling Hawke's left eye with blood.

"That's one eye closed, Grandpa, now I'm going to shut the other one. You ready? Get ready!"

Desmond began jabbing wildly, dancing around the half-blinded Hawke, hurling insults and laughing loudly as Hawke's punches went wide. The crowd was on their feet again, into it now, smelling the blood of an Englishman.

Hawke knew he was in serious trouble. His shots to the head weren't connecting. The kid's hand speed was lightning fast, and Hawke couldn't see much anymore. His mind was scrambling, searching for anything useful he could dredge up from his brief boxing career. A phrase, something his coach used to beat into all of them in training, began to take form in his mind, and then suddenly he had it.

Kill the body, the head will die.

He stepped into the man and struck suddenly, viciously, and without warning. He threw two ferocious left hooks, delivered mercilessly, one to Desmond's liver, the other to his ribs.

He saw a much surprised Desmond spit blood from the two body shots. The Jamaican had been wisely protecting his liver, keeping his elbows tucked in close. But Hawke had seen a fraction of an opening and had struck hard. And now the blood was surely bubbling up inside his opponent's body. Desmond coughed, expelling a great looping gout of flying blood.

Hawke took one step backward and dropped a straight right hand directly on Desmond's chin. The blow staggered the Jamaican, knocked him backward, arms pinwheeling, and he almost went down. Two old fellows leaped out of their seats and grabbed Desmond by the elbows, keeping him on his feet, one of them hissing in his ear, "Des, you going to let this old white candy-ass bastard kick your ass? No, you ain't, boy! C'mon, now, fight! You a Jamaican, son, you a champion!"

Desmond stepped back into the fight. His eyes were moving around in his head, and Hawke could see he was forcing them to focus.

"Had enough, son?" Hawke said, keeping his feet moving. He had his breathing going now, feeling good, into it, the blood lust starting to rise.

"Just beginning to piss me off, mon. Thass all you be doin'."

Hawke saw the anger flash in the kid's eyes and knew he had a slight chance to win this. Get them mad, that's how you win fights.

Suddenly, the kid charged him, windmilling, throwing a flurry of wild punches. Hawke got his hands up, catching punches on his arms. Out of the corner of his eye, he saw the real punch coming from down low. A haymaker right hook. It was coming up fast and looked as if it could knock over a tall building.

But Hawke slipped that punch and countered with another pair of lethal left hooks to the kid's ribs. He heard a loud crack, the whole room did, and felt the man's bone break under his fist. Desmond stopped breathing, but Hawke stayed right on him and threw a fast four-punch combination to his face, *wham-wham, wham-wham.*

Hawke stepped back. One of his punches had caught Desmond over his right eye, now bleeding profusely, and loops of blood were flying out of both nostrils.

Hawke was vaguely aware that Harry Brock was circling the ring, considering whether or not to step in and stop the fight. But Harry hesitated. He could sense that Hawke must be seeing some fight left in the kid. Hawke clearly wasn't backing off. He wanted to throw one last shot.

"You want me to stop this?" Brock asked Hawke.

"He hurt my friend. An eye for an eye, a bone for a bone," Hawke said out of the side of his mouth, his eyes focused only on his target. He wanted more.

Hawke wound up and delivered a big right hand to the jaw. The Jamaican, his jaw broken, folded up like an accordion, collapsing to the filthy floor strewn with broken glass and chicken blood, adding a little of his own to the mixture.

Hawke backed away, saw Harry Brock bending over Desmond's unconscious body. Harry gave Desmond a fair ten count, allowing him every chance to get back on his feet.

". . . Ten!" It was over.

Brock whirled around and grabbed Hawke's right wrist, thrusting his hand into the air in victory.

The Jamaicans went wild, some of them coming out of their chairs to cheer the victorious Hawke. They didn't care much who'd won; it had been a hell of a fight. Collapsed in a chair against the wall, Congreve raised his fist in the air, saluting the victory. Sir David even stepped into the ring, pounding his man on the back, shouting into Hawke's ear words he couldn't hear because the blood was pounding so hard inside his head.

Hawke saw the defeated Jamaican on the floor, his arms flung out as if someone had thrown him away. He was now stirring about, eyelids fluttering open, moving his lips, and he stepped over to have a word. Desmond's father, who'd been tending to his son, turned away in disgust. Hawke took his arm and spun him around.

"I don't want to see your crew on my tail anymore. You understand me? What will happen if I do?"

Coale nodded yes and walked away, defeated.

Hawke then bent over the boy and looked into his blood-filled eyes. He spoke softly, just loud enough so the boy alone could hear him.

"It's not about age, son, it's about desire.

You had it once and lost it. Maybe you should think hard about trying to get it back."

"Thank you, Alex," Congreve said as they stepped outside into the cool night air. "A few more blows to the bum leg with that tire iron, and I'm afraid I'd have been totally out of commission. As it is, I think I'll need some help getting back to the boat."

The three Englishmen and Harry Brock had left the building full of drunken Jamaicans behind and were making their way through the dark underbrush toward the sea. Trulove and Hawke had Congreve between them, supporting his weight as they made their way across the rocky ground. Harry was at the rear, covering their retreat with the SAW.

"Are you managing all right, sir?" Hawke asked Sir David. He was huffing and puffing a bit, Congreve being no featherweight these days.

"Indeed, I think I am," C said. "No teeth missing, just a split lip. Ambrose and I are both in far better shape than the chap you left back there on the floor. Or that fellow out there facedown on the dock. Did you see him, Alex? I demanded medical attention for him, of course. Not that there was much likelihood of it."

"He's dead," Hawke said. "A man named Hoodoo."

"You know the victim, Alex?" C asked.

"I do, sir. I know who he is, at any rate. Have you any idea what he was doing out here in the middle of the night?"

"Yes, we do," Congreve said through his pain, speaking slowly and breathing rapidly. "He was delivering weapons to these chaps. Russian machine guns, now stowed in a locked room in the basement. Apparently, there was some disagreement about remuneration, as best we can surmise."

"Before we were discovered, we'd been hiding under the dock as the guns were being unloaded," C said. "We couldn't understand a lot of what was being said, of course — even Ambrose doesn't speak this particular Jamaican Rasta dialect — but we did hear a name. A man who may be the one selling them these weapons."

"Who?" Hawke asked. "What name?"

"Chap named Korsakov," Ambrose said. "Russian. Lives somewhere here on Bermuda. Ever heard of him?"

"Name rings a bell," Hawke said. "I think that's who's been having me followed by the Rastas."

"Why?"

"No idea, but I intend to find out."

"Alex? I think you'd best put me down for a moment," Congreve said. "I'm feeling a bit lightheaded."

Trulove and Hawke gingerly lowered their

friend so that he was seated on a soft clump of grass, his back against the smooth red bark of a gumbo limbo tree.

"Can you make it back down the hill to the dinghy, Constable?" Alex asked his oldest friend, kneeling down beside him.

"I think if I just rest a moment, yes. Should do. It's a bit — painful, you know."

"Breathe deeply. Try to relax. We'll get you to a doctor as quickly as possible." Hawke had tied his shirt round Congreve's leg wound, cinching it tight. The blood flow appeared to have ceased. After an already long and difficult recovery, this fresh injury was a serious setback for his old friend.

"Bloody doctors. I thought I was through with them."

"Anybody smell smoke?" Brock asked, sniffing the air.

"I do," Trulove said. "Fire somewhere. Where's the smoke coming from?"

"Down by the water," Hawke said, "where you left the yawl anchored. We'd better get moving. Ambrose?"

Congreve nodded his head. Sir David and Harry Brock got Ambrose back on his feet and began to descend the steep pathway, Hawke taking the lead.

"Harry and I can take care of Ambrose. You go on ahead, Alex," C said. "Make sure there are no more unpleasant surprises awaiting us."

Hawke raced down the steep path and was the first to reach the clearing and the little cove where Diana had left her boat at anchor.

He was the first to see *Swagman.*

She was adrift and afire.

It looked like a Viking funeral. Someone had loosed her free, torched her, and trimmed her sails to carry her away.

Swagman was already well out, far beyond the reef line, running dead before the wind with all of her blazing sails flying, every last one of them burning brightly. She was lighting up the night sky, afire now from stem to stern, the orange and red flames licking out the windows of her cabin house and racing up her mainmast, and her mainsail had mostly burned clean through, falling away in flaming tatters as she sailed off ablaze toward the black horizon.

"Good Lord," Congreve said, the three men suddenly at his side.

"Yes," Hawke said. "Little we can do now I'm afraid."

"The ring," Congreve said, all of the life, all of the fight, gone out of his voice.

"What?"

"Diana's engagement ring. The D Flawless. You told me to stow it somewhere safe until I was ready to present it to her. I wrapped it in one of my handkerchiefs and stowed it forward of the anchor locker. A little cubby hole in the bow."

"It's a diamond. We'll buy her another."

"It belonged to my mother, Alex. It's all I have from her."

"Then we'll find it."

"Are you sure?"

"Of course I'm sure," Hawke said, and put a comforting arm round his friend's shoulder. "We'll get you in the dinghy and back to the airport. You're going straight to hospital, and then I'll take you home and we'll split a bottle of rum. Sound good?"

"It does, Alex," he said, his eyes filling with tears as he watched the beautiful old *Swagman* sailing for the far horizon in flames.

"Undeserved fate for a lovely old boat," Hawke said, his eyes on her.

"Diana will be devastated," Congreve added. "*Swagman* will burn to the waterline and then slip beneath the waves forever."

And his mother's precious diamond would become just another bauble among countless jewels scattered across the sandy floor beneath the turquoise sea.

30

"Pelham?" Anastasia said, as the weathered cedar door swung inward to reveal a sweet-faced man, quite elegantly dressed in a white dinner jacket and black bow tie. He had a fringe of soft white hair and the palest blue eyes, and he held himself very erect. He did have the loveliest smile. This was Hawke's "partner"? He had to be eighty if he was a day. In the beginning, she'd been exceedingly curious about Hawke's roommate. Now, based on recent events, she found herself considerably more than curious.

"I'm Asia Korsakova. How do you do?"

"Very well, indeed, Madame. Won't you come in?"

The invitation from Teakettle Cottage, surprisingly engraved on a stiff cream-colored card from Smythson of Bond Street, a good London stationer, had arrived with her mail yesterday. Her beautiful beach bum had his stationery engraved at Smythson's? It had said "Dinner at Eight." She was a little early, she knew, but she'd been unsure of finding her way through the maze of sandy lanes that wound through the overgrown banana groves. She knew that one of them would lead eventually to Teakettle Cottage, but which one? So here she was, at his door at a quarter to the hour.

"You may want to keep your wrap," Pelham said. "You'll be dining al fresco, and it's a bit cool out on the terrace this evening."

"Thank you, I will."

She followed him into a large circular room with high ceilings and lovely old beams supporting the domed roof. In the fireplace, a blazing fire took the damp chill off the room. The views of the ocean and sky beyond the terrace were beautiful in the evening light. The sun had set over the turquoise sea, leaving a stage backdrop of brilliant pinks and corals.

"May I offer you something to drink, ma'am? A cocktail, perhaps? I've been accused of making a mean Dark and Stormy, if I may say so."

"Lovely. But I'll have vodka and tonic. Over ice, please."

Pelham nodded and went behind the curved monkey-wood bar. There were two sturdy bamboo stools, and she perched on one while he fixed her drink.

"Slice of lime for you, then?" Pelham asked, regarding her out of the corner of his eye.

"Why not? So. How many are you two expecting this evening?"

"I beg your pardon, ma'am?"

"How many other guests for dinner?"

"Just you, Madame."

"Just me?"

"Yes, Madame."

"Oh. Well. I thought it was to be more of a party."

"I've no doubt it will be, Madame."

"Ah. Well, then."

"Here you are, a lovely vodka and tonic. I hope it will prove satisfactory."

Pelham went silently about his mixology as she sipped her drink, tidying up, slicing some more limes, getting out a beautiful old sterling cocktail shaker, filling it with shaved ice, black rum, and ginger beer.

"Interesting pictures," Asia said, leaning forward to look more closely at a particular photograph. Any number of black-and-white framed candid shots hung on the raffia-covered wall adjacent to the bar. The old photos, mostly of American and English film stars, were faded and water-stained and looked as if they'd been hanging right where they were for centuries.

"Errol Flynn, isn't this one?"

"Yes, ma'am. All former tenants and guests at the cottage, mostly. The subject of a good deal of gossip, I gather."

"I adore gossip," she said, and downed the

rest of her drink. She slid the empty glass toward him. "Any of the good stuff left?"

"A pleasure," Pelham said, reaching for the Stolichnaya. For the first time, he noticed her long red fingernails. He was acutely aware that she was an extraordinarily beautiful woman, prodigiously possessed of what they used to call, in his day, animal magnetism. Suddenly, a good deal of his lordship's recent behavior came into somewhat sharper focus.

"Pelham, may I ask a rather personal question?"

"I endeavor to be candid on any subject, Madame."

"How long have you two been — together. You and Alex, I mean."

"Together?" he said, seemingly surprised by her choice of words.

"Yes. Together. I mean, how long have you and Alex been . . . close? I'm just curious about the length of your . . . relationship. The duration. Roughly speaking, of course."

"Well, I can be very precise about it. Come December 24, at precisely seven o'clock in the evening, it will be thirty-three years to the minute, Madame."

She put down her drink, a little vodka sloshing over the rim of the glass.

"*Thirty-three years?* Is that what you said?"

"Precisely. I was present at his birth. He was born at home. His mother was having a rather difficult time, you see, and the doctors required me to —"

"His birth?"

"Yes, Madame. How time flies. Hard for one to believe that his lordship will turn thirty-three in just —"

"His what?"

"I beg your pardon?"

"Sorry. What you just called him. Called Alex. I thought I heard you use the phrase 'his lordship'?"

"Yes, ma'am."

"Charming. A joke between you two?"

"I beg your pardon, Madame? A joke?"

"One of your pet names for each other, I mean. I know couples do that after years together."

"Couples? I have no idea what you're talking about, Madame. I don't wish to be rude, but I must say this conversation is —"

"You don't mean to say he's titled?"

"Indeed, Madame."

"My beautiful beach boy is, in fact, Lord Hawke?"

"He is Lord Hawke, indeed. I'm hardly surprised you were unaware of it. He prefers not to use the title. If I may be so bold, I suggest you refrain from using it yourself, Madame. I myself absolutely insist upon this form of address, only as I believe it de rigueur for someone of my station."

"And what, if I may be so bold, exactly is your station, Pelham?"

"I am in service, ma'am. I should have thought that much, at least, would have been somewhat obvious. I've been in service to the Hawke family for most of my eighty-four years. As, I daresay, were my father before me and his father before him."

"In service. A butler, do you mean?"

"Rather more than that, Madame, but I suppose that appellation will suffice."

"So you're not . . . roommates? Partners?"

"Roommates?" Pelham said, almost choking on the word. His starched collar suddenly seemed far too tight, and indeed his face had turned a startling shade of red.

"Are you all right?" Asia asked, fearing he might be suffering from a coronary event or worse. She hurriedly poured him a glass of water.

Summoning every ounce of his dignity and with his exquisite patina of noblesse oblige barely intact, Pelham was able to croak in a strangled voice, "Hardly roommates, Madame."

At that moment, Alexander Hawke strode into the room. He was naked save a small towel wrapped precariously around his waist. His body and his dark hair were still damp from the recent shower, and he wore a creamy white beard of shaving cream. In his hand was an old-fashioned ivory-handled straight razor.

"Oh, terribly sorry. I'd no idea you'd arrived," he said, glancing at Anastasia. His eyes moved to Pelham, who seemed a bit rattled and was shakily knocking back a goblet of water or perhaps something stronger.

"My fault entirely," Ansastasia said, swiveling her stool toward him. "I thought I'd get lost finding you, so I arrived far too early. Pelham and I have been having a grand time."

Hawke and Anastasia stared at each other for a few long moments, neither of them willing or able to speak. Finally, Hawke's face broke into a wide grin.

"Ah. Good. Good for you two to have some time to chat. Get to know each other a bit. Well. Perfect. I'll be with you shortly. Pelham, you don't have something brewing back there with my name on it, do you?"

"Indeed, m'lord," Pelham squeaked.

Pelham came out from behind the bar with a frosted silver julep cup on a silver tray. Hawke took it and smiled at Asia. "My 'dresser,' you see. I always have a wee cocktail while I'm suiting up for dinner."

"Good idea," she said, smiling. "It's reassuring that you haven't finished dressing."

Hawke looked at her, then down at his towel, seeming to have momentarily exhausted his gift for dialogue.

"Well, I'll leave you to it, then. Give me ten minutes or so. You look stunning in red, by the way."

She nodded and watched him disappear

down the hallway that led, she imagined, to his bedroom. When she turned her glance back to Pelham, her eyes were softer than before.

"Are you quite all right?" he asked her after a few moments of silence.

She looked up at him, her eyes shining.

"There's an awful lot of little boy in that big man."

"Most perceptive of you, Madame Korsakova."

"A sad little boy, I'm afraid. What was he like, Pelham? As a child? Was he a very sad little boy?"

"His boyhood? Sad? Indeed, I suppose it had some of that, as everyone's does."

"Would it be terribly indiscreet of you to talk about him? You hardly know me, after all."

"I know you well enough, I think, Madame. At least, where he's concerned. We do have a few minutes before he returns."

"Tell me a story, Pelham," Anastasia said, leaning forward and resting her chin in her hands. "About the little boy you knew." Her green eyes, shining and moist, had a lustrous depth, Pelham noticed for the first time.

It was only with some difficulty that he avoided falling into them himself.

"Shall we move out to the terrace?" she said. "The fresh breeze off the ocean is lovely."

■ ■ ■ ■

"Lord Hawke was born healthy and boisterous as a three-ring circus on Christmas Eve around seven o'clock in the evening. He was born to a somewhat absent father, a career Navy man, and a doting mother in a leafy corner of Sussex," Pelham said quietly. Anastasia sat back against the cushy linen sofa and placed one of her thin red cigarettes in a carved ebony holder. Pelham pulled up a chair and leaned forward to light it, an old Dunhill table lighter somehow appearing in his hand.

"His lordship spent a rather normal childhood in the company of various corgis and terriers, stern-faced maiden aunts, and an unending parade of frowning nursemaids, all supervised by yours truly.

"But how his eyes would light up at the sight of his mother. Often, she would venture upstairs to his nursery for his bedtime prayers, dripping with dewy raindrop pearls that never quite fell, whispering the softest 'Good night, sleep tight,' before vanishing again.

"On warm summer afternoons, Alex was always brought down to her rooms at tea time. The windows were opened to the gardens, and bees buzzed in and all about. She would read to him, stories of pirates and knights and fair damsels in distress. He loved them all. Rather fancied himself a swashbuckling pirate, I daresay.

"Eventually, they would both die, of course, Lord and Lady Hawke. Murdered by real pirates aboard their yacht on a family Caribbean vacation. Alex was only seven when it happened, but he witnessed the murders. It was horrible, ma'am, horrible beyond words. I don't think he's ever quite recovered. I — I know he hasn't.

"He spent those awful months following the funeral at the shore below his grandfather's home, building elaborate sand castles, tears streaming from his eyes. When a castle was complete, perfect, he trampled it, kicking away the turrets and battlements until it was just sand again. Then he would wander off along the sand and start another castle somewhere. So many ruined castles. So many sad days.

"The boy's happiest early recollections would be of the great heaving blue sea beyond his windows. I can see him even now, ma'am, wheeled outside, on a small bluff directly overlooking the sea. He would sit bolt upright in his formidable navy-blue pram (it was made of steel, his first battleship, really) enraptured for hours on end.

"When storms came, nursemaids would squeal with fright and wheel their small charge back indoors. The young master, red-faced with fury at this removal from his beloved perch, would beat his small fists against the steel-sided pram, raging at the injustice of it all. He adored foul weather, always has.

"Around the age of sixteen, he left home for good. He studied first at the naval preparatory school, Homefield, in Surrey. The regime was harsh, with a curriculum geared to the needs of future midshipmen and commodores. He excelled and was accepted at the Royal Naval College in Dartmouth. He was a natural leader of men. He excelled on the athletic fields. He adored reading military history and the classics. Still does. Later, in battle, he learned that he was naturally good at war."

"He's a soldier?"

"He was. A pilot, Royal Navy. Now, he's in business. Family enterprise. Quite extensive."

"Is he happy?"

"In the absence of war, his spirits seem to go into steep decline. Sunshine and salt air help. It's partly why we came to Bermuda. To try to mend —"

"Oh, hullo!"

Pelham stopped in midsentence and looked up.

"Fascinating stuff," Hawke said, smiling at Pelham. "Please don't let me interrupt."

31

"So, you like war, do you?" Anastasia asked, once they were alone on the terrace.

"There is nothing quite so exhilarating as being shot at without effect," Alex Hawke said, escorting her to the little red-checkered table, drink in hand.

"Churchill?" she said.

"Good for you. Winston nailed it, as usual. All right, then, who's hungry around here? I'm famished!"

Dinner was served at the table for two overlooking the moonlit sea. A single candle inside a hurricane glass illuminated Anastasia's face in a flickering umbra. They had simple fish, freshly caught in the grotto below, and a clean, cold white wine. Hawke had found cases of the stuff in the musty cellar.

"Delicious," Asia said, putting the napkin to her red lips.

"Tell the chef," Hawke said, smiling, "I think he's already completely in love with you."

"You don't say? Silly me. Here I was, all the while thinking it was Pelham who cooked the dinner."

"Very funny," Hawke said, smiling at her.

"Bad joke. Anyway, it's you he loves, Alex, not me. You're very lucky to have such a kind and obviously devoted friend. To Pelham."

She raised her glass, and he his.

"Anastasia, since the other day, that . . . stormy afternoon, I just want to tell you that I haven't been able to —"

"You know what? Sorry. Let's please change the subject, all right?"

"What do you mean?"

"I mean, I think we're talking about us, Alex. Let's not talk about us tonight. I'm afraid of us. Scared to death of it. And it's already far too romantic out here, anyway. So tell me about you, your life. What you do. I thought you were a simple beachcomber, a lost soul without two rubles to rub together. But I don't think so anymore. Who are you, Alex Hawke? Tell me who you are, what you do."

"Do? My friends all claim I wake up in the morning and God throws money at me."

She laughed out loud at that one.

He sipped his wine, looking at her above the rim. Her dark blonde hair in the candlelight, the chunks of gold at her earlobes, her green eyes gleaming. She was lovely, but she needn't worry. He wasn't in love with her.

How could he be? Love was strictly reserved for the innocent.

"Alex?"

"Yes?"

"I asked you a question. Tell me who you are."

"Oh, yes. Sorry. Well. No one special, really. Another perfectly ordinary English business-man. Half American, to be honest. My mother was an actress from Louisiana."

"An ordinary businessman? I don't think so. Your body has too many suspicious scars for a businessman."

"Oh, that was just a bit of nasty business. I got shot down over Baghdad. I got a taste of Iraqi hospitality before I checked out of my suite at the Saddam Hilton."

"And now just an ordinary businessman."

"It's true. You should see me marching around the City with my tightly rolled um-brella and my battered briefcase. My family has a number of interests, none of which interests me very much. I've managed to hire enough captains of industry to steer the vari-ous ships without me. So I came out here to Bermuda for a while. Decided I liked it. I've actually got a small company here, a start-up. Blue Water Logistics. Quite exciting, really."

"Logistics. It's one of those words I've never really understood. What does it mean?"

"Fairly straightforward. People, future clients all, I hope, make various things.

Things that need to get moved around the planet. Sometimes huge numbers of things at great expense. Pipe for pipelines. Nuts and bolts, steel and timber, oil. You make it, we move it. That's my new motto."

"You should meet my father. He makes a good many things. You might find him a good client for your Blue Water."

"What does he make?"

"He's an inventor, primarily. A scientist. He invented a computer cheap enough for the whole world. Called the Zeta machine. Perhaps you've heard of it?"

"The Wizard? I've got the latest one sitting on my office desk in London. Amazing little gadget. Changed the world. He invented that? You must be very proud of him."

"He's an amazing man. The most brilliant on earth, I think. A scientist. A humanist. A philanthropist. He's made billions and given most of it away. He's built schools and hospitals, not just everywhere in Russia but in every corner of the earth. India, Africa. He uses his money to try to make the world fit his view of it."

"What is his view of it?"

"A natural philosopher's view. That mankind should be in harmony, like planets orbiting stars, electrons around neutrons, like nature itself. That there should be peace, equilibrium, order. That the clouds of war need never blot out the sun."

"A romantic idealist."

"Perhaps. You might decide differently if you met him."

"I should like that very much. Where does he live?"

"In the sky."

"Ah. So he *is* God."

Asia laughed. "No. He has an airship. A very special one that he designed. She's called *Tsar,* which is the acronym of his scientific company, Technology, Science, and Applied Research. He travels the world aboard her. Of course, he has houses everywhere, including one here on Bermuda that you may have seen."

"The converted fortress on Powder Hill. So that's what the big mast is for. To moor his airship?"

"Yes. He spends some time here. And some years ago, he was kind enough to give me Half Moon House, where I live and work part of the year."

"Where are you from, Asia?"

"Russia, obviously. I grew up in the country. A large estate we have outside St. Petersburg. It's called Jasna Polana, which means 'Bright Meadow.' Tolstoy called his country house that, too. My father is a great admirer of Tolstoy. We have a lovely palace there. Orchards, meadows, stables, many streams. Do you shoot? Fish?"

"I do, occasionally."

"Then you must come and stay with us. You and Father could have a nice business talk. Would you like that?"

"I think I should like it very much indeed."

"Good. Consider yourself invited."

"Asia?"

"Yes?"

"Stay here tonight. Stay with me."

"What is that song playing now?"

" 'Smoke Gets in Your Eyes.' The most beautiful song ever written."

"And who is singing?"

"Charles Aznavour."

"Shall we dance, Lord Hawke?"

"Please don't use that title."

"I forgot. Only Pelham is allowed to use it. Get on your feet and dance with me, Hawke."

"I should be delighted."

"Yes, you should be."

A small window directly above Hawke's head proved accessible to sunrise; a fiery parallelogram now appeared on the far wall. The room was filling to the ceiling with the oils of sunrise, light containing extraordinary pigments, washing the whitewashed stone walls around Hawke's bed with brilliant shades of gold and pink. He loved waking up in this room.

"Are you awake?" he asked her in the stillness of the early morning, stroking her thick golden hair. Her head was still on his chest, right where she'd last fallen asleep.

"Hmm."

"Thinking of going for a swim."

"Hmm."

"Can I ask you a question?"

"Maybe later," she said, her voice furred with sleep.

"No, now. It can't wait. I have to ask you about Hoodoo."

"Poor Hoodoo. A lovely man. He's dead. Murdered."

"I know. I'm trying to understand why."

Asia sat up in the bed, rubbing the sleep from her eyes. "What they said in the paper. You read it. He was killed by those awful Jamaicans living out on Nonsuch Island."

"Yes, but why was he there?"

"It wasn't in the papers?"

"No. You tell me."

"My father sent him. To deliver a warning. My father wants those people off that island. It's a nature sanctuary. They are living there illegally."

"Why didn't your father call the police?"

"My father never calls the police. He prefers to handle things himself. Besides, the police wouldn't do anything anyway. My father says someone at the top in Government House is taking money from the Jamaicans. That's why they're allowed to stay."

"I heard a rumor there were illegal weapons involved. That the murder was an arms sale gone awry."

"Hoodoo? Selling weapons? Ridiculous. People say anything to sow discredit upon my father. I stopped listening long ago."

"Ah."

"Do you normally grill your suspects before they have a chance to wake up, detective?"

"Sorry. I'm a beast."

"I'm beginning to wonder."

"Come here. Look at this."

Hawke rolled naked off the bed and lifted the ring attached to the circular section of flooring that concealed the top of his fireman's pole and the blue grotto below.

"What's that?" she said, flopping forward on the bed and staring at the hole in the floor.

"It's called a fireman's pole, for somewhat obvious reasons. There's a hidden grotto just below us. You slide down the pole and into the water. I do it every morning. Great way to wake up."

"Wait. Why are you so curious about Hoodoo?"

"Tell you later," Hawke said, and then he disappeared through the floor.

"Hold on, I'm coming, too!" she cried, leaping from the bed. Grabbing the pole with both hands, she slipped down into his waiting arms.

32

Miami

Raining cats and dogs used to be true. Back
in Robin Hood's day, Stoke had read somewhere, the domestic animals used to sleep
curled up inside the thatched roofs. When it
rained really hard, down they came, *wham* on
the dinner table. Hello, Sparky, hey, Ginger!
It was raining that hard now. Luckily, except
for a few Seminole tiki huts, there were very
few thatched roofs in Miami today.

It was just after two in the afternoon when
Stoke turned the GTO off Collins and onto
Marina, headed for the Miami Yacht Group's
showroom. It was located almost kitty-corner
from Joe's Stone Crabs. Big glass showroom
with red, white, and blue flags standing out
stiff from the tall poles surrounding the lot.

The weather today, finally, was perfect for
what Stoke had in mind. Blowing hard out of
the southwest, a big tropical depression
headed up from the Keys, the leading edge
about over Islamorada now. As he drove

slowly through Miami Beach, palm trees were bent over backward, crap was flying around in the streets — no cats or dogs, though, at least he didn't see any.

He'd taken a good long look at the ocean from the balcony of his penthouse apartment. Blowing like stink out there. Huge rollers, whitecaps with the crests whipped off soon as they peaked. He'd been waiting all week for weather like this.

Today's the day, he thought, smiling at himself in the mirror, sliding the knot on his Italian designer silk tie up to his Adam's apple. He adjusted his wraparound sunglasses. Would Sheldon wear sunglasses on a day like this? he'd asked himself. Yes. He had the whole Sheldon Levy thing down now. Hell, he *was* Sheldon Levy.

Traffic was light on a stormy day, and he'd made good time getting over the causeway. Miami Yacht Group looked just like a car dealership, except it had boats where all the cars would normally be. Big boats, little boats. The littlest ones were out front on trailers. The medium ones would be inside on the showroom floor. The big go-fast ones he was interested in, those of the Cigarette persuasion, they were in the water at the docks located on the marina side of the glitzy glass and steel showroom.

Soon as he walked through the front door in his shiny sharkskin suit, Elsa Peretti tie,

Chrome Hearts wraparound shades and pointy-toed alligator shoes, a salesman was on him like sucker fish on a mako.

"Good afternoon!" the guy said.

"You, too."

"And how are we doing today, sir?"

Stoke smiled at him. Tall and angular and blond. Blue-water tan. Faded khakis, no socks with his bleached-out boat shoes, collar of his navy-blue polo shirt turned up on the back of his neck. Two little crossed flags on his shirt with the words "Magnum Marine" underneath. Talked funny, too, through his teeth, like his jaw was permanently wired shut.

"I'm good, I'm good," Stoke said, looking around the showroom.

"Heckuva storm out there, isn't it? Golly!"

Golly? When was the last time you heard that word? Seriously.

"Golly is right, darn it," Stoke said, as he bent over and peered out the big plate-glass showroom windows, as if noticing the weather out there for the very first time today.

"Nothing a Magnum Sixty couldn't handle, I'll bet," Stoke said, clapping Larry Lockjaw on the back. "Right?"

"Well, n-now," the salesman said, staggering a bit before recovering his balance, "you'd have to be pretty darn plucky to go out on a day like today. But you know what? Your timing is perfect. We've got a pre-Christmas special going on, and I —"

"Call me plucky, but I want to rock one of those Magnums right now!"

"Well, gee, you know, I don't think today is ideal for —"

"Actually, you know what? I'm here to see one of your other salesmen. Piss, I think his name is."

"Piss?"

"Yeah, Piss. Like — take a piss? I've got his card somewhere in my wallet."

"I'm sorry, sir. My hearing's terrible. Are you saying Mr. Piss?"

"Yeah, Piss. Pisser, something like that."

"You're looking for a Mr. Pisser? I'm afraid —"

"No, wait. Urine. That was it. I knew it was something like that. Like piss, I mean."

"Oh. *Yurin,* you mean?" the guy said, sort of chuckling. "Right, sir, that would be Yuri Yurin. He's our divisional sales manager here at the Miami Yacht Group."

"He around?"

"Matter of fact, he's on his lunch break. But I'm sure I can help you. I'm Dave McAllister, by the way."

"I'm sure you could help me, Dave. But, you know what, I came here to see this Yurin guy."

"Well, in that case, let me go back to his office and see if I can get him. May I tell him who's asking for him?"

"Sheldon Levy."

"I'm sorry?"

"Sheldon Levy. No, no, don't apologize. I get that all the time. I don't look all that Jewish, do I? But then, look at Sammy Davis, Jr. Know what I'm saying?"

"Don't go anywhere, Mr. Levy. I'll be right back with Mr. Yurin."

Two minutes later, Yurin came out on the floor, wiping the mayo off his lower lip. Big boy, good-looking blond bodybuilder. He still had a little piece of shredded lettuce in the corner of his mouth. Big Mac, Stoke thought, seeing the guy eating one at his desk, wolfing it down, when he heard he had a fish on the line. Russians couldn't get enough of Big Macs ever since Mickey D had opened that first one on Red Square. Beat the hell out of borscht, you had to figure.

"Mr. Levy!" he said, shaking Stoke's hand, Yurin trying to figure out where the hell he'd seen the huge black guy before. He knew he'd seen him, you didn't forget someone Stoke's size easily. But where? Like all the black-shirted security guys at the Lukov party, Yurin was muscled up, beefy, anyway, going to fat around the middle courtesy of the good life in sunny south Florida. Too many stone crab dinners at Joe's.

"Yurin, Yurin, Yurin, good to see you again, man. You don't remember me, do you?"

"No, I do, I do. I'm just trying to remember

408

where we met."

"The Lukov birthday thing. You gotta remember that. *Kaboom?*" Stoke clapped his hands together loudly when he said it, and both of the salesmen flinched, McAllister actually taking a couple of steps back.

"Ri-i-i-ght," Yurin said, drawing the word out, deep Russian accent, still no clue. It was the suit, tie, and sunglasses Stoke was wearing, that's what was throwing him.

"Fancha's manager? Suncoast Artist Management?" Stoke said.

"Fancha! The beautiful birthday singer! Of course! So, what can I do for you, Mr. Levy? Dave says you're in the market for a new Magnum Sixty."

"I certainly am," Stoke said, holding up a genuine crocodile satchel with his right hand. "Man, what a machine. I want to get Fancha one to celebrate her new movie contract. We just cashed the first check," Stoke said, holding up the croc case again just for emphasis.

"You are in luck today, Mr. Levy. I just happen to have three brand-new Sixties in stock. Factory fresh. Pick your color. Diamond Black, Cobalt Blue, or Speed Yellow."

"Is there a question? You got to go with the Speed Yellow, you got any style at all, right, Yurin?"

"Speed Yellow it is! Let's go back to my office and work up a sales order, Mr. Levy. Or can I call you Sheldon?"

"Call me Sheldon."

"Call me Yuri, then," he said, big smile, fish already in the boat, easiest damn yacht sale in the entire history of South Florida yacht brokerage.

"I kinda like Yurin. Let's stick with that, okay? You know who you look like, Yurin? Just came to me. Dolph Lundgren. The movie star? *Agent Red*? *Red Scorpion*? No? Doesn't matter."

A momentary look of confusion crossed Yurin's face, but he grabbed Stoke's biceps, or tried to, and steered him back toward where all the sales guys had their little offices. This guy Yurin was obviously used to being the biggest kid on the block. You could see he didn't care for second place at all.

"Yurin, hold up a sec," Stole said, stopping dead in his tracks just outside the guy's office.

"Whassup?" In a Russian accent, the tired old hip-hop expression sounded funny instead of cool.

"Here's the thing, Yurin. I truly want this boat. And I've got the money to pay for it right here. Cash."

"We take cash," he said, like a joke. Being funny didn't come naturally to most Russians.

"But, of course, I'll want to take her for a quick spin first."

"Hey, no problem, Sheldon. We can arrange

for a sea trial whenever you're ready."

"I'm ready."

"Okay, what day should I schedule you for?"

"Today. Now."

He laughed. "Good joke. Funny."

"No joke, Yurin. I want to take her out there in a blow. See how she performs when it's kicking up like this."

"Kicking up? You're looking at gale-force winds out there. It's got to be blowing thirty, thirty-five knots. Gusting to fifty. Small-craft advisory warnings have been up since ten o'clock this morning."

"Sixty feet's not all that small a craft, Yurin."

"Yes, I know, Sheldon, but this is an extremely high-performance racing boat with a planing hull. She likes flat water."

"Yurin. Ask yourself one simple question. Do you sincerely want to sell a boat today? Say yes or no."

"Yes."

"You're not afraid of a little wind and rain, are you, Yurin? Like my grandmother used to say, rain won't bother you unless you're made of sugar."

"Afraid?" The look said it all. He was going.

Stoke clapped him on the back hard enough to rattle his molars. "All right, man, cowboy up, and get your goddamn foul-weather gear on, little buddy, we're going sailing!"

411

33

The big yellow Cigarette was bobbing pretty good, even still moored in her marina slip. Like a bronco in the chute, Stoke thought, boat saying, "Cut me loose, cowboy, I dare your ass." Although the Miami Yacht Group's marina was pretty well protected from the ocean, it was still choppy with whitecaps inside the breakwater. Sailboat masts swung wildly, a forest of aluminum sticks, whirling and twirling in the storm. The skies were now very dark purple with a funny greenish cast to them.

Perfect.

Like some pretty ladies of Stoke's former acquaintance, the Magnum 60 was all bow and no stern. She had a small open cockpit aft, inside which were four deeply contoured bucket seats, bright yellow like the hull, with harness equipment like you might expect on the space shuttle. Along her sleek flanks, she had five oval portholes forward, meaning there was built-out space below.

What you do down there, Stoke thought, is not take little nappies or read spy novels and do crossword puzzles. You go down there to take care of business with Mama once you get offshore and shut two engines down and crank up a third, the Johnson. Boat like this was all about testosterone, a little too much or a little too little, depending on the owner.

"Looks like a Chiquita banana on steroids," Stoke said, uncleating a spring line and heaving it aboard. The Russian guy fake-laughed, going for the stern line.

He said, "This is the sister ship to the boat that won the greatest sea race in the world, Sheldon. The Miami-Nassau-Miami at an average top speed of over eighty-five miles per hour. You know what sister ship means?"

"Lemme think a sec. Identical twins?"

"You are a very intelligent individual. You've heard of *Bounty Hunter*? Don Aronow's *Maltese Magnum*? These magnificent boats are names out of racing history."

"Don't I know it," Stoke said, as if he had a clue.

Yurin started to climb down into the helm seat, and Stoke stopped him, grabbing his shoulder with a gentle squeeze. "I'll drive," he said. "You ride shotgun. You know what shotgun means?"

"Shotgun?" the Russian asked.

They already had their helmets on and two-way radio communication. It was the only way you could talk aboard these monsters, even when there was no hurricane blowing.

"You want to drive?" Yurin said. "Are you serious, man?"

"I just want to putt around. You know, here inside the marina. Get a little feel. Don't worry about it."

"You think you can handle this thing? You have some experience with this kind of boat? Any kind of boat?"

"Navy SEAL operations, Team Two. Riverine patrol boats in the Mekong Delta. Three tours."

The Russian looked at him with different eyes.

"Good enough," he said, and went around to the dock on the vessel's port side, loosening the stern, spring, and bow lines. "Climb aboard," he told Stoke. "I'll cast you off and jump down."

Stoke saw that the helm seat had no seat to speak of, only a curved backrest with a narrow bench you parked your butt on. The sides wrapped around you nice and snug, especially snug for him, but okay. He turned on all three of the battery switches, checked the fuel level and oil pressure. All good to go.

She had twin 1800-horsepower Detroit racing engines, and when he turned the key on number one, the response was one sharp *blat* and then a deep vibrating rumble. Followed by the second engine, the feeling of power

414

coming up through the soles of his shoes was something else entirely.

Yurin freed the last line and leaped aboard as Stoke started reversing out of the slip. There was so much power on tap you had to handle the throttles like surgical instruments. Tiny adjustments.

Yurin was strapping himself into the port-side seat as Stoke got the big Magnum turned around and headed toward the mouth of the harbor.

"Where the fuck are you going?" Yurin said. "Gale-force winds coming right up the Cut! We'll get knocked on our asses out there."

"Relax, Sunshine," Stoke said, looking over at him. "I think we'll poke our nose out in the Atlantic. Just get a touch of it, see how she handles the rough stuff."

Yurin started to say something, thought better of it, and just shook his head. He planted his feet and held on to the stainless grab handle mounted on the dash in front of him.

"That's it. Just hold on, Yurin. We'll be back in your office signing papers before you know it."

Stoke lined up in dead center of the narrow channel, aiming for a spot midway between the two massive cement breakwaters that enclosed the marina. The entrance was funnel-shaped, with the narrowest part on the seaward side. Beyond the entrance, the

Atlantic looked like really convincing special effects, pretty much the way it did in that movie *The Perfect Storm.* Mountainous crests, cavernous troughs, the wind rising to a wailing gale, ripping the crests off waves, well-defined streaks of foam marching off to the southeast. A boiling black sky overhead.

Stoke eased the throttles forward until he saw the tachs reading 2,500 rpm, mentally preparing himself like a bull rider in the chute.

"Ready?" Stoke said, glancing over at Yurin. They were mid-channel, almost out in open water, about to enter the funnel.

No reply. The copilot was wearing the thousand-yard stare, wondering what the hell he'd gotten himself into, if his life was worth a measly million bucks for a plastic play toy.

Stoke suddenly firewalled both throttles, and the boat came screaming out of the water, leaping forward with a thunderous roar of exhaust as the big props grabbed water. The boat went flying through the chute, wide open. At the other end, an oncoming wave was building, rushing toward them. It looked to be a green frothing wall about twenty, thirty feet high, and it was just getting started.

"Watch out!" the Russian screamed.

"Not a problem," Stoke said calmly in his lip mike.

The Russian's eyes went wide with terror. His client seemed intent on slamming the

Magnum head-on into the oncoming wall of water. They were going to smash it like a bullet to the forehead. Wave had to be forty feet high now. The water was glassy green, so clear you could almost see through it to the other side. The props whined as the sharp prow of the Magnum struck the wave, pierced it, and then Stoke just drove the boat right through the wall, the bow eventually emerging from the other side.

The bow was suspended in midair, the back half of the boat, including the cockpit, was momentarily still inside the wave, and then they were through and pitching forward, the nose dropping and the bottom of Stoke's stomach falling away as they went screaming down the wall of another big wave, into the trough of a brand-new wave just starting to build.

"Holy fuck," he heard Yurin say, sputtering. Stoke looked over at his drenched passenger and liked what he saw. Fear.

What was left of the boat's curved windshield was a mangled piece of chromed frame wrapped around the Russian's chest, sheets of broken safety glass in his lap and on the deck around his feet.

"Not bad, huh?" Stoke said. "I thought we'd lose a lot more than just the goddamn windshield. Look, we've still got the spotlight up on the bow. Now, that's good construction."

"Are you out of your fucking mind?"

"Easy, Yurin. No way to speak to a prospective customer."

"Go back!" Yurin said. "Turn us around. You're going to snap this thing in two out here!"

"I'll go back, but first I've got a couple of questions."

"Questions? About the boat?"

"No. About you."

"Me? I'll tell you about me. I'm going to fucking kill you, okay? I'm going to rip your ugly head right off your —"

He was clawing at his safety harness, desperate to get out of his seat and remove Stoke's head. Stoke looked over at him, smiling.

"Look, just calm down, okay? Let me explain something. Only take a second. You're an asshole, all right?"

A sudden surge threw both men back in their seats, snapping their heads back. They were angled sharply upward now, Stoke was using the powerful engines to climb the nearly vertical face of another building wave. And keep Yurin firmly planted in his seat.

"What?" Yurin shouted. "What the fuck do you want to know?"

"You're Black Beret, right? All you security guys at the birthday party. Russian Black Berets?"

"I don't know what you're talking about.

Just turn around and go back to the marina before you kill both of us!"

"I will, but bear with me a sec. Spend a lot of time in Chechnya, Yurin? Whupping Chechen ass?"

"Never been there."

Stoke put the wheel hard over to port, and the boat fell off the steep climb and started skidding sideways down the wave. Then the wildly cavitating props caught water, dug in, and she was headed on a better diagonal course down into the trough. Stoke had just enough control for a second to pull the 9mm Glock from inside his foul-weather jacket. Yurin saw the gun, and it seemed to make his already perfect day even more complete.

"Yurin, listen up. Get out of your harness."

They were in the trough for the moment. Stoke pulled the throttles back to idle and unsnapped his own seat harness. If you planted your feet wide, you could probably stay on them. At least long enough to do what he had to do.

"What?"

"You heard me. Get your ass down on the deck. On your knees, Red Rider. You've got three seconds before your brains won't work so good anymore. One . . . two . . .

"Three," Stoke said. He turned and fired a round about a foot in front of Yurin's nose.

"Fuck!" Yurin unbuckled the fasteners and slid out of the harness, one hand still clenching the sissy bar, what the Navy called the "oh-shit bar." They were still moving uneasily along the trough. The Magnum was rocking and rolling, and it wasn't easy, but the Russian managed to kneel on the deck between the two seats without getting thrown out of the boat.

"Jacket off. Everything off, waist up."

"Jesus. A fucking giant black homo with a death wish."

"Now."

Stoke tapped him gently on top of the head with the pistol butt. Yurin ripped at the zipper on his yellow slicker, somehow managing to get it off. The wind whipped it right out of the cockpit, and it disappeared aft in a cloud of spume.

"Now the shirt."

He was wearing a black T-shirt, the same kind he had on the night of the party. Macho muscle-boy crap. People who had Ferraris didn't wear Ferrari shirts. And people who had real muscle didn't wear muscle shirts.

The shirt came off as Stoke carefully moved around behind him and jammed his left foot into the back of Yurin's neck, shoving him forward, facedown on the deck, the man's neck and shoulder muscles all thick cords and knots bulging as he tried to squirm away. Made the image Stoke had expected to see a moving picture, but yeah, there it was, all

right. He saw just what he thought he'd see.
The Head of the Tiger.

34

The tiger's head was tattooed right between Yurin's shoulder blades. Stoke had to admit it was impressive, even though it was only about the size of a softball. But it was the work of an artist, beautifully etched into the skin. Below the scowling tiger's face was the tattooed name Stoke had been thinking about ever since he'd first met Yurin and his black-shirted bully boys at the birthday blast.

OMON.

The Russian special forces, the so-called Black Berets. Death squads who had roamed Chechnya before and after the carpet bombing of Grozny, killing anything and everything in their path that remained alive. Elite forces during the war, paid killers after. He'd kept his mouth shut, hadn't told Brock about his suspicions that night. He thought he'd pry around the edges a little and see what broke loose first. But he'd been doing his research.

Now that Putin's second Chechen war was long over, OMON worked for the new dark forces of the interior ministry inside the Kremlin. They roamed Moscow in armored personnel carriers, wearing their trademark black and blue camo fatigues, doing odd jobs for the powers that be. When they got bored, or loaded, they picked up gutter drunks in Red Square, hauled them off to the tank at Lubyanka in the APCs, and beat the shit out of them. Or worse.

Stoke leaned down to speak directly into Yurin's ear. He kept his foot planted on the guy's neck, just to keep him from getting any frisky ideas. The kid had stopped squirming and bitching, but only because Stoke had put a little more weight on the back of his neck, compressing his vocal cords.

"What brings you bad boys all the way to Miami?" Stoke asked.

"Sunshine," Yurin croaked as Stoke increased the pressure. And leaned down again to scream into his ear.

"You want to go home tonight, Yurin? Hit the vodka? Sleep in a nice warm bed? Or do you want to be just another accidental drowning in a storm? Too many beers, taking a piss off the stern, oopsy-daisy. A tragic mistake, officer, happens all the time. Your call."

"What's your fucking problem?"

Stoke's immediate problem was that he felt the Magnum starting to roll over on her beam ends as the sea started piling up rapidly on the port side.

"Whoops, another big one coming. Hold on, Tiger."

Stoke grabbed the back of his seat, struggling to stay upright with one foot braced against the Russian's head and the other on the deck. They were in free fall again, speeding down the face of a huge wave, rudder amidships, but now no one was at the wheel. Stoke couldn't let go of the seat to grab it for fear of being thrown from the cockpit. The boat's motion was ridiculously violent and disorienting, but Stoke had seen worse. He'd once ridden out a mid-Pacific typhoon solo in a two-man Zodiac. Six days of that, this little blow was cake.

"Who do you work for, Yurin? I want a name!"

"Get the boat out of this c-crazy-shit ocean, and m-maybe I'll t-t-talk," he sputtered, his nose and lips mashed against teak decks that were now awash, seawater sloshing in and out of his damn mouth, just the kind of modified water-boarding technique Stoke had been shooting for out here.

"Talk now, before we bury the bow again and wash both our asses into the drink. Who do you work for?"

"The Dark Rider."

"The what?"

"Dark Rider. What he's called. No one knows his real name."

Stoke leaned forward and grabbed the spinning wheel. He held it hard over, keeping the nose from burying itself and instead starting up the next wall on a reasonable angle.

"You get orders from somebody. Who?"

"Directly from General Arkady Zukov. Retired now, from the KGB. A great Russian patriot. We are all patriots, working to restore Russian pride."

"Shitty job so far, Yurin."

"Piss off."

"Rostov? Is Rostov the Dark Rider?"

"No. Not Rostov. Higher."

"Higher than the president?"

"Maybe."

"What was that? I can't hear you."

The boat was totally out of control.

"I said yes! Higher!"

"Here's the big one, Yurin. Ready? What the fuck are Russian OMON troops doing here in America?"

No answer.

Stoke shifted his foot to the back of Yurin's head, driving his face hard into the deck as they crested the thirty-footer. In a few seconds, they'd drop sickeningly down the other side.

"Tell me about OMON. Now!"

"Fuck. A mission. We're here training for a mission."

"What kind of mission you on, Yurin?"

"Hostage rescue."

"Like you rescued those schoolchildren in

Beslan?"

"Fuck you. Shoot me."

Stoke mashed his nose hard into the deck and heard a howl of pain.

"Where you training?"

"Oh, shit! Out in the Everglades. An abandoned airstrip."

"OMON is going to rescue hostages here in Miami? Is that it? Why doesn't that make any sense to me, Yurin? Unless maybe you're training to *prevent* a hostage rescue, know what I'm sayin'?"

Yurin was silent.

Stoke removed his foot from the back of the big Russian's head, stepped over Yurin, and carefully slid back into the helm seat. He didn't have it all, but it was a good start. It was enough to get Harry Brock's attention. Harry was headed to Bermuda for a high level powwow with Hawke. Stoke had gotten what he'd come for, good hard intel. Russia was on everybody's mind now, especially Alex Hawke's.

"We're going back," Stoke said, steering off the wave crest, taking a diagonal back down the face. "Get up. Slowly. See if you can get back in your seat without getting tossed into the drink, all right? I'm not in a rescue mood right now."

The big yellow race boat was pointed sharply downward on the foamy green face of the wave at a forty-five-degree angle.

"Jesus," Yurin said, managing to get to his feet by holding on to the bar. He slid back inside his seat, buckled up. Stoke kept the Glock in his hand, in case the guy got courageous. But he was a little green around the gills now, his nose mashed over to one side, the blood and spittle trickling out the sides of his mouth blown backward on both cheeks, not looking too sporty.

"Your nose is broken, Yurin. You want me to fix it? I can do it back at the dock. What I do, I jam my two little pinkies straight up your nostrils and, *pop-pop, voilà,* straight as an arrow again. Hurts like a bitch, though, I gotta be brutally honest."

Yurin didn't reply, didn't even look over.

It wasn't easy getting through the narrow end of the funnel with a fiercely following sea, but Stoke managed it, just surfed a big roller all the way through the chute.

When they were back in the relative calm of the marina, the seriously pissed-off Russian said, "Any reason why we couldn't have had that conversation in my office?"

"Just two," Stoke said, nosing the big Magnum back toward the Miami Yacht Group docks. "Number one reason, I'm a habitual thrill seeker."

"Yeah? You Americans haven't seen anything yet."

"That's a threat?"

"That's a promise."

"What's your problem with Americans, Yurin?"

"You people are a fucking error that needs correcting."

"So, I guess you don't want to hear the second reason."

"Yeah, yeah. What?"

"Me being just a fucking error, like you say, I guess you wouldn't want to sell me this boat?"

"What?"

"I guess you don't want to sell me the boat, Yurin."

"You serious? You actually want to buy it?"

"Of course I want to buy it."

"Jesus. You are serious. I thought Moscow was crazy. Miami is the freaking moon."

"Windshield will have to be replaced, of course."

"Of course."

"Give me a number," Stoke said, smiling at the Russian guy for the first time all afternoon.

35

Mayor Monie Bailey spooned the last little bit of macaroni and cheese into her four-year-old daughter's mouth and then used a dish-cloth to remove the rest of Stouffer's finest from her child's hair, ears, cheeks, and the scruffy terry bib hanging by a thread below her chin.

"More," Debbie Bailey demanded, banging on the plastic high-chair tray with a wooden horse. "More mac."

"All gone!"

"No! More!"

"All gone, I said. Night-night time!"

"No night-night! More!"

"You ate the whole thing, Debbie. The whole Family Size. You must have worms."

"No worms. Yucky!"

She plucked the child from her chair in the kitchen and carried her upstairs to the room she shared with her older sister, Carrie. The room always made her smile. It was what she'd always wanted as a girl but was never able to have. A pink powder-puff dream, walls, rugs, curtains, duvet covers, even the two dressers and the mirrors above them, all the same pale shade of pink. And the pink lampshades everywhere just made everything glow.

Carrie, who'd turned nine last week, was propped up against her fluffy pink pillows, reading. She'd received a hardcover illustrated *Black Beauty* for her birthday, but that remained uncracked, jammed in among all the shelves of well-thumbed graphic novels and paperbacks in the pink bookcase beneath the window.

"Hi, Mom," Carrie said, her eyes never leaving the page.

"*Street Girl,*" Monie said, eying the book's lurid cover. "Interesting. What's that one about?"

"Hookers. Well, not really hookers. See, their moms are all hookers, and their kids all sort of grow up in the life, you know? You know, they, like, copy the behavior of the parents, or parent in this case, since there don't seem to be a whole lot of dads in this book. Just gangsta pimps, mostly. But this one girl, Amanda, she's, like, the hero, and —"

"Heroine."

"Right, *heroine,* and she's determined to break out of the vicious cycle and make something of herself, you know, beyond just shooting smack and hooking."

"Isn't that great?" Monie said, tucking Debbie in, pulling the duvet cover up under her chin. It was supposed to get really cold tonight, dip down into the teens. "A girl with spunk, huh? If you like girls like that, you should try Nancy Drew, girl detective. Talk about spunky."

"She's cool. I like her."

"Nancy Drew? You do?"

"Noooo-a, Amanda, silly. Now, shush, Mom, I'm at a really good part. Amanda's about to get caught with her mom's crack pipe in her purse at school. She didn't put it there, of course. Her mom's scag boyfriend, Notorious Ludacris, did it."

"Sorry, Charlie. Lights out. Tomorrow's a school day, remember?"

"Okay, okay, Mom. Just lemme finish this chapter, okay?"

"Now. Lights out."

"My God! We are, like, so strict in this household, it's just pathetic!" She closed the book and put it on the nightstand.

"Go to sleep. Sweet dreams, you two."

"More kissing!" Debbie cried.

"Kiss-kiss, now go to sleep."

Monie flicked a wall switch by the door that turned all the lights off.

"Night-night, Mommy," Debbie said.

"Night, Mom," Carrie said. "Love you."

"I love you, too, sweetie. Both you guys."

She pulled their door closed and walked a few feet down the hall to her husband's study. George was at his desk, staring at his computer screen. EBay Motors, most likely. George spent every evening he wasn't playing fantasy football or watching the Golf Channel on that damn eBay, chasing his dream car. She walked over and stood behind him.

Yep, eBay.

"How's it going, hon?" she asked.

"Aw, hell. You know that dirt-cheap '58 Vette I was bidding on? The maroon one? White interior?"

"Uh-huh."

"Some butthead aced me out at the last second. I mean, the very last second. One second before the time expires, he slips in there at five hundred over my final bid. Damn it!"

"Aw. Did you have a good day at the office?"

George turned around in his swivel chair and smiled up at her. "Isn't that an oxymoron?"

"Probably."

"Kids asleep?"

"One down, one to go."

"One X-Men flashlight shining under the blanket?"

"Yep. That'd be my guess, five minutes after lights out. She should be clicking it on right

432

about now. She's started a new book."

"*Black Beauty*?"

"Dream on, clueless dreamer. She's reading *Street Girl*. By the beloved author of *Ho Town*."

"Sounds bad."

"Mmm."

"Hey. You want to fool around?"

"How'd you know?"

"I don't know. The way you're standing with your one hip cocked out. Usually a reliable indicator. How's the mayor business?"

"Endless meeting with the Civic Association. Annual report from the Public Relations Committee. You know my definition of a committee?"

"A group that keeps minutes and wastes hours."

"Correct. Well, guess what the chairman of that committee told me at the end of his annual report? At the end of his endless two-hour PowerPoint presentation?"

"No clue."

"He said that after an exhaustive study, it was the unanimous recommendation of the PR Committee that the town of Salina not toot its own horn."

George laughed. "The PR Committee guy said that?"

"Yep."

"Isn't the very definition of PR tooting your own horn?"

"I thought so."

"So, what did you do?"

"I disbanded his committee on the spot."

"One less committee for mankind."

"You can search every park in every town in America, and you will never, ever see a statue of a committee."

"That's my girl. Disband 'em all. Don't leave a single one standing."

"Turn that thing off and come to bed," Monie said, running her fingers through George's soft but thinning brown hair.

In the bathroom, pulling a shorty see-through black negligee over her head, she remembered the phone call while she was taking the mac and cheese out of the nuker.

"Honey," she said, cracking the door an inch or two.

"Yeah?"

"Did I forget our anniversary or something?"

"Nope, that's next week. Why?"

"I got a call from some bakery. Said they were delivering the surprise and wanted to make sure someone was home."

"The bakery? Not me."

"That's weird. I thought maybe you were springing some big news or something. That promotion I keep hearing about."

"I'm springing something big, all right. Come out here and have a look."

"George! You ought to be ashamed of yourself!"

At that moment, the front doorbell rang.

"Who the hell could that be? It's almost nine o'clock," George said, pulling her to him, pressing his erection against her belly.

The little nightie that could, Monie thought, smiling up at him. "Probably the bakery."

"What did you tell them?"

"I said I hadn't ordered anything. Of course, I wasn't completely sure you hadn't."

"I'll go get rid of them," George said.

"Not with that thing sticking out, you won't. I'll put a robe on. As for you, mister, go directly to bed. And hold that thought."

George went to the window and peeked under the shade at the driveway below. "Bakery, all right. Big white truck."

She grabbed her blue terry robe from the hook on the bathroom door, slipped it on, and padded down the stairs barefoot, knotting the sash around her waist.

"Hello," said the very fat bakery man when she opened the front door. He was all in white, even his shoes. You could barely see his face because of the huge white box in his hands, tied with a bright pink ribbon.

"Hey. I think you guys made a mistake," Monie said. "We didn't order anything."

"This is the Bailey household, correct? You're Mayor Monie Bailey?" he asked, peering at her over the top of the box.

"It is. I am."

"Well, then, ma'am, this is the right place."

"But, like I said on the phone, we didn't order anything."

She felt uncomfortable and realized the guy was staring at her breasts. Not openly, but she'd caught him looking. She was suddenly aware of how cold she was and looked down. Well, no wonder. Her sash had come undone somehow, and her robe had fallen open. The little black see-through wasn't covering up much cleavage. Her "strategic assets," as George called them. She quickly pulled the robe together at the throat and managed to tie the sash with one hand.

"That doesn't mean someone somewhere doesn't want you to have a very special surprise, does it, now?"

"N-no, but we — look, it's nine o'clock, and we're plumb tuckered out, so could you just —"

"Could I just come in and set this beauty down? It weighs a ton. And it's definitely for you."

"Well, I — okay, what is it?"

"A cake. A gorgeous chocolate cake with coconut icing."

"And who ordered it for us?"

"Name's in the envelope inside the box. You have relatives in Topeka?"

"Only my mom. Oh, Mom, that's it, her

old-timer's kicking in again. She's starting to get dates mixed up lately. And next week is our anniversary, so I bet — come on in. Sorry to keep you standing out there in freezing cold. Put it in the kitchen, if you don't mind. Right through there."

"Sure thing, lady," the fat man said, moving past her toward the kitchen.

"Through the swinging door," Monie called out, turning on a couple of living-room lights and following him toward the kitchen. She paused at the foot of the stairs and called up to George.

"It's okay, honey. I've got it. It's a surprise from Mom. One week early."

"Okay," came the muffled reply from upstairs, and then she was through the dining room and pushing open the swinging door into the kitchen.

He'd put the box down on the butcher-block center island and was leaning back against the counter by the sink. He had a big smile on his face and, what the hell, a gun? It was black and stubby in his chubby white hand.

It was pointed straight at her heart.

"Oh, my God."

"My name's Happy. I'll be your worst nightmare this evening."

"Sweet Jesus, what is this all about?" Her heart was suddenly pounding against her ribs, threatening to splinter them. She flashed on

Debbie and Carrie upstairs in their beds and knew she had to stay calm somehow, suppress the sudden terror and panic threatening to overwhelm her sanity, and somehow get through this alive, get this maniac out of her home.

He smiled.

"Not good, is it? Ruin your day, something like this."

"Omigod, omigod, omigod. Who — who are you? What do you w-want?"

"Well, that depends. I only came here to make a delivery. But sometimes life throws you a bone. *Bone.* Get it?"

"What the hell do you want? Huh? Tell me! It's yours! Money? Jewels? Just take what you want and leave, okay? Please. Just, just leave."

"First I want to see exactly what you got on under that robe. Then we'll get to the other stuff I want."

"Oh, Jesus, oh, sweet Jesus. My God, a stalker. You're a stalker? You've been following me? That it?"

"Just a week."

"A week? Why? Why me?"

"The robe, honey. Now."

"My husband's upstairs. If I scream, he'll —"

"He'll what? Come running down here to find a guy with a gun more than happy to put his brains on the wall? C'mon, mayor. Take the robe off, and we'll see how this plays

438

out. Maybe everybody gets out of this alive, you play nice. Otherwise, maybe not."

Her entire body was suddenly shaking uncontrollably. Terror. Anger. The freezing cold. All of the above.

"Look, if it's money you want, we've got plenty. There's a safe. I'll show you. Hidden behind a mirror in the linen closet. There's twenty thousand in there. Cash. And all my jewelry. Take it all, and get the hell out of here. I'll even give you an hour head-start before I call the cops."

He pulled back his sleeve and showed her the chunky gold Rolex with the diamonds encrusting the dial. He'd bought it at the Blue Diamond King on West Forty-seventh with his first paycheck since the new job. "I'm up to my ass in jewelry right now. What I want is for you to lose that robe. Do it. I got a gun in my hand and a rap sheet two miles long, cupcake. One more dead broad in my life just ain't all that significant, believe me."

"Oh, God . . . can't we —"

"Do it, lady!"

36

With trembling hands, she loosened the terry sash. Then she shrugged out of the robe and let it fall to the floor, puddling around her bare feet. She'd turned the heat off downstairs. It was already freezing in the kitchen. She could feel goose bumps all over. She saw the wooden knife block sitting on the counter. Eight brand-new German knives from Kitchenworks.com. Knife against gun? Paper against scissors, but better than nothing.

"Nice," he said, staring at the nipples hard against her sheer black nightgown, her breasts like cantaloupes encased in silk. "You know how much I could get for you in Saudi? Dubai? Whoa!"

"What are you talking about?"

"I'm not really a baker, as you may have guessed. I'm an old-fashioned iceman. Professional-grade button man, born and bred on the streets of Brooklyn, New York. But I do a little flesh peddling now, sell women on the side. Damn good business, too, Ukrainian girls, mostly. Beautiful. But not as pretty as you. Some sheik of Araby would pay top dollar for those tits."

"Look. Whatever you want from me, just do it, okay? Do it. Then leave. I won't scream. I won't make a sound." She was trying to picture getting him preoccupied, then grabbing one of the big butcher knives out of the block.

"I don't mind a little screaming now and then, tell you the truth, mayor."

"Mayor? Why'd you call me that?"

"I like to bone up on my targets, you know, do my research. Part of the fun."

She looked behind her at the swinging door. It had a small porthole window she'd had installed back in the day when they could afford a cook. She knew she'd never get through that door alive.

"Please. Hurry up and get this over with. My husband could come down any second."

"Come over here, bitch. And lose the nightie, okay?"

"Okay. Okay. You win."

She walked around the center island, pulling the flimsy nightgown up over her head. *There is only one way out of this nightmare,* her brain was screaming. Give this asshole what he wants, and pray to God she could get hold of that butcher knife on the counter. If that didn't work, what? Anything to get him away from the house. Far away from her children. Anything. She would do — she dropped the nightgown on the floor — anything, she realized, to save them, save her family.

"There," she said, positioning herself in front of him, where she could maybe lean forward and grab the knife. "Is this what you wanted? Go ahead. It's all yours, Happy. Have at it. Then get the hell out of my house."

He stayed put. He kept the gun on her, then reached out with his free hand and squeezed her left breast, testing it like fruit at the market, gently kneading the flesh but pinching her nipple hard, harder. And still harder, waiting for some reaction in her eyes that she would never, ever give him.

She could feel his hot breath on her, the scent of testosterone suddenly filling a family kitchen so recently smelling of macaroni and cheese. He was hurting her now. She suddenly took his free wrist, guided his hand down between her legs, let his fingers pry apart the soft flesh, while she backed against the counter, put her hands behind her, spread her legs wide. Her right hand was now maybe three feet from salvation.

He looked at her and smiled.

"Looks like I came to the right house."

"Do it," she said, calculating how and when she might lunge to grab a weapon. She knew she'd only get one chance. Happy was smiling at her.

"Do what, honey? Ask for it."

"You want me to suck it? Is that it? Okay. I'll do it. I'll do it right goddamn now."

She reached out, found the zipper under the protruding belly and yanked it down. Hooked her index fingers inside his stretch waistband and pulled his white baker's pants down to his knees. His penis was standing straight up, just like George's upstairs. Then she bent her head to him, took him in her mouth, and gave him what he wanted.

Somehow, she'd have to get him when he used both hands to pull his pants up. That would be her only chance, catch him when —

"What the hell?" a new voice somewhere said.

George. He was at the kitchen door. She stood up, wiping her mouth with the back of her hand. Her husband was standing there in the doorway in his striped woolen robe, a look of total incomprehension on his face. He looked at his naked wife, then at the fat baker, then back to her.

"Monie? What's going on?"

"He's got a gun, George. But it's okay. He got what he wanted. Now he's leaving. Go back upstairs. I can handle this."

"Go back upstairs?" George said.

"The flashlight, George. Check on the X-Men flashlight. Make sure it's off and nobody can ever get to it. Got that?"

"Check on the X-Men flashlight," George

said robotically.

"You know what, George?" Happy said, moving away from her so he could keep an eye and his gun on both of them. Then he was hitching his trousers up and zipping up his fly. "We're all going back upstairs. You're going to show me the safe, and then we'll take it from there. How's that sound?"

"You said you'd leave if —"

"Lady, I didn't say shit. You did all the talking. Remember? It was your idea, not mine. Let's go. And leave the robe and the nightie there on the floor. We might need them later. George, do me a favor. Bring the cake up, will ya?"

George, carrying the cake, was first up the stairs, then Monie. Then Happy, a step behind her with the gun. She could feel his eyes on her naked bottom all the way to the top.

"Which way's the master bedroom?" Happy asked.

"Left," George said, on automatic pilot. He took a left and walked down the hall toward their room.

"Kids are in there?" the baker said, pausing as they passed the pink door of the girls' room.

"We don't have any kids," Monie said, striving mightily to keep her voice even.

"Really? I counted two."

"Neighbors' kids. I pick them up at school

sometimes," she said. "Their parents are dead. Not dead. Away."

"In here?" George asked, reaching their bedroom.

"Right in there, George. You, too, cupcake."

She hesitated a beat, and he nudged the muzzle of the gun into her right butt cheek.

"You bastard," she hissed. "I've got an entire police force under me that's going to tear your fat ass to shreds for this. They'll boil the meat right off your bones."

"Spunky, huh? We'll see about that. Okay, George, put the cake on the dresser there near the bed. That's right. Now, you and little wifey-poo here climb in the bed and pull the covers up. But keep your hands out where I can see them. Got that?"

"In the bed? Together?" George asked.

She looked at her husband's eyes for the first time. He was in a complete state of shock. No help there. *Thanks, George.* She was waiting for another break. She just needed a distraction. Anything that would let her go for the gun. Or, wait, scissors. She had a pair of crimping shears, big ones, in the top drawer of the dresser, right beneath where George had put the cake box.

"At least let me open my surprise," she said, moving quickly toward the dresser before he could say anything.

"You want to open it? Why not? Go ahead, it's for you, after all."

In the mirror, she saw him watching her move. Enjoying this. Saw George climbing into the four-poster bed, still in his robe. He pulled the covers up and splayed his hands out on top. Then he put his head back against the pillow and closed his eyes.

"George?" she said to his reflection, "You may not have noticed, but we've got a shit-for-brains psycho doughboy in our bedroom. He's going to rape me and kill us all. And you're in bed with your eyes closed? Jesus, George!"

Her husband of twenty years never even blinked.

And she could see Happy in the mirror, too, his eyes were still all over her. She tried to shield her hand with her body as she pulled open the small sock drawer where she kept the scissors. She reached in, dug through the socks, all the way to the back, her fingers desperately searching but coming up empty. Wait, maybe the other drawer? Where she kept her bundle of old love letters from George? Yeah. The scissors were right on top.

"Whatcha doin' over there, honeybun?" he said.

She glanced in the mirror. He'd pulled up a chair and was sitting now, watching her, into the live nude show, the gun loose in his right hand.

"Scissors," she said, holding them up so he could see them. "To cut the ribbon."

"Oh. Sure, why not?"

But now that she had them, what was she going to do with them? Charge him? She'd be dead before she took three steps. No. She'd open the box, try to palm the scissors somehow, hide them behind her back, wait for her chance. She cut the pink grosgrain ribbon and ripped it away. Then she lifted the top off the box and dropped it to the floor.

"Bring the box over here," he said, his voice flat and thick with lust now.

"Okay." She lifted it and turned toward him, the scissors still in her left hand.

"Leave the scissors on the bureau. So you're not tempted to be a bad girl. You know what happens to bad girls."

"Sure."

She carried the box to him, her mind clawing for another weapon, another plan, a little hope here, please. The box was full of red crepe paper and heavier than a box with a cake should be.

"Put it on the floor. By my feet."

She did it.

"Look inside. Take a peek at what you got."

She pulled the paper away and felt something metal, smooth, heavy, shaped like a small drum. She lifted it out and stood up with the thing in her hands. Okay. Smash him in the face? Bring it down hard on the hand with the gun? Which? Now! She had to do it now, or —

She heard the click as he cocked the trigger back.

"Silly girl," he said, the gun pointed at her face. "Put it on the floor, and get into bed with your husband."

"What is this thing?" she asked, looking at the object in her hands. The silver drum had a small fan built into the lid, beneath a wire mesh. And there was a dial and some buttons.

"I'll tell you when you're all tucked in under the covers with Georgie, okay?"

The bad dream wouldn't end unless she ended it. She looked at him one last time, searching his feral eyes for God knows what, mercy, sanity, and then she slammed the metal drum down on the top of his head as hard as she possibly could.

He screamed in surprised pain and tilted the chair back to get away as she raised the drum again, blood pouring from a deep gash in his forehead. They could both tell the chair was going over backward with his weight, and she dropped the drum and dove for the gun with both hands, trying to wrench it from his fingers as he hit the floor.

"George!" she screamed. "Go get the girls! Get them out of the house! Run! Now!"

Happy was on his back on the floor now, dazed but still functioning. She pounced on him, knees in the middle of his chest. She had one hand around his wrist and the other around the barrel of the pistol. She slammed the hand against the wooden floor, hard, once, twice, trying to shake the gun loose. But the goddamn barrel was so short she couldn't seem to get good enough leverage to pry it out of his fingers.

"Let go!" he said, his voice surprisingly calm.

"Fuck you!" she screamed. She gave up on the gun and went for his eyes with her fingernails, raking his face with both hands, ten bright red stripes appearing instantly on his face.

"Bitch!" he screamed, and then she was flying backward, slamming into the dresser and collapsing to the floor. She saw George on his feet, coming toward her, no shock in his eyes now, coming to help her.

"George, watch out! He's still got the —"

"Good-bye, George," the baker said, and shot her husband in the head, a fine red mist where the top used to be. Her husband staggered and fell, his body sprawled across hers. He was dead. She had to get him off. She had to get to the kids, she had to —

The man who had killed her husband and was now going to kill her was standing above her, the gun pointed at her head. His face was shredded, and the blood was pouring down his white baker's shirt, splashing onto her. He put the muzzle of the pistol in the middle of her forehead.

She was going to die now without saving her children.

"Good night," he said. But instead of pulling the trigger, he brought the butt of the gun down hard on the top of her head.

Sometime later, she opened her eyes. She was in her bed, her head on a blood-soaked pillow. She tried to move her hands, but they were tied to something. Bedposts. Feet, too. The baker had pulled the chair up next to the bed, facing her. He had the metal drum in his lap. She couldn't see his face anymore because of the mask. It had two glass eyes and a protruding round mouthpiece that made him look like a giant insect.

"Know what your surprise is?" she heard him say through the mouthpiece, lifting the drum. His voice was distorted, making him sound like a computer recording or something. Her head hurt terribly, and she wanted him to go away. She hurt in another place too, and knew that he'd abused her while she'd been unconcious.

"No," she murmured, "please."

"It's a sleep machine," she heard him say.

"What does it do?"

"Puts people to sleep. Either for a few hours or forever, depending on the strength of the formula. It's new. I'm testing out different strengths for my company. Your family is helping out with our little experiment."

"Oh. Strengths of what?"

"Same stuff we used on the Chechens in the Moscow theater siege. Remember that? We pumped it into the theater through the air-conditioning system to disable the Chechen terrorists. Kolokol 1, the stuff is called. An opiate-derived incapacitating agent. What I'm doing, my job here, is testing the various levels of lethality for use in a hostage-rescue situation. At this level, my guess is it takes effect very rapidly. Certainly with children. Probably within ten seconds or so with adults. We'll see."

"Oh," she heard herself say again.

"I'm turning it on now."

She heard the click of a switch and the whirr of the little fan on the lid.

She fought the restraints, twisting and turning her body on the bed, feeling the thin plastic cuffs cutting into her wrists, her ankles, knowing it was useless but fighting it until she had nothing left.

He watched her, looking down at her struggles with amused detachment.

Exhausted, she let her head fall back against the pillow, felt hot tears running down her cheeks, looking up at the monster looming over her bed, defeated.

"What about my — what about my children?"

"Already sound asleep," he said, taking a clear plastic nose cone attached to a long hose and placing it over her nose and mouth. She screamed again and twisted her head violently from side to side, holding her breath, knowing she couldn't allow this stuff down into her lungs, because if she did, she would surely just . . .

A moment later, she was asleep forever, too.

37

Bermuda

Pippa Guinness stuck her pert blonde head inside the door of Hawke's new office at Blue Water Logistics. The Dockyard offices were nice enough. His own space was bright and airy, a corner office on the top floor, with sunny views on two sides overlooking the open ocean to the north and Hamilton Harbor to the south. On the ramparts, huge cannons stared out to sea. Furniture was a bit *"moderne"* for Hawke's taste, but it looked appropriate for a start-up enterprise, he supposed. Eventually, he'd fill the empty shelves with books and ship models, and that would help.

"Alex? They're almost ready for you in the Tank. C says ten minutes?"

Hawke and Harry Brock both looked up and nodded in her direction. She was wearing a short pink linen skirt and a tight-fitting blouse opened at the neck, and Hawke was viscerally aware of Brock's spiking blood pressure.

"Ten minutes," Pippa said again, smiling sweetly at the two men seated by the window, and then she pulled the door closed behind her.

"Who the living hell was that?" Harry Brock asked Hawke. Harry was leaning back in the ultramodern leather and steel Eames chair. His feet, shod in wildly inappropriate flip-flops, were propped up on the black leather ottoman covered with newspapers, sailing and motorcycle magazines, a few shipping trade papers, and copies of *Tatler* and *The Spectator*.

"That?" Hawke said, affecting an air of boredom. "That, Harry, was Pippa Guinness. Why do you ask?"

"Why do I ask? Are you kidding me? That is the single most gorgeous piece of ass on the big blue planet, and you are asking me *why?*"

"She has her good points."

"Two at the very least. That is one tasty little creampuff, boss."

"A creampuff made on a welding machine," Hawke replied, skimming through his folder for the upcoming meeting.

"What's she do around here, anyway? And don't tell me that's your secretary. I will have you killed, m'lord."

"She runs the joint, actually."

"I thought you ran the joint."

"I do. Off the books. But Pippa is the acting chief of station. I plan to travel a lot, as
you know. She'll mind the store while we're
in Russia. Ambrose, when he recovers enough
to leave his wheelchair, will pitch in as well."

Harry clasped his interlocking fingers
behind his head and started singing, "Back in
the U.S.S.R., boys, you don't know how lucky
you are, boys," he said, almost getting the
Beatles tune right.

"Yeah. It's been a while for me. I'm guess-
ing Moscow has changed a bit."

Harry laughed out loud.

"You will not believe your eyes, comrade.
The Communist Party World Headquarters
is now a dilapidated two-story dump on a
side street. They serve warm champagne in
the lobby, trying to get people to come inside.
Read all the fascinating Stalin, Lenin, and
Trotsky FAQ brochures."

"I wonder what the most frequently asked
question about Trotsky might be."

"As if anyone had any questions at all
anymore." Harry laughed. "Right across the
street is the new Ferrari-Maserati dealership.
Much better brochures over there, believe
me."

Hawke smiled and got to his feet, glancing
at his watch.

"How's Stoke doing down in Miami,
Harry? Happy?"

"Over the moon. His fiancée just got this

big movie deal, but I'm not so sure about the two guys she's signing with. The fucking Russian oligarchs bought the whole Miramar motion-picture studio with cash and are signing every beauteous babe in Miami, Vegas, and La-La."

"Have they actually made a movie yet?"

"Hell no. But she's signed on to do some singing gig on an airship. Flying with a bunch of celebs across the Atlantic. Something to do with the Nobel Prize, I think."

"Airship?"

"Yeah. Called *Pushkin*. Carries seven hundred passengers. Most amazing damn thing you ever saw."

Hawke looked at Brock but didn't say anything. *Airship?*

"Let's go, Harry. Doesn't pay to keep the king waiting." Hawke slipped into the grey and white seersucker blazer that he'd hung on the back of the door.

"The king? Is there a problem between you and your boss I should know about?"

"Yeah. Pippa. She's driving me crazy. Always looking over my shoulder. But I can't do a damn thing about it right now. C wants her here to keep an eye on things. Which means keep an eye on me, basically."

"Want me to take her off your hands?"

"How would you do that, Harry?"

"Offer her a glamorous new life as the new

Mrs. Harry Brock. Take her away from all this."

"I thought you were already married."

"My divorce finally came through. Only took seven years. It's high time I married somebody else I hate and gave her a house."

"But you were obviously in love with the Brazilian special forces woman we met in the Amazon. Saladin's sister, Caparina. Now, there was a woman, Harry."

"I am in love with her. Love is exponential, Alex. You should know that at your age."

"Let's go, Harry."

The Tank was the secure conference room on the second floor. It was in the very middle of the building, accessible only from the third floor by a single private elevator. The lift had a keypad and required a retinal scan to operate. Outside the secure room were cubby holes for all cell phones and BlackBerrys. There was a metal detector at the door and two Royal Marines standing guard on either side. This single room was probably the most secure place on the Atlantic Ocean, Hawke imagined.

C looked up as Harry and Hawke entered. He smiled, got to his feet, and shook hands, first with Alex, then with Brock. Hawke noticed three other men at the table, plus, of course, Pippa Guinness. He'd also noticed Sir David's black eye, courtesy of the Jamaicans on Nonsuch Island. It seemed better today but was still visible. Ambrose had been in bed ever since that night, but he was recovering nicely.

"Welcome, gentlemen. Would you like any coffee? Tea?" Sir David said.

Brock and Hawke both declined and took the last two seats available at the round table in the center of the small, completely sound-insulated room.

"I'd like to introduce our friend Professor Stefanovich Halter, just arrived from Moscow," C said, smiling at a tall, portly man who immediately stood up and shook hands with Hawke and Brock. His face was handsome in a classical way, strong-boned, with sharp, dark eyes. "He's here to brief you on the current political situation in Moscow and offer further assistance to Red Banner as we redouble our intelligence efforts there."

"Please, call me Stefan," the Russian said, in a pitch-perfect rendition of the upper-crust Oxbridge English accent. Hawke found it impossible not to notice his tattered tweed blazer and the old school tie, unusual here on Bermuda.

Professor Halter was known to Hawke only by reputation, but the man was legendary inside the British service. Twice posted to England by the KGB on long, deep-cover assignments in London and, later, teaching at Cambridge University, the elegant Russian spy had been recruited by MI-6 whilst at Cambridge. He was now a double agent on C's payroll and had been working both sides of the aisle ever since, currently serving as a mole deep inside the KGB. When not operating inside Russia, he was a teaching fellow at Cambridge, with several doctoral candidates in Western studies under his tutelage.

Despite a number of incredibly close scrapes, this large, perfectly urbane and charming fellow had managed not only to survive but to play the most dangerous game at a level even few in it could understand.

He was currently working for President Vladimir Rostov's new KGB in a far less esteemed job, having been caught in a compromising position with the wife of a high-ranking KGB officer. He'd been temporarily removed from the operational work he so loved and remanded to the analytical division, where he spent long hours developing and refining reports no one ever read.

Still, he was a treasured MI-6 asset inside the Kremlin and had been generous in helping Red Banner as it began to re-build a network in that savage city. Many of the former Russian agents who'd secretly played for England's side were now dead, either of natural or other causes.

"Can't help but admire your tie, Professor Halter," Hawke said with a smile. It had a dark blue background and diagonal light blue stripes with the Eton College heraldic shields between the stripes.

"Old Etonian, are you?" Halter replied.

"Not me, my father. But I'm delighted to meet you. My father, in his unfinished memoir, speaks very highly of you."

"Thank you, Alex," the Russian said. "As it happens, I was deeply involved in one of your father's rather ticklish adventures. That single-handed raid of his on the Arctic Soviet SOFAR installation during the Cuban missile crisis. It is still the stuff of legend, you know. How he survived that dreadful business, no one knows to this day."

Hawke smiled, trying hard to remember his father as he had lived and not how he had died, murdered at the hands of drug-smuggling pirates aboard his boat in the Caribbean.

The Russian spy seemed to pick up on the younger man's feelings and said brightly, "Well, Alex, Sir David thinks I might be of some help to you when you arrive in Moscow."

"Any assistance will be most appreciated," Hawke said.

"Yes, Alex," C said. "I thought we'd just give Stefan the floor this morning, let him give us a bit of an update, and then I'm sure he'd be happy to take any questions. Does that suit everyone? And let's keep it informal, shall we? If you have a question, pipe up."

They all nodded, and Halter picked up a slender remote from the table. Suddenly, a slide appeared on a heretofore invisible wall-sized screen at the far end of the room. An old photograph of Vladimir Putin filled the wall.

"Dear Volodya," Halter began. "Now wasting away at a hideous island prison off St. Petersburg called Energetika. A very bad business, indeed. A sad end, I must say, for a man who did do an enormous service for his country, despite his many flaws."

"What service?" Brock said, somewhat aggressively. Putin, in his book anyway, was an ex-KGB tough busy building a police state when he'd been disappeared. Shutting down the free press, arresting dissidents like Kasparov, and throwing them into Lubyanka with no access to attorneys. Among other things.

"You have to look at it from the Russian perspective. Is he pro-democracy? Not exactly. But — the country was in free fall. A kleptocracy, run by criminals throughout the nineties, thieves who shipped countless billions offshore, bankrupting the country. Humiliated by the loss of the Cold War and what was seen as American arrogance. Putin restored order, gave the people back their pride, put the oligarchs in prison or at least out of the way. That's a service."

"If I may add to that," Sir David said, "it

461

was Putin who put the final nails into the Communist Party's coffin as well."

"Still, democracy never had a chance," Pippa said, looking at Stefan for confirmation.

"Yes, actually, it did, Pippa. But there was no infrastructure to support it, and so, sadly, it led to chaos. And at any rate, as I say, Putin was never a Western-style democrat at heart. He was a professional KGB officer. You must remember the KGB, wherein he grew up, isn't remotely interested in ideology. It's interested in power. And law and order. And that, frankly, is what the Russians craved after all those years of drunken disorder inside the Kremlin and blood in the streets. They were shamed and humiliated. That's why the country has now reunited so strongly against the West."

Another slide appeared. The current president, Vladimir Rostov.

"Our fearless leader," Halter said. "He's basically pursuing Putin's goals but with a much more aggressive anti-Western posture. I assume you're all familiar with the term *irredentism?*"

Hawke, Trulove, and Brock came up with blank stares.

"Irredentism," Pippa Guinness said in a sing-song schoolgirl manner Hawke found especially irritating, "the annexation of territories administered by another state on the grounds of common ethnicity and/or prior historical possession, actual or alleged."

"I was going to say that," Harry Brock said, and Hawke smiled at him across the table.

"Can you use *irredentism* in a sentence, Harry?" Hawke asked.

"No. And you can't make me."

Both men laughed out loud, earning a stern look from C, who continued.

"Miss Guinness is quite correct. I believe Rostov is a determined imperialist who won't stop until the old borders of the former Soviet empire are restored. Eastern Europe, the Baltics, et cetera. He, too, grew up as a KGB man in the Cold War. All he understands is conflict, the clash of two systems. He doesn't give a bloody fuck about personal ethics, it's all about the conflict. You're either with us or against us."

"Precisely right," Professor Halter said, nodding vigorously.

"Revanchist Russia wants a fight, any fight," Sir David Trulove said. "Witness their recent bullying of independent Ukraine and Georgia, two former vassal states, both desperately hopeful of joining NATO. Rostov also wants to take on the West now, because he sees it as weakened. Win, lose, or draw, Russia is back on stage as a world power. And, because of their vast energy holdings, and the price of oil, they've got enormous cash reserves. They can also shut off the flow of energy to Europe at the slightest provocation. They won't be bullied, I daresay."

"Quite true, Sir David. Now, these men," Stefan said, flipping through slides of various Kremlin personalities, "are called the *siloviki*. The president's hand-picked innermost circle. There used to be twelve, but two were recently eliminated for crossing the line. All are former military and KGB cronies of Rostov's. They are like a brotherhood. A secret fraternity. They look the same, talk the same, think the same. And they now have unassailable control over the levers of power. They control the Duma, the parliament, all the governors and mayors throughout Russia, the legal system, the tax system, and, of course, the military and the KGB."

"A one-party system?" Hawke asked.

"Exactly. Two-party politics is finished in Russia. The Kremlin now has unchecked power. They've got all the instruments at their disposal, and it is a very, very dangerous situation. Washington-Moscow nuclear tensions are at the highest levels seen since the end of the Cold War."

"What's Moscow's current attitude toward the U.S.?" Brock asked, "I mean specifically."

"Are you familiar with the Russian word *nashe,* Mr. Brock?"

"Sorry, no."

"Roughly translated, it means 'ours.' As in 'ours' versus 'yours,' meaning American.

Nashe is a buzzword in Moscow these days. Anything *nashe,* anything Russian, is good, anything American is bad. Music, politics, culture, what have you. It's all about Russian pride reasserting itself."

"So, negative feelings toward America."

"Extremely negative. Within both the government and the general population. Everyone in Russia feels betrayed by America. The media is full of anti-American propaganda, of course. Day and night, because all media is state-run now."

"What are they saying?" Hawke asked.

"That the Americans are stupid, greedy, and the cause of more instability around the world than any other nation. That they rubbed Russia's nose in it at the end of the Cold War, but now Russia is strong and rich once more. And now the revanchists shall have their revenge."

"Revenge?" Hawke asked. "Revenge for what?"

"For kicking their bloody arses in the Cold War, Alex. And then having the cheek never to let them forget who's boss," Stefan said.

"And do we have any idea how they intend to exact that revenge?" Hawke asked.

"No. Exactly what they intend, we've no idea. We're hoping that Red Banner will help us find out."

"The Pentagon doesn't see them starting a shooting war," Brock said. "They're in no position to do that now. Someday soon, perhaps, but not now."

"What about the so-called Third Man?" Hawke asked.

"Now you're getting to it, Alex," Stefan Halter said. "You're referring to the three chaps Yeltsin met with at that Belarussian hunting resort. The vodka-fueled meeting where they unilaterally decided to abolish the Soviet Union. There was Kravchuk from the Ukraine and Shushkevich from Belarus. And a third man, as you say, who has never been identified."

"But who has long been rumored as the power behind the throne," C said. "A virtual Tsar who rules but is never seen or heard. A man who destroyed the old Soviet Union so that he might one day reign over the New Russia."

Stefan Halter smiled at the group assembled. "He's called the Dark Rider by the KGB."

"Stefan," C said, "perhaps a brief explanation of the Dark Rider concept would be helpful."

"Certainly. Historically, two types of leaders rise to the pinnacle of power in Russia. In my country, we call these two types pale riders and dark riders. The pale rider is a benevolent soul, weak-willed, concerned more about the well-being of his countrymen than the welfare of the state. The last Tsar,

466

Nicholas II, who forfeited his entire empire to the Bolsheviks in 1917, is a good example.

"A more recent example would be Yeltsin, a corrupt, good-hearted drunkard. A dark rider always comes on the heels of a pale rider. He is tough and single-minded, interested only in consolidating power and in the security of the state. The power of the state to enforce its will on the people is his raison d'être. He will sacrifice all, including personal ethics, honesty, and human lives, for the good of the state. Putin was a dark rider. But not quite dark enough for some. That's why they got rid of him."

"And Rostov?"

"So, too, is Rostov, a few shades darker. But rumored to drinking heavily lately and getting long in the tooth, I think. The natives are restless, from what I gather."

"And the Third Man?"

"The darkest of the dark. It would save a great deal of time if I could tell you his identity. Unfortunately, I cannot. It's the most closely held secret in the Kremlin."

"Where do we start looking?" Hawke asked. "Russia is a sizable country."

"My lack of an answer constitutes my single greatest failure as a counterintelligence agent, sir. I have no earthly idea. But I can tell you this. Rostov may be strong and tough, but he comes with strings attached. He is still a puppet. Perhaps one of the *siloviki* is pulling his strings. Or an outsider we know nothing about. But working in the Kremlin as I do, I sense a rising tide of anxiety inside the walls.

"Maybe the military has gained the upper hand and will attempt to seize power. Maybe there will be some preemptive Russian strike against the West. That revenge motive we discussed is very powerful right now. I simply do not know. But if you can learn the identity of the real power behind the throne, you will gain critical understanding of what is going on within the Kremlin walls. That knowledge is vital to Red Banner's mission. Key to it, in fact."

Hawke thought for a moment, then looked directly at Halter.

"Stefan, have you heard of a man named Korsakov? Count Ivan Korsakov?"

"Of course. Korsakov is one of the most interesting figures in modern Russia. Not so much beyond our borders, as he is a very private individual. An absolute genius, from an ancient family rich beyond measure. Beloved across the width and breadth of the country for his philanthropy, his kindnesses to the poor. But you won't find his name on any schools or hospitals. Always anonymous."

"What's his background? Is he political?"

"Not at all. First and foremost, he's a scientist and inventor. Recently nominated for a Nobel. But he's a great businessman. A poet, a gifted composer as well. As I said,

468

he's a descendant of one of Russia's oldest, most powerful families. The Korsakovs rose to the heights of power around the time of Peter the Great, who in 1722 made them barons and later counts. They conquered Siberia, for one thing, brought it under the control of the Tsars."

"I see."

"Why are you so curious about him, if I may ask?"

"His daughter, Anastasia, has recently become a friend of mine. She has invited me to visit their country estate outside St. Petersburg. I was thinking of going for a few days' visit before my arrival in Moscow. I was wondering if it would be worth the time. Her father will apparently be there."

"Alex, if you have the opportunity to meet and gain the confidence of Count Korsakov, you will have advanced the cause of Red Banner enormously. No one knows more about what really goes on inside Russia than that man. He is privy to the darkest secrets imaginable. He may even be able to lead you to the Dark Rider."

C had lit one of his poisonous black cheroots. He inhaled, expelled a cloud of smoke, and said, "Just how close are you and the count's daughter, Alex?"

"She's invited me for some Christmas house party, that's all. They have some kind of winter palace out in the countryside. Why?"

"Just curious. If you have a relationship with her, it could be very helpful to the cause."

Hawke stared at his superior angrily but said nothing. C hadn't put him in this position. He'd brought it on himself.

Pippa smiled at Alex. "She's a painter, isn't she? Anastasia, I mean."

"Yes. She is."

"I've seen her work at a small gallery over on Front Street. Male nudes. Some figure studies that looked vaguely familiar, Alex. Quite exciting. There was one large one that I almost thought could have been —"

Hawke's eyes blazed.

"Pippa, may I speak with you privately for a moment?" Alex said. "Outside?"

"Of course," she said, following him to the door.

"My apologies, gentlemen," Hawke said, trying to keep the anger out of his voice. "I'll be back momentarily."

"Fucking hell, girl," Hawke said to her when they were safely outside the soundproofed room and away from the Marine guards. He had to restrain himself from slapping her face.

"What is it, Alex?" she asked, an innocent smile flitting across her face. "Have you fallen in love with this little Russian princess?"

"Damn it, Pippa."

"Don't be embarrassed, darling. You know

I'd recognize your — I mean, you — anywhere."

38

The president's trim, blonde secretary, Betsey Hall, walked quickly down a short hallway to the small White House reception room, where the secretary of state and her security entourage had just arrived.

"Betsey, good morning!" Consuelo de los Reyes said, standing to embrace her good friend. The two single women often spent time in each other's company. Dinner once a month at 1789, long one of Georgetown's popular restaurants, and sometimes an evening of ballet viewed from the secretary's private box at the Kennedy Center. They never talked politics. They talked men, and they were seldom complimentary.

"Madame Secretary, welcome," Betsey said, shaking hands with her friend and smiling at the security team. "Good morning, everyone."

"Is anyone else already in the Oval?" de los Reyes asked.

"Yes, but they were early. You're right on time."

"Who's here? The vice president?"

"No, the McCloskeys are down in Miami. They're taking that airship cruise to the Nobel ceremony in Stockholm. The president was invited, but his schedule didn't allow it."

"So, who do we have in there?"

"His crisis team. General Moore from the Joint Chiefs, CIA Director Kelly, FBI Director Mike Reiter, the new Director of National Intelligence, Simon Pinniger, and a couple of guests. Brits from MI-6."

Consuelo's eyes widened. "Alex Hawke is in there?"

"Sorry, no," Betsey said, patting her friend's shoulder. She knew how Consuelo felt about the dashing British spy. Their on-again, off-again affair had been rocky from the beginning. From the look on her friend's face, Betsey knew nothing had changed. Off again.

"Who, then?" she asked.

"It's Sir David Trulove and his new assistant station chief from Bermuda."

"Bermuda? What's his name?"

"It's a she. Pippa Guinness."

The secretary of state rolled her eyes and whispered in Betsey's ear. "Bermuda. That's where Alex Hawke is living now, damn Miss Guinness to hell."

"I know, dear. Sorry."

"How does the little bitch look these days?"

"Restless as an eel."

The secretary laughed out loud. Then she straightened herself. "Oh, well. Nothing new, I suppose. He is who he is. What's the weather like in there this morning?"

"We had a nasty nor'easter blow through here earlier this morning — Senator Kennedy — but now it's all sunshine and roses in there. He's in a great mood. Feisty."

"He must not have seen the new polls this morning."

"Of course he did. You know what he said?"

"Can't even guess."

"He said, 'Well, I guess I'm never going to be popular, so by God, Betsey, I'll just keep on being right.' "

The secretary laughed and headed toward the private entrance to the Oval Office. She was looking forward to her weekly meeting with the president. It was always informal, kept deliberately small, and anyone could bring up any topic they wished. And she was naturally curious about the crisis du jour.

President McAtee stood as the beautiful Cuban-American secretary swept through the door. The members of the president's team all stood and extended their hands in greeting. Pippa also stood and smiled, but Consuelo pointedly ignored her.

"Conch, good to see you!" the president said. "Congratulations on your Mideast trip. I think we made a lot of progress."

"I think we made as much progress as we can make with the Saudis and the Iranians, Mr. President. At least for the time being."

When everyone was seated and the steward had served more tea and coffee, President Jack McAtee said, "Conch, I want to save your recent trip for last. We're all looking forward to hearing your insights and points of view. But Brick is just back from a meeting in Estonia with our new ambassador there, Dave Philips, and picked up some insights into our Russian friends that I think we should discuss immediately. Brick?"

"Thanks, Mr. President," the lanky, red-haired Virginian said in his slow drawl. He leaned back in his armchair and stretched out his long legs. The director was wearing, as always, beautifully polished cowboy boots with his navy suit.

"Based on my two days with Ambassador Philips, I'd say we've got trouble on the Russian front. Just a quick anecdote. Dave went to a reception at the French embassy in Tallinn with the Russian ambassador a week ago today. He's become friendly with the guy, they've gone out drinking a few times. Anyway, the ancient Russian ambassador shows up in uniform. He was a general under Stalin. And he's wearing his old uniform."

"Odd," the president said. "What's that all about?"

"Dave asked him. He said all Russian

ambassadors had received a directive from Rostov himself. From now on, they are to wear their military uniforms to all official state functions."

"Speaks volumes," General Moore said. "They are going to a war footing."

"You believe that, Brick? War? With us?"

"It could all be posturing, you know, on the part of a resurgent Kremlin. Part of their new public relations campaign to climb back onto the world stage. They might be just sticking their toe in the waters of the Baltic. See what we'll let them get away with."

"What's the military assessment, Charlie?"

General Moore handed each of them a thin blue folder marked "Most Secret." Moore started speaking as the group began flipping through the folders.

"Here are the most recent satellite passes over Eastern Europe and the Baltic. And what you'll see isn't posturing, it's Russian troops. Three divisions have massed along the Ukrainian border, here, here, and here. Another two divisions are poised here along the Estonian border. And most troubling of all, here you see five divisions moving into place at the Latvian and Belarus border. From our recent war gamers' perspective, and from where those troops and tank corps are positioned, it's a straight shot through Lithuania and back into Poland and the Czech Republic, where we're deploying our antiballistic-missile batteries."

Brick Kelly said, "Sir, you'll remember that only recently, Rostov threatened to deploy cruise missiles in the tiny Russian enclave of Kaliningrad, if we go ahead with missile defense in his backyard."

The president said, "Tell me again where Kaliningrad is, Brick? I swear I'm bad at geography. Always have been."

Kelly got up and spun the globe. He stopped it at Eastern Europe. "It sits right there between Poland and Lithuania. One Kremlin ploy might be to say they were sending troops in to reinforce their threatened enclave. It's all tap-dancing and saber rattling right now, but I don't think we can afford not to take it very, very seriously, Mr. President."

"Jesus," the president said, loosening his tie. "Didn't anyone see this coming?"

"It was a sudden movement, but clearly the planning for this operation has been under way for some time," the CIA director said. "We should have caught something, but we didn't. We're playing catch-up ball in Moscow, Mr. President. It's going to take a while before we can get our field-agent network back up to where we were during the Cold War."

"Britain's doing the same thing, Mr. President," Sir David Trulove said. "As you well know, we've recently joined forces with

Langley to create something called Red Banner. A secret division to deal with the resurgent Soviet — excuse me, Dr. Freud, I meant Russian threat. Based in Bermuda and headed up by Alex Hawke, whom I'm sure you remember."

"How is Alex bearing up, Sir David? He was quite ill for a while, I know."

"Well and good, sir. Living the good life in Bermuda these days until I darkened his door."

"Yanked him out of early retirement, did you?"

"I keep him busy."

"Give him my regards, will you?"

"I'll do that, sir. Thank you."

At that moment, Betsey Hall entered the Oval through her private door. Her expression was grim, and she went immediately to the president, bent from the waist, and whispered something into his ear. McAtee listened intently, nodded his head, and got to his feet.

"I need to take this call," he said. "Urgent. No need to leave, sit tight. Please excuse me for a minute."

McAtee walked behind the historic *Resolute* desk. In 1850, the British HMS *Resolute* had gotten lodged in Arctic ice and was long abandoned before being discovered adrift by an American fishing vessel that towed her to port. Congress purchased the vessel, refitted her, and presented her to Queen Victoria as a token of peace. *Resolute* served in the Royal Navy for twenty-three years. After decommissioning, Queen Victoria ordered two identical desks built from her timbers, presenting one to President Rutherford B. Hayes in 1880 and placing the twin in Buckingham Palace, where it stands today.

McAtee sat at the historic desk, flanked by the two flags, and picked up the receiver on the phone that was blinking.

"This is the president," he said.

He listened impassively, his expression giving little away to anyone in the room who glanced his way. A few minutes later, he said, "Thank you very much. You'll be hearing from me shortly."

He stood and crossed the room, returning to his favorite chair by the fire. He sighed deeply and leaned his head back against the cushion of the chair. No one knew quite what to say, and a lengthy silence ensued.

"That was the governor of Kansas," McAtee said. "Along with Bill Thomas at NSA. Last night, the mayor of Salina, someone I knew personally, was murdered in bed, along with her husband and two children. There are no suspects, and Monie Bailey didn't have an enemy in this world. It was the work of terrorists. The husband was shot dead, the other three were gassed."

"Gassed?" Mike Reiter said as he leaned

forward. "Terrorists? In Kansas? Good Lord. Will you excuse me, Mr. President? I need to make a few phone calls." McAtee nodded, and Reiter quickly left.

"A cell phone was left on Monie's body. There was a message on it. It came from a member of a group calling itself the Arm of God. NSA has already traced the call. It came from another cell. The caller was in an apartment complex in a suburb west of Tehran when the call was made. We have assets on the way to that building now."

"Unbelievable," General Moore said.

"It gets worse," Jack McAtee said.

"Sorry. Go ahead, Mr. President."

"The caller, whose voice was electronically altered, said that at precisely six o'clock Tuesday morning, Central Standard Time, that's tomorrow morning, the town of Salina, Kansas, will no longer exist. He said evacuation of the entire population should begin immediately. Then he 'allahued Akhbar' three times and hung up."

The room sat in stunned silence.

"Salina, Kansas," Moore said. "Why? It doesn't make any sense. There's nothing there."

"Except churches and schools and families with little girls and boys," McAtee said, his expression blank.

Brick Kelly stared at the still-spinning globe. He stuck out a finger and stopped it, found Salina on the map of the U.S., and said, "This is interesting. Salina is in the absolute dead center of the country. Look. Right square in the middle of the north-south axis and the east-west axis."

"A shot to the heart?" General Moore said. "Some kind of warning shot to the heart of America?"

"Maybe," the president mused. He'd been thinking along the same lines.

"What does NSA think, Mr. President?" Sir David asked. "Is this threat at all credible?"

McAtee nodded gravely. "Very credible. They say I should authorize immediate evacuation. This radical group, this so-called Arm of God, has a blood-soaked history. They're a Soviet-sponsored terror network headquartered in Iran. Lately, they've been training foreign fighters to infiltrate Iraq and Afghanistan with ever more sophisticated IEDs. And they're the ones currently negotiating with the Russians on the purchase of new shoulder-fired missiles to bring our Ah-64 Apache choppers down."

"The Russians. Why do they keep coming up?" Consuelo de los Reyes said, to no one in particular.

"I'm sorry. I've got to call the governor," Mc Atee said. "I'll have to cancel the remainder of this meeting, I'm afraid. There are forty-two thousand souls in that town whose

481

lives are at stake. I want to thank you all for coming and we'll regroup soon, I promise. I'll keep you abreast of this situation as it develops. Betsey will call your offices with a time to reconvene."

The president stood, and so did everyone else. As they were filing out, he stopped Sir David and said quietly, "Could you stick around another minute or so?"

"Certainly, sir."

When the room had cleared, McAtee said, "I want you to promise me something, David, all right?"

"Anything."

"This man of yours. Hawke. He's heading up that new division for you. What's it called again?"

"Red Banner."

"Right. I trust Alex Hawke. Completely. A couple of years ago, he single-handedly saved my life up on the inaugural platform. Not only mine but my wife's and everybody in the damn government, most likely. We've got nobody like him, David, nobody who operates at his level. I want Hawke inside Russia. Tonight, if possible. If anyone can figure out what the hell these mad Russians are up to, it's him. Quote me. Tell him I said that. And tell him there's not a second to lose."

"You seriously think the Russians may have something to do with this Kansas situation, Mr. President?"

"It's possible. But I'm beginning to think the Russians have something to do with everything on the damn planet lately. Nothing those people do would surprise me at this point. They've pulled out of the arms treaty, they're flying long-distance bomber sorties over Guam again, they've got troops massing on the NATO borders, they're retargeting European cities with their missiles, and they're selling advanced weapon systems to our most feared enemy, Iran. Friend or foe, David, you call it."

The president took a deep breath and sat back in his chair, looking at the chief of British intelligence. "Sir David, I'm sorry. I've got to get back on the phone with the Kansas governor. Get those poor people out there in Salina to safety. I'll speak to you soon. Safe journey back to London."

"Good-bye, Mr. President. Thanks for your time. And good luck to you. It looks as if we may stand together yet again."

"It does, sir, it certainly does."

The president was distracted, already on to his next call, his next crisis, but he looked Trulove in the eye and spoke from his gut.

"We're it, you know, Sir David. Our two countries. The last barricade. We're all that's left. God help us."

■ ■ ■ ■

PART TWO:
WHITE NIGHTS

■ ■ ■ ■

39

Russia

Hawke pressed his forehead against the icy window of his small train compartment. He cradled a mug of lukewarm tea in both hands, grateful for the small amount of heat it offered. The train was slowing, wheels screeching, the air beyond the frosted glass smoking with snow, clouds of frothy white whirling about outside, obscuring everything. From somewhere ahead, the plaintive cry of the train's whistle, a hollow call that could have sprung from the bottom of his heart.

Were they finally arriving?

He was on the last leg of his journey to Anastasia. He'd been at his window for hours, staring out at the frozen tundra, mesmerized by the view and thoughts of the new woman in his life. Hours had passed since he'd awoken from a sleep as deep and dark as the grave itself. He'd climbed down from his warm bunk and sprung to the window, his heart hammering. Was it love he was feeling, or was it merely the thrill of the game? Perhaps both? He knew this grip of conflicting emotions was powerful enough to paralyze him if he weren't careful.

So he sat by his window and forced himself to look at things he could actually *see.*

He saw Russia. He saw its fields, steppes, villages, and towns, all bleached white by the moon and bright stars. He sat for hours on end and watched as Russia flew past, wrapped in glittering clouds of snow and ice.

It had been nearly twenty-four hours since he'd received his orders and begun his onward journey. He'd said good-bye to Diana and Ambrose at the Bermuda airport and climbed aboard an RAF transport. He'd slept in the rear, freezing, on top of the mailbags, all the way to RAF Sedgwick, then caught a commercial flight into Russia, landing at St. Petersburg. He presented himself at immigration as Mr. A. Hawke, senior partner, Blue Water Logistics, Bermuda. He had a Bermuda passport that, even to his jaded eye, was a work of art. A four-color brochure inside his briefcase described the worldwide shipping capabilities of his new company. Just in case anyone was interested.

Since boarding the train at St. Petersburg's Moskovsky Vokzal station, he'd had nothing to eat but Ukrainian sausage, which resembled a kilo of raw bacon coated in herbs, and some smoked cheese, which he found he simply couldn't stomach. The kind of meal that you only want to see once but worry might resurface at any moment.

The Russian beer, however, was delicious. At the last big station, all of the passengers had jumped from the train and run for the buffet. He'd followed and had purchased a loaf of black bread and a bottle of Imperia vodka, primarily for warmth, he told himself. It was long gone.

Alone inside his compartment, despite its faint stench from the lavatories, not quite neutralized by the eau de cologne of some recently disembarked passenger and the smell of some fried chicken, pieces of which he'd finally found stuffed under the seat cushions, wrapped in dirty grease-stained paper, he was quite content.

He'd bought a ticket for a *kupe* class compartment. This entitled him to a set of bunks, a small table, storage space, and, most important, a lockable door. By Russian standards, this was relatively cushy train travel. The next class down was a bed in an open train carriage with about forty other passengers, mostly Russian or Mongolian traders with stacks of bags of their stock in trade. Not much sleeping went on back there, rather a lot of beer drinking and fighting over the use of the toilet. The lavatory attendant, a grumpy elderly babushka, kept the one clean toilet on the carriage locked for her personal use.

Hawke knew he was back in Russia.

He glanced at the green glow of his wristwatch. It was after two o'clock in the morning, but the night was lit up like day. The citizens of St. Petersburg called their midsummer evenings the White Nights. That beautiful town, the northernmost city of any size on earth, is so far north that the sun never really quite dips below the horizon during midsummer. This, of course, was December, but still, it was the whitest night Alex Hawke had ever seen. He could easily be reading by his window, and beyond it, a full moon on snow, not the sun, created the white night flying by his window.

He found himself bewitched by the luminous, enchanting landscape. As time passed, the succession of huge views from his window aroused in him such a feeling of spaciousness that it made him think and dream of the future. One that might well include the beautiful Russian woman whose face he so longed to see.

But, he reminded himself again, he was in Russia on a mission. It was no time for lovesick dreaming. It was time to reimmerse himself in the hard reality of Russia and all that menacing old word Russia once more implied.

It was time, he knew, to rearm, to steel himself for whatever lay ahead. What the British secret services had long called the Great Game with the Russians was afoot once more, and he was headed deep into the thick of it. Harry Brock was already waiting for him in Moscow, meeting with Red Banner's newly recruited case officers and speaking with potential targets Stefan had indentified within the KGB. Spies with a price were not hard to come by in the new Russia.

In Bermuda, Ambrose Congreve, much improved every day, was happily ensconced in Hawke's office at Blue Water. Appointing the former chief inspector of Scotland Yard temporary chief of station for the fledgling MI-6 division had been C's idea, and Hawke thought it an inspired one. Especially when he learned that Ambrose was always summoning Pippa Guinness to his office, asking her to have this or that typed, or, better yet, please bring him a fresh pot of tea, no lemon, thank you. He was still in a wheelchair, but had said his leg seemed to be healing nicely.

As the endless miles rolled by, Hawke remained at his window, trying to summon his old memories of Russia. His mind found an ugly landscape of crumbling factories and idle collective farms, back streets of towns crowded with prostitutes, beggars, hawkers, hustlers, and peasants, all humming with activity, a scant few worthless things for sale in clogged lanes of shops with mostly barren shelves, selling matches and salt, sweatshops making T-shirts and plastic shoes.

But for the occasional intrusion of police, life went on. Politics was merely a nuisance you tolerated, with mostly bemused indifference. And what looked at a distance like total anarchy and chaos? Close up, it was meticulous order.

He wondered how much country life had changed in the years since the collapse of the old Soviet ways. Out here, probably not at all. The New Russia you read about existed only in places like Moscow, St. Petersburg, and Kiev. The New Russia was all about money and power, and there was precious little of either to be found out here, where field was followed by field only to be swallowed up by another black forest.

He could make out an occasional farm building, buried under a mantle of snow. Or now and then, at a desolate country crossing, he'd catch a glimpse of snowy lane, winding back up a hill, disappearing amid a copse of frosted trees. It wasn't until you got beyond the great cities of Russia, he now realized, that you could sense the vastness of this ancient land. Its true size, its scope, its immensity, were literally unimaginable.

There was never any vehicular traffic at these infrequent crossings, ever. No trucks, no cars, no tractors. Were there simply no combustion engines outside the cities? None at all? A few hours earlier, they'd slowed for a crossing, and he'd seen a mule cart with an ancient driver on his box, bundled against the freezing north wind, the reins clenched in his frozen fingers. The man was so still on his perch that Hawke feared he might have simply frozen to death while waiting for the long train to pass.

The train slowed further, and he guessed by the hour that they might finally be approaching his destination, a tiny country station on the way to nowhere.

He stood and gathered his few belongings. He was already wearing his long black woolen greatcoat against the cold and his thick black cashmere scarf and his Russian fur cap, purchased from a kiosk at the St. Petersburg station. He reached up to the top shelf for his luggage.

He had with him his old leather Gladstone portmanteau, primarily because of its twin false bottoms. The two visible compartments were filled with clothing and shoes and his few books. Two secret compartments contained one pistol each, twin SIG Sauer 9mms, plus enough Parabellum ammunition to start a small war. Another, smaller compartment housed his powerful Iridium Globalstar satellite telephone. The guns and the phone had been waiting for him in a luggage storage locker at the St. Petersburg train station.

The train lurched to a stop, and he leaned

over to peer out his window. The window framed what looked like a charcoal sketch. There was the tiny station house with its puffing chimney. Beside it were birch trees, laden with hoar frost. Their branches, like smoky streaks of candle wax, looked as if they wished to lay down their snowy burdens on the building's steeply pitched roof.

The dimly lit sign over the doorway read "*Tvas.*" The stationmaster's office was lit from within, and inside the yellow room, he saw the silhouette of a tall woman bundled in furs, pacing back and forth. His heart leaped at the sight of her, and he raced from his compartment, careened down the narrow corridor to the platform, where he jumped from the train.

Her face was at the stationmaster's window, peering out at the arriving train, as he grasped the doorknob and pushed inside, instantly grateful for the warmth of the small stove glowing in the corner.

Anastasia turned from the window and smiled at him.

"You've come" was all she said.

She was covered head to toe in white sable, an abundant coat reaching the tops of her snowy boots. Her head was covered with a matching sable cowl, and her golden curls fell beside her cheeks, still rosy with the cold. Her hands were clasped inside a white fur muff, which she let drop as she moved quickly toward him across the scuffed wooden floor.

"Oh," she said, suddenly remembering the stationmaster who stood beside his counter. He was a small fat man who wore a grey Tolstoyan shirt with a broad leather belt, felt boots, and trousers bagging at the knees. He looked a kindly enough fellow, but a tiny gold pince-nez on a wide black ribbon quivered angrily on the end of his nose.

"Nikolai, this is my new friend whom I've been telling you about."

The Russian bowed, saying something under his breath to Anastasia.

"He says you're very handsome but that I shouldn't have come all this way for you on such a night. He's very protective. I've known him since I was no taller than a poppy."

"Come here," Hawke said to her, dropping his portmanteau to the floor and spreading his arms wide.

She ran to him, and he enfolded her in his arms, burying his face against hers inside the warmth of her furry cowl, inhaling the fresh outdoor scent of her, the perfume of her skin, finding her lips and kissing them, at first softly and then with a sudden urgency that surprised even him. He'd struggled mightily to banish her from his mind for all the long hours on the train, and now he was overwhelmed at the strength of the feelings suddenly welling up inside.

"You look so — beautiful," he said, aware of the word's ridiculous inadequacy, holding her away from him so he could look into her brightly shining green eyes, hardly able to believe anyone could ever be or look or seem so lovely.

"And you, handsome prince." She laughed. "Come to Mother Russia at last, have you? Come along, now, we've got a long journey yet."

"Are we walking?" Hawke said. "I saw no sign of a car. Or a road, for that matter."

"A car?" She laughed again. "You think an automobile could travel two feet in snow this deep? Get your bag and follow me, bumpkin."

She bent to retrieve her dropped white muff, then hurried to the still-opened station door, turned and said good-bye to the stationmaster, then rushed outside. Hawke grabbed his bag and followed her, catching up with her under the single lamp illuminating the snow-covered platform. It had begun to snow again, snowflakes coming down one by one. They spun slowly and hesitantly before finally settling like fluffy white dust on the sparkling blanket of already fallen snow.

"Kiss me again," she said, and he did, standing under the lamppost, aware of old Nikolai peering out at them from a corner of the window. She saw him, too, and pushed Hawke away.

"Now, follow me, sire. Your carriage awaits."

He followed her, matching her determined march through the deep snow stride for stride, their boots making a great crunching sound. They made their way around the side of the station house to the rear, their angular shadows preceding them across the new-fallen snow. There in the moonlight, three white stallions stood abreast of each other, harnessed to a magnificent gold and blue sleigh. A troika. He hurried toward this apparition, having never seen a conveyance quite so marvelous in his life.

He ran his hand along the steaming, glistening flank of one the three enormous stallions. The restless horses were snorting great clouds of white steam from their flaring black nostrils and pawing the snow impatiently. As he approached the sleigh and ran his fingers over the bodywork, he could see that it was a dark blue decorated with shooting stars and comets, all the wonders of the heavens, carved into the wood and picked out in gold leaf.

"My God, Anastasia, what a lovely thing."

"Isn't it?" she said, climbing up into the sleigh. "It was a gift from Peter the Great to one of my more illustrious ancestors. Baron Sergei Korsakov gave Peter a billion rubles to help him defeat Louis XIV. Luckily for us, Peter won. As a reward, the Tsar also built for us the roof you're going to be sleeping under tonight."

Hawke laughed and slung his bag into the rear of the sleigh behind the leather-upholstered bench seat. The sleigh was smaller inside than he'd imagined, just room enough for two, filled with blankets of sable and mink. He climbed up and joined her inside, pulling a mink blanket over both of them.

"I'm fast," she warned him, taking up the four reins.

"Fast is good," Hawke said, watching her carefully and inspecting the unusual rig. He'd never seen a troika up close and was fascinated at the complicated arrangement of the horses. "Usually," he added, striving for nonchalance.

"Shall we go?" she asked him, smiling, flicking the reins lightly.

"Ever onward."

She spoke a few urgent words to her chargers, and they were off at breakneck speed, careening wildly through the trees and then racing down across the face of a broad, snow-covered meadow. At the bottom of the vast meadow, a narrow lane led off into the hills to the south. The tinkling sound of the many silver sleigh bells added to the magical quality of their journey, and Hawke was content to remain silent, sucking the cold air down into his lungs and watching the girl, the horses, and the white clouds scudding across the face of the fat yellow moon.

The center horse, between the wooden shafts, was clearly the lead. He was trotting. The two outside horses, with one rein apiece, were harnessed at slightly divergent angles so that all three animals were arranged like a fan. The horse on the far right was galloping furiously, while the one on the left was more coquettish. It was a style of coaching developed over many centuries, and it worked.

Hawke noticed she never used a whip but spoke to the three stallions, calling on each one continuously, urging them onward with a combination of flattery and invective.

"What are their names?" he asked her, leaning close so she could hear.

"Storm, Lightning, and Smoke. My favorite horses."

"Which is which?"

"That's my great galloping Storm on the right. Smoke does all the work in the center, and Lightning canters on the left. You! Storm! What are you looking at? Get on with you! Go!"

Presently, they came to a stop under a stand of birch trees at the top of a hill. Below them lay a small valley. There was a frozen lake, gleaming white, and standing along its banks was a magnificent palace, ablaze with light glowing from hundreds of windows. It was three stories of gold and grandeur, a mix of the best of Russian and European architecture, with galleries and flanking wings that stretched along the lakefront for at least 900 meters.

"My God, Anastasia," Hawke said, gazing down at it, his eyes wide with delight.

"What is it, darling?"

"Don't look now, but we're living in some kind of bloody fairy tale."

"I've been living in one since the afternoon I discovered a naked man sleeping on a beach. Might I tell you a great big secret?"

"Yes, you might."

"I might be falling in love. Not with you, of course. But with my life again," she said.

"Life's lousy in bed, darling. You'll need men for that."

She laughed, kissed his cheek, and, snapping the reins, said, "Storm! Are you awake? Home! Fly away! Fly!"

40

Salina, Kansas

All Beef Paddy liked to whistle while he worked. Now he was whistling one of his favorites, an oldie but goodie called "Be True to Your School." Beach Boys. After he'd finished cleaning up over at the Bailey household, he'd gone back to the little riverside park the next morning, where he kept his truck hidden in the bushes, then hiked through the woods to his deserted motel and caught some Z's. Must have slept six hours. He'd seen a couple of cruisers on the way, parked, uniforms having their morning coffee gabfest, and managed to avoid them.

Now he parked his white Happy Baker Shoppe truck, fitted with carefully counterfeited Kansas plates, in the Cottonwood Elementary School parking lot. He loaded up his dolly and hurried inside to make his delivery. Even though the entire school, like the parking lot, like the whole damn town, was completely empty by now, he had boxes and boxes of delicious doughnuts on his dolly.

Under the doughnuts, in the bottom of every box, was a little surprise. Just like Cracker Jacks, only much, much more surprising.

Paddy, still in his white Happy the Baker outfit, was not even slightly surprised to find one of the side doors to the school unlocked. Seemed like every door in town was open, half of the ones he'd tried, anyway. He was on his third elementary school and had only Central High School left to do before he, too, got out of town in a hurry. A busy baker is a happy baker. Busy, busy, busy.

Paddy had waited patiently all day, till the police had got everyone cleared out. Then he'd started driving around, making his doughnut deliveries. He'd been driving all night, all over town, lights out, of course. Office buildings, shopping malls, the town hall, the water works, you name it. It had been fun. He loved playing cat and mouse with the local cops. They were having a tough time, trying to do a murder investigation in the middle of an emergency evacuation. He'd counted on that, and he'd been right.

They had cruisers out patrolling the streets, mostly looking for stragglers, not coldblooded murderers, and Paddy had gotten really good at avoiding them. If he even saw headlights coming, he'd pull into a lot or just to the side of the road and slump down below the windows. He had his little snub-nose .38 handy in case anybody got nosy, but so far, nobody had.

Everybody had left town in pretty much of a hurry when, twelve hours ago, the bodies had been found. And the cell he'd left on Monie's body. Then the police had started cruising up and down the streets of Salina with loudspeakers blaring, giving the order to evacuate because of some unspecified threat to the town. He had his radio tuned to a local talk show. Rumors were flying. Some callers said it was a problem out at the fertilizer factory, some said it was a natural-gas problem, and a few even said it was bird flu. Everybody was busy packing up and getting the hell out of Dodge.

What nobody was saying was that it was terrorism. The police were mum on that subject. Besides, terrorism just didn't seem to be on Salina's radar, and you could see why. It was the most white-bread place Paddy had ever been to. Very few raisins in this batter. And the tallest building in town was, what, ten stories maybe, not exactly World Trade Center material. Who the hell would want to blow up Salina, take out a freaking Kmart? Puh-leeze, right?

These al-Qaeda creeps were crazy, you could tell the people of Salina thought, but they weren't crazy enough to have Salina, Kansas, high on their priority target list.

By now, the police were busy looking into the Arm of God and Tehran connection, Paddy thought, laughing to himself as he drove his bakery truck west. He cruised under Interstate 135 on West Magnolia, headed for the deserted parking lot of the Salina Municipal Airport. It looked sad and empty, the airport did, like a spot that could use a few doughnuts.

I-135, the interstate that ran north and south, and I-70, the one that ran east and west, had immediately turned into parking lots as 40,000-plus people tried to blow out of town at once. Now the interstates, too, were empty. Highway Patrol had shut them down, ten miles outside the city limits. All roads leading into town had been closed when the evacuation warning went out.

As he wheeled his dolly down the school's center hallway, rolling past all the empty classrooms, he liked the echo of his song off the linoleum tiles of the long, empty corridor. There were Christmas decorations everywhere, and he sort of got into the spirit. It was fun having an entire town all to yourself. Sort of like being invisible. He started whistling "Jingle Bell Rock," getting into it.

He entered the principal's office and saw that they'd all left their Wizard computers right on their desks, so no delivery there. He strolled next door to the science lab and saw that there were still a few computers at the workstations, but most of them seemed to have disappeared along with the kids. So, he placed a half-dozen doughnut boxes on the dissecting tables and moved on to the library, where he knew most of the computers would be — that is, if there were any left.

His deliveries complete, he headed back to the truck with an empty dolly. It was now just after five o'clock in the morning, and the sun was breaking over the little town of Salina. Paddy had been here, what, a week, staying at a Motel 6 on the outskirts of town, following the mayor around, scoping out her daily routine.

He'd also been watching the local news, keeping abreast of the situation so he could report in. Now that the country knew about what was going on, it was nonstop news on CNN and Fox. But they weren't letting any new crews inside the barricades surrounding the town, so all you were left with was talking heads who didn't know what the hell their heads were talking about.

He climbed up behind the wheel and cranked the engine. He was just pulling out of the lot, planning to hit the high school over on East Crawford Street, when the flashers lit up in his rearview, and he knew party time was over. He smiled, got the little snub-nose pistol out of the pocket in his baker's jacket, and stamped on the go pedal. No way he could outrun the local PD's Crown Vic, but he could get where he wanted to get to, at least. He didn't speed, just kept going, acting like he didn't know there was a squad car right on his ass, blinkers and sirens going.

"Pull over!" he heard from the loudspeaker. Pull over? Were they crazy? The whole town was going to go up in smoke in a nanosecond or so!

He hung a right on East Iron Street. It led all the way up a hill to a town park he'd staked out earlier. It was just some trees, a creek, and a baseball diamond, but it sat up high overlooking the little town, and he thought it would be a perfect place to bring his mission to an exciting conclusion. He slowed going up the hill, taking his time, watching the rosy dawn spread across the doomed village. The cops dropped back, content to follow him up the hill, see what the hell Happy the Baker was up to. They were probably running his plates, too. Which was good. They'd see the plates belonged on a 1973 Chevy truck, just like the one he was driving. The devil was in the details.

It was five-thirty a.m.

The deadline his guys in Iran had put in the cell phone he'd left at the mayor's house was six a.m. Central Standard Time. Half an hour. Plenty of time to enjoy the moment.

He crested the hill and drove under the little arch that said "Hickory Hill Park," his hideout. He wound around a little, cops right behind him, until he came to the spot he'd chosen that first evening, before he started stalking the mayor and her family. It was what they called a scenic overlook, and he parked right out at the edge of the little lot there. Then he killed the motor, slipped the snub-bie into his pocket, and sat there waiting for the fuzz to come bust him.

Come to Papa, boys.

41

He watched the cops exit the cruiser in his rearview. They got out with their guns drawn, approaching him from the rear on either side of the truck. When the guy on his side was abreast of the driver's window, he rolled it down, gave the young cop a big smile, and said, "Was I going too fast?"

"Sir, I'd like your driver's license and registration, please."

"Absolutely, officer," Paddy said, handing him the fake license and registration papers.

"Your real name is Happy? That right?"

"Yessir. Named after my old man. He was Happy, too."

"Sir," the cop said, looking from his license photo to him and back again, "are you aware that this town is under an evacuation order?"

"I was wondering where the hell everyone went. Evacuation, huh? What's going on?"

"How did you get this vehicle past the police barricades, sir?"

"Weren't any barricades up when I arrived."

"And when was that?"

"Few days ago."

"And in the meantime?"

"You mean since I arrived?"

"Correct."

"I've been asleep."

"You've been asleep for three days?"

"Correct."

"Where?"

"At the Motel 6. Real nice place."

"Sir, no one sleeps for three whole days."

"I do. I get these dang migraines. Once I get 'em, I just pop a bunch of Dalmane pills and nod on out. If I wake up, I take another handful. *Wham,* I'm out like a light. Hell, I just woke up a few hours ago."

"And what exactly are you doing?"

"Delivering doughnuts."

"To an empty town?"

"Well, see, here's my thinking on that. Are you familiar with the franchise system?"

"Franchise system."

"Yeah. My thought is this. I'm a baker. I bake the best damn doughnuts west of the Mississippi. And my business plan is to take my product direct to the consumer. I've delivered product in Junction City, Wichita, hell, all the way to Topeka. Don't charge a nickel. I just deliver the boxes and let folks discover them for themselves. Now, I've got my Web-site address right on top of every box. People eat them, like them, and want more. That's my strategy. Right now, I'm a one-man distribution system. But pretty soon, hell, folks are going to be knocking my door down. I'm going to open up a string of Happy Baker Doughnut Shoppes from here to Canada."

"They do smell pretty darn good back there."

"You see? That's just what I'm saying! And you know what? They taste better than they smell. I've got some fresh glazed back there, you and your partner want to try a couple."

"Hey, Gene, you want a warm doughnut?" the young cop said to his older, and much fatter, partner.

"Damn right I do, Andy," Gene said. "You can smell them things a mile away."

"There you go," Paddy said with a smile. "Let me go around and open up the truck. We'll have us a nice hot breakfast up here on the hill. I got a thermos of steaming black New Orleans French Quarter coffee back there, too."

"Well, I guess we can do that. Not much else we can do. Andy, go back and get on the radio, will you? Tell them we've got a gentleman up here needs assistance, and we'll be standing by in case, you know, anything happens."

Happy climbed out and opened up the

back. He slid the loading platform out and opened up a box of glazed, a box of cream-filled, and a box of jelly.

The two cops dug in, and while they did, he poured all three of them steaming cups of black coffee.

"Dang!" Andy said, polishing off a glazed in two bites. "That is one hell of a doughnut."

"You feel happy, Andy?"

"I sure do."

"Good. 'Cause that's my new advertising slogan. 'Eat Happy.' You like it?"

"Love it. Can I have another one of the cream-filled?"

Ten minutes later, they were all sitting on the platform, talking football, whether or not the Chiefs would make the playoffs, and, of course, the war on terror. Andy said he thought the whole evacuation thing was a crock. Something dreamed up to scare ordinary Americans and make a laughingstock out of a whole town. That was the town consensus, he said.

"Yeah?" Paddy said. "Well, maybe you're right. Will you excuse me a sec? I got to get my smokes. Call me crazy. I can't drink my morning coffee without my smokes."

"Go ahead. We'll hold down the fort back here. See if the town blows up," the young cop, Andy, said.

"Yeah," Gene said. "I can hardly wait. What a damn deal we got here. If she blows, we're screwed. If she doesn't, we're a national joke."

It was five-fifty-five a.m. when Paddy unlocked the glove compartment and took out the rectangular black plastic box that had been sent from Moscow, through Iran, and delivered to him by courier in Miami a week ago today. It represented the very latest in remote-detonation technology. Every Zeta machine built had a GPS broadcast device built in, as well as the eight ounces of putty-like explosive called Hexagon. The machines also broadcast an ID number, much like the squawk system used by aircraft. So you always knew which machines were where before you decided to arm them or detonate them.

The box Paddy held in his hand contained dual microprocessors in addition to the radio-signal command that would cause the Zetas to explode. The system was currently preprogrammed to detonate only those devices now inside the city limits of Salina, Kansas.

"Hey, Happy," Andy called, "c'mon back. You're going to miss her if she goes."

"Yeah, right," Gene said, laughing, "Miss the whole shebang. The whole damn shooting match."

It was five-fifty-nine a.m., coming up on six a.m.

"I won't miss it, Andy. I can't find my damn smokes, that's all. You got any?"

"Hell, no. Cops can't smoke for insurance

reasons. Besides, my wife'd up and kill me she thought I was puffing on them cancer sticks. Why, she'd —"

Paddy was walking back toward the rear of the truck with his finger on the button, eyes glued to the red digital display that was spinning down to zero.

Now.

You could feel the ground shaking, even up here on Hickory Hill. The three men stood and stared down in wonder at the little town as it exploded. It was like watching a movie of a building coming down, only it was all of the buildings, all of the neighborhoods, and they were all coming down at once, sending a huge cloud of smoke rolling skyward as the noise and sheer force of the blast came rolling up the hill and rocked the truck, spilling the coffee from all three cups and sending the doughnut boxes flying off the back of the truck.

"Holy shit!" Andy screamed, walking out to the edge of the overlook. "They freakin' did it! The goddamn A-rabs blew up our whole goddamn town!"

Fires broke out everywhere. Power lines sparked, ignited, and came down, writhing like angry snakes in the streets. Underground gas lines exploded up through asphalt intersections, the power station was sparking into yet another inferno, and every last filling station in town had turned into a brilliant fireball that climbed into the dawn sky and lit up what used to be Salina like the Fourth of July fireworks every summer up at Hickory Hill.

Paddy had his snubbie out, was looking down the barrel at the backs of the two Kansas policemen. He could easily put a bullet in each of them, shots to the back of the head, walk away. He raised the pistol, put a pound of pressure on the trigger . . . and then changed his mind.

Having admired his work from afar, Paddy climbed up into his truck and stuck the key into the ignition. He had a long way to go and a short time to get there. He was catching the next thing smoking out of Topeka to Miami. There was a lot to be done before *Pushkin* lifted off in a matter of hours.

He left Officers Andy and Gene standing there at the edge of the bluff, looking down at what was left of the town they'd both grown up in, tears already drying on their cheeks.

Happy had mixed emotions about sparing the lives of Officers Andy and Gene of Salina PD. But, but, but. He was a professional. He didn't kill people for fun. Only for money. Or for a good reason. And he could see no good reason to off these two guys. If the two cops identified a crazy baker delivering doughnuts to a deserted town, so what? He'd be long gone before anyone could tie him to the

514

multiple explosions that had flattened the place. And he seriously doubted anybody ever would.

Anyway, by the time anybody had a clue what had blown Salina to smithereens, the world would be an entirely different place. A lot of America might look like the blackened ruins smoldering at the bottom of the hill. And Happy? Hell, he'd be sailing the skies above the blue Atlantic, enjoying the many pleasures of the floating pussy palace on what promised to be a very interesting voyage to Stockholm.

The Happy Baker, his mission accomplished, silently rolled away, gone in a flash.

Taking care of business, baby.

TCB.

42

Miami

It was gone.

The whole damn town, just flat gone.

Standing beneath one of the giant monitors mounted on a granite lobby wall, Stokely and Fancha, along with everybody else, were watching CNN images of a small Kansas town that no longer existed. Rumors were flying.

The buzz inside the teeming *Miami Herald* lobby was this, it was that; it was al-Qaeda, it was Hezbollah, no, it was the Iranians, some kind of small nuke, a dirty bomb, hell, no, it was simply a main gas line under the town that had blown, a fertilizer factory, some even theorized a fertilizer bomb, set off by some home-grown disciples of Timothy McVeigh, antigovernment militia still simmering over Waco and Ruby Ridge.

The real truth was, nobody knew what the hell had happened to Salina, Kansas. Especially not the talking heads on CNN, in

Stoke's opinion, anyway. Anybody who did know, wasn't talking to the media.

On the oversized monitors throughout the lobby, the all-too-familiar banner "Breaking News" was running beneath devastating live pictures of what used to be the little town of Salina, Kansas, population 42,000. Salina was now a charred, smoking ruin, with nothing standing but a few brick chimneys and a blackened water tower.

"What's this all about, Stokely?" Fancha asked, a worried frown on her face. "Terrorists?"

"I don't know, baby. Could be terrorists. Maybe just a chemical plant or an underground natural-gas main. Could be anything. But we've got to be getting aboard, anyway. We'll get more scoop soon as we're settled in our stateroom."

"A whole town? Just gone?" she said, staring at the monitor. "Unbelievable."

"Yeah, but the town was completely evacuated before, right? So somebody knows something, and whatever it is, they ain't saying yet."

One thing Stokely Jones did know for sure: this might turn out to be very, very bad news. For America. For the whole damn world. Say it wasn't a simple accident, gas main or whatever. Some terror group takes out an entire American town? That's a message, no matter who sent it. But he'd cleared this trip

517

with Brock, check out Tsar and besides, he'd promised Fancha he'd accompany her, and a promise was a promise.

He gave her waist a squeeze.

"Let's go, baby, this is going to be fun."

She was nervous as a cat about this trip, and she was counting on him, big time. Hell, he'd been smiling since the second he woke up that morning, making breakfast, making bad jokes, trying hard all day to keep things upbeat. He took her elbow and steered her toward the short lines waiting at the elevators to the rooftop. They were a little late, and most of the passengers were already on-board.

"You believe all the famous faces we're rubbing elbows with?" he said.

"You don't rub elbows with faces, Stokely."

"You don't?"

"Faces don't have elbows. People have elbows."

"True enough."

Still, the lobby was celebrity-packed, filled to overflowing with the rich and famous and their entourages, all of the remaining people who would shortly be boarding the giant airship *Pushkin* for her maiden voyage to Stockholm and the Nobel awards ceremony four days from now.

"You excited, sugar?" he asked her, leaning down to whisper in her ear.

"Now that you're coming, I am. I only feel

safe when you're next to me, Stoke. I need you by my side. That's the Lord's truth."

"I'm there for you, baby, you know that."

"What about you, Stoke? Aren't you even a little excited?"

"Honey, you know me. I only got two emotions. Hungry and horny. You see me without an erection, quick, make me a sandwich. Hey, look. You see who I see coming through the door? The Marlboro Man himself."

The vice president of the United States, a tall, rugged-looking rancher who hailed from the western slope of the Colorado Rockies, was entering the lobby. Tom McCloskey had come to see his wife, Bonnie, off. The veep was originally supposed to go on the voyage himself, but something had come up at the last minute. Stoke had been shaving early that morning when he'd heard on the radio that the vice president's wife would now be traveling alone.

Now Stoke figured it was maybe this disaster in Kansas that was keeping McCloskey close to home. Washington probably knew more than they were saying? Security was tight, crew-cut guys talking into their sleeves everywhere. Hell, Stoke had never seen so many Secret Service personnel in one room in his life. "M&M is in the lobby, moving to the elevator bank," he heard an agent say. M&M, Stoke knew, was the Secret Service call sign for McCloskey. It was based on a moniker the agents had given McCloskey when he first arrived at the White House, Marlboro Man.

Of course, any number of Washington types, senators and their wives, were on the trip. Congressmen, God knows who all, but players, mostly. He saw the governator of California and his pretty Kennedy wife, big-time business magnates like Michael Eisner and that Apple guy, Steve Jobs, people like that. And there were Hollywood people, of course, big-time producers and a few movie stars, a few he even recognized.

Plus, you had all the geeks and brainiacs. The Nobel Prize winners and nominees from around the world and their families. A lot of former Nobel laureates had been invited, too, according to the fancy formal invitation Fan-cha had received at her home on Low Key. Stoke had actually read it. This trip would be the biggest congregation of Nobel laureates ever assembled.

You could understand the excited buzz in the air. Hell, you had media everywhere, celebs mixing it up with geniuses, people thinking and acting as if they were part of history. And they were. The first ocean cross-ing of the world's biggest airship, the largest vessel to ever cross the Atlantic. Kinda like the maiden voyage of the *Titanic,* back in the day, Stoke was thinking, but he quickly shoved that bad thought aside.

They'd finally made it to the front of the line, next ones to board the elevator. There were monitors on the walls here, too, some kind of a press conference going on. Stoke ignored the hubbub and listened carefully, but there still didn't seem to be much new information.

Clearly, nobody, including the state trooper captain in Kansas, had a clue yet to what had happened. He was now holding forth at a podium on a hill overlooking the town.

"Stoke, did you remember to pack your —"

"Hush a second, baby, I want to hear this."

"Sir, first question," a young female reporter said. "How's the mayor doing? We hear she's suddenly gone into seclusion."

"That's correct. Mayor Bailey was taken violently ill sometime during the night. She's at an undisclosed location with her family now, and they have asked that the media please respect their privacy."

"Where are they, sir?"

"I'm afraid I'm not at liberty to say."

"No truth to the rumor that there was foul play involved? That her disappearance is somehow tied to all this?"

"None at all."

"Sir, moving on from the mayor, how long ago did you get the order to evacuate?" an NBC talking head asked.

"The first call came in at four o'clock this morning, Central time."

"Who made that call, sir?" another reporter asked.

"That would be the governor. The second call came direct from FBI headquarters in Washington, D.C."

"And what did the FBI tell you?"

"To evacuate the town immediately."

"Why?"

"There was a threat."

"From whom?"

"Didn't say. Unspecified. But credible, that's what they said. Credible."

"Al-Qaeda?"

"Like I say, unspecified."

"And you were able to evacuate everyone in time?"

"Yessir, we were. Salina PD, working with my folks, did an outstanding job. I've got the Salina police chief arriving here in about twenty minutes, and a couple of his officers. They were the last ones patrolling inside the town before she blew. They'd be happy to answer —"

The elevator doors slid open, and Stoke and Fancha moved quickly to the rear. Stoke remembered that it opened at the back when it reached the roof. When it did, he and Fancha stepped out into the brilliant Miami sunshine and looked up at the moored airship, her gleaming hull strung with red, white, and blue bunting. Stoke didn't say anything, but he thought the stars and stripes sort of clashed with the big red Russian stars painted on the ship's tail sections.

There were velvet ropes on either side of the red carpet leading to the moving stairs at the stern of the ship, lots of cameras pointing and clicking as he and Fancha walked by. Not clicking at him, at Fancha.

Ten minutes later, a white-coated steward was showing them their stateroom on the promenade deck, portside. It was a beautiful room, paneled in walnut, with a king-size bed and a sofa, table, and chairs sitting under three big opening portholes flooded with light and blue sky. On the coffee table was a huge arrangement of white flowers with a little envelope on a plastic pitchfork. Also a silver bucket with a bottle of Roederer Cristal champagne on ice. Hollywood, Stoke thought. Had to be, right?

He handed the steward a twenty and asked where the TV was. The young fellow picked up a remote from the bedside table and hit a button, and an oil painting over the dresser slid up into the ceiling revealing a flat-screen Toshiba.

The steward bowed, said something in Russian, and left. Fancha, who seemed happy enough with their room and her flowers, began unpacking, and Stoke sat on the edge of the bed, figuring out the remote. Finally, he got Fox News, live from Salina, breaking news. News was always breaking, Stoke thought. Problem was, there was nobody left on the planet smart enough to fix it.

The state trooper had turned it over to the police chief, who seemed to be wrapping up his remarks. Stoke was sorry he'd missed the chief's remarks. This was a big story, and he was about to be completely out of the loop for the next four days. He wanted to know what the hell was going on.

The chief was saying, "Thank you, and now I'd like to turn it over to two of my finest young officers. These two young fellas standing behind me were the last two on patrol inside the city. They'd be happy to take your questions. This is Officer Andy Sisko, and Patrolman Gene Southey. Officers?"

Stoke saw two uniformed patrolmen, clean-cut Midwest guys, step up to the podium, both looking a little nervous about all the cameras, being on national television.

"Officer Sisko, you were the last man to leave Salina?" a reporter called out.

"Yessir, I was. Me and Officer Southey were assigned to the last sweep."

"You're certain the town was completely evacuated? There were no remaining civilians?"

"Well, that's right. Our fellow officers and the staties did a fine job. They made sure they got everybody out. Everybody."

"Dogs and cats?"

"Very difficult. Most people took their pets, if they could find them. They left in pretty much of a hurry. So I'm sure some stray animals got left."

"Officer Southey, even when a hurricane is bearing down on a town, we saw this in Key West last year, you still get a large number of people refusing to leave their homes. You didn't see any of that in Salina?"

"No, sir, we did not. Folks here were real cooperative. Everybody just loaded up and vamoosed. We did run across one fella, though. He was still out there on the street, but we got him out in time, too."

"Someone who'd refused to leave his home?"

"No, sir, he was making deliveries."

"Deliveries? To a deserted town? What was he delivering?"

"Doughnuts. Bakery goods. He had a truck full."

Stoke leaned forward on the edge of the bed, turning up the volume with the remote.

"You mean you had someone delivering doughnuts in an empty town? Under an emergency evacuation order?"

"Yessir. He'd slept through all the warnings is what he told us. Didn't know anything at all about any warnings, any evacuation. Just going about his business."

"Do you have his name?"

"Sure do. His name was Happy. Happy the

Baker. Nice fella. Gave us breakfast on his truck right about here where I'm standing now. My partner and I had coffee and doughnuts with him right before she blew."

Stoke's jaw dropped, and, eyes riveted to the screen, he said to Fancha, "Happy the Baker, baby. That big guy who delivered the cake at the birthday blast here in Miami."

But Fancha was already in the head with the door closed, changing her outfit. Didn't hear him.

Stoke's cell phone vibrated in his pocket.

"Hello?" he said, flicking it open.

It was Harry Brock. Calling from Moscow, where it had to be the middle of the night.

"Stokely, you watching this? Television? CNN?"

"Yeah, Harry, I'm watching. Happy the Baker."

"Damn right, our old pal Happy the Baker from the birthday party in the Grove. Jesus Henry Christ. Happy the freaking bomb baker. He blew up that town, Stoke. That's all there is to it. Why else would he be there?"

"Why the hell does he blow up a whole town?"

"Good question. How soon can you get out there?"

"To Salina?"

"Of course, Salina. You're the only one on the planet who knows this guy on sight. Knows what he looks like, talks like. I need

526

you out there now, Stoke. Is there a problem?"

"I'm onboard the *Pushkin,* about to take
off. Check out this Tsar operation on the airship going to Stockholm. With Fancha. I told
you about it. She wants me —"

"Stoke, listen carefully. Ever since the party,
I've been looking hard at your boy Happy.
He is a Russian-American. A made *mafiya*
assassin from Brooklyn. His real name is
Paddy Strelnikov. He's undercover KGB, is
what they're saying at Langley. The bombing
of Salina was intended to look like an Iranian
operation. A group calling itself Arm of God.
But it's not Iranian, damn it, that doesn't
make any sense. The ayatollahs are scared
shitless of the U.S. right now. So, maybe it
really is a goddamn KGB operation. Fucking
Russians, I wouldn't put it past them these
days. Anyway, look, I want you to get out
there and find Happy's fat ass or find out
where he went. Find him, and bring him in.
The Russians might be making some kind of
move, Stoke, a big move. This might be part
of it. That's all I can tell you now, okay?"

"I'm on my way."

"Get this guy, Stoke. He's critical. One
more thing. Before he blew up the town, he
murdered the mayor and her family in their
beds. Husband. Two little kids. Left a cell
phone with a phony Arabic message on one
of the corpses. That information has not been

released to local law enforcement."

"Christ," Stoke said.

"You're going?"

"I'm gone."

The phone went dead in his hand just as Fancha opened the door to the head. She'd changed into a beautiful turquoise skirt and blouse. She'd never looked prettier. That smile, the one he loved, the one that meant she was happy. She spun around, and her skirt flared out like a ballerina's.

"Hey, baby, why isn't that champagne opened yet? This girl is thirsty."

"Oh, yeah. I should have opened that. Sorry."

"Stokely, honey, you don't look so good. Is something wrong?"

"Yes, baby. Something is wrong."

"How wrong?"

"Really wrong. Bad wrong."

"You're not going with me."

"No, honey, I'm not. I can't."

She turned around and went back inside the bathroom and closed the door. Didn't slam it. Just closed it. And locked it.

Stoke picked up his unpacked suitcase and rapped softly on the bathroom door.

"Fancha? I'm sorry, baby. Let me explain."

No response. He pressed his forehead against the door and spoke softly.

"Baby? I'm so sorry. Let me just kiss you good-bye. Okay? Please."

Nothing.

"It's business, honey. National security. What am I supposed to do?"

He could hear her in there, sobbing.

He left the stateroom without another word, pulling the door closed behind him, seriously disgruntled.

War isn't hell, he thought to himself, charging angrily down the corridor to the airship's aft elevators.

Hell, no.

Sometimes it was much, much worse.

43

Korsakov's winter palace was plainly visible now, countless lighted windows winking through the dark, snow-laden forests. The blisteringly fast troika flew across an arched wooden bridge spanning the frozen river. The sleigh went airborne for a long moment at the top, and Hawke found the speed, the fierce cold, the ringing sleigh bells, and the snow-spangled forests sparkling in the starlight exhilarating.

He glanced at Anastasia, sliding his cold hand under the fur throw and placing it on her warm thigh. She slid closer to him, never taking her eyes off the hindquarters of the three flying horses. She watched their every movement, like a pilot casting her eye over her instrument panel, and whispered corrections as they flew over the landscape at impossible speeds. Hawke was mesmerized by her art, her precise skills at something he'd never known existed.

"How much of this enchanted forest is Korsakov property?" Hawke asked. For the last half-hour or so, there had been endless miles of dry-stacked stone walls and small cottages in neatly fenced fields. Now a high yellow wall lined the left side of the snowy lane.

Asia laughed. "Alex, you were on Korsakov land two hours before your train arrived at Tvas station."

"Ah. Sizable holdings."

She cast a quick smile in reply and flicked the reins.

"Not really. We used to control all of Siberia — Storm! What's gotten into you? Pay attention! Lightning, get along with you! Turn! Turn! We're home at last!"

Nothing had prepared Hawke for the sheer grandeur of the Korsakov winter palace.

The troika suddenly careened off the snowbound country road and raced under a great arch of stone and wrought iron, the entrance a heavily filigreed black arch surmounted by golden two-headed eagles. The horses, now in sight of their stables, surged ahead beneath the snow-packed *allée* of trees leading to the palace.

The sense of power and opulence only grew as they got closer. It seemed too vast to be practicable as any kind of home. Hawke couldn't even guess at how many rooms, but it dwarfed a European's notion of parliaments and museums. And every window was ablaze with light.

"A party?" Hawke asked. "Just for me?"

"A dinner and concert," Anastasia said. "Five hundred guests."

"Only five hundred? Cozy."

"Half of Moscow is here."

"Really? Which half?"

"The half that counts. The half holding the reins of power. My father means something to this country, Alex. He stands for the New Russia. Strong, powerful, fearless. They revere him here, Alex. He's like a — a god. Like a —"

"Tsar?"

"That's not as far-fetched as you might think."

Hawke looked at her a moment and decided to let that one pass. "Are you as hungry as I am? Near starvation?"

"We're too late for the Christmas feast, but we can enjoy some of the concert, perhaps. And no, the party is definitely not for you. We're celebrating Papa's Nobel award and the coming debut of his new symphony."

The sleigh careened into a large snowy courtyard, and Anastasia reined in her three chargers. The trio swerved to a stop at the foot of a wide set of steps, the runners throwing up a great shower of glistening snow. A host of liveried footmen instantly surrounded them, helping both Anastasia and Hawke to step down from the ice-encrusted sleigh and whisking Hawke's luggage away. Considering its contents, he would have preferred to carry it himself, but it was too late.

Hawke stood for a moment, stomping his boots on the hard-packed snow, trying to get some feeling back into his feet.

Anastasia stood stroking Storm's mane as grooms covered the other two horses with blankets and led them away to the stables. She was quietly giving orders to a tall bearded fellow, obviously the man in charge. Once they were alone again, mounting the broad stone staircase to the main entrance, she whispered, "I instructed Anatoly to put you in the Delft Suite on the third floor. It adjoins my own rooms with a connecting door. I hope you don't find that too forward of me."

"Forward, certainly, but perhaps not too forward."

She took his hand and hurried him up the steps. Crimson-uniformed servants with gold braid and bright brass buttons swung the double doors open wide. Hawke saw a massive illuminated Christmas tree standing at the center of the gilded and white-marbled entrance hall. The ceiling vaulted four stories above it, upheld by fluted columns the size of grain silos. Two curving marble staircases led to the second and third stories, where piano music tinkled, mixed with the muted laughter of hundreds of guests.

Hawke entered his own room and found it surprisingly and refreshingly small. The walls were entirely covered in blue and white Dutch tiles. Peter the Great, Hawke knew, had been a huge admirer of all things Dutch. Hawke's room was, so Anastasia had informed him, the very room in which Tsar Peter slept whenever he was a guest of the Korsakovs. A cozy fire had been lit in the tiled Dutch oven in the corner. He removed his ice-coated black greatcoat and quickly shed all of his sour-smelling travel attire, washed himself with hot water from a bedside jug, and dressed.

He'd found a set of perfectly tailored evening clothes laid out on his four-poster bed, and to his amazement, the shirt, trousers, and waistcoat, everything, fit perfectly. Nestled at the foot of the bed was a pair of black velvet evening slippers with the Korsakov coat of arms embroidered in gold thread. Unsurprisingly, they fit.

He saw his Gladstone bag on a settee in a darkened corner. He crossed the room and checked to see that the combination locks were intact and that the bag containing his weapons had not been tampered with. It seemed that it had not; at least, the number combination he always left the two locks set at had not been altered: 222, February 22, his late parents' anniversary date.

He was, he assumed, an honored guest of this great household. But then again, this was still Russia.

Suddenly bone tired, he kicked off the slippers and stretched out fully dressed on the vast down-filled bed. The flickering firelight cast cartoon shadows on the underside of the bed's canopy. It had been a long, uncomfortable voyage from Bermuda, and he was overcome by an overpowering desire to sleep here, now, submerged in all this sumptuous featherbed comfort.

At some point, Anastasia rapped on his door loudly enough to wake him. She was wearing a deeply low-cut gown of midnight-blue silk, her hair in ribbons and her throat wreathed in sparkling diamonds. The deliciously warm scent of Dior wafting up from her pale white bosom was almost overpowering.

"I thought I'd lost you," she said.

"Mmm," he said, unable to think of a real word.

He thought perhaps he'd slept a few minutes. A glance at his watch showed he'd been out cold for more than an hour.

"Comfortable?" she asked, stepping inside and taking him into her arms.

"Mmm. Very."

"White tie becomes you, Alexander. You should wear it more often."

He kissed her upturned lips, surprised at their warmth and softness. He pulled her to him, crushing her half-exposed bosom against his chest, inhaling the sweetness of her hair, her skin.

"Comfortable except for the bed," he said, whispering into her ear. "Mattress is a bit firm for my taste. I'd like to try yours."

"Down, boy," she said, feeling his erection hard against her thighs. "We have to put in an appearance. I want you to meet my father tonight. I think he's expecting it. And my brothers are dying to meet you. Come along, now, Alex. Don't tarry."

He followed her down the grand gilded staircase and found himself moving in Anastasia's wake from one glittering room and mirrored gallery to another. They were in search of her two younger brothers, Sergei and Maxim. The sounds of stringed and percussion instruments, clarinets, and French horns, Count Korsakov's new symphony, could be heard throughout the rooms they passed through. The twins, she told Alex, were not fond of symphonic music. They liked hard Russian rock, a group called the Apples, on their iPods. *Nashe,* they called this music. It meant "ours." Western rock was definitely over in the New Russia. Western everything was over.

"They could well be playing in here," she said.

"Playing? How old are they?"

"Twelve. Twins, you see."

"And their mother? Your mother?"

"She died in childbirth. The boys barely made it. We were lucky they survived."

"I'm so sorry, Asia. I'd no idea."

They entered the great Hall, where the ceremonial feast clearly had just taken place. Guests and servants had long since departed, but the enormous baroque room was still full of wonders. The barrel-vaulted hall was stunning in its abundance of mirrors and glittering gold. An unbounded sea of mirrors in gilded frames were reflected in other mirrors, creating a magical, endless space in which hundreds of wax candles still burning in the spaces between the windows and the mirrors gleamed.

"Perhaps they've escaped to the kitchens," Anastasia said. "Wait here for a moment, and I'll go and fetch them."

Hawke paused at the table, picking up a spotless crystal goblet and deciding to fill it with blood-red wine from one of the many silver carafes. He sipped and found it delicious. So, too, was the leg of roast duck he removed from a half-eaten carcass and began to gnaw at ravenously.

The table, which stretched to shadowy infinity down the hall, had not been completely cleared. The white linen tablecloths were hung with ribbons of many colors and glorious rosettes. In the center of the table towered a massive construction resplendent with symbolic sculptures, monograms and crowns of various ancient courts of Europe.

The massive carved silver candelabras, which marched down the table into the shadows, were all still blazing with candles. Around the bases were woven Christmas holly and berries, artificial flowers made of red silk. Fresh flowers covered the branches of tiny potted trees or were woven into garlands that hung above miniature fountains, the waters still playing right there on the table.

Candlelight gleamed, reflected in the gold and silver tableware and on the great tureens, whose lids took the shapes of boars' heads, stags, or pheasants. This magnificent table, Hawke decided, was itself a work of art. And perhaps a political statement as well. Such grandeur would surely reignite for Count Korsakov's guests the dreams and glories of an ancient Russia that no longer existed but had once reigned triumphant.

This was the table, Hawke decided, not of a mere billionaire nor of a wizard, a genius of science, art, and music.

This was the table of a Tsar.

Did Count Korsakov dream of Tsardom? Is that what Anastasia had been trying to tell him in the sleigh? The restoration of the Tsars was not wildly implausible, Hawke knew. There was vast nostalgia in the country for the power and glory that the times of the Tsars represented.

The last of the Tsars, the Romanovs, were feeble, weak, and wholly incapable of ruling this huge country. But the Korsakovs, based on what he knew and had seen, were clearly powerful enough to do just about anything they damn well pleased.

C had been correct, he mused. He had needed to come here, needed to see all of this for himself. He could sense enormous changes coming in this country, a seismic shift in the balance of —

"Look out!" he heard Anastasia shout.

Something, some fat silver missile, was headed directly for his head.

He ducked and watched the thing go by. It was a flying model of an airship. About three feet long, it had Nazi swastikas emblazoned on the tail, and the red lights on the fuselage were blinking. You could even hear the faint whirr of its multiple propellers as it sailed away.

"What the hell?" Hawke said.

"It's a race," Anastasia said, suddenly at his side. "Watch out, Hawke, here comes the *Hindenburg.*"

Now a second radio-controlled miniature airship came weaving its way between two of the flaming candelabras, the ill-fated zeppelin in hot pursuit of ZR-1, the German airship that had caused such destruction in London.

"Sergei, Maxim, please land your craft and come down and introduce yourselves to Alexander Hawke. He's our guest, so be polite."

"Where the hell are they?" Hawke asked, peering into the gloom. He couldn't see another soul in the cavernous candlelit room.

"Up there," Anastasia said, pointing to a balcony high above them. It was clearly where the choir and the dinner musicians had entertained during dinner.

Two identical boys leaned over the railing and waved down at Hawke. They were both good-looking, and both had shoulder-length blond hair.

"How do you do, sir?" the twins said in unison and in very good English. "Sorry, we're racing!" one added.

"Very well, indeed," Hawke called up to them. "Don't mind me. Keep racing. Who's winning?"

"The *Hindenburg*," one excited boy said. "She's about to lap ZR-1! For the third time," he added, laughing.

Hawke laughed, too, and said, "Come on, now, ZR-1, don't humiliate yourself!"

Anastasia took his arm, saying, "I've located Father by telephone. He's finished his concert, sadly, but is having brandy in his study. He's most anxious to meet you."

And off they went.

44

"Lord Alexander Hawke," Count Ivan Korsakov said, striding across the Persian carpet, his smile as warm and radiant as the fire in the hearth. "I can't tell you how delighted I am to meet you. My daughter has told me so much about you, I feel we've known each other for years."

"Count Korsakov," Hawke said, shaking the man's hand. "The reverse is also true, sir. I'm honored. Most kind of you to invite me."

"Has Anastasia shown you around? The two-ruble tour?"

"I haven't had time, Papa," she said, moving to her father and putting her arm around his waist. "We're so sorry to have missed your concert."

He glanced lovingly at her, and Hawke had a split second to appraise the man. Impossibly good-looking, mid-fifties, the light in his pale blue eyes otherworldly. In this man, the blood of the Golden Horde, the Tatar and the Boyar had mixed to good effect. He was broad-shouldered, tall, and lean, with shoulder-length snow-white hair. He was elegantly dressed for the evening in a nineteenth-century suit of dark blue velvet, with breeches and white stockings. His command of English was flawless, the Russian accent lightly applied.

"Were you brilliant at the keyboard, Papa? Incandescent?"

Korsakov kissed Anastasia's brow. "I may have missed one or two complete passages, I suppose, but the audience feigned appreciation throughout. Brevity being the soul of after-dinner concertos, eh, Lord Hawke?"

"Alex will do, please, sir, if you don't mind. I don't use the title."

"Those who stand on ceremony seldom deserve the platform."

"Well said, Count Korsakov," Hawke said, with a slight nod of the head.

"All right, Alex, what can I get you to drink?"

"Rum would be lovely. Gosling's if you have it."

"Gosling's, of course. Spoken like a true Bermudian."

He went to the drinks table, poured Hawke a beaker of black rum, and filled his own snifter with brandy from a heavy crystal decanter. "And you, my dear girl?" he asked his daughter.

"Just water, please. I'm not staying. I'll let

you two rivals for my affection battle it out in private. And may the best man win." Hawke tried to smile at his lover's father but could not catch his eye.

Hawke had spied a large painting over the mantel and wandered over to inspect it. It was similar to the one in Bermuda, same subject, but the setting was a fox hunt. Count Korsakov sat astride a splendid mount, dressed in a pink jacket, surrounded by his baying hounds. He squinted at the signature in the lower right corner and saw Anastasia's distinctive swirling initials.

He thought of his own portrait, now apparently complete, which he'd not been allowed to set eyes on. No mystery there, he thought. He'd not be astride a great steed or dressed for the hunt or battle or anything else, for that matter. Bloody hell, what had he got himself into?

She came gliding up behind him, whispering, "Don't stay up past my bedtime," into his ear before turning to her father and saying, "Papa, I will see you at our usual breakfast. Perhaps we'll go riding afterward and let Mr. Hawke sleep. He's been on a tiresome journey, poor man."

"Lovely. Sleep well, dear."

She blew him a kiss, then pulled the ornate doors closed behind her.

Korsakov had taken one of the two leather armchairs on either side of the cavernous fireplace, and Hawke took the other, stretching his feet out toward the crackling logs.

The count raised his glass and said, "For your health, sir!"

"And yours, sir."

They sipped in silence for a moment, and then Korsakov said, "I owe you an apology, Alex."

"Really? What on earth for?"

"When I first learned you were seeing my daughter on Bermuda, I was deeply concerned. I'm very protective of her. She's been badly hurt in the past, and I won't let that happen again. I'm afraid I had you followed."

"The Disciples of Judah are in your employ?" Hawke said mildly.

"For many years, yes. When I first came to Bermuda, many of the Jamaican immigrants worked on my banana plantation. Hardworking, loyal, very religious. Especially old Sam Coale, who was my tally man for decades. He, his children, and a few others eventually joined my private security force. Of late, they have become problematic. There were rumors of drug dealing, arrests, other scandalous misdeeds. You are no doubt aware of the sad fate of Hoodoo, a trusted employee and friend of long standing."

"I am."

"I've had Sam Coale and his two sons arrested for his murder and incarcerated in Casemates Prison. My friends in the local constabulary are building a strong case against them. The other inhabitants of Nonsuch Island, primarily rabble, have all been evicted. I consider the case closed. But again, I apologize for any inconvenience I may have caused you in the past."

"Inconvenience? Only if one counts kidnapping, torture, and the destruction of a beautiful old yawl belonging to a friend of mine an inconvenience."

Dark anger flared in the count's eyes, but he said only a quiet "I'm so sorry. I was foolish to trust these men."

"I see."

Hawke regarded the man in a silence that lengthened to the point of discomfort. He was thinking of bringing up the issue of the Russian arms Hoodoo had stowed aboard the launch. After a moment's consideration, he said, "You say Anastasia has been badly hurt. I want you to know that I care very deeply for your daughter and would never allow any harm to come to her."

"I believe you," Count Korsakov said, his hard, bright eyes never leaving Hawke's.

"Would you mind telling me what happened? To Anastasia? How was she hurt?"

"She's strong-willed, as you've no doubt noticed. Sometimes, frequently, her heart leads her head. She married a man wholly unsuited for her. I was vehemently opposed. I even threatened to disinherit her. But of course, that old ploy never works when they think they're in love."

"I wouldn't know."

"At any rate, she had a short, unhappy marriage that ended in tragedy, all as I had predicted."

"How did it end?"

"The man was killed. In a hunting accident."

"How awful."

"Yes. I actually saw it happen. We were in Scotland, shooting pheasant and partridge. I have a small shooting estate there, midway up the Spey Valley at the junction with the River Avon. Ballindalloch Castle? Perhaps you've heard of it."

"No, sorry."

"No matter. At any rate, Anastasia's husband was accidentally shot by one of my other guests. Shot to the head, died in the field before help could be summoned."

"Horrible. Still, accidents happen, do they not?" Hawke forced a smile, not at all sure this had been an accident.

"Yes. But come, let's talk of more pleasant things, shall we? These are precious holidays, meant to be festive. I understand you've started a new company on Bermuda. Blue Water Logistics, I think it's called?"

"Indeed. I'm most excited about it. I've two young colleagues in the venture, Benjamin Griswold and Fife Symington. We've great aspirations, at any rate."

"But your primary interests remain in London. Your family interests?"

"Yes. A large, diversified holding company. I'm trying to ease my way out of those responsibilities and have hired some splendid managers to remove most of the day-to-day burden. Blue Water allows me to live as I please on Bermuda with a new business challenge to occupy my mind."

"You're ex-military, are you not?"

"You seem to know quite a bit about me."

"Does that surprise you? Given the circumstances?"

"Not really, no."

"You were a Royal Navy man. A pilot? Held the rank of commander, I believe."

"Yes. I flew Harriers. Saw some action in the first Gulf War."

"And now?"

"Now?"

"You've severed your military connections?"

"Yes."

That little three-letter affirmative hung in the air for a seeming eternity. Hawke and Korsakov seemed content to stare into the fire in silence, sipping their drinks, thinking their separate thoughts. Suddenly, Korsakov slapped his right knee and spoke up.

"I may drop by Blue Water one day, when I return to Bermuda. If that suits you."

"I'd be delighted."

"You know about these computers of mine? The Zeta machines? Popularly known as Wizards these days?"

"I daresay the whole world knows of them. You're rather the Henry Ford of the computer era, you know."

"Well, you flatter me, of course. But TSAR, my company, does ship millions of these things all over the world from our factories here and in China. Perhaps the Zeta might be of interest to your new logistics firm?"

"It certainly would."

"I wonder. Have you any written material on your new enterprise? Any brochures or things like that I could peruse?"

"As a matter of fact, I do. I'll give them to you first thing in the morning."

"Excellent. And now, I must confess, I'm a bit tired. It's been a rather long evening. You could do with a bit of rest yourself after your travels."

Count Korsakov got to his feet and raised his arms over his head, unable to stifle a surprisingly noisy yawn.

"I could sleep for a week," Hawke said, rising as well, though in truth, his one-hour nap had completely refreshed him. Naps were the secret of life, as his hero Churchill had discovered during the war.

The count put his arm around Alex's shoulder, and together they moved toward the door.

"One curious thing, Alex," he said, pausing in midstride. "Speaking of shooting in Scotland. You're a sportsman, obviously. I wonder. Do you ever visit the island of Scarp? Up in the Hebrides?"

"I do. I've an ancestral hunting lodge there. I do a bit of stalking now and then. Why do you ask?"

"My older brother Sergei, you see, was a great one for stalking. Tragically, he disappeared while on such a hunt. On Scarp, as a matter of fact."

"On Scarp? Surely you must be mistaken. It is a very small island, mostly uninhabited. Only a few crofters and farmers. I'm sure I would have heard of his disappearance."

"Oh, no, this was years ago, Alex. Back in the drear dark days of the Cold War."

"How did he come to choose Scarp, of all places? Most forbidding place on earth."

"Sergei was a Soviet intelligence officer, on leave from the military, and had sailed his small sloop to the island for a day's stalking. We never saw him again."

"Really? What year was this?"

"Oh, I hardly remember. Let's see, October 1962 or thereabouts. We were impossibly close, my brother and I, and I miss him dreadfully. We were both away at a school in Switzerland, you see, just the two of us. Le Rosey, perhaps you've heard of it. The dormitory caught fire one night when I was about seven years old, Sergei was eleven. The old wooden building burned to the ground. Only the two of us boys survived. Sergei was badly burned saving my life. I owed him everything, and his loss haunts me to this day."

"I'm terribly sorry."

"Your father was a British naval intelligence officer, I believe, wasn't he?"

"He was."

"Probably did some stalking himself, I'd imagine, used the family lodge on Scarp from time to time?"

"He may well have. He was a great one for the outdoors. I was only seven when he died. I don't recall hearing much about Scarp. There was a great stag he mentioned once or twice, a big red stag. That's about all I remember."

"Not called Redstick, was he? This red stag?"

"No. Monarch of Shalloch, he was called, I'm sure."

"Hmm. Fascinating. Extraordinary to think that their paths might well have crossed at some point, isn't it? Two Cold Warriors?"

"Yes, I suppose it is."

"Well, off you go, then. Sleep well."

He pulled open the tall walnut doors. There was a man waiting in the hallway, looking as if someone should put him to bed. His eyes were bloodshot, and he looked a bit unsteady on his pins. Frowning, he looked Hawke up and down and said, in furry English, "You're the Englishman."

"One of them, at any rate, sir. There are millions of us, you know."

"Hmpf," the man muttered, unamused.

"Vladimir, my very good friend," Korsakov said with a forced smile. "Come in and have a drink."

"Aha! There you are," the man said angrily to Korsakov. "I've been looking all over for you. I'll have a word, if you don't fucking mind."

"What did you say to me?" the count said, the words seeming to come from another being.

Hawke looked at Korsakov, astounded at the raw animalism in the man's face. For the tiniest instant, his hard blue eyes flashed with the glint of incalculable malice. He'd caught only the briefest glimpse of what lay hidden beneath the polished veneer, the genteel mask of the philosopher king. But he had seen a monster, sacred and profane, a strange, arrogant, terrifying glimpse of evil at full throttle. Hawke believed that had he made a sudden, threatening move at that moment, Korsakov, like a dog, would have bared his teeth in a furious snarl.

When he looked again, the count was once more the picture of beneficent charm, so convincing that Alex wondered if he only imagined what he'd seen.

"Yes, yes, of course," the count said, "First, please say hello to Alex Hawke, Vladimir. Alex, this is my old comrade, Vladimir Rostov."

"Good evening," the Russian said, badly slurring his words and not offering his hand.

"Good evening," Hawke said, standing aside so that the man might enter Korsakov's study. He recognized him now, the current president of the Russian Federation.

Once President Rostov was safely inside, the count quickly closed the door, and Alex was left standing alone in the great vaulted hallway. There was a good deal of shouting in Russian, and he desperately wished Ambrose were at his side translating. He heard the word *Amerikanski* a number of times, from both men, and so at least the subject matter of their violent disagreement was known.

He decided to linger a moment, see if he could pick up anything interesting. A moment later, he heard the inebriated Russian president shout something in English. "The Americans will annihilate us for this insanity!"

For what insanity? Hawke wondered, but the shouting match had quickly reverted to Russian. What the hell had the Russians done now?

He looked down at his hand and saw a tumbler of good black rum. *That's a bloody waste,* he said half aloud, quaffing it at one draught. The count and the president seemed to have moved deeper into the study, their voices no longer audible through the door. He looked left, then right. He realized he hadn't the faintest notion how to get through this architectural wonderland to his bloody room.

To the right, he thought, lay the Great Hall, where he'd met the twins. He'd start there, if he could find it, and do a little exploring on his way to bed and Anastasia. Snooping, really, but then, he was a natural-born spy and couldn't help himself. He had noticed a very large hangar out beyond the stables, a corrugated-aluminum structure that looked large enough to accommodate the real *Hindenburg.*

If this bloody snowstorm would just ease up a bit, and if he could find himself a warm fur coat and a pair of size-twelve Wellies in a mudroom somewhere, he thought he just might go out and poke around a bit.

He looked at his watch. No, he had more important things to do than snoop about the count's hangar. With the time difference, he could still make a few calls via his sat phone. Yes, it was still early enough in London to catch C before he went to bed. He thought C would find the confrontation between Korsakov and an angry Rostov most interesting. He'd call Ambrose in Bermuda as well, bring him up to speed on recent developments.

Red Banner had a lot to talk about.

Harry Brock was waiting for him in Moscow, staying at the Hotel Metropol under an assumed name. Simon Weatherstone, as Harry's passport now described him, was holding secret meetings around Moscow with the small cadre of newly recruited agents of Red Banner. Hawke decided he'd call Harry's room at the Metropol first thing in the morning, rather than wake him in the middle of the night. Harry and his new Red Banner resources might come in handy in ferreting out the source of Rostov's anger.

Insanity? American anger? What could that mean?

45

Count Ivan Korsakov stared in angry disbelief at the raving lunatic standing before his fireplace, pounding his fist on the wooden mantel, sending a few precious silver-framed family photographs crashing to the floor. He'd known Vladimir Rostov for many, many years and had never seen him so enraged. Such fury made his drunkenness almost incidental, comical, were it not so late in the evening and so much to be done by morning.

He glared at the Russian president, now stomping on broken glass.

"The Americans will annihilate us for this insanity!"

"Calm down, Volodya. Enough," the count said, reverting to Russian. He listened in hostile silence to this calumny, his anger building.

"Enough? Have you lost your fucking mind?" Rostov bellowed, looking wildly around the room, as if answers to his shouted questions might be hiding in dark corners or floating up near the ceiling. His eyes were rolling around in his head like marbles.

"Now, you listen to me," Korsakov said, as calmly as he could. "You are a guest in this house. I won't be addressed in this manner. Sit down in that chair, and shut up until you can compose yourself."

"Do you realize what you've *done?* Do you? Answer me! This leads to annihilation, I tell you! Annihilation!"

Korsakov, furious, came out of his chair, grabbed the irate man by his shoulders, shook him violently, and then wrestled him down onto a large leather sofa. He held him there, his hands around his throat, squeezing, until Rostov's arms and legs stopped flailing.

The president lay back against the cushions, red-faced and breathing heavily, but he was no longer shouting at the top of his lungs.

"Are you quite finished with this outrageous behavior?" Korsakov snarled, removing his hands from the president's reddened throat. He'd had countless men shot, poisoned, beheaded, and even impaled. But he had never killed a man with his bare hands before, and he could see the attraction.

"I asked you, are you finished?"

"Yes, yes. Just leave me alone for a moment."

The count crossed the room and picked up the receiver of a telephone sitting on his desk. He whispered a few words into the mouthpiece and hung up. He looked angrily at the broken picture frames and shattered glass on the stone hearth floor, then collapsed into the same fireside chair where he'd been sitting earlier. After a few moments' contemplation, he leaned forward with his hands on his knees and stared at the drunken president until he had his full attention.

"Now, in a slow, calm voice, I want you to tell me what in God's name you are so incensed about. If you raise your voice, even slightly, I shall have the servants throw you out in the snow. Do we understand each other?"

"Damn it to hell," Rostov said, sitting up and shakily pouring himself a drink from the decanter on the table. "Why wasn't I informed of this decision? I'm still running this country, unless I missed a meeting."

"I make a lot of decisions in a day. Which one are we speaking of?"

"What decision? Your decision to blow up an entire American town! Wipe it off the face of the fucking map! You know they will trace this back to us. Twenty-four hours. Maybe less. And then what? War? War with America? You know as well as I the number of American nuclear submarines even now prowling the Black Sea."

"There will be no war with America, Volodya, I assure you."

"No? You know the Americans have back-channeled the Syrians, the Iranians, and others. Told them that if any act of terror on American soil can be traced back to Damascus or Tehran, the capitals of those countries will cease to exist within twenty-four hours. You know that as well as I!"

"Syria and Iran are not Russia."

"Thanks be to God. Jesus. We all want to go against the Americans. Every one of us. And we will. But, not *now,* Ivan. We're not ready, damn it, we're not even close!"

"I think we *are* ready. Destiny is an impatient mistress."

"You don't think repositioning our troops to the Baltic and East European borders is provocation enough? You don't think we have already pushed the White House to the limit? Already they are making noises at the Security Council. You think the UN, pitiful and pathetic as it may be, will just look the other way? Or NATO? Really, it all defies belief. The Duma will have your head for this one, Ivan. That I can promise."

"Or it may be that I will have the Duma's heads, Volodya."

Rostov stared at him in disbelief. This form of treachery far exceeded anything he'd thought possible. Even that lunatic Stalin had shown restraint when it came to —

They were interrupted by a knock at the door. A uniformed man strode through, shut the door, and locked it.

"Volodya, calm down. Look, here is your old friend General Kuragin, come to join our little party. Nikolai, bring my special carafe of vodka from the drinks table, and join us, won't you?"

General Nikolai Kuragin, a longtime aide to Rostov, had for years been secretly the head of Korsakov's own private army. He did as he was told and moved to the drinks table. A skeletal man who looked more Teutonic than Russian in his sharply tailored black uniform, he was utterly ruthless. There was a large black leather case in his right hand, attached to his wrist by a stainless-steel chain and bracelet.

Inside the general's black case was an electronic device, one of only two in existence, which carried the codes to initiate detonation of every single Zeta bomb on the planet. The one he carried was to be used only as a backup to the primary, that one always in the possession of Korsakov himself. Kuragin knew the codes as well. They were permanently inscribed in the folds of his brain. He'd never even written them down.

"Good evening, Mr. President," Kuragin said to Rostov, with a sharp nod of the head.

Rostov glared at him. "You're part of this, aren't you, Nikolai? You lying bastard. All these years, all I've done for you. You've pretended to be my friend and ally. And now you betray me for this perverted megalomaniac?"

"Watch your tongue," Kuragin barked at him, and Rostov sank even deeper into the cushions. It was over now, he knew. All was lost. All.

Korsakov looked at Kuragin, a wry smile playing about his lips. "The president thinks we may have gone a bit over the line destroying the American city, Nikolai."

"Really? Why does he think that?"

"He's afraid of the American reaction. NATO. And the UN."

"He's afraid of shadows," Nikolai said. "Always has been."

"He needs courage, perhaps. Pour him another drink. From my carafe."

Kuragin took Rostov's glass from his hand and filled it from the silver carafe emblazoned with the Korsakov coat of arms. Handing him the glass, he said, "Drink."

Rostov needed little encouragement at this point. He swallowed the contents in one gulp, then held out the crystal tumbler for a refill.

"Another?" Kuragin said, his eyes on Count Korsakov.

"Coals to Newcastle. Why not, Nikolai?"

His glass full once more, Rostov tilted it back, swallowed, and wiped his mouth with the back of his hand. He glared at the two men who'd betrayed him.

"And tonight this fucking fox in the henhouse?" he managed to croak.

"Fox?" Korsakov asked the president. "Henhouse?"

"This Englishman you invite into your home! Who is he? Do you even know? He could well be a spy."

"Oh, we know this fox quite well, do we not, Nikolai? We've had this particular fox in our sights for a very, very long time. Here. Have another drink, Volodya."

President Rostov staggered to his feet, stood for a moment, then collapsed back into the deep leather cushions.

"You two want war with America, do you?" he said. "Ha! You know her submarines encircle us, like wolves underwater. With missiles aimed straight at our mothers' hearts. You provoke whom you should appease, comrades. At least, until . . . until . . ."

He made a harsh choking sound and could not continue. His head fell back, and he stared at his two tormentors, glassy-eyed. The empty glass in his hand fell to the floor, smashing to bits on the stone.

"Are you all right?" Korsakov asked, looking at him carefully.

"Agh. A horrible headache. I feel . . ."

"Volodya. My dear old friend and comrade. I'm afraid it's time you took your leave from this mortal coil," Korsakov said, crossing his legs at the knee. "Your passing is premature, I'll grant you. I was going to bid you farewell in the morning when the helicopter arrived to ferry you back to the Kremlin. But now —"

"Tomorrow?" the man croaked.

"Yes. A doomed flight. Tragic. A crash in the Urals. A state tragedy. A world tragedy. But my dear Volodya, such things happen. Life goes on."

"Doomed?"

"You are dying, old friend. Poisoned. Not slowly and painfully like our erstwhile friend Litvinenko in London some years ago. This method shouldn't take long. Perhaps, what do you think, Nikolai? Twenty minutes?"

"Cyanide prevents the body's cells from using oxygen so death should arrive in short order."

"Time enough, then, to show him the future?"

"The future belongs to us, sir. We have more than enough to share." Kuragin smiled.

"Ivan?" the dying Rostov repeated, his eyelids fluttering. "Are you there?"

"Volodya, can you still hear me? You see the case General Kuragin carries? Do you wonder at it? Our very own nuclear football, as the Americans would have it. I call it the Beta machine, or simply the Black Box."

"Yes, Ivan, I see it," Rostov said weakly, peering at the case Kuragin carried.

"You've been drinking cyanide, Volodya. Call me old-fashioned, but sophisticated nuclear poisons like polonium I find unnecessarily messy. Unless one wants to send a message. There is no message here tonight, Volodya. Only the future burying the past."

"The Americans, I tell you." Rostov gasped. "Will annihilate us."

"Let me assuage you in your final moments. Nikolai, open your case. Show it to our dying friend."

"Yes, sir," Nikolai Kuragin said. He detached the leather case from his wrist and placed it on the low table, where Rostov could see its contents. When he entered a code into the keypad, the case popped open, and then the lid rose automatically. Inside the lid was a vivid CRT screen displaying a real-time satellite map of the world in three dimensions. Pinpoints of light, hundreds of them, thousands, millions, flashed on every continent.

"These lights represent countless Zeta machines, each broadcasting its precise GPS location and a unique identification number," Korsakov said. "As you can see, they are everywhere on earth. Numberless millions of them, in every city, town, village. And inside each of them is eight ounces of Hexagon, Volodya, a powerful bomb waiting for my detonation signal."

"Bombs everywhere," Rostov mumbled.

"Everywhere on the planet. Many are controlled by my agents in the field on a strictly limited, as-needed basis. But on a worldwide basis, the millions are controlled by this single unit. Here, let me zoom in on a city. Which one? Paris? Honolulu? Bombay? No. L.A."

Korsakov manipulated the controls to bring the city of Los Angeles forward to full screen. It was a solid mass of tiny blinking lights.

"This number here in the corner of the screen represents the number of Zeta machines within the Los Angeles city limits. As you can see, there are exactly three-point-four million units in this one city alone. Should I choose to, now, I could detonate any one of them in an instant. Or, more dramatically, *every* one of them in the same instant."

Nikolai Kuragin laughed. "We could, at this very moment, do exactly to L.A. what we did to Salina."

"Or London, Honolulu, Buenos Aires, or Beijing," Korsakov said, scrolling rapidly through those cities, their skyline images coming up on the screen.

"You're insane," Rostov whispered, and they would be the last words he would utter in this earthly realm.

"Do you want me to remove him?" Nikolai asked, staring blankly at the corpse.

"Later. But have him incinerated tonight. And his remains placed aboard the helicopter as soon as it arrives in the morning. Along with his luggage, where I have already packed a Zeta. They'll find his ashes and tiny shards of bones in the mountains with the burned-out wreckage."

"Yes, sire."

"Sire. I like the sound of that. So, Rostov is finally no concern of ours. Good. Now, tell me about the mood at the Duma. I plan to go before them tomorrow evening, as you know."

"I don't anticipate any problems with your succession to president. In fact, I anticipate unanimous support. Rostov is now gone; it's the obvious thing to do. You're revered throughout the country. Most of the embittered Communists, members of the Other Russia, and other parties who would be opposed have already had their minds changed with offers of money, property, or positions in your new government. Those who refused, or balked, have already gone far away."

"Never far enough. Dispose of them."

"It will be done."

"And how is our old friend Putin these days? Enjoying his forced retirement to Energetika Prison?"

"Glowing with enthusiasm, I should say." Nikolai laughed. "Still, I wonder why you don't simply introduce him to the tree with no limbs."

"Impale him? No, too quick an exit. I want him to sit in that cell and rot slowly, lose his hair, his teeth, and finally, when he's fried from within, then he can wither and die and never trouble us again."

46

Salina, Kansas

Stoke flew commercial from Miami to Topeka, connecting through Charlotte. There was a young FBI guy waiting at the end of the jetway when he landed at Topeka airport. Navy-blue suit, white shirt, dark tie, buzz-cut sandy-colored hair. Spit-shined black lace-up shoes. Stoke liked him on sight. He had a solid Midwestern smile, and even better, he looked as if he could have made the Olympic wrestling team if he hadn't chosen law enforcement. He couldn't have been more than twenty-four.

"Stokely Jones?" the kid said, extending his hand.

"Yep," Stoke said, giving him five of the best.

"Special Agent John Henry Flood, sir," he said, flashing his badge. "I've got a chopper waiting right here at the airport to take us up to what used to be Salina."

"Let's go get 'em, John Henry Flood,"

Stoke said. All he had was a carry-on with one change of clothes, his shaving stuff, and his SIG Sauer nine with two extra mags of ammunition. Special Agent Flood was already moving like a running back through the crowded concourse, and Stoke had to hustle to catch up. Kid was on a mission. Good.

They came to an unmarked exit off the concourse, and Agent Flood hung a left. A uniformed airport security guy was watching the door, and he opened it for them, right out onto the tarmac. The jet-black whirlybird was sitting right there, all warmed up, rotors spinning at flat pitch.

"Only way to fly," Stoke said, smiling at Agent Flood. "Unmarked black choppers."

Stoke ducked under the whirling rotors and followed the special agent around behind the tail. They scrambled aboard through the starboard-side hatch. The pilot nodded at them, shaking hands with each man as he climbed aboard. John Henry folded himself into a rear seat, and Stoke sat up front on the right. Both men donned their headsets and quickly got strapped in.

"Morning, gentlemen," they heard the pilot say in their headsets.

"Morning," they replied.

"Short trip, here we go."

The pilot smiled at the two men, gave them a thumbs-up, and increased the collective pitch. The little bird lifted off the tarmac, climbed quickly, and took a northerly course, fast and low, skimming over a group of hangars and climbing rapidly en route to Salina.

Stoke turned in his seat and smiled at the FBI kid.

"You go by John or John Henry?" he said into his mike.

"My mother named me John Henry, sir."

"No need to 'sir' me, John Henry. Call me Stoke."

"Deal. Glad to have you aboard here. You're Langley, right, you're CIA?"

"Nope. I got a small private security operation in Miami called Tactics International. Work with the Agency, Pentagon, on special assignments. Mostly for a guy named Harry Brock. Heard of him?"

"Oh, yeah, we've heard of him, all right. Kinda legendary. He's the one asked the Bureau to bring you in."

"What have we got up there, John Henry? How do you see this thing?"

"A mess, sir. A quadruple homicide, the town mayor and her family murdered in bed, and a town wiped off the map."

"Any leads?"

"A cell phone left on one of the victims. Had a message in Arabic to vacate the town by six a.m. yesterday. We traced the call to a cell tower in Tehran. Group called Arm of God claiming responsibility."

"Verified?"

"No, sir."

"Any idea why the Iranians would want to provoke us? I mean, they're already walking a fine line, building nukes and threatening Israel with extinction. The ayatollahs giving us a perfect excuse to take them out doesn't make a whole lot of sense right now."

"No, sir, it does not. We're hoping you can shed some light on this. Harry Brock told my boss you might have a whole different angle on this Salina situation."

Stoke nodded but didn't reply. He wanted to see and hear what the FBI knew before he told them about the baker. He was thinking about the last time he'd seen Happy, when he was delivering his surprise birthday cake. The explosion had been huge. And Harry Brock had said the baker was a Russian-American assassin. Maybe KGB. What the hell was the KGB up to in Salina, Kansas?

Salina and Hiroshima had a lot in common. Stoke and Agent Flood drove silently through streets full of downed and blackened trees, block after block of houses and buildings burned to the foundations, piles of burned debris that filled entire intersections. The smell was unbelievable. A raw, choking cloud of smoke and rot hanging over everything. He saw charred corpses of dogs and other animals that had been left behind, now stacked in piles on what used to be street corners. A storm had moved through the night before, and the streets had a patina of grey mud and matted black dirt.

The day was cold and bright. When the sun peeked out from behind the clouds, there was an odd glittery quality to the surfaces of the black and desolate acres, as if it had rained glass an hour ago, or some giant had flung great handfuls of tiny silver coins over the town after it had been destroyed.

John Henry's face was somber, and the conversation was minimal. He was staring straight ahead; he'd obviously seen enough of this wasted town to last a lifetime. Flocks of birds circled overhead, and it occurred to Stoke that they simply had no place to land.

"Where's the first stop?" he finally asked John Henry.

"We've got a temporary HQ set up. A trailer up top of that hill over there. A state park called Hickory Hill. It's a heavily wooded area, but it escaped the fire because of its height above the town. Also the Motel 6 where I've booked you a room. Not great, but it's the only thing still standing."

Stoke was gazing out his window, having a hard time dealing with such complete destruction. A fine old American town, with a lot of history he didn't know and now never would. Gone.

"You know this is the heart of America,

John Henry?"

"What do you mean?"

"I mean this town is, was, exactly halfway between the East Coast and the West Coast. And halfway between the northern and southern borders. Smack dab in the middle of the country when you open up a map. Right in the crease."

"You think that's intentional?"

"Yeah, I do. They wanted this to hurt."

"Well, they sure as hell succeeded."

"You had kin here?"

"I grew up in a big yellow house with green shutters, used to stand right on that corner."

"I'm sorry."

They drove up a narrow winding road that led to the hilltop overlooking the town. Near the edge of the cliff was the big silver Winnebago doubling as FBI headquarters. Stoke grabbed his door handle and smiled at Agent Flood.

"John Henry, I want you to cheer up," Stoke said. "We're going to catch this slimeball and nail his balls to the wall, okay? Don't you worry about it."

"How are we going to do that, sir?"

"Well, for starters, I know exactly who he is."

"That'll help," John Henry said, smiling for the first time since they'd landed at Salina.

47

"Mr. Jones, welcome, I'm Agent in Charge Hilary Spurling," the attractive blonde FBI lady said as Stoke and John Henry entered the trailer. It was cold as hell outside, and it felt nice and warm inside. Spurling was in her thirties, all business, but still a babe. She introduced him to the rest of the group. It included Bruce Barnett, the Salina PD's medical examiner, a guy from the FBI's Explosive Unit Bomb Data Center in Washington named Peter Robb, and the two uniformed officers Stoke had seen on CNN.

"How's everybody doing?" Stoke said with a smile. "This the team?"

"This is the team," the ME said.

Spurling said, "Mr. Jones, let's cut right to the chase. I understand from my director, Mike Reiter, and our colleagues at both Langley and Homeland, that you and Agent Brock may have some information that would help us in this investigation. Is that correct?"

"Yes, ma'am, it is. But if you don't mind,

before I share that information, it would be helpful to hear what you've got so far. Is that all right with you?"

"Certainly. Won't take long, because we haven't got much. Why don't we start with you, Bruce? Dr. Barnett here is the state ME assigned to the multiple homicide by Salina PD."

The medical examiner pushed his glasses up on the bridge of his nose. "Yes, well, there were no casualties from the explosion, as you know, Mr. Jones. So, I've spent the last twelve hours with the four murder victims at 1223 Roswell Road. The home of Mayor Bailey and her family."

"Who found the bodies?" Stoke asked.

"The housekeeper when she arrived at work that morning," Bruce Barnett said.

"Is she available? I might want to talk to her."

"Yes."

"Tell me about the crime scene."

"No forced entry. The killer was freely admitted into the home. So, he was known to the deceased or used some ruse to gain entry. Two of the victims, children, female, ages four and nine, were found in their beds. The husband died of a gunshot wound to the head. Mayor Bailey died the same way her children did. Poison gas."

"Jesus," Stoke said. "He gassed them?"

"Yeah," Spurling said. "It gets worse. He

had some fun with the mayor before he killed her."

"Tell me," Stoke said.

"Raped and sodomized."

Stoke looked away for a second. "You guys anywhere near identifying the gas?"

"Some kind of incapacitating narcotic, administered at a lethal dosage level. Best early guess is a formula based on the drug fentanyl. We sent lung-tissue samples from the victims to the Bureau's lab in D.C., see if we get any database matches with known material. So far, all I can tell you is it's of foreign origin, nothing of ours. We're waiting to hear."

Stoke looked at the bomb-squad guy. "What the hell kind of nonnuclear explosives could cause the kind of destruction I just saw?"

Peter Robb said, "First of all, it wasn't one bomb. It was hundreds."

"Hundreds?" Stoke said.

"Maybe a thousand. Maybe more. EU-BDC's primary responsibility is forensically examining bombing evidence to identify bomb components. Looking for a signature. So far, all we've got is this." He handed Stoke a small, jagged piece of very thin metal. Silvery, glassy, almost like mirror. He tried to bend it and couldn't.

"What is this stuff? I saw it everywhere."

"Checking on that now. But it was found at every single scene. The whole town is littered

575

with it. My men are now doing materials analysis on it, looking for explosives residue, and performing accelerant examinations. So far, we're coming up empty. It's the craziest crime scene I've ever seen, Mr. Jones, and I've been doing this a long, long time. Whatever this bomber used, it's like nothing we've ever seen before."

"What do you mean by that, Mr. Robb?" Stoke asked.

"Multiple bombs strung like firecrackers. All connected by one fuse and all going off simultaneously. I know it doesn't make any sense, but it's the only way I can explain it."

"Thank you," Stoke said, turning his attention to the two uniforms. "And you two men were the officers who located the straggler? The guy delivering doughnuts, right? You spoke with him. You were with him when the bomb went off."

"Yessir," Andy Sisko said. "Patrolmen Sisko and Southey."

"And you got his name?"

"Happy," Officer Gene Southey said. "Happy the Baker. Had it stitched on his shirt. Said he'd been in town a few days. Sleeping off a migraine and never left his motel."

"What did he say when the town blew up? What was his reaction?"

The two cops looked at each other. "What did he say, Andy? You remember?"

"I don't think he said a damn thing," Sisko replied. "I think he just got in his truck and drove away."

Stoke looked at him. "Big white truck? 'Happy the Baker' on the side?"

"Yessir, that's it, all right."

"And he just drove away. Leaving two witnesses behind."

"Witnesses to what?" Southey asked.

"His crime. Happy the Baker blew up your town, officer. I don't know how or with what, but he's your guy."

"Holy shit, I mean, damn! We were sitting right there with the guy!"

Agent Spurling said, "Mr. Jones, please tell us what —"

"Hold on a sec," Stoke said whipping out his cell phone. He speed-dialed Sharkey's number at his new Coconut Grove office in Miami. The phone rang four, five times. Stoke could see his office, the little pink stucco bungalow hidden by the banana trees, all the windows open, the bamboo chaise where he'd take a nap when things were slow. He could even see Luis there now, snoozing on those soft green and white cushions.

"Tactics," Shark finally said, too cheery, trying to sound awake.

"You napping on the job, son?"

"No, sir, I was in back, you know, a pro'lem with the air conditioner and —"

"Time to jump and scatter, Shark. We've

got something out here."

"Tell me, and it's done."

"Luis, listen carefully. That tape we shot a week ago in the Grove. That night from the boat? Not all of it. But pull every scene that includes Paddy Strelnikov, a.k.a. Happy the Baker. It's at the very end of the tape, coming out of the house with the cake. Edit. Burn a disc. I want you to email that footage to, hold on, what's your e-mail address, Agent Spurling?"

She told him, and Stoke gave it to Sharkey. "We need this stuff now, okay? Keep the disc as backup. FBI's got to get this guy's face on the national wire right now. Call Barry Pick at Miami-Dade. Tell him cake boy did Salina. Tell him to watch the airport, Happy could be coming home or even there already. You cool?"

"Cool runnin', mon."

"Later, Shark."

Spurling was looking at him.

"You've actually got tape on this guy?"

"Lots of it. We were surveilling Chechen Russian mob guys on another matter and picked him up accidentally. He's involved with a guy we're looking at for something else. Yurin."

"Urine?" Agent Spurling said, a puzzled frown creasing her brow.

"I know, I know. It's confusing, isn't it? But it's Yurin with a Y. All Beef Paddy, that's Happy's moniker, was delivering a bomb in the form of a birthday cake. This was at a party where this guy Yurin was running security. Did you put out an APB on the white truck?"

"Happening as we speak, Mr. Jones," Spurling said, snapping her phone shut.

"You have to figure he dumped it nearby. Way too easy to spot. He hides the truck somewhere, steals an abandoned car, heads to an airport. I'd get everybody available working that truck. Five-mile radius."

"Yeah. Sorry. We didn't even begin to make this guy as a suspect. Just a nutjob. Who the hell is he?"

"His real name is Paddy Strelnikov. American-born Russian. *Mafiya* type from Brooklyn. We think he's KGB. A sleeper assassin, possibly working directly for someone in the Kremlin. The last time I saw Paddy, he was in Miami. He killed a Chechen terrorist responsible for attacks against the Russian population and the threats against the Kremlin."

"Holy shit," Officer Southey said. "Russians in Salina?"

"Yeah, you two are lucky to be standing here. John Henry, I want to talk to the manager of the motel where Paddy was staying. See his room."

"That's easy. You're staying there. Motel 6."

"Let's go."

John Henry had parked the FBI car at the same overlook where Paddy and the two cops had watched the town blow up.

"This is where the three of them, the suspect and the two officers, observed the explosion. The bakery truck was parked right where you're standing."

Stoke walked to the edge of the cliff, looked down at the smoking, glittering remains of Salina. Then he turned around and stared at the dense woods behind him. He saw a couple of dirt roads, almost overgrown, leading into the park's interior.

"Where's the motel? Up here on the cliff somewhere, I'd guess?"

"Yessir. It's just on the other side of those woods. Right on the state highway. Maybe a mile, mile and a half. Nothing up here on the bluff was touched. Only reason the motel and the park survived."

"Can you drive a car through that stuff? Or do we have to drive around to get to the highway?"

"I don't know that you could get a car through there, sir. Those are nature trails. Pretty thick."

"Let's take a walk, John Henry. I love nature."

Five minutes later, glancing up as he

walked, Stoke said, "Lots of broken branches back in here. Both sides of the trail. High up, too."

"Yessir, I noticed that."

"Looks almost like a damn truck came through here recently, doesn't it, John Henry?"

"There it is. Down in that ravine."

Stoke looked to his left. At the bottom of a very steep ravine, he could see the white bakery truck. It was on its side, the cab partially submerged in a swiftly running creek.

"Let's go," Stoke said, and ten minutes later, they'd managed to work their way down to the truck. It was banged up pretty bad, glass gone from the windshield, water running right through a portion of the cab. One of the two rear doors was hanging ajar.

"Accident?" John Henry asked.

"I think he ditched it. Long gone, I think, probably hiked through the woods to the motel, changed clothes in his room, and then stole one of the abandoned cars in the lot and boogied. But go through the cab, okay? Best you can. Check the glove compartment, and check under the seats. Might find something helpful, though I doubt it, many times as this bad boy's been around the block. I'll look in the back."

He lifted the rear door and looked inside. Doughnut boxes, a lot of them, as if they'd been through a cement mixer. Most of them still sealed, but a lot had popped open, and there were hundreds of gooey cream, chocolate, glazed, and jelly doughnuts stuck to the ceiling, the walls, lying around. Stoke resigned himself to going through every last one of the damn boxes. After all, it was Happy's MO, wasn't it? The last time he had delivered a bomb, it had been inside a bakery box.

"John Henry," he called out ten minutes later.

"Yessir," came the reply from the cab.

"Come back here and take a look at this, will you?"

"Nothing in the cab, sir," John Henry said a minute later, peering into the gloom inside the truck. He could see Stokely sitting in the midst of hundreds of opened doughnut boxes. Gooey stuff all over him.

"Gimme a hand in here, John Henry," he said. "Help me get out of all this crap. Can't even stand up, the floor's so bad."

"Disgusting."

"That's one point of view. Elvis would've thought he'd died and gone to heaven in here."

Agent Flood took Stoke's hand and helped the big black man scramble out of the upended truck. Stokely stood with one foot in the icy creek, his entire body covered in

582

creamy caramel icing and sprinkles from head to toe.

"Check this out," Stoke said, wiping icing from his eyes with his one free hand.

He held up a small, silvery object, like a desktop sculpture of a human brain, stem and all. But the thing about it that caught John Henry's eye was that it was as shiny as a brand-new mirror. Like the little piece of metal he'd seen back at the trailer. And the stuff sprinkled all over his dead town.

"What the heck is it?" Flood asked.

"It's a Zeta computer. Called the Wizard. Sell 'em all over the world for about fifty bucks apiece. Even cheaper in Third World countries."

"Oh, yeah. I've seen those."

"Damn right you have. Millions of them have been sold in the last few years. We've got to get back to the trailer and show this thing to that bomb-squad guy. What's his name?"

"Robb. Peter Robb."

"Yeah, Robb. Show it to him."

"Why's that?"

"Because, John Henry, I think this computer's got a bomb inside it. Hell, more I think about it, maybe this isn't the only one."

"Bombs in computers."

"That'd be my guess, yeah. I could be wrong."

John Henry was turning the thing over in

his hands, staring at it in disbelief. "My kid's fifth-grade computer class uses these."

"Scary thought, ain't it?" Stoke said. "We've got to talk to Robb. Get the whole damn FBI on this. Find out how many of these damn computer bombs might be out there."

Stoke's cell hummed in his pocket. He whipped it out and flipped it open.

"You're talking to him," he said.

"Stoke, it's Luis."

"Shark. What's up?"

"Miami Dade PD just called two minutes ago. Friend of mine there picked up on some info he thought we should know about. They tracked our baker boy, All Beef Paddy Strelnikov. He's back in Miami, all right. One of the local officers who had seen the APB photo made him at the *Miami Herald* building. Dressed as an exterminator. Carrying two large canisters on his back, like oxygen tanks or something."

"He's back in Miami?"

"Not anymore. He gave them the slip. They searched the building top to bottom. *Nada.* They think he might have gotten aboard the airship, the *Pushkin.*"

"Listen to me. Did anyone actually *see* him board?"

"No. But he was in a stairwell to the roof minutes before that thing was getting ready to go."

"Tell me it's not gone yet, Shark."

"Left for Stockholm hours ago. Man, I woulda called you sooner, you know, but I just found out myself."

Stoke snapped his phone shut.

"Canisters?" he said, looking at Flood. "Oxygen tanks?"

"What?"

"Those tanks were full of gas, not oxygen. He was experimenting with poison gas on the mayor and her family. See how much it would take to put them to sleep before it was lethal. What the Russians did at that theater rescue in Moscow, pumped gas through the AC to put everyone to sleep. But they got the formula wrong, and most of the hostages died. Happy may have smuggled his god-damn poison gas aboard the airship."

"I'm sorry, but what are you talking —"

"Fancha," he said under his breath, and then he started scrambling up the steep ravine faster than John Henry Flood would have ever believed a man his size could move.

48

Tvas, Russia

Early-morning bars of gold light streamed across the gilded furniture, the sumptuous bed, and the Persian carpets. Anastasia swept into the room and found Hawke alone in her big canopied bed. He had the quilted blue silk duvet pulled up under his neck, wearing nothing but a grin.

"Hawke, get up!"

"Are you quite sure I'm not up already, darling?"

He'd barely managed to reach down and slide his portable sat phone under the bed without her noticing. He'd just rung off with Harry Brock. It had been a most disturbing conversation. He'd told Brock about last night's confrontation between Rostov and Korsakov. And thanks to Harry, he now knew what President Rostov had been so angry about the previous evening. What the "insanity" had been. An entire American town had been obliterated. Rostov's rage could mean only one thing, however far-fetched it might seem. The Russians had been behind the bombing of an American city. Which meant they were clearly willing, ready, and able to risk all-out nuclear war with the United States.

Korsakov had clearly ordered this unprovoked attack without the Russian president's knowledge. Last night, Hawke had witnessed a power struggle at the very pinnacle of Russian politics. Brock was now communicating this intelligence to his superiors at Langley and the Pentagon. The White House would soon be buzzing as well.

And Hawke? Korsakov's gorgeous daughter was standing at his bedside, treating him like a naughty schoolboy, her dainty foot inches away from the sat phone hidden beneath the bed.

As a distraction, he flashed what he hoped was a winning smile.

"Alex! There's no time for that. Seriously. Come along, now, go into your room and get yourself dressed. And packed. We're leaving in one hour."

"Leaving? We just got here."

"Out!" Anastasia whipped back the duvet. The sight of her aroused lover, naked in the morning sunlight, was almost sufficiently diverting to advance Hawke's cause.

"Look at you."

"Hmm."

"*Nyet, nyet, nyet.* Get up and go. I mean it. Papa will be furious if we're not ready." She grabbed his wrist and began to pull him from her bed.

"Okay, okay, I'll get up," Hawke said, laughing. "Beautiful morning, isn't it? God's in his heaven and all that?"

Hawke climbed down from the bed and slipped his arms into the silk robe she held open for him, surreptitiously kicking the phone further beneath the bed. He'd fetch it later. He then turned inside her embrace, kissed her on the mouth, and patted her lovely rounded bottom. She was still in her dressing gown, he noticed, and naked beneath it. Ah, well, time's winged chariot, nothing to be done.

"Okay, I give up. Why on earth are we leaving, by the way? I was just getting accustomed to this palatial life you filthy-rich Russians seem to enjoy."

"Papa just called me to his room. He needs to get back to Moscow. Political events there require his presence. He's invited you and me to go with him, and I accepted. He's offered to give us his box at the Bolshoi tonight. *Swan Lake* with Nasimova. Her opening night. It will be spectacular, I promise. Now, go."

"How are we getting there, by the way? Troika, one hopes . . ."

"Even better. We're taking his private airship."

"How wonderful. I've been dying to climb aboard that thing and have a look. Do you think he'll let me fly it?"

"The famous Royal Navy flyer? I should think so. Now, get moving."

She rushed into the bathroom, and Hawke snatched his phone from beneath the bed before going to his own room to pack.

Hawke watched with open admiration as the ground crew slowly backed the gleaming silver zeppelin out of the massive hangar, each blue-uniformed man handling one of the many cables hanging down from the fuselage. She was extraordinary to look at, four hundred feet in length, he'd guess, with a gaping round opening at the front. Quite a radical design, he thought, but then, it had sprung from the mind of quite a radical guy.

Her name, appropriately enough, was emblazoned on her flanks. *Tsar.* At her tail section, from which a boarding staircase was now emerging, the bright red Russian stars adorned each fin. In the brilliant snow-reflected sunlight, she was a gleaming machine from another world.

"What do you think?" Anastasia asked, suddenly appearing at his side. She was wrapped in her white sable and matching hat and looked lovely.

"Stunning."

"We can board now, if you'd like. Our luggage has already been taken aboard and stowed. Father is already aboard as well. He's having a series of private meetings with his closest business associates. I'm afraid we won't be seeing much of him until we arrive in Moscow."

"Ah, well. I'm glad I had a bit of time with him last evening. Got the chance to get acquainted."

"So is he."

"How fast is *Tsar*? Remarkable-looking thing, I must say."

"A hundred and fifty miles an hour is pretty much her top end. But the captain tells me we've got a good tailwind this morning. We should be in the capital for lunch."

"I should make arrangements for a place to stay," Hawke said. "Do I have time to make a call?"

"Already taken care of, darling. I booked you a suite at the Metropol. Just adjacent to Red Square and very close to the Bolshoi. Shall we go aboard? I think Father would like to get going as quickly as possible."

"What's going on in Moscow?" Hawke asked, taking her arm as they crunched through the snow toward the hangar.

"I never ask," she said with a wry smile. "And he never tells."

Once aboard and aloft, they went all the way forward to the Jules Verne Observation Lounge, a semicircular room below the nose of the ship. It was all glass and steel, comfortably furnished with leather club chairs. A steward took their breakfast order, and they sat back to enjoy the spectacular view. Speeding silently over the vast white landscape, flying in such comfort less than a hundred feet above the endless snowy forest, was hypnotic. Hawke, however, was most interested in seeing the inner workings of the airship, especially the pod containing the flight deck.

As soon as they'd finished breakfast, he left Anastasia alone with her American novel (he'd brought her a copy of *Huckleberry Finn* along as a present) and went exploring. He went from stem to stern, only avoiding those areas where security forces looked at him forbiddingly and shook their heads. But Anastasia had made a call to the bridge and arranged a visit with the captain.

The airship's flight deck was a separate pod, hung beneath the central fuselage, an elongated crystal-clear egg in the embrace of perforated metal girders connected to the underside of the ship. A circular staircase led from the lowest deck down to the bridge deck. The single security man at the top smiled and said, "They are expecting you, Mr. Hawke."

A minute later, Hawke saw they'd gained some altitude. He was standing behind the captain's right shoulder, staring down between his feet at snow-covered mountains two hundred feet below. Off to the right, there was a deep gash in the snow, a partial fuselage and black pieces of wreckage scattered about. He saw a long black blade protruding from the snow like a huge runaway ski and put it together. A chopper had gone down. Recently. The charred main wreckage was still burning a bit, black smoke spiraling upward in the clear blue air.

"What happened down there?" Hawke asked the man at the helm.

"A crash," the man replied, in a blinding glimpse of the obvious, his English softly laced with Russian. "We've just radioed it in. Looks as if it happened just a short time ago."

"No sign of survivors?"

"None. But medevac rescue teams are already en route."

"Captain Marlov, I'm Alex Hawke. I believe Anastasia Korsakova may have told you I might be stopping by the bridge for a quick look round this morning."

"Yes, yes, of course!" the captain said. He was a slight fellow with a shock of blond hair under his cap. He wore a sky-blue uniform with four gold braids at his sleeves. "Welcome aboard, sir. Enjoying the voyage so far?"

"Indeed. Mind if I just hang about for a few minutes? Watch you fellows at work?"

"Not at all. As you can see on the digital readouts displayed above, we've got a lovely day for flying. A good stiff breeze on our tail, and we're making nearly one hundred sixty over the ground."

"How much gas does it take to keep this monster afloat?"

"We carry thirty million cubic feet of helium," the captain said proudly. "*Pushkin* carries three times that."

"Still use helium, do you? I thought it was explosive."

"On the contrary, helium is a natural fire extinguisher. And while it was once rare, it is available worldwide as a byproduct of natural-gas production."

"Fascinating."

Hawke smiled and let his gaze drift over the controls and the instrument panel. Fairly straightforward and a fairly simple craft to fly, he decided after watching the crew at work for ten minutes. The deck he was standing on was made of thick, clear Lexan, shaped like an elongated egg. In the center was a large round metal hatch with a stainless-steel wheel for opening and closing. About a hundred feet of coiled nylon line encircled the hatch.

"Escape hatch?" Hawke asked the captain.

"*Da, da, da.* For the crew in an emergency. Also for the passengers on the decks above, should a fire break out somewhere aboard that blocked the normal exits."

"Where do you head from Moscow, captain?"

"To Stockholm. For the Nobel ceremony. We are meeting our sister ship there. The great passenger liner *Pushkin*. Perhaps you've heard of her. She's en route to Stockholm now, from Miami."

"A magnificent vessel, from pictures I've seen. You should be very proud."

"One day, the count hopes to see hundreds of these great airships crisscrossing the world's oceans and continents. It's a marvelous way to travel, as I'm sure you'll agree."

"It's a very civilized mode of transportation. Captain, thank you. I'll leave you to it, then. Pity about those chaps in the chopper, isn't it?"

Hawke was still mulling over the downed helicopter when he returned to the observation deck, where Anastasia remained engrossed in her novel. He picked up an English edition of *Pravda* and scanned the headlines. Nothing hinted at the unrest inside the Kremlin walls. No surprise, since the government controlled all the media. He picked up an ancient copy of *Sports Illustrated,* pretending to read it, privately going over recent events.

He planned to call the White House as soon as he could. He needed to speak to the president himself, tell Jack McAtee what he thought was going on.

The rest of the short voyage was uneventful. Only the mooring inside the walls of the

Kremlin brought Hawke out of his reverie. He went to the window and peered down at a snow-covered Red Square. "Red Square is such a surprisingly beautiful place," Hawke said. "Pity it's still saddled with that discredited old Commie name."

"Red has nothing to do with Communism," Anastasia said.

"No?"

"No. It's been called that for centuries. Red, in Russian, means beautiful."

"Beautiful Square. Well, that's much better."

The square was filled with throngs of people looking upward as the great airship descended slowly toward the mooring mast. They seemed to be cheering.

"What's all that about?" Hawke asked Anastasia, who had joined him at the window.

"I'm not sure. There's to be an emergency session of the Duma this evening. Papa was asked to appear. We'll find out more after the ballet, I'm certain."

"I'm sure we will," Hawke said, gazing down at the cheering masses waving up at the airship. Near Lenin's Tomb, on the periphery, a few protesters, mostly elderly Communists waving tattered red banners, were closely watched by OMON security forces in their trademark blue and black camo. Their armored personnel carriers were parked nearby. *Tsar*'s mooring lines had been heaved, and a ground crew had taken control of the ship as she neared the mooring mast. Hawke felt a shudder aft and assumed the boarding staircase was being lowered to the ground.

He was still thinking about the burning chopper in the mountains. It figured in this, but how?

"What time shall I pick you up for the Bolshoi?" he said, stroking Anastasia's cheek.

"Oh. Are you off, darling?"

"Yes. I've got to meet a friend at the Metropol. Sorry, I should have told you earlier. Blue Water is doing a new business presentation tomorrow, and I need to make sure we're ready."

"Who is your friend?"

"Simon," he said, hating the lie but unable to say Harry Brock's name. "Simon Weatherstone. An American. He's staying at the Metropol. I'm supposed to meet him in the bar."

"Meet me in front of the theater a few minutes before seven. Since we've got Papa's box, we don't need to arrive early."

He said good-bye, kissing her lips, hating himself for lying to a woman he might be falling in love with, knowing he had no other choice, still finding it an utterly distasteful part of his chosen career.

War was hell.

With a side order of heaven.

49

Moscow

Inside the lower house of the Russian parliament, the state Duma, the mood of the emergency session was initially somber and tense, then increasingly restive. Rumors were rampant. Supporters of the late President Rostov were already claiming privately that he'd been assassinated. His helicopter having crashed mysteriously en route to Moscow from Korsakov's winter palace in perfect weather, there were many eager to lay the blame at the count's feet.

The *siloviki,* the ten most powerful men in the Kremlin, and many more, were more than ready to defend Korsakov, angrily denying such blasphemy and implying political or even physical threats should these blasphemers not immediately cease such sacrilege against the revered man's name.

Naturally, in such a power vacuum, there was an enormous amount of jockeying going on inside the chamber. Some of the Nationalist Party lawmakers, given to near-hysterical rhetoric, were eventually shouted down. Others, mainly Communist diehards, who threatened to turn violent, had been forcibly removed by Gennady Seleznyov, speaker of the Duma. The Ten, of course, sat silently, stoic, holding their cards very close to the chest.

Rostov's most likely and logical successor, Prime Minister Boris Zhirinovsky, had been at the podium for more than two hours, striving for a ringing rhetoric that had fallen woefully short of the mark. He needed three hundred votes to secure his position. He had perhaps half that. And those numbers were going down, not up. He droned on, and a sleepy stupor descended over the ornate, rococo-style room.

Now, a fresh rumor swept the great hall. The airship belonging to the reigning hero of all Russia, Count Ivan Korsakov, had arrived in Moscow. Reports said he was even at this hour en route to the Duma to make a plea for reason and calm in the wake of the morning's tragedy. A prescient few guessed he had other, far more ambitious agendas to place before the legislature.

The prime minister, oblivious to all this, droned on.

Suddenly, the wide doors at the rear of the chamber were flung open, and a large cadre of heavily armed OMON security forces in full camo regalia marched inside, their heavy boots marking quick time on the marble floors, half of the men moving rapidly along the far left aisle of the room and the other half going right. They positioned themselves exactly one foot apart, backs to the wall, weapons down, eyes forward as if awaiting further orders.

Entering the room like a conquering hero was General Nikolai Kuragin, resplendent in his sharply tailored black uniform, a black leather briefcase attached to his wrist. He strode alone down the center aisle toward the podium, head high, jaw thrust forward, his eyes on the prime minister.

Upon seeing his approach, the prime minister stopped his speech in midsentence, struck mute, unable to continue. The room erupted in pandemonium. After a moment, the speaker ushered the prime minister away from the podium and returned to call for order. When the four hundred legislators in the hall had calmed to a dull roar, he invited General Kuragin to the podium and asked him to address the assembly.

The general cleared his throat and gazed out at the assembled legislators with the look of a man whose hour had come at last.

"My great good friends, patriots all, I've come here today in grief but also in hope," the general began. The reaction was instantaneous and overwhelming. Applause, loud and sustained, greeted this declaration. Some already knew and many were beginning to guess at what was to follow.

"My good friend President Vladimir Vladimirovich Rostov served our nation with great distinction and honor. We, in turn, honor his memory and mourn his tragic passing. But at this historic —"

"Murderer! Liar! Murderers, all of you!" shouted a female voice somewhere in the audience. A small white-haired woman was on her feet, screaming at the general. He nodded his head, and two OMON soldiers quickly made their way toward her from either end of the row where she stood. They lifted Rostov's widow off her feet, still screaming, and carried her quickly to the nearest exit.

When the ensuing hubbub had died down, the general continued his speech as if nothing had happened.

"We, in turn, honor his memory and mourn his tragic passing just a few short hours ago. But at this historic moment in our motherland's heroic history, we cannot dwell on the past even for a short time. Events allow us no such luxury. Russia must look to the immediate future. And the future, my dear colleagues, is entering the room even as I speak. Please welcome Count Ivan Ivanovich Korsakov, who humbly begs permission to enter this chamber and address this august body."

The eruption was predictable. Save for a few naysayers scattered here and there among the rows of chairs terraced up the rear, the four hundred members of the Duma rose to their feet to cheer and applaud, turning to watch the great man enter the chamber.

Korsakov, dressed in a formal grey suit and wearing a long grey cape that draped from his shoulders, paused in the doorway for a moment, acknowledging their welcome with a modest smile, then strode down the center aisle to the podium. Reaching it, he turned and bowed deeply to those assembled. The roar that greeted this gesture was deafening, and he used the moment to replace General Kuragin behind the podium. Korsakov raised his hands in a futile effort to quiet the assembly.

The general remained at his side throughout, his sharp eyes moving over the crowd like the trained security man he'd once been. If there was to be any assassination attempt, it would come now, and he and his troops were ready for it. Many of the security men surrounding the podium were more than ready to take a bullet for their leader if it came to that. Not so Nikolai Kuragin. He wouldn't take a bullet for anybody.

"I am a proud Russian citizen," Korsakov began as the room finally hushed. "I've been one all of my life. And I have never been more proud of my country than I am at this moment. We have accomplished much since the end of the Soviet era. President Rostov and his predecessor, President Putin, deserve the lion's share of the credit for this progress. Now we stand together on the threshold of greatness such as we have never known.

"My friends, Russia is once more a great power in this world and gaining strength every day. It is my will that she will become even greater. Her time has come at last, comrades. I stand before you today, a humble patriot but also a man ready to lead you to where a great and luminous future beckons. And that is Russia's historic place, is it not? At the very forefront of the world's great nations! This is where I vow to take our beloved Mother Russia!

"Therefore, I am privileged and deeply honored to place my name before you as a candidate for the presidency of the Russian Federation."

He bowed his head briefly and waved to the crowd, stepping aside to let Kuragin return to the podium.

"Count Ivan Ivanovich Korsakov has allowed his name to be put forth as a candidate for the presidency. All in favor, signify by saying aye. All opposed, please stand."

A chorus of ayes rose in the room and reverberated throughout the chamber. Korsakov, delighted, smiled benevolently at his supporters. It was happening, all of it, just as he'd always dreamed it would.

Once the noise had died down, a strange silence fell over the room as, one by one, trembling men opposed to Count Ivan Korsakov's presidency rose to their feet.

Only a few stood up, of course, the hardened opposition, consisting mainly of diehard Communists and members of Kasparov's New Russia party. The men who rose were brave indeed. They stood erect, their faces grey and shining with sweat, but their eyes were staring at the podium as the OMON troopers made their way to the ends of the aisles, waiting for a signal to drag them away. There was no shouting, no resistance from them, even though they knew that by standing in defiance, they'd sentenced themselves to life in the gulag.

Or worse.

Korsakov, his eyes scanning the faces of the men who dared oppose him, made a slight hand gesture, and the OMON troops withdrew and resumed their positions along the walls.

A thunderous explosion of applause greeted this show of magnanimity and mercy. Here, then, at long last, was a ruler for all the people!

"Ladies and gentlemen," Kuragin said, "it would appear that Russia has a new president! President Korsakov, would you say a few words?"

Then, from one of the last rows in the great hall, came a single voice, rising above the rest.

"Tsar!" the man shouted. "Tsar! Tsar! Tsar!"

The chanting of that word in the chamber was startling. It had remained unused in Russia since that terrible night in an Ekaterinberg basement in 1917, when the last Tsar and his family had been executed, their bodies dumped in a well deep in the forest.

But the men and women of the Duma remembered how to say that word, and the swelling of it grew until it filled the hall, every single one of them stamping their feet and shouting at the top of their lungs.

"Tsar! Tsar! Tsar!"

President Korsakov had moved away from the podium. He stood quietly, hands clasped behind his back, his head lifted high, his eyes shining. After a time, he thought the chant might go on for hours if he didn't stop it, so he stepped back up to the podium and said nine historic words into the microphone.

"I accept with honor this ancient and noble title."

Pandemonium, joy, and glee greeted his words.

Russia, after ninety-plus years, had a new Tsar.

Hawke remembered elephants onstage, but that was all he could recall of Giuseppe Verdi's *Aida,* the first and last opera he'd ever attended. He'd been six years old at the time, seated between his parents in the Royal Opera House at Covent Garden. Opera and ballet were not his bailiwick. He'd happily never seen a ballet in his life and was hardly looking forward to this one.

But nothing had prepared him for this moment.

From the very instant Nasimova appeared as a beautiful white swan gliding serenely across the frozen wintry pond, he'd been mesmerized. Perhaps it was simply Tchaikovsky's genius at work, the full orchestra dipping and soaring with his inspiration. Perhaps it was the corps of ballerinas, each a white swan lovelier than the next. But whatever it was, Hawke felt a deep stirring inside, something moved within him that he'd not imagined even existed.

Rhapsodic, that was the word for how he felt, reaching for Anastasia's warm hand in the dark. And a new sense of wonder at the mysteries of the schizophrenic Russian soul. It produced unholy monsters like Stalin, capable of murdering millions of his own people. And it produced men capable of imagining this loveliest of dreamlike fantasies.

Alone in the dark of the private Korsakov box with Anastasia at his side, he was entranced. He was actually leaning forward from his plush velvet seat, his elbows on the curved balustrade, his chin resting in the cup of his palms, his eyes sweeping the stage, not wanting to miss a single movement, a single note of the glorious music.

"Do you like it?" he heard Anastasia whisper softly, leaning into him.

He tore his eyes away from the stage, from Nasimova flying above Swan Lake, to look at his lover's beautiful face. She was especially radiant tonight, a glittering diamond tiara in her golden hair and tiny waterfalls of diamonds suspended from each earlobe. She wore a dark blue silk gown with a plunging neckline, the silk contrasting with her full pale bosom, her whole being luminous in the soft blue artificial moonlight streaming from the stage.

"I can never thank you enough for this, Asia," he said, kissing her lips. "I didn't know there could be anything so beautiful."

"My love," she said, her eyes shining with a depth of feeling he had never seen.

"What is it?" he asked, falling into her eyes. All day, he'd felt she had something to tell him and that she'd been waiting for this moment.

"There is . . . something else I must tell you. But I am — afraid. I know I love you. I must have loved you from the moment I saw you. And I think you have feelings for me, too. But now, something has happened. Something that may make you run from me.

The timing, you know, it's just too soon for you, and now I am so afraid you will go away, and all this joy will end for me."

"How beautiful you are . . . what is it, darling? Don't be afraid. Tell me."

"Something more beautiful than one woman could ever be."

"Tell me."

"We are making a baby, darling Alex. I am pregnant with your child."

Hawke looked at her, saw the tears well up and begin to roll down her cheeks and all the questions and hope in her eyes. He wiped her tears away and kissed her mouth, mixed emotions racing through his mind so rapidly that he had no time to think, and so he just said what was in his heart.

"How wonderful, darling. How absolutely marvelous."

"You are happy? You won't run?"

"Deliriously happy," he said, kissing her eyes, her cheeks, her lips.

"We made our baby during that storm over Bermuda, darling. I know it. That magnificent storm. He will be magnificent, too. Thunder in his heart and lightning in his veins. Just as you are."

"Are you sure it's a boy?"

"As sure as I can ever be. I know in my heart."

Two hours later, they emerged from the

theater, both of them still glowing with the ballet's lingering beauty and the bright promise of her news. Hawke had his arm around Anastasia, holding her close to him, protecting her and his child as they made their way through the bustling crowd streaming down the staircase toward the exit.

It had begun snowing, heavily. A warm front from the Mediterranean had brought high winds, colliding with a cold front from Siberia. A serious storm, exhilarating.

Storms and babies, he thought, smiling down at her, and he felt as happy as perhaps he had ever been. That a life marred by so much tragedy as his could have moments like this one made it all seem worthwhile. The whole night lay before them, and their lives would be forever entwined and filled with limitless wonder and possibility. He realized at that very moment that he truly loved this woman. And that his badly broken heart had at long last healed enough to take her inside.

"Isn't it beautiful?" he said, looking out at the frosted city.

Moscow looked its best under a blanket of white. The city was made for snowy nights like this one, and he was eager to make his way to the Pushkin Café, just five or six blocks from the Bolshoi, where he had booked a cozy table in the Library on the second floor. There they would drink champagne and plan their future together.

He was halfway down the steps when he felt the sharp pain in his ribs. He looked down and saw that a short, squat man in a black overcoat had thrust his hand inside Hawke's own coat. It was the muzzle of a gun, he could feel it now, pushing between two ribs.

"You're under arrest," the man said, not even looking up, just jamming the gun harder into his ribcage.

Hawke made two moves at once. With his right hand, he gently pushed Anastasia out of harm's way. His left hand he brought down hard, palm flat, on the back of the man's thick neck, driving his head down, only to meet Hawke's right knee coming up under his chin, breaking his jaw. The move sent the little fellow flying.

"Alex!" Asia cried. "What is —"

Hawke never had time to reply.

Instantly, he was surrounded by five more men similarly dressed in black overcoats, but these were big men, burly types. They were all armed, and they pressed in close, letting him see the pistols they carried.

"Come with us," one of them hissed in his ear.

"Where?"

"You'll know soon enough."

They had his arms now and were moving him quickly out into the snowy street. He didn't have to wonder where the KGB thugs were taking him. He knew.

Lubyanka Prison.

Hawke twisted his head around, looking for Anastasia. She was standing where he'd left her on the steps, looking down at him, both hands to her face, terror in her eyes.

"Find the American!" Hawke cried out to her. "The one I told you about at the Metropol!"

He felt a blow to the back of his head and then nothing more. His last thought before he went out was that on the airship, he'd managed to give Anastasia the assumed name Harry Brock had registered under at his hotel.

Harry would find him. Help him.

Maybe.

50

Aboard Pushkin *at Sea*

Fancha was singing when the lights went out. She was singing *"A Minha Vida,"* her biggest hit from the *Green Island Girl* album, which had just gone platinum. The dinner crowd was really with her, she could feel it, and so she went ahead with the beautiful song, singing in the dark, thinking this lighting thing was just some kind of a dramatic flourish by the very flamboyant Russian stage director named Igor. She'd seen him backstage before the show started, sipping vodka from a flask with one of the musicians.

Or maybe it was just a temporary power outage aboard the giant airship?

They were sailing far out over the Atlantic now, just north of Bermuda, she thought. Past the point of no return, like in her favorite John Wayne movie, *The High and the Mighty.* She'd been afraid of flying ever since she'd seen it, but she still loved it, still found herself whistling the haunting theme song now and then.

When she ended the song, there was a lot of applause and even shouts of "Brava! Brava!" from some of the French and Italian people onboard. Had to be the smartest audience she'd ever performed for, most of them Nobel Prize winners, after all. And Vice President McCloskey's wife, Bonnie, was sitting right up front by the little stage, clapping louder than anybody.

She took a deep bow, even though nobody could see her.

The sudden darkness was startling and complete. It was a moonless night, and even though there were big windows in the ship's ballroom, she couldn't see much other than the silhouettes of the three hundred or so people in the audience. They were mostly all seated at tables of four or more, but a large number of couples were still circling the dance floor, the small band onstage behind her going into an unfamiliar riff.

Dancing in the dark?

People just kept clapping, probably thinking, lights go on, lights go off. Happens all the time on shipboard, right? A lot of liquor had been consumed at the cocktail reception and a lot of wine at dinner. She didn't drink herself, but later, she'd remember that she still wasn't scared at that point, thinking it was all sort of fun.

"If someone will light a candle, I'll sing another song," she said to a ripple of nervous laughter.

Someone called out, " '*Ave Maria*'!"

She began to sing the beautiful aria, feeling the power of her instrument, waiting for the violinist to catch up.

Then the lights came back on.

And someone screamed.

The terrorists, for that's what they were, had entered under the cover of darkness, but many were still pouring into the room from every doorway. They were all dressed in heavy boots and black combat fatigues, but it was the guns everybody was looking at. They all carried big, complicated-looking assault rifles, cradled in their arms like babies, but they had multiple layers of weapons, sashes of bullets, flashy knives, all kinds of smaller guns holstered to thighs or sticking up from belts.

The thing that really spooked her was the gas masks. They all wore black insectlike gas masks pushed back on top of their heads.

Gas? Then she saw the fat man come in with the two canisters on his back. The baker. The one from the birthday party. The one who'd brought the bomb inside the cake. The baker stood beside the muscular blond guy, another face she thought she recognized from the party, the security guy. He seemed to be the leader. He was shouting orders and threats at the frightened, terrified passengers. People were too shocked to panic yet, but husbands were searching for wives, people were speaking rapidly to each other, considering what to do and abandoning strategies instantly, paralyzed with fear, realizing the utter uselessness of their plans.

"Attention!" the blond man yelled, raising his rifle above his head and waving it about. "You are now all hostages of the Chechen Liberation Front. Do exactly as you're told, and no one will die. Disobey my orders, and you all will be killed. We are now flying at five thousand feet. For any one person who disobeys orders or causes trouble, five passengers, chosen at random, will be thrown out of the airship."

Oh, Stokely, she thought, feeling her whole body tremble. *Oh, baby, where are you now?*

The blond guy, the leader, kept shouting orders, making threats. She remembered his name suddenly. Yuri.

There was a commotion on the dance floor, where people were moving and sliding against each other, everybody knowing that at worst they were dead, at best they were at the beginning of a long ordeal. A husband and wife were arguing now in the middle of the crowd, and she heard the woman scream at her husband, "Do something, God damn you! Do something!"

Fancha heard herself saying into the micro-

614

phone, "Everybody try to stay calm. Do what they say, and we'll be okay."

But the woman who wanted action slapped her husband hard across the face and turned from him, pushing through the panic-stricken crowd on the dance floor, shoving people, trying to move toward the leader. People were slipping and falling, scrambling to get out of her way.

"Stop right there," Yuri said, seeing that she was headed for him. He pulled a large .45 automatic and aimed it at her head.

"Kill me!" she said, shouting at the top of her lungs. "Go ahead and kill me, you fucking bastard!"

"Stop now, I warn you!"

"Remember United Flight Ninety-three, asshole? That's me! That's who I am!" She looked around at the crowd behind her, her eyes wild, and said, "Let's roll!"

She kept pushing forward, ignoring the gun pointed directly at her. When she broke through the perimeter of the crowd and was maybe six feet from the blond guy, one of the nearby terrorists, who couldn't have been more than twenty, stepped forward with his knife and slashed her throat, almost severing her head, the blood gushing out onto her white evening gown.

She collapsed to the floor in a heap. The crowd was stunned for a moment but then started screaming in renewed panic, pushing one another out of the way, thinking there had to be some kind of escape, still some way out of this nightmare.

As Fancha desperately looked around for a way out, shots were fired. She didn't see who was shot, because right then the lights went out again.

The leader was screaming at them to get on the floor, *now,* or they would all be killed. This time, people listened, and she could sense them diving to the floor. In the darkness and pandemonium, her eyes began to adjust. And Fancha saw her escape.

There was a small backstage area behind the velvet curtains. A door back there led to the kitchen, and from the kitchen she knew she could find her way to the main staircase and down one deck to her cabin. She silently stepped around the musicians, who seemed rooted to their chairs, and slipped through the tiny gap in the heavy velvet curtains. It was totally dark and deserted backstage, but she could see a thin strip of light beneath the door to the kitchen.

The kitchen, too, was deserted. Maybe the staff had all been gotten rid of, or maybe they'd just fled in panic. She raced down the center aisle, sidestepping pots and pans on the floor where people had dropped them, and came to the swinging door to the corridor. She pushed through it, bracing herself for more armed men beyond, but the hallway was empty, too. Right, left? Which way? She was breathing hard, and her heart was pounding. Disoriented now, she took a deep breath and placed one hand on the wall, willing herself to calm down.

Think, Fancha.

Left. The stairs were to her left, at the very end.

She ran all the way, took the steps three at a time down to the promenade deck. Her cabin was number 22, five or six doors down on the left. Her luck was holding. The corridor to her room was empty. Usually, there were one or two of the beautiful Slavic housekeepers pushing their trolleys up and down the hall.

Key, where's the key? It was a card key, and it was still where she put it, in the inside pocket of her black velvet bolero jacket. She pulled it out and slipped it into the slot, praying for green, because sometimes the damn thing flashed red and she'd have to go looking for the steward or a housekeeper to let her in.

Green.

She pushed inside, just the sight of her turned-down bed and the lamp glowing softly on the bedside table doing wonders for her. She turned and double-locked the door, falling against it, her forehead against the cool wood, and then just let the tears come. She didn't make any noise; she couldn't allow herself that satisfaction, someone might be passing outside, so she just stood there crying silently, her shoulders shaking involuntarily.

Sweet baby Jesus, she whispered to herself, wiping her eyes, finally done with the tears.

She sat on the edge of the bed, looking at herself in the mirror over the dresser. And that's when she remembered the phone, the sat phone Stoke had unpacked and placed on the dresser. He'd left without it, and she'd put it in the top drawer. He'd shown her how to work it once. It was pretty easy.

She pulled the drawer open, grabbed it, and lay down on the bed, her head propped up on two pillows.

She could hear it ringing in Miami, once, twice, three times.

Pick it up! Pick it up!

"Hello?" It was Stokely.

"Baby, it's me," she said, her voice breaking.

"Honey? You okay? Talk to me, baby . . ."

"Not so okay, Stoke. Not okay at all."

"What is it? Tell me what's happening."

"I was singing, you know, and the lights went out. When th-they, when they came back on, the room was full of terrorists. Guns, knives, wearing g-gas masks and — shooting."

"Who are they? They identify themselves?"

"Chechen Liberation, some damn thing like that."

"Where are you? I mean now? How are you calling?"

"I'm in our stateroom. On the sat phone you left."

"Oh, God, baby. I'm so sorry."

"What do I do? I don't know what to do, Stokely!"

"You got the door locked?"

"Uh-huh."

"And nobody knows you're in there?"

"I don't think so . . ."

"Listen, baby. In the closet. On the top shelf. My canvas carry-on bag is up there. I forgot it."

"Yeah."

"My gun is in the bag, baby. The one we took out to the range together. The Heckler and Koch nine-millimeter. The one I showed you how to shoot at the range, remember?"

"I do."

"I want you to get it down. It's loaded. All you have to do is chamber a round, just like I showed you. There are two extra clips in the bag with fourteen rounds each. You get a chair facing the door, and you don't let anyone inside, okay? Somebody comes through that door, you shoot, okay?"

"Okay."

"Tell me what happened, best you can."

She gave him the short answer. Her heart

was pounding again.

"They already killed one hostage?"

"One that I saw. With a knife. But I heard shots just as I was leaving the stage. Maybe more are dead now . . ."

"Tell me about the leader again."

"Blond. Big muscles. He looks familiar."

"Yurin? The security guy at the party?"

"I don't know for sure, but yeah, I think so. Chechen Liberation Front, that's what he said."

"Chechen? Or Russian?"

"He said Chechen, but he's Russian, right?"

"Right."

"Baby, I'm so scared."

"You're going to be okay. Now, what about the baker? Happy? The fat man who brought the cake to the party. You see him?"

"Yeah, he's with them. He had two — two, uh, tanks strapped on his back. He had his mask down over his face. For the gas, I guess."

"Gas? What about gas?"

"They're all wearing gas masks, Stoke. They're going to gas us? Is that it?"

"Baby, they ain't going to do a damn thing. We are working on this right now. I just found out the baker might be aboard. I already told the CIA, the FBI, and the Pentagon. So right now, everybody in Washington is figuring out the best way to save you. The vice president himself is forming a rescue task force. Is his wife okay? I need to tell him."

"I think so. She was when I left."

"So, all you have to do is stay out of sight until the rescue, baby. And shoot anybody tries to come through that door. Can you do that?"

"Rescue how? They said if a plane or boat came within a radius of fifty miles, they'd start throwing people out the door, one at a time."

"When we come, they won't know what hit them, honey. Trust me. I am going to get you out of this."

"Are you coming?"

"You damn right I'm coming. You hold on, okay? I'll be there before you know it."

"I told you I didn't want to come on this damn trip without you."

"I know you did. You were right. I'm sorry."

"I need you, Stokely. We all do. You never saw such a scared bunch of people in your life."

"I'm coming."

"I'm going to hang up now, Stoke. Get the gun. But you answer the second you see this phone ring. You're all I've got to hold on to."

"I love you."

"I love you more."

"No way."

" 'Bye, baby. Be strong."

" 'Bye."

51

President Jack McAtee said good-bye to the British ambassador, hung up the phone, shook his head wearily, and looked at the crisis team he'd assembled in the Oval Office. Those present included the vice president, Tom McCloskey; the chairman of the Joint Chiefs, Charlie Moore; the secretary of state, Consuelo de los Reyes; the new director of the National Security Council, Lewis Crampton; FBI Director Mike Reiter; and the director of the CIA, Patrick Brickhouse Kelly, better known as Brick.

His team.

The mood was tense. They had an American city in ruins, and the evidence pointed to a Russian terrorist as culpable. If that were true, and McAtee found out the Kremlin was even remotely involved, military confrontation with Russia was back on the table for the first time since Kennedy had stared down Khrushchev over Cuba fifty years earlier, sitting at this same desk.

And now there was news coming out of the Salina investigation that an airship carrying hundreds of VIPs and Nobel laureates, not to mention the vice president's wife, might be a target for the same terrorists who had murdered Salina's mayor and her family and destroyed the town. A key suspect had been seen in Miami just before the airship departed.

"You guys ready for this one?" the president asked, trying to smile.

McAtee was tired and looked it. He saw events spiraling out of control and knew he was powerless to stop them. All he could do now was try to learn as much as he possibly could about exactly what the hell was going on and make the very best possible decisions he could under the circumstances.

The only good news was that his White House team had been in crisis situations before, maybe not as bad as this one, but they'd weathered the storms, come through well enough. It they were all smart, kept their heads and wits about them, they might get through this one, too. But it was a bitch, no doubt about that. The Russians seemed out of control — and they still had thousands of nuclear warheads aimed at America.

"What is it, Mr. President?" Brick Kelly said.

McAtee said, "That was the British ambassador. He says he just got a WTFIGO cable from London. Anybody know what that stands for?"

"What the fuck is going on?" Lew Crampton said.

"Bingo, Lew. He says the MI-6 intel currently coming out of Moscow is going from weird to completely insane. One, the president, Rostov, just died in a helicopter crash. Clear weather, military chopper, very suspicious. Two, the Duma is in emergency session, locked down, no media, rumors flying. Three, one of the British service's top operatives, an old friend of Brick's and this office, was just arrested coming out of the Bolshoi ballet."

"Not Alex Hawke?" Brick Kelly said.

"I'm afraid so, Brick."

"Jesus. The KGB's got him? Not good."

Brick Kelly said, "As you well know, he's gone undercover, sir. A new division of MI-6 called Red Banner. Designed to counter the resurgence of Russian intelligence. Hawke is in Moscow because —"

"He's in Moscow because I sent him there, Brick." The testiness in his voice bore witness to the tension in the room. "I was fully briefed on Red Banner by Sir David Trulove when he last visited the White House."

"Sorry, Mr. President, I should have assumed that. At any rate, one of my agents is liaising with Hawke and Red Banner. He's in

Moscow now. Harry Brock. I'm sure he can help."

"Ah, yes, Harry Brock. Well, that's reassuring, Brick, knowing you have a man of that caliber inside the enemy camp." The president's sarcasm was not lost on anyone.

"He's different, I'll admit, sir. But he's damn good in the field. I'll contact him and the American ambassador when this meeting's over. See if we can't get Hawke released as quickly as possible."

"Good. Thank you, Brick," McAtee said.

The president rose from his desk, walked to his favorite armchair to the right of the fireplace, and sank down into it.

"Anybody got any ideas?" he said.

As usual, no one in his government agreed with anyone else about what the hell they should be doing at the moment. That's why he'd assembled his team this morning, to try to make some wise collaborative decisions about how best to proceed through the current minefield.

"The primary card the Russians hold right now is energy," the secretary of state said, shifting her weight around on the sofa. "One, the petro-rubles make them immune from certain threats. And two, if pushed, they can throw the switches at Gazprom and Rozneft and turn out the lights in all of Europe."

"Not to mention the Baltics, East Ukraine, et cetera," the vice president added. "Bastards. They think they've got us in a corner. Rule one: Never corner a rat or the American military."

Tom McCloskey, the former Colorado rancher, was smart and tough, and he could focus. That's why McAtee had put him on the ticket, a decision he'd never regretted once.

The president looked at Kelly. "You've got human assets inside both Gazprom and Rozneft, isn't that right, Brick? Deep cover?"

"Yes, sir, we do. Three Russian engineers manning the on/off switches are on our payroll. Unnumbered accounts in Geneva."

"Could these guys actually stop this thing? If the Kremlin tried shutting everything down in Europe? Or the former Soviet republics?"

"Stop, no. Delay, yes. At least, they could buy us valuable time in a crunch. That's why they're there."

McAtee smiled. "Well, good news at last. We're on a roll. Anybody else?"

General Moore leaned forward, looking at his boss. "I ordered our overhead capability rerouted this morning. All sixteen of our low-level birds are now operating over the Russian mainland, Mr. President. Total satellite coverage."

"Good work. We'll need —"

"Mr. President?" Betsey Hall said, interrupting. McAtee's secretary had cracked the door and stuck her head inside.

"Yes, Betsey?"

"An urgent call for you. From Moscow."

"Who is it?" McAtee asked, looking at the blinking light.

"Someone named Korsakov. I believe he's the late President Rostov's successor."

"Turn on the tape, Betsey," McAtee said, returning to his desk, punching a button, and picking up the receiver.

"This is President McAtee," he said.

"President McAtee, I am Ivan Korsakov. I've just been selected by the Russian Duma as the new leader of our government. You are the first person I've called."

"Well, I'm glad you called. Congratulations, President Korsakov."

"Actually, I've been proclaimed Tsar."

"Tsar, is it? Well, that is interesting. Historic, one might say."

McAtee covered the phone and said to his team, "They've got a Tsar now. Holy Christ."

"Mr. President, I'm delighted we have this chance to speak," Korsakov said. "And I look forward to working with you. Striving to build a better world."

"I'm so glad to hear you say that, given recent troubling events."

"Mr. President, the people of my great country are relying on me to restore Russian pride and honor. All Russian people, whether they are in the Baltics, in Estonia, Lithuania, East Ukraine, wherever, they are all relying on me to restore the cohesion of the Russian nation."

Restore cohesion?

McAtee paused a moment to gather his wits and then said, "I'm sure over time, we will be able to work through your issues and still develop a plan that will retain the current integrity of Europe."

"Mr. President, I am not entirely sure of your meaning, but let me tell you what we feel we must do to reunite our citizens in the Baltics and East Ukraine."

"This sounds an awful lot like irredentism, and I don't think you —"

"If by that word you mean someone who advocates the restoration to their country of any territory properly belonging to it, then yes, that is exactly what I am saying to you. I am only speaking now of the territories mentioned. We can discuss Moldova and the 'Stans' at a later date."

"I must be misunderstanding you. Surely you're not proposing to alter the national boundaries of the European Community?"

McAtee looked up, surprised. His entire team had gotten up and gathered around his desk, lending him support. He smiled at them, grateful. He needed it.

He continued, "What you're suggesting would cast us back into the confrontation we put behind us at the end of the Cold War."

Secretary de los Reyes nodded her head,

vigorously approving the tack the president was taking.

Korsakov said, "Now, now, Mr. President, please. There is no need for confrontations. Let's not even speak in those terms."

"Frankly, Mr. Korsakov, we don't know each other. But let me assure you that you cannot expect me to remain silent and inactive while you prepare to cast aside all precedent and all the legal instruments that have given this world the stability it enjoys today. You are talking about illegally absorbing millions of citizens now happily part of other nations."

"Mr. President, this is not a negotiation. I had hoped to avoid just this sort of overheated rhetoric. But then, perhaps you haven't considered the security dimensions of the moment we seem to have arrived at?"

"Security dimensions? Is that a threat?"

"You are aware of the terrible incident at Salina, Kansas."

"Of course, I'm aware of Salina. An unfortunate development. We're sure it's not likely to happen again."

"On the contrary, that is exactly what is likely to happen again. But this time to a major population center and without benefit of advance warning."

"Mr. Korsakov, think extremely hard about what I am about to say. You yourself are not nearly so immune to certain actions as you seem to think. Reprisals could be swift and overwhelming."

"You are in no position to threaten me, I assure you."

"I'm not?"

"No. Trust me, as you will soon learn, you are not."

McAtee searched the faces of his team before replying. Each one of them made a slashing motion across the neck.

"I'm sorry, Mr. Korsakov. I am unable to continue this conversation any longer. Our ambassador will be in touch."

He hung up.

"Play that back on speaker, will you, Betsey?" he said after a moment.

The team stood around the desk and listened as both sides of the conversation were played. Jaws dropped, eyes rolled, but no one spoke when it was over. The implications of what they'd just heard were too profound to be assimilated in an instant. The world had just shifted on its axis, and the floor beneath their feet felt as if it might give way at any moment.

"Well?" the president said. "Welcome to the parallel universe. We've fallen through a wormhole. I always wondered if things could get any crazier. Now I know."

"Good Lord," the vice president said, managing a grim smile. "We're back to October 1962. Maybe worse."

"Definitely worse. This man is insane. A genius, perhaps, but a raving megalomaniac. Khrushchev was merely a Commie thug with a grade-school education," Mike Reiter said. The good-looking young director had only been on the job a few years. But he was a major history buff and had taught Russian studies at Georgetown before joining the FBI.

Consuelo de los Reyes felt her cell phone vibrate and stepped a few paces toward the Rose Garden windows to take the call. She listened for a few moments, then turned back to face the group, shaking her head, her face drained of all color.

"And the vice president's wife? Is she all right?" they heard her say. She listened and then looked at McCloskey, nodding, giving him a brief smile that said she was okay.

"Tell us what's happened, Conch," the president said when she'd ended the call.

"The airship *Pushkin,* en route from Miami to Stockholm for the Nobel ceremony, has just been taken over by Russian terrorists. One of the hostages managed to get to a satellite phone and call her fiancé in Miami. A man named Stokely Jones who does contract work for the Pentagon."

"Friend of Hawke's," Brick Kelly said. "Ex-Navy SEAL. Hostage-rescue specialist."

"My God, poor Bonnie," the vice president said, wandering dazedly over to a sofa and collapsing into it. "She's okay?"

"Yes. That's what the hostage told Mr. Jones. She had seen her, and she was okay."

The president stood up, staring at Charlie Moore.

"Everyone, listen carefully. I want you and your teams to initiate the following measures immediately. Lock down all Russian assets in this country. Everything. Seize all bank and real estate assets, detain and arrest the crews of every Russian ship in every U.S. harbor. Euro Command in Germany needs to crank up, now, General Moore. I need you to ascertain our offensive strike capability as of right this minute. Have the chief of naval operations send a flash message to the fleets, putting them all on high alert worldwide. Tell the CNO we need to know where all of our subs are, in the North Sea, around Kiel and St. Petersburg, also on the other side, Vladivostok. Tell him to get our carriers out of harm's way immediately. With me so far?"

"Yes, sir."

"Next. A flash message to the Air Force. We need to know exactly what our immediate bomber and fighter capabilities are and where. And we need to activate the capacity to jam the Russians' low-level combat satellites, and do it now. Yes?"

"Yes, sir."

"Okay, that's all I can think of at the moment. I'm sure you people will have more ideas as the situation develops. Let's get moving."

Moore, already headed for the door, paused and said, "One more thing, Mr. President. I'm going to get the SEAL hostage-rescue team working on this hijacking immediately. They'll come up with something if anyone can."

"Good idea. Now, Brick, you and Mike listen up," the president said. "SEAL HRT needs every bit of information you guys can get on that airship hostage situation. How the hell do you deal with something like that? It's not like a plane. Something that runs out of fuel and has to land sometime. Something SWAT hostage-rescue teams can board and overwhelm. A damn zeppelin can stay aloft indefinitely. So, what the hell do we do?"

Mike Reiter said, "I've just been thinking about that, Mr. President. And I don't have a goddamn clue."

52

Energetika

Hawke awoke to a scream. A terrible, masculine scream that stretched on forever. It started high and went low, as if the dying author had jumped off a cliff. It was a death scream. Whoever he was, the poor bastard was now among the departed. And he'd gone out the hard way. The man hadn't been far away, somewhere to Hawke's right, maybe only fifty yards or so. What had happened to him?

The windows of the darkened machine Hawke found himself in were coated with a thick rime of frost. It was bloody freezing inside the military helicopter. He could see his breath in pale blue lights that shone down as if from high walls looming up beside the chopper. Groggy, he tried to raise his hand to wipe clear a porthole on the glass beside his head and found he could not lift it. His wrists were bound with plastic flex cuffs and lay helplessly in his lap.

He looked down. His wrists were connected by a thin steel chain to cuffs around his ankles. How long had he been out? He could feel the drugs still coursing through his veins, but the effects seemed to be wearing off. He observed himself to be all alone, abandoned by his captors. This was his fate? To freeze to death in the back of a Russian helicopter? It hardly seemed fitting or even fair.

Where was he?

On the ground. Certainly not Lubyanka. He had no sense of being in Moscow or any city, for that matter. Outside, the wind was howling, and he could smell the sea nearby, hear waves crashing against rock. He'd been drugged and flown here in a helicopter. But where the hell was here? He leaned his injured head, now bandaged, back against the metal bulkhead behind him and tried to get his brain rebooted.

As the fog inside his head gradually lifted, he dimly recalled the last conscious moments outside the Bolshoi. He'd been arrested. Dragged away from Anastasia. Before he'd blacked out, he'd been sure they were taking him to Moscow's most notorious prison, the KGB's private gateway to hell. But no, he was sitting all alone in the back of a helicopter freezing to death. And outside, not too far away, a man had just died in agony.

There came the sound of heavy boots crunching on snow outside. And wavering fuzzy discs of lights, flashlights in the hands of four or five men, laughing drunkenly as they neared the chopper. One of them, the pilot, yanked the forward left door open and clambered up into his seat. Frigid wind blew through the cockpit. Instantly, Hawke heard the whine of the turbo engine spooling up. The pilot yelled something in slurry Russian to the men outside.

The right rear door was pulled open, and a flashlight was shoved into his face, a foot from his nose. This was cause for further hysteria among the men outside.

A red-faced man leaned inside and shouted something incomprehensible in Russian. Hawke ignored him, finally interrupting his tirade to say, "Get somebody who speaks English, for God's sake."

There was more shouting, and now someone else was yelling at him.

"Out!" a younger guard shouted in English.

"Sod off," Hawke replied. He was sleepy. His head hurt. He wasn't going anywhere.

Hands reached inside for him and yanked him bodily out onto the frozen ground. He stayed on his feet but felt faint, as if he might collapse. Then someone shouted more Russian and jabbed him with a rifle muzzle. He managed to stagger forward a few feet and remain upright.

He looked around. The helo, now lifting off with a roar and a great rotor downdraft, had landed inside some kind of courtyard. There were high stone walls surrounding it, punctuated every fifty yards or so by towering black Gothic spires. Lights showed at the very tops, men moving around inside. Guard towers. He was in some kind of prison. On an island, he thought, for he had no sense of any mainland, and he heard the sea all around him now that the chopper had tilted its nose down and disappeared into the black night.

"Go!" the English-speaking guard said, prodding him in the direction of a large four-story building that looked as if Charles Addams had been the principal architect. It was all spires and gargoyles, black with soot. Because his ankles were bound, he could only take small, painful steps through the black and crusty snow. The result was more prodding and shouted insults in Russian.

He saw human wraiths wandering around inside the yard, barely clothed; they were all wall-eyed, hairless men and women who seemed lost and demented. One of them, a female perhaps, loomed up in front of him, ghostlike, and opened her toothless mouth in a silent scream. A guard slammed her to the ground and kicked her out of their path.

He was passing through what appeared to be a forest of thick round stakes. He squinted his eyes in the blowing snow, trying to believe he was only imagining what he saw. The bodies of both men and women straddled the tops of the stakes. The stakes disappeared inside their groins. Some of them were still writhing and moaning in agony. Some of them, with the sharp points of the stakes protruding from their chests or necks, were mercifully dead.

Impaled.

He knew enough history to know that impaling had once been the favorite method of execution in this part of the world. A sharpened stake, penetrating the rectum, would kill you slowly, maybe in two or three days, before finding and piercing a vital organ. A dull stake, slowly inching upward as the weight of the victim did gravity's work, could take a week or more. Ivan the Terrible earned his moniker by impaling thousands. Peter the Great had impaled his share as well. Not to mention Vlad the Impaler, more popularly known in legend as Dracula.

But Hawke, as he staggered through this gruesome forest, had had no idea this barbaric method of execution was still in use.

Just when he thought it could get no worse, a guard lurched drunkenly toward the nearest stake, jumped up, and grabbed some wretched woman by the ankles, yanking her down a foot or more further onto the bloody stake. She screamed in agony, and the guard let go, collapsing to the ground in hysterics. Hawke, unable to control his rising gorge, wrenched himself free of the guards, bent forward from the waist, and retched, his vomit spattering his shoes, staining the freshly fallen snow.

He now knew the probable fate of the poor bastard whose cries had woken him up from his drug-induced sleep. He closed his eyes and remained still, swaying on his feet until he was prodded forward toward a set of steps that led up to a massive wooden door, blackened as if by fire but still intact.

And so he entered the vile prison known as Energetika. It seemed as if the fires of hell must be raging below. Those blackened walls outside. And inside, the floors, windows, walls, even the heavy old furniture were covered with layers of black soot. Yet there was no industry anywhere near this island. If Energetika wasn't hell on earth, surely it was close enough.

The jailer, a man with a stupid face beneath his green eyeshade and grimy, sooty clothes, sat behind a great carved desk littered with papers. He barely looked up when Hawke was presented to him. He took a swig of vodka from an open bottle on the desk, scrawled a notation on a random piece of paper, and pointed to a dark corridor leading off to the left.

"Why am I here?" Hawke shouted at the man as they tried to drag him away. He planted his feet and twisted free of their clutching hands.

"Why? Because you're under arrest, of course," the jailer replied.

"You speak English?"

"Obviously. We have schools in Russia, believe it or not. Even universities. Very civilized."

"On what charge?"

"Espionage against the Russian state. Our new Tsar, he doesn't tolerate spies. He executes them. I'll see you at dawn, Englishman. They're cutting a fresh stake for you now."

"New Tsar?" Hawke cried as they grabbed him again. "Who is he? What's his name?"

"His imperial majesty, Tsar Ivan Korsakov, that's who."

"I know him! We're friends! I must talk to him."

"Talk to the Tsar, he says?" the man said, and he and his comrades exploded with laughter. "Take him away," the jailer said, wiping tears of mirth from his rheumy eyes.

Hawke's new home was underground, three endless sets of steep stone steps that led downward into deeper gloom. A steel door was opened, and he was shoved inside, the door slammed shut behind him. He was alone inside a small, barrel-shaped cell whose bare, oozing walls seemed to be impregnated with tears. A flickering lamp stood on a stool in the corner, its wick swimming in fetid oil, illuminating his quarters.

He stood a moment and took inventory. A bucket for waste. A slab of metal secured to the wall on which lay a thin mattress blackened with age and God knew what else. He went to it and sat down, determined not to go mad before morning, determined to survive, whatever it took.

He had a son, after all. He was going to be a father. He held that moment in his mind, Anastasia whispering the joyous news in the dark, and used it to build his fortress, thick walls and ramparts high and mighty. Against the world.

At some time during the night, he must have fallen off, slept. He felt rough hands pulling at him and shouting. A dream? No, it was just the moon-faced jailer and two other foul-smelling lackeys, come to fetch him. Somewhere, a red dawn must have been breaking.

It was time.

"Where are you taking me?" he demanded. Terror was rising in him now, unabated. He knew from previous experience that only through sheer force of will would he be able to subdue it and face whatever was coming like a man.

They pulled him to his feet.

"Just tell me where you're taking me," he said again, hearing the pathetic weakness of his pleas, but he couldn't stop himself.

He had this irrational need to know. Was

this it? The end? Yes or no, which was it?

If the end is near and there's not a damn thing you can do about it, old sport, he thought to himself, *buck the hell up. Stiff upper.* And yet —

"*Tell me,* God damn you all!"

"Silence!" the jailer shouted, shoving him roughly toward the door. Hawke struggled with the plastic cuffs, knowing in his heart it was useless. There were three of them, two of them armed. What could he do? He had to think of something. But what? He deliberately dragged his feet, stumbled, fell forward with his bound hands outstretched to break his fall.

He rolled onto his back, and as a guard bent to lift him, he brought his knees up and caught him smartly under the chin. For his trouble, he got the butt end of the rifle across his jaw and was hauled to his feet again.

Hawke knew where they were taking him, of course. It must be dawn by now. Had to be.

And he was headed straight for a stake in the impaling yard.

53

But at the end of the corridor, instead of turning to the right and climbing upward to the yard, the guards steered him left and began descending another steep stone staircase leading down. And then down another, the steps progressively harder to see in the guttering light of lanterns hung from the walls. His escorts seemed in an inordinate hurry for Hawke's taste, and he could but wonder where they were going now.

"What fresh hell lies this way?" Hawke asked, not expecting a reply but feeling an overwhelming sense of relief that any new hell could hardly be worse than the one he'd believed most assuredly he was headed for.

"The dungeon," the moon-faced jailer said simply.

"The *dungeon?* And what, pray, do you call where I slept all night? With wee beasties scratching their way across my floor? The bridal suite?"

His attempt at gallows humor elicited no

reply, but it lightened his own heavy spirits as he descended into whatever subterranean inferno they had planned for him. The *oubliette,* most likely, a traditional feature of ancient forts, a deep well where a man was thrown and simply forgotten.

What the hell, he thought. He had to get off the bloody ride at some point. If this was his stop, so be it.

They passed along a few very grim corridors indeed, arches along both sides, each enclosing heavy wooden doors with small barred windows.

"This is us," the jailer said, pulling out a huge key ring and inserting one of them into the lock. It clicked, and the door squeaked open. Hawke followed the jailer inside, still in the grip of the guards. They lowered him to the stone floor, first to his knees and then letting him fall over on to his side.

"I am back in one hour," the jailer said, and with that, he and the two guards left, a great thud and a metallic clang as they pulled the heavy door closed behind them.

"Hello?" Hawke said, knowing he was not alone.

It was pitch black, but to his right, he saw the orange glow of a cigarette glow brighter and then dim as the smoker inhaled and exhaled.

"Good evening," a disembodied voice said pleasantly. Heavily accented English. "If you can manage to crawl over here, you'd be better off sitting up here next to me on the cot."

Hawke managed to sit upright on the damp floor, facing the strangely familiar voice.

"And why is that?" he asked, straining his eyes in the dark to see whom he was addressing.

"I've got a lead-lined mattress."

"Sounds comfy, but no thanks."

"Suit yourself. This prison was built on top of the deadliest radioactive dump in Russia. The Navy's been dumping poisonous nuclear waste here for fifty years. Eat a fish caught anywhere in these waters, and you'll glow in the dark for weeks."

"Surely you're not serious? A prison built atop a radioactive-waste site?"

"Fiendish, isn't it?"

"Helps me understand our cultural divide."

"You Brits lack Mongol blood. It's your great weakness."

"Perhaps I'll join you up there after all. A bit chilly down here on the floor."

"Deceptively chilly. Quite hot, in fact. One of the secrets of survival here is staying off the floor as much as possible This lowest level of Energetika is as close to hell as you can get."

"Survival is possible? But how?"

"Sorry. I should have said postponing the inevitable."

Hawke immediately clambered to his feet.

"I've definitely decided to accept your offer."

"Here, I'll move over. Plenty of room."

"Where are we?" Hawke asked his fellow prisoner, taking a seat next to the man on the lead-shielded cot.

"A small island off St. Petersburg. Energetika was originally a fortress built by Peter the Great to guard the approach to Kronstadt Naval Yard."

"Might I have a cigarette?" Hawke asked, getting as comfortable as he could, his back against the cold stone wall, his shackled legs dangling over the edge of the thin mattress.

"Hmm, of course. How rude of me. I should have offered you one."

The man leaned forward with the pack, the cigarette still in his mouth, and in the red glow, Hawke finally realized whom he was speaking to.

"Thanks," Hawke said, raising his manacled wrists and pulling a smoke from the pack. He stuck it between his lips, opened the matchbook, and lit up, puffing hungrily.

"Not at all," Vladimir Putin replied. "I've got an endless supply. That jailer's on my payroll. As are a majority of the guards. Vodka?"

"Good God, yes."

The former president of the Russian Federation produced two small tin cups and a bottle of Stolichnaya. He filled both cups to the brim and passed one to Hawke. He took a small, burning sip despite his urge to down it all at once. Nothing had ever tasted so good, so pure, so absolutely necessary before. Nothing.

Hawke said, "I'd heard you were in residence here. Never expected to pay you a visit, of course. I'm Alex Hawke, by the way."

"Oh, I know who you are, Lord Hawke, believe me. I've been expecting you."

"Call me Alex, won't you?"

"Doesn't care for titles," Vladimir Putin said, and extended his hand. "I recall that now, from your file. Alex, I am called Volodya." Hawke shook it with both of his. The man's grip was firm and dry and somehow reassuring.

"You've been here for some time, yet you've still got your hair and teeth, Volodya," Hawke said. "Unlike most of the poor wretches I saw wandering around up in the yard."

"My lead-lined mattress, you see. Miserably uncomfortable, but it serves its purpose. And I've got lead liners in my shoes as well. I can't stay here forever, but I'm all right for the time being."

"If you call this all right."

"Better than the forest of limbless trees up in the yard, believe me. I'm sure you saw it? Our orchard of death."

"The orchard of death. Good God, impaling. Who's responsible for that barbarism?"

"Your new friend, of course. Count Korsakov. Or Tsar Ivan, I should say. An old-fashioned Russian, he quite enjoys the spectacle of impaling. I'm sure he plans to attend your introduction to the stake, whenever that should happen."

"They really made him Tsar?"

"Hmm. It's been his plan all along. Now that he's eliminated every obstacle and hint of opposition, it's reality."

"He put you here?"

"He did. Or rather, he had Kuragin do it. Korsakov prefers to stay in the background while others achieve his ends. Fancies himself the wizard behind the curtain. Never dirtied his hands once in all the years I've known him."

"What was your crime? The world never knew why you disappeared. Even Auntie Beeb was stumped on that one."

"Auntie Beeb?"

"Sorry. Slang for the BBC."

"Success was my greatest failing in Korsakov's eyes. I brought Russia back from the brink of absolute chaos. And naturally, he loathed the fact that I was a democrat."

"You? A democrat? That's hardly our perception of you, sir."

"You in the West never understood me. I was in the process of building democracy, but doing it at my own speed. At a pace suitable to a country with a centuries-old tradition of autocracy. You saw what happened when we rushed headlong into democracy. Utter disaster and chaos. The greatest political disaster of the twentieth century. Anyway, that's ancient history. The simple truth is, I was far too popular and thus too powerful for a man who dreamed only of autocracy, of Tsardom."

"Sounds like he's come out swinging now."

"He has, certainly. He'll rule the world, you know. It's only a matter of time."

"We've heard that before. I believe Stalin and Lenin had similar notions. The great workers' revolution it was called back then."

"Korsakov is different. He's a legitimate genius. Nobody can stop him now. Even the Americans blasting satellites out of the sky with all their secret Star Wars weaponry can't touch him. More vodka?"

"Yes, please. Perfect. Thank you."

"I've got to say, under the circumstances, you're the cheery one, aren't you, Lord Hawke? Sorry. I mean Alex."

"Cheerfulness in the face of adversity. You've heard that one, I'm sure."

"No."

"Comes from our Royal Marines ethos. The four elements of the commando spirit: courage, determination, unselfishness, and my all-time favorite, cheerfulness in the face of adversity. My father taught me all four when I was six years old. I've tried to take them to heart all my life."

"Your father was an admirable man," Putin said, raising his cup.

Hawke clinked it with his own and said, "Well. A bit of dirty weather ahead, that's all. Nothing for it but to batten down various hatches, right? We all cross the bar sooner or later."

"There's an oil lamp hanging above my head, Alex. If you'll return my matches, I'll provide a bit of light for you."

Hawke handed him the matches, and Putin lit the wick, throwing shadowy silhouettes of the two men against the farther wall. Putin looked at him carefully in the flickering lamplight, as if he were coming to some kind of decision.

"Do you know why you're here, Alex? Here at Energetika, I mean."

"No idea. I'm a simple English businessman on a business trip. Like everyone else in prison, I'm completely innocent of any and all crimes."

"He put you in this poisonous hole, you know."

"He?"

"Korsakov, of course. Have you met him?"

"I have. Very charming but with the eyes of a fanatic."

"He wants you dead."

"Why? What have I ever done to him? I'm madly in love with his daughter, for God's sake. I plan to marry her."

"And she's in love with you, I'm told. Part of the problem."

"What problem?"

"You are a highly unsuitable match for Anastasia, princess of Russia. Your background is wholly unacceptable."

"Unacceptable? I'm descended from some rather scandalous pirates, I'll grant you, but that shouldn't be held against me. On what grounds?"

"Your father, to begin with."

Hawke almost choked on his vodka. "My father? He died when I was a boy of seven. After a long and distinguished naval career, I might add. What on earth has he to do with any of this?"

"I can answer in one word," Putin said as he emptied his cup. "Scarp."

"Scarp," Hawke said, and leaned back against the wall, savoring his cigarette and his vodka.

"Scarp," Putin repeated. He liked saying the word, liked the harsh sound of the single syllable.

"Funny, that," Hawke said. "That's the second time in three days that benighted rock has come up in conversation. Korsakov was going on about it, too, at his winter palace. Something about stalking on the island during the Cold War. I had no earthly idea what he was talking about. Sounded a bit daft on the subject."

"Korsakov keeps a list. People he wants to kill. Naturally, I'm on it. That's why I'm here. Doing the slow burn, they call it. But you, well, you've been on the list since the day you were born."

"Have I, indeed? I understand you being on it. Politics. But what the hell's he got against me?"

"In October 1962, your father killed the only man Ivan Korsakov ever loved. His older brother, Sergei."

"My father killed a man on Scarp? Ridiculous. How? It's not possible. My family has had a shooting lodge there for generations. I've been going myself for years. It's a tiny island. Any kind of foul play or disappearance would have been reported. I've never heard a thing. My father, by the way, killed any number of people in the line of duty. But he was no murderer."

"Who said anything about murder? Ivan's brother was KGB, like all of us. During the height of the Cuban missile crisis, it was learned that your father figured in a British plan to infiltrate a secret Soviet facility up near the Arctic Circle. Operation Redstick. This was at a very critical moment in the standoff. Khrushchev couldn't allow our operations to be penetrated. Colonel Sergei Korsakov was dispatched by KGB to Scarp to eliminate your father."

"And?"

"Obviously, your father eliminated Colonel Korsakov."

"And the body?"

"Your father buried him, I suppose. Kept his mouth shut about it. That's what I'd have done."

"And so I'm tossed into the dungeon, like some latter-day Count of Monte Cristo, thrown into the bloody Château d'If for a crime I did not commit?"

"Yes. A great irony, isn't it, that it was the Tsar's own daughter who discovered you on that deserted beach and delivered you up to her father's sacrificial altar."

"I suppose it is rather ironic. Revenge, is it, then?"

"Exactly. Revenge of the very best kind. Keenly anticipated and long awaited."

"I'm surprised he hasn't done away with me sooner."

"Ah, but our Tsar likes to savor his revenge. Anticipate it. In any case, there were hundreds of political enemies who needed exterminating at the stake, all ahead of you on the list. You he sees as mere fun. He wants to toy with you, a cat-and-mouse game."

"How much time for fun have I got left?"

"Until your execution? You're scheduled for a dawn exit. If not this one, the next. But relax, Alex. I'd give you at least forty-eight hours. Our new Tsar is tied up with celebratory receptions and meetings in Moscow and then this Nobel ceremony in Stockholm. Then he'll show up here in his great airship, and you will be shown to the stake, I'm afraid."

Hawke shuddered.

He'd never been afraid of dying. In his dirty line of work, he'd always known a quick and brutal death might come his way at any time.

But not this way.

Not the bloody stake.

The orchard of death struck something akin to pure terror in his heart.

54

Hawke sipped his vodka and said, "How have you managed to avoid it so long? The stake, I mean."

"Now you have asked a good question," Putin said, putting a match to a fresh cigarette. "Despite Korsakov's abiding desire to see me slowly turn to soot and ash in here, I'm protected, you see."

"By whom?"

"Powerful people who think Ivan Korsakov is a madman who will see Russia a smoldering ruin after a ruinous world war with the West. I, of course, share that opinion." He took a puff. "Insanity."

"These people would like to see you return to power?"

"Obviously."

"Why don't they get you out of this bloody hole, then?"

"I wouldn't live twelve hours on the outside. An army of Korsakov's assassins lies beyond those black walls. The Third Department, he calls them. So long as the Tsar lives, the safest place on earth for me, oddly enough, is right here at hell's gate. And so I'm content to bide my time, knowing it will come."

"Bit difficult to bide one's time contentedly when, like me, one only has forty-eight hours to live. Or less."

"Yes. That's why I sent for you tonight."

"You mean it's not dawn yet? I assumed the sun was up."

"No." Putin pushed a button, and his watch glowed. "It's only two in the morning."

"Why *did* you send for me? Not that I'm not extraordinarily grateful."

"I wanted to meet you. You're a legend."

"A legend? Hardly."

"When one's life comes down to facts versus legend, go with legend every time, Alex, trust me. In any event, you have a first-rate reputation inside the KGB. You are an extraordinarily well-respected intelligence officer. I've followed your career closely for years. When I was head of KGB, I tried to recruit you over to our side. You will remember a certain statuesque blonde in a café in Budapest, what, six years ago now? You two adjourned to the Hotel Mercure in Buda for the evening. Room 777."

"Katerina Obolensky. I will never forget her."

"Of that I made certain. But alas, you had some stubborn sense of loyalty to your mother country. Later on, at the Kremlin, I continued to follow your exploits. Cuba, China, the Middle East, et cetera. One of the reasons I was so looking forward to this encounter. 'Talk shop' is the expression in English?"

"Yes. There were other reasons?"

"It is very much in my interest to help you escape from here. Now that we've spoken, I'm convinced my preconceived notions about you were correct. I think you're one of the few men alive who stands even a ghost of a chance against Korsakov. And now that you know how and why you were consigned to a horrible death in this hellhole, you have a very good incentive to kill him before he kills you. Should we be able to get you out of here, of course."

Hawke took a deep breath, trying to accept the very pleasing notion that an agonizing death was not inevitable and that somehow salvation might actually be possible.

"Let's go down that road, shall we? I was wondering, you know, how the guards come and go. Clearly, they can't all stay out here for extended periods, I mean, if they are to survive the radiation."

"They rotate frequently, Alex. Four-hour shifts three times a week. Twelve hours a week isn't lethal. Two ferries are running continuously back and forth to St. Petersburg. Like shuttles, I believe that is the English word.

One ferry arrives as the other is departing."

"That could work."

"No. These boats are not under the control of my 'friends' here. Very tight inspections going and coming. You'd never make it."

"I could go out in a laundry basket. It's been done."

"In films. Not here. No one has ever gotten out of here alive. Some have tried to swim it, believe it or not. Three attempts since I've been here. Eight miles to the mainland. They prefer hypothermia and drowning to prolonged radiation sickness. Or, certainly, the stake."

"Good information."

A lengthy silence ensued.

"Are you thinking?" Hawke asked Putin.

"I'm always thinking."

"Anything interesting come to mind?"

"You'll be the first to know."

The two men sat side by side in silence, puffing and sipping and thinking. It occurred to Hawke that he and Comrade Putin were getting just the slightest bit pissed. It was quite pleasant, actually.

Suddenly, Putin sat forward on the cot.

"I'm going to show you something I've never shown to another guest down here. Take it as a measure of my trust and respect."

"What is it?"

"The other room."

"The *other* room?"

"Watch and grow wise," Putin said, and pulled a slender remote-control device from beneath his fried mattress. He pressed a button, and a razor-thin rectangle of light appeared in the wall opposite the bunk where the two men sat. There was a pneumatic hiss, and a large section of stone swung out from the wall, revealing a small, lighted room beyond.

"Wonders will never cease," Hawke said, becoming convinced that they would not. He was still alive, for one thing. He was sitting in a dungeon sharing a bottle of vodka with the former prime minister of the Russian Federation. And the new princess of all Russia was pregnant with his child. Wondrous.

"What's in there?" Hawke asked.

"My lead-lined room. Constructed in total secrecy and at vast expense with the help of my jailer. The man who brought you down here is on my payroll. Former KGB assassin who worked for me in East Germany. Looks like a common thug, dumb as a post, but he's actually quite brilliant."

"What's in it, your secret lead vault?"

"Hmm. A real bed. Music and DVDs. My books and a few mementos. And a small refrigerator full of good vodka and a quantity of golden Sterlet caviar."

"And your plan for my salvation is?"

"There's also a satellite telephone. So I might maintain communication with my underground commanders, even now planning my triumphant return to power."

"And might I use this telephone? Call in the cavalry?"

"You are such a clever fellow, Hawke. Yes, you may use it. It's in the top drawer beside my bed. One call. You'd better make it a good one."

Hawke got to his feet. "I might actually get out of here," he said, smiling at Putin.

"Vastly preferable to a sharp stake up the sphincter, I assure you, Lord Hawke."

Three hours later, Hawke was shivering in the yard, crouched in a darkened alcove beneath one of the watchtowers, freezing his butt off. The sky above was shot pink with the approaching dawn. No sound could be heard from the poor devils in the orchard of death. Frozen stiff during the night, if they were lucky. He looked at his watch. He should have heard something twenty minutes ago. Where the hell was the cavalry?

He heard the approaching chopper before he saw it, the deep *thrump-thrump-thrump* announcing some helo's imminent arrival. *Harry? Let it be Harry. Please.*

Guards emerged from stations on the wall, machine guns slung from their shoulders. One raised a pair of binoculars to his eyes, tracked the approaching chopper for a few moments, and then signaled okay to his comrades. They immediately retreated back inside the warmth of their tower stations. Okay? Why would they signal that? This was a bloody rescue attempt, wasn't it?

No.

Damn it to hell!

The helicopter, Hawke saw as it flared up over the yard, did not look remotely like anything Harry Brock would be flying. No, it was a Russian Army Kamov Ka-50 Black Shark, bristling with antitank missiles and 30mm machine guns hung from small mid-mounted wings amidships. A damn Russian military chopper! Where the bloody hell was Harry?

When the pilot was six feet from touch-down, a typhoon of snow in his downdraft, someone flung open the starboard-side pas-senger door.

And inside, beckoning to him, was a wildly grinning Harry Brock.

Hawke stayed low and bolted through the shadows across the yard, head down, sprint-ing beneath the spinning rotors. A second door on the right side popped open, and Hawke dove inside, not even waiting for the jet-black combat chopper to land. He caught a glimpse of the guards on the walls, peering out the windows. One or two raced outside and along the parapet, shouting something inaudible, lost in the wind and roar of the chopper's powerful engines spooling up.

The helo pilot immediately lifted off, banked hard, and roared out over the wind-whipped Gulf of Finland, heading toward mainland Europe.

"Harry, you crazy sonofabitch, how did you pull this one off? A Russian Army combat helicopter? These are pretty tough to come by for American civilians."

"You think those guards back there would have let me land a Bell Jet Ranger with the stars and stripes on the tail?"

"No, but I mean, how the hell, Harry? Seriously."

Brock hooked his thumb toward the rear of the chopper. "Ask her royal highness back there, boss. Daddy's little princess gets what she wants."

Anastasia, dressed in a fleece-lined Army jumpsuit, was waiting in the rear. Hawke scrambled aft and almost landed in her outstretched arms. She pulled him to her. He was shaking with the cold, and he embraced her, letting her warmth and fragrance begin to wash away the ugly images of the last twelve hours.

"My poor darling," she said, holding him at arm's length. "I was so terrified. I couldn't reach Papa to tell him about your ridiculous arrest until a few hours ago. He was outraged. Whoever did this to you will be severely punished, Papa will see to it."

Hawke was considering how best to respond

to this bit of awkwardness when he heard Harry say, "I gotta ask one question. They allowed you an effing phone call from inside that burned-out freakhouse?"

"Not really allowed. It's a long story."

Brock said, "Anastasia was with me when you called my cell phone. We were having a drink at the Metropol bar, figuring out who to invite to your funeral. Short list, you'll be sad to learn."

"Funeral postponed indefinitely," Hawke said, reaching forward to squeeze Harry's shoulder. "Thanks, old buddy, I definitely owe you one. Where are we headed?"

"No rest for the weary," Harry said, turning around in his seat. "We're going direct to Ramstein Air Base in Germany. Two FA-18 Super Hornets are gassing up right now to take us to Bermuda. We hook up with Stokely on the ground there."

"Why on earth are we going to Bermuda?"

"Hostage-rescue mission, boss, all I can say. It's too noisy to talk in here," he said, casting a meaningful glance at the Russian Army pilot. "I'll fill you in when we get on the ground at Ramstein."

"And what about you, darling girl? Are you coming to Bermuda?" Hawke asked Anastasia, taking her hand and holding it to his cheek. The Gulf of Finland, garlanded with wind-blown whitecaps, was disappearing beneath the chopper at an amazing rate.

"No, darling, I can't. I'm returning to Moscow. A gala reception for my father tonight at the Facets Palace inside the Kremlin, and then we board the airship in a day or two for the short flight to Stockholm. For the Nobel ceremony, you know?"

"I hear he's the new Tsar," Hawke said, with a heartiness that rang with terrible falsity in his ears. "You must be very proud."

"It's so wonderful, Alex. Not for him but for my country. Russia will be a great nation once more," she said, beaming at him. "The first Tsar to receive a Nobel. I am so very proud of him. Promise me you'll come that night, Alex! Come to Stockholm for the Nobel dinner? I'll save a seat for you."

"Of course I'll come, Anastasia. If you want me there, I will be there."

"Might be a lot of empty seats at that Nobel ceremony," Harry Brock said, looking meaningfully at Hawke, but neither Alex nor Anastasia had any idea what he was talking about. Hawke let it go. Clearly, Harry had a great deal to tell him. He'd just have to wait and find out what when they landed at Ramstein.

Alex Hawke spent the rest of the trip staring down at the sea, all the way to the frozen white fields of Germany. He was oddly troubled for a man who'd just escaped a horrible death. Something was stuck in his craw, and for the life of him, he could not figure out what the hell it was. Half an hour later, he had it. An offhand remark Putin had made last night, a simple sentence that had seemed innocuous enough at the time.

It's a great irony, isn't it, that it was his daughter who found you and delivered you to the sacrificial altar?

Alone on a deserted beach? One of hundreds just like it? No. How could he doubt her love? She'd just saved his life. This marvelous woman who was carrying his child. She was truly beautiful. And true beauty, as she'd told him one afternoon at Half Moon House, came from deep inside.

He reached over, took her hand, and gently squeezed it.

"I may not have mentioned this," Hawke said, whispering into her ear, "but I want to thank you for saving my life."

"I had nothing to save until I found you. Now I have you, I have everything."

55

Moscow

It was snowing.

A beautiful winter's night. Anastasia rushed through Cathedral Square to the Grand Kremlin Palace, her long white sable coat trailing behind her in the powdery snow. She was late, breathless, and completely happy for perhaps the first time in her life. Her heart, she knew, was full at last. Every palace window was aglow. Nothing had never looked so dazzling.

Lofty and majestic, the Moscow residence of the Tsars dominated the southern part of the Kremlin. The windows of the main wing faced the dark Moskva River, brimming with ice floes in mid-December. There were great throngs of people lining the quay and the bridges despite the heavy snow, all eyes gazing up at the glittering palace. All of Moscow seemed aware that this was a truly historic night not to be missed. The city seemed frozen in place; even the traffic had come to a complete stop.

For the first time in more than ninety years, Russia had a Tsar. Bells were ringing loudly from every church tower, and in some places, crowds had gathered and were singing ancient Russian folk songs, passing bottles of vodka to stave off the chilly night air.

The Grand Kremlin Palace overshadows all other Western European palaces of the period in terms of sheer size and ornateness. It was only fitting, she thought, that her father's greatest triumph should be celebrated in such a glorious setting. She hurried up the white marble staircase leading to the State Parade Chambers on the second floor. This entrance was closed to the public tonight but, tonight, Anastasia was not the public.

She was the princess.

Two guards in their most festive regalia stood at attention on either side of the ancient wooden door in the huge east wing of the palace. The door was fifteen feet high, a masterpiece of nineteenth-century Russian carpentry, made from the wood of nut trees without using a single nail or any glue.

A chain of halls named for the old Russian orders lay behind this door: the St. George, St. Vladimir, St. Catherine, St. Andrew, and St. Alexander Halls. Anastasia paused at a cloak room just inside the entrance and gave the attendant her sable coat, hat, and muff. Also her furry boots, which she exchanged for the pair of heels in her bag.

Then she hurried through the vast octagon of St. Vladimir Hall, her heels clicking on the parquet floors. One of the arches opened onto a passage leading directly to the largest and most festive hall in the palace, St. George Hall. The dimensions of the lovely cloister vault were gigantic, nearly two hundred feet long and sixty feet wide. At the far end was the orchestra, and she noted with pleasure that they were playing, not Tchaikovsky or Rachmaninoff, but her father's new symphony, *Light of Dawn.*

She pushed through the sea of beautiful gowns and splendid uniforms toward her father. Above the crowd, six massive gilt chandeliers lit with more than ten thousand electric candles cast a lovely glow. She saw him! He was standing with a small group on a raised podium just in front of the orchestra, in one of his most splendid white uniforms.

She hurried toward the new Tsar, her eyes shining.

"Father," she said, embracing him. "I'm so sorry I'm late. You look wonderful."

"My dear girl. I've just asked for a waltz. Will you join me out on the floor?"

"I should be honored, Papa."

He took her outstretched hand and stepped down from the podium. As they made their way to the center of the floor, a lovely Strauss waltz began, and the crowd parted magically, every eye on the new Tsar and his beautiful daughter in her shocking crimson gown. She looked at her father, dazzling in his uniform, and remembered something Alex had said to her that night in the troika.

Don't look now, but we're living in some kind of bloody fairy tale.

It was true, she was. As she'd made her way through the palace's many halls, she'd heard the words whispered over and over as she passed. "The princess! Do you see her? How beautiful she is!"

And then her father was waltzing her around the suddenly empty dance floor, the crowd having moved to the sides of the hall, leaving the Tsar and his daughter alone to bathe in the adulation of all of Moscow. And no one in the ballroom that night would ever forget how heartbreakingly beautiful the new Princess of Russia had looked, waltzing with the Tsar.

"Oh, Papa, isn't it magical?"

He pulled her close and whispered softly into her ear. But his words were a cruel shock.

"How dare you?" he hissed. "How *dare* you?"

"What?" she cried, pushing away so that she could look up into his face. "How dare I what, Papa?"

She had never seen such anger as flashed in those eyes, and she tried to shrink back, but he held her tightly around the waist with one

669

hand, the other hand cruelly squeezing her fingers. And so they danced on, the enraptured crowd blissfully unaware of the drama unfolding before their eyes.

"Betray me, of course," he said, his voice low but full of menace.

"I? Betray you? Never!"

"Ah, and now you lie. You little bitch."

"Tell me, then! Tell me what I have done."

"This fucking Englishman. The one you invited into our home. You think he loves you? Ha! He is only using you to spy on me. He is an agent of MI-6! I had him arrested and sent to Energetika, where he so richly deserved to be. Only to find out that he has been rescued! And not by his comrades, no! By my very own daughter!"

"Papa, what are you saying? It was you who had Alex arrested? Because earlier, when I told you he'd been taken, you said it was all a mistake. That you would have him freed!"

"This was a matter of state security. It is not incumbent upon me to confide to you in matters of state."

"Papa, Alex is not a spy. He's much too gentle a soul for that kind of work. Besides, I would never betray you. I thought you wanted his freedom. So I took it into my own hands. He's the man I love, Father. The man I want to marry. I wanted him to meet you because I love you, too. And I am so proud of you both that I wanted to —"

"Silence! You don't know what you are talking about, you silly little fool. Listen to me carefully. I never want you to see him again. Ever. *'Smert Shpionam,'* Anastasia. Remember that. 'Death to spies.' And anyone who conspires with them. Understand me?"

"And now you threaten me? Your only daughter?"

"I care only for the state."

"Father, please, I beg of you. Can we not discuss this later? At some quiet place and not here in front of all Moscow?"

"There is nothing more to discuss. You are the daughter of the Tsar. You are the Princess Anastasia. One day, you will be Tsarina and sit upon the throne. I will find you a suitable husband, don't worry. But I will have an heir worthy of my legacy. Do you understand me?"

"Papa, I am already carrying his baby. I am pregnant." Her voice broke, and the tears came.

"You'll just have to get rid of the little bastard."

"Oh, Papa."

"Stop this blubbering! What will people think?"

"I'm sorry, Papa, I cannot help it. I-I don't know what to do now. What am I to do? I love him with all my heart. And he loves me. I want to have his baby, Papa. You must let me have his baby."

"Never!"

"Oh, God. Oh, God," she sobbed, and her father quickly saw that she was nearing hysteria. He held her tightly to his chest and whirled her about, whispering feverishly into her ear.

"Listen, my darling. Perhaps you are right. We should talk about this later when there is not so much attention focused on me. After the ceremony in Stockholm, we will go away somewhere for a few days. Like we used to do. A father-and-daughter vacation. Perhaps on the fjord in Sweden. Our old summer place at Morto. There we will try to resolve this unfortunate affair in a way that is acceptable to both of us. How does that sound?"

"Oh, Papa, you must believe me. I would never do anything to hurt you. Yes. Thank you for trying to understand. We will talk later when we are both not under so much pressure. I understand what you are saying. I will try to make you happy with me again."

"That's my girl."

"I love you, Papa. I know you will make a wonderful Tsar. Wise and kind. The father of our country."

He released her then and bowed to her, deeply, from the waist. The crowd burst into long and sustained applause.

"Her imperial majesty, the Princess Anastasia!" the Tsar cried out, and then the crowd went simply mad. She smiled, turning so that she might gaze into the gathered faces, waving at them all, saying "Thank you, thank you" in a small voice that no one could hear but everyone understood.

"Thank you for the dance," her father said coldly as they walked back to the podium.

Russia's new princess couldn't stop her tears. But she kept her smile.

56

At sea

Alex Hawke had the best seat in the house. He was just aft of the pilot. Under normal circumstances, his was the Weapon System Officer's seat. Hawke's WSO position, the Yank flyboys called it wizzo, was slightly elevated above and behind the pilot, so he had a good view ahead over the pilot's helmet. The WSO who normally resided here was the air navigator, involved in all air operations and the weapon systems of the aircraft. The plane was an American Navy F/A-18 Super Hornet, the two-seat F model that flew its first combat missions in 2002.

But these were not normal circumstances. There was no need for any wizzo on this flight. This F model had been heavily modified and was one of a small number of twin-canopied fighters built by the Navy for black ops missions like this one.

Two Super Hornets were streaking wingtip-to-wingtip just above the wave tops at 1,360 miles per hour, flying beneath any possible enemy radar, the heaving blue Atlantic a blur fifty feet below the aircraft. Off Hawke's starboard wingtip was an identical, heavily modified fighter aircraft. Harry Brock was riding wizzo in that one. The two fighter jets, having arrived on station, were operating approximately fifty miles due north of Bermuda. Suddenly, in tandem, both aircraft hit the afterburners and, pulling serious g's, went into a steep climb.

Ascending rapidly to a new altitude of 5,000 feet, the fighters immediately leveled off and hit the air brakes. Hawke checked his gear, deliberately slowing his breathing. Since they were maintaining radio silence, he looked over at Harry and gave him the okay hand signal. It was returned. It was almost time.

There was a bit of static in Hawke's headphones, and then he heard the slow West Texas drawl of the pilot, Captain Leroy Mc-Makin.

"Howdy, folks, this is your captain speakin', up here in the front of the airplane. Certainly has been my pleasure having you onboard today for our short flight from Germany to the middle of nowhere. Like to thank y'all for choosing Black Aces Air today. We do know you have a choice of air carriers, and we sure do appreciate your business."

Hawke laughed. American Navy pilots,

always a breed apart.

"Thanks for the ride, Cap," Hawke said, craning his head around to look at the surface of the sea below.

"Well, we want to wish you a pleasant stay here in the middle of the Atlantic Ocean or wherever your travel plans may take you, and if your future plans should call for air travel, I sure do hope you'll think of the Black Aces."

Captain McMakin craned his head around and smiled a big Yankee grin at his passenger. Hawke gave him a thumbs-up in return.

Hawke reached down for one of the two oh-shit handles built into the sides of his padded seat bucket. He pulled one of them up into firing position. He waited a beat. Then he pulled the trigger. For one long second, nothing happened. Then the canopy ejection initiator fired, causing the single aft canopy to jettison. Next, the rocket catapult under the seat fired with a roar of flame, ejecting a strapped-in Hawke and his seat out of the aircraft, 300 feet, straight up, pulling three g's.

He was now riding a Zero-Zero ejection seat, capable of saving his life even if deployed at zero velocity and zero altitude.

Two-tenths of a second after the catapult fired, the seat stabilization gyros canceled asymmetric forces producing seat tumbling and rotation. Six-tenths of a second after the seat left the floor of the aircraft, his seat-separator system activated. Hawke's lap belt released, and he was forced away from the seat, into thin air. His chute popped and began his descent toward the sea under a normal canopy. At the same time, a survival kit and a small raft had deployed.

Hawke had never ejected before.

It was a unique experience, having the wind blast whip the air out of your nose sideways. In the old days, when he'd first learned to jump out of airplanes, it was a bit less exciting. You were supposed to be facing the ground with your head a little lower than your feet when you pulled the chute, so that when the lines paid out and your chute opened, the risers would swing you under, and you wouldn't get that terrific grab up through the crotch that could be so unpleasant in so many ways.

Hanging in his straps, he saw Harry's chute deploy. He checked his watch.

So far, so good.

Ten minutes later, he was paddling his raft toward Harry. Harry was in his raft but seemed to be having a few problems separating from his chute.

"Harry!" Hawke called out when he was twenty feet away. "You all right?"

"Yeah, yeah, yeah. If I could get rid of this damn harness."

Hawke nudged his raft up next to Brock's. Harry had a vicious-looking knife out and was sawing away at one of the straps.

"Some thrill ride, eh, Harry?"

Harry finally got rid of his harness and shoved the tangled mess over the side. He looked up at Hawke.

"It was all right, I guess. Hell, I been kicked in the ass harder than that."

The two men drifted around each other for a few minutes, bobbing along with the rollers, staring at the vast blue sea and sky.

"Well, this is fun," Brock said finally.

"Yep," Hawke replied, trailing his fingers through the water. "Beats the hell out of Energetika, trust me."

"Got any ideas?"

"Afraid not. You?"

"Know any games?"

"What kind of games?" Hawke asked.

"You know. We could play Twenty Questions."

"I'd kill you," Hawke said.

"How about I Spy?" Harry asked. "Ever play that? I spy with my little eye —"

Hawke laughed. "You're funny, Harry. Really. It's the only reason I put up with you."

At that moment, a few hundred yards away, the deep blue sea began to boil. It heaved upward in a frothing white mushroom, as if deep below the surface, some underwater volcano had just blown its top.

"This us?" Harry asked.

"Better be. If it's not, we're in deep shit."

The sleek black prow of a giant nuclear submarine broke the surface at a forty-five-degree angle, water sheeting off its flanks. It was a magnificent sight, Hawke thought, one you never tired of seeing.

It was the old SSBN-640, all right. The USS *Benjamin Franklin,* commissioned in 1965, Captain Donald Miller commanding. Formerly a fleet ballistic missile sub, she'd been extensively modified to support Navy special operations missions. Her entire ballistic missile section had been removed and turned into living quarters, a space where embarked special operations personnel could rest, train, and plan operations in relative comfort.

Now registered as *Kamehameha,* she was based at the Royal Dockyard, Bermuda, and permanently attached to the joint U.S.-U.K. intel group known as Red Banner.

57

"Like to begin by welcoming Commander Hawke and Mr. Brock aboard the *Kamehameha*," Stokely Jones said. They were in the sub's SPECWAR wardroom. Stoke stood in front of a blackboard. On the wall beside him were blown-up pictures of the hijacked airship from every possible angle. The men around the table included Hawke and Brock plus two fourteen-man platoons of SEAL counterterrorist commandos.

The hand-picked members of the U.S. Navy's elite counterterrorist group and hostage-rescue team, SEAL Team Six, had begun training for this mission ten minutes after the president had learned of the hijacking. Training normally consisted of lessons learned from experience. But no one had ever assaulted an airship before.

No one. Ever.

The sub had been steaming submerged for more than an hour since they'd picked up Hawke and Brock. They were positioned directly beneath the airship now, at a depth of two thousand feet, immobile. A tiny video camera mounted on an invisible needle-thin antenna from the sub's conning tower provided a continuous live feed of the airship. The ship was dark for the most part, very few lights aboard as the sun set and darkness fell.

"The situation is this," Stoke said, offering a quick summary for the two new arrivals. "We've got four hundred terrified passengers aboard this damn zeppelin. We think they're still being held here, in a large ballroom on the promenade deck. Guarding the hostages are approximately twenty heavily armed terrorists, highly trained members of OMON, the Russian special forces. There is also the possibility that a Russian-American assassin named Strelnikov has brought poison gas aboard the *Pushkin,* an incapacitating narcotic based on the drug fentanyl, administered accidentally at a lethal dosage level in the Moscow theater siege. Any questions so far?"

"What the hell do they want?" Hawke asked. "The Russians?"

"They want the U.S. and its European allies to butt out of their business, basically. While the new Tsar reclaims all the territory they lost when the Soviet Union dissolved."

"Have troops crossed any sovereign borders yet?" Hawke wanted to know. Obviously, he hadn't seen any news in days. No CNN in

Energetika.

"Not yet. But the Russian Army's got ninety divisions massed on the various borders, from the Baltics to East Ukraine. Washington thinks Estonia is where they'll move first. Close the border bridge over the Narva River to anything but military traffic. Jam the whole country's Internet there like they did a while back, fake a Russian citizens' protest and then shoot a few Russian citizens to create a false crisis for the ethnic Russian population living there, start moving tanks and troops across the bridge to 'rescue' them."

"And if the West responds?"

"They start to kill all the airship hostages. Throw them out. One by one, including the wife of the U.S. vice president, until the West backs off. Any more questions?"

"Just one," Brock said. "How the hell do you guys plan to get those people out of there safely?"

Stoke smiled. He'd known Harry Brock for years. Harry liked to cut to the chase.

"These OMON guys have ordered a no-fly zone, fifty-mile radius around the airship. Any aircraft violates it, they start tossing hostages out the door. Same thing with surface vessels."

"What altitude is the damn thing?" Hawke asked.

"Hovering at five hundred feet."

"Stationary?"

"Last time we looked."

"Look, I've been aboard an identical but smaller version of this thing called *Tsar*. From that underside picture there, it seems there's an identical circular hatch in the floor of the control pod. Looks like no exterior handle, no access from outside. So, what's our point of entry?"

"We've got a couple of options, including that hatch," Stoke said, moving his laser pointer. "Here, here, and maybe here."

"They all look bad," Brock observed.

There was a lot of eyeball rolling from the SEALs around the table. One of them piped up and said, "I'm sure you have a better idea, sir."

"Damn right," Brock said. "And I'll tell you what it is as soon as I think of it."

Stokely frowned. "Look. Enough of this shit. We all know this isn't going to be easy. But we got two things working for us here. One, surprise. They don't know we're down here. Not a fucking clue. Two, we got someone inside the ship. We got a hostage aboard with a sat phone."

"Really?" Hawke said, seeing the first ray of hope. "Someone inside? How'd you pull that off?"

"She was invited," Stoke said evenly, looking straight at Hawke. "Friend of mine."

"Oh," Hawke said, instantly realizing the

world of hurt Stokely had to be in. Fancha, his fiancée, that's who was on the inside. For Stoke, the already incredibly high stakes of this rescue operation were right through the sub's roof.

It was personal for Stoke, and that was not good.

Hawke checked his watch. The commando team would commence rescue operations in six hours. At midnight. There was no moon, few stars. At least some of the hostages would be asleep. Maybe only a skeleton OMON crew standing guard, if they were really lucky.

Luck? Luck was for losers. They were six hours out, and they didn't have a goddamn plan.

Hawke needed to talk to Stoke alone, and fast.

58

"Doesn't feel good, Stoke, none of this," Hawke said from his perch on the upper bunk, his legs dangling near Stokely stretched out on the bunk directly below.

"No shit, boss."

They were in Stoke's tiny cabin, just aft of the forward torpedo room, the only place on the sub where they could find any privacy. Putin had given Hawke a pack of smokes, and he shook one out and lit it now.

"Oh, great. Now you're smoking," Stoke said. "Good thinking."

"I might well be dead in a few hours. Perfect time to start smoking."

"Now, that's what I call inspirational leadership. Shit, I'm feeling better about this whole mess already. I'm psyched. Happy, you and Urine better watch your asses up there. Man coming after you got himself a death wish."

"Urine?" Hawke said, puzzled like everybody else about that confusing Russian name.

"With a Y. Yurin. He's the one I told you

about who was training these OMON guys down in Miami. Big blond muscle-boy type. Badass, though. Probably killed a couple thousand Chechen children when he was there."

"You think he's running the show up there?"

"I know he's running the show. Total professional killer. They've been training for this for months, out there in the Everglades. One of the many reasons I'm feeling down on my luck."

Hawke nodded and took a deep drag on his smoke. He couldn't remember a time in his career when he'd felt such apprehension over an impending operation. SEAL Team Six, now officially known by the less harmonious DEVGRU, was about as good as it got. One of their first deployments had been the hijacked cruise ship *Achille Lauro.* Boats and oil rigs were common fare for Six. But they'd never mounted a maritime combat boarding operation with situational parameters remotely like this one.

A bloody airship!

Enough to make any rational man start smoking, he thought, taking another puff and blowing it at the ceiling. He'd been thinking about this rescue attempt until his head hurt, the whole flight from Ramstein. The Russian ploy was brilliant. A dirigible presented huge logistical problems, insurmountable problems, maybe, to any hostage-rescue operation. There had to be a way, though. There always was. But damned if he could think of one.

"Damn right it doesn't feel good," Stoke said after a long silence. "Hell! I never should have let the girl go on the damn zeppelin in the first place. She didn't want to go, you know. I made her go. Anything happens to her now, hell, I don't know what I'll do."

"Stoke, I'm just as worried about Fancha as you are. But I mean this operation doesn't feel good."

"You think I don't know that, boss? It sucks, is what it does. SEAL Team Six? The best HRT on the planet. You get a hostage situation on a goddamn cruise ship or a 747 sitting out on a runway? Team in, team out, in a heartbeat, tangos dead, freed hostages not even scratched. But this shit? A fucking zeppelin suspended in midair? Nobody on the planet is trained for that."

"Exactly why he chose it," Hawke said.

"Why who chose it?"

"Korsakov. The new Russian Tsar. He built the goddamn airship, maybe with this eventuality in mind. No, make that *probably* with this in mind."

"Smart man. So, how the hell are we going to do this without getting our asses kicked and taking a couple hundred hostages down with us?"

"I have a thought on that. You're not going to like it."

"Yeah? Try me. I'd like anything better than what we've got. We've been sitting out here submerged in this old boat going crazy with this for two days. We could use some fresh ideas. SEALs don't get discouraged easily. That team in there? They are discouraged."

"You've got to call Fancha, Stoke. I hate to say it. She's our only chance."

"I'm listening."

"That hatch in the floor of the control pod. It's the only good way for us to insert. The rear staircase doesn't work. The fore, aft, and midships emergency egress doors in the fuselage don't work. All bad. Right?"

"Right. You'd have to use choppers and fast-roping down to the airship from above, and you do that, invade their no-fly zone, they start heaving elderly geniuses out the door from five hundred feet. Water's like concrete from that height."

"So we go up through the control-pod hatch. But it's locked from the inside. How do you plan to get in?"

"Blow it. Charges on the hinges only way."

"Might as well ring the doorbell, Stoke. Hey, Yurin, you got company! Start heaving hostages out the door."

"Think I don't know that?"

"Hostages will be tossed out, shot, or gassed before we get even three guys through

688

that hatch."

"Yeah. So tell me your idea before I kill myself."

"Fancha has to open the hatch."

"What? How the hell is she going to do that without getting herself killed? Her cabin is two decks up and half the damn ship away from the bridge. I think you forgot the part about the twenty-some-odd armed killers wandering around that ship looking for trouble."

"I don't know how she does it yet. I wish I did. But she's got to try, Stoke, she's got to. It's the only way to do this. Believe me, if I had a better idea, I wouldn't even suggest this."

There was a long silence from the bunk below.

"She's got a gun," Stoke said softly.

"She does? Well, hell, man, that's great. What kind of gun?"

"My H & K nine. Two extra mags of hollow-point meatpackers."

"Silencer?"

"Yeah."

"Perfect. How'd that happen?"

"I left my gun bag in the stateroom closet by mistake. Thank God I did."

"Can she shoot?"

"A little. Took her out to Gator Guns a few times. Just range shit. But she knows the gun."

"So, bloody hell, she's got a chance, Stoke. The ship is mostly dark. With any luck at all, she'll make it down to the control pod without even being seen. There'll be someone down in the pod, but maybe not. The ship's not moving, so you don't need a pilot. Not much to do down there, just monitor the radar looking for bogies inside the no-fly, check the airship's elevation, and adjust for windage, right? Maybe one guy down there? Two max?"

"Yeah. Maybe two. Certainly not expecting anybody currently aboard to make a move on the damn bridge. Hell, most of the passengers are in their seventies. All of them with IQs in the thousands. The whole bunch way too smart to do anything as stupid as what we're talking about."

"Listen. I've been down in an identical pod. She'll have a clear shot from the circular hatch at the top of the ladder. So she takes them out before she even goes down. Then she opens the hatch for us. That's it. Done. We're in. The best HRT team in the world with the element of total surprise. A walk in the bloody park, Stoke."

"Sounds so easy a child could do it, doesn't it? I don't even know what I'm so worried about."

"Stoke, look. I know you love this woman. I know it's dangerous as hell, what I'm asking her to do. But it's the only chance we've got, man. Not only to save four hundred people's lives but to counter Russian aggression that could trigger a world war. You know that, don't you?"

"Fancha saves the world. Man, shit I get myself into hanging around with you."

Stoke got up and picked up the sat phone lying on the tiny grey desk, punched in a number, sat down on a corner of the desk, a look of pained concern in his big brown eyes.

"Hey, baby. How you doing? I know, I know. But we're coming to get you, okay? Soon, that's when. That's what I'm calling about. Now, calm down and listen. I've got a way maybe you can help us out . . ."

Hawke dropped lightly to the floor and slipped out of the cabin, quietly pulling Stoke's door shut. He didn't want to hear this conversation. If things upstairs went badly, as they frequently did, there'd be only one person to blame, and he didn't have time to think about that right now. He sprinted aft along the narrow companionway. It led to where Brock and Captain Jack Stiglmeier, XO of SEAL Team Six, were meeting in the sub's NAVPSPECWAR wardroom, where all the missiles used to be.

He had to get to Brock and the SEAL Team Six exec officer, work out some kind of operation that had even a minute chance of actually working. Before any SEAL mission, the assault force plans routes that will be used to gain control of the target. On surface vessels where hostages are held, the bridge is usually the assault-and-rescue team's first objective, since it's the nerve center of the vessel. Movements are conducted in a "bounding overwatch" mode, where one part of the team is always covering the other. Any enemy sighted can be taken under immediate fire without others having to move and shoot at the same time.

Having an armed hostage aboard willing and capable of neutralizing the bridge and give the boarding team a viable insertion point was critical to the plan the three men now worked out. The success of this assault, Hawke knew, would be immeasurably more problematic should Fancha fail to reach the bridge alive.

A long, sweat-soaked hour later, Hawke shoved his chair back, put his feet up on the table, lit another of Putin's cigarettes, and smiled at Brock and Stiglmeier.

"Yeah, okay," Hawke said. "God help us, I think we're finally good to go. You guys good? Everyone ready?"

"Good," Harry said, looking down at a diagram of the pod he'd drawn on a legal pad, outlining the two teams' plans of action. Harry would be going up with Stoke's squad, acting as his second in command.

Stiglmeier said, "I'm good. And ready."

"Let's go to work," Hawke said, looking at

his watch. "You want to call a time, Jack?"

"I still like midnight."

"Then we ride at midnight," Hawke said, smiling at the team.

59

Fancha was ready, too. She had exactly fifteen minutes to make her way aft, down two decks to the bridge deck, get away from anyone who tried to stop her, find the control pod, and open the hatch for Stoke and his men at the stroke of midnight. She checked her watch again. If she was lucky, she'd reach the bridge a few minutes early. If she was unlucky, well, nobody blames you for being late if you're dead.

She had Stoke's gun and the sat phone both stuck uncomfortably in the small of her back, inside the belt holding up her black jeans. She wore her dark red blouse untucked so it would cover the two items. She had no idea what to expect once she stepped outside her cabin, but she thought having the gun and a phone in her hands was probably a bad idea when and if she encountered one of the terrorists.

She looked at herself in the mirror one last time.

"You can do this, girl, you can do this," she said to herself, and she almost believed she could. God knew she'd said it enough times since she'd hung up from talking to Stoke.

She'd not cracked the door in almost three days, living in constant fear the terrorists would conduct a room-to-room search for her. Luckily, they'd either forgotten about her, or decided she wasn't worth the effort. She'd had nothing to eat but snacks, sodas, and beer from the minibar. But she understood what Stokely wanted from her, how important it was, and she was determined to succeed or die trying.

She unlocked the double locks on the door, grabbed the knob, and turned it. Slowly, as quietly as she could, she pulled the door open, an inch, two inches. Someone was coming! She pulled the door shut and leaned against the wall, her heart pounding.

There had been a sound from the corridor, coming toward her from the left. Someone whistling. A woman. It sounded like one of the housekeepers. Could they really have the staff continue to clean the damn ship while people were being held hostage? Maybe even being killed? She supposed they could. This was, as Stoke had told her when they were boarding, a "tight ship."

And these "housekeepers," as they called themselves, didn't look much like housekeepers. The majority of them were young, mid-twenties, blonde, and all uniformly beautiful. Ukrainians, mostly, the ones she'd talked to, but there were pretty girls of every race, creed, and color aboard. All trained to walk and talk the same, pretty much indistinguishable. The Stepford Maids, she called them.

It was some high-class form of white slavery, she supposed. Dirt-poor girls from small towns, desperate to get out. Horrible but not nearly as bad as what happened to thousands of other girls like them around the world. These women were the lucky ones; the unlucky ones got sold.

She put her ear to the door. The whistling woman was just passing by. Fancha pulled the gun from her waistband, opened the door silently, and stepped out into the hall.

"Excuse me?" she said, approaching the woman from behind. The housekeeper stopped, but before she could turn around, Fancha had brought the butt of the gun down on top of the woman's head, swinging it just as hard as she could. She crumpled to the floor, out like a light.

Fancha bent and grabbed her under the armpits, quickly dragging her back inside her stateroom. She shut the door and locked it. She stared down at the unconscious woman, breathing hard, unable to believe she'd done this to her. She grabbed her wrist and felt for a pulse. Strong. But wait just a minute. This woman was wearing a uniform. Black satin, with a frilly white apron and a frilly white cap. The size wasn't perfect, but it was close enough.

She bent down and started unbuttoning the woman's blouse.

It took all of two minutes to disrobe the maid and herself and put on the housekeeping uniform. She looked at herself. She'd tucked her dark hair up under the cap as best she could. Stuck the gun and the phone inside the apron strings, where they were tied tightly in the back. Found a long black cardigan sweater in her closet and put that on. It was just long enough to cover up everything back there. She'd pass for one of the housekeepers, she thought, if nobody looked too closely, remembered her face.

There were two terry robes hanging in the bathroom. She took the sashes from both and used them to bind the unconscious woman's wrists and ankles. She used a hand towel as a gag, tying it tightly, knotting it at the back of the girl's head, praying it was enough to keep her quiet when she came to.

She cracked the door, saw that the dimly lit passage was empty, and headed for the stairs at the far end. She didn't run, because housekeepers didn't run. She tried to take her time. And tried to whistle, as they all seemed to whistle. The maid encounter had cost her precious time. But the uniform also might save her life, she thought, hurrying up the steps to the deck two floors above. Her first job was to determine if the hostages were still being kept in the ballroom. Stoke guessed they were. The terrorists would want them contained, where they could keep a close watch over every move they made.

She'd had an idea, and maybe it was a good one. First, go back through the kitchen, which she managed without seeing a soul. Next, go backstage, look for the small door that opened onto a tiny staircase leading up to the projection room. The ballroom was also where they showed movies every night. She had a hunch there'd be no movie tonight, and the projection room would be empty, and she was right.

Peering down through the tiny window next to the projector, she saw the hostages. They were mostly crowded on the floor, sleeping on blankets, although some were seated at the tables. They looked as bad as you would expect. Little food, little water, little sleep. And there were ten armed terrorists stationed around the perimeter of the room, just in case anybody got any ideas. She headed back to the kitchen and quickly made her way down to B Deck.

Stokely had told her where to find the bridge deck pod. It was the clear plastic egg she'd seen suspended from the bottom of the airship's hull. Stoke said to go to the very center of A Deck, and there she'd find the entrance ladder down to the control pod.

B Deck aft where she was now, was mostly crew quarters. Zero décor. Pretty grim compared with the luxurious spaces above. Two jumpsuited crewmen were headed her way. Laughing, arms around each other, drunk. She took a deep breath, kept whistling, smiled at them as they approached her. The one nearest her reached out, leering, and grabbed her arm. She hissed at him, something low and threatening, and wrenched her arm away. "Asshole!" she said, giving it her native Cape Verde accent. She was clearly more trouble than she was worth. They kept moving.

She kept moving. All the way to the end of the corridor, down a set of service steps to the A Deck. Then she started back toward the middle of the ship. It was steerage down here, crew quarters even less appealing than the deck above.

"Hey! Stop!" someone called out in English as she passed an open door. She'd caught a glimpse inside and speeded up a little bit. There had been at least a couple of men in there, playing cards, it had looked like, a huge cloud of smoke over their heads, noisy, drunken laughter from inside.

"Hey! You deaf? I said stop."

She did, her heart pounding. If she ran, he'd catch her. It would be over. She turned around.

The guy was at the door, leaning out into the hall, a half-empty bottle of vodka in his hand. He looked vaguely familiar. Oh, yeah. Happy the Baker, God help her.

"Come back here."

"Okay," she said, using a universal word and trying to give it a bit of an island accent. She turned around, walking toward him, head down with her hands clasped behind her back. A perfectly obedient little Stepford Maid but one with her finger on the trigger.

"Haven't seen you before. What's your name, honey, you look familiar."

"Tatiana."

"Whatever. Come on in, baby. Join the party," the big fat man said, slapping her rump as she stepped through the door and into the smoke-filled room. He turned and locked the door.

Not a good sign.

Two fourteen-man teams of commandos huddled at the base of the steel ladder inside the conning tower. They'd been exhaustively briefed over the last hour. The mood was good. They had a workable mission plan now, and they had confidence in the two men who'd lead the assault. One was American, Stokely Jones, a legendary SEAL in his day. The other was a Brit named Alex Hawke, and it was obvious he'd been there, done that, and, besides, they liked what they saw in his eyes.

The absolute animal willingness to kill.

Each man was clad in black rip-stop Nomex with lightweight Kevlar and ceramic body armor. Their faces were smeared with black camo face paint. They carried a lot of gear, including the new M8 assault rifle, maybe the deadliest such weapon in the world. The SIG Sauer P228 pistol, carried in a low-slung tactical holster just below the hip, would act as backup. Pistol magazines hung precariously from gun belts, M8 mags rode in thigh pads for quick access. Some members carried the M4-90, a magazine-fed tactical shotgun. A street sweeper if ever there was one.

In addition to the knives and ammo hung from their web belts, they were equipped with flashbang stun grenades. These nonlethal explosives could incapacitate targets through blinding light and an excruciating 180-decibel noise. And they had smoke grenades to screen movement or disorient targets when necessary.

Each man wore a Kevlar helmet headset with an earpiece that fitted snugly inside the left ear and a filament microphone that lay just below the lower lip. They had their Motorola wireless sets turned off now, most of them practicing how to say "Drop the gun!" and "On the floor!" and "Shut the fuck up!" in phonetic Russian.

Hawke, Stoke, Brock, and Hynson stood to one side of the group, going over last-minute instructions with the skipper of the submarine. Timing was going to be absolutely everything now, and they couldn't afford even the slightest error on anybody's part.

Hawke checked his watch. Ten minutes out.

They were ready. Now all they had to do was wait and pray for Fancha's call.

Happy the Baker. That's who the guy was, all right. The one at the birthday party in Coconut Grove, whom Stoke said the FBI called the Omnibomber. A guy who went around the world blowing up people the Russians at the Kremlin didn't like.

Happy and two other guys were sitting around a card table littered with overflowing ashtrays, empty bottles, and dirty glasses. Russian engine-room crewmen, by the looks of them. They were wearing oil-stained "wife-beater" undershirts, the ones with shoulder straps. By the sweat and stink rolling off them, there wasn't a lot of bathing going around here.

One of them looked her up and down, picked up an ashtray, and upended the contents onto the rug.

"Oops," he said, laughing, the other two finding the whole thing hilarious. They looked at her through lowered lids, their hands moving down to the crotches of their

702

greasy work pants.

Happy the fat boy, his little pig eyes narrow, nuzzled her ear, his hand on her ass, mercifully too drunk to recognize her from the party in Miami.

"Clean it up, bitch," Happy said, his voice thick with alcohol and lust. He was standing close behind her, his foul breath on her neck, his rough hands kneading her buttocks, reaching up under her arms to squeeze her breasts hard enough to make her wince. He wasn't close enough to feel the gun yet, but he was getting there.

She had to get him, get all of them, out in front of her.

Now.

"Okay," she said, moving quickly away from Happy.

She dropped to one knee and swept the butts and ashes back into the ashtray with her hand. Then she rose and carried it over to the table between the two unmade beds. She placed it on the table and sat down on the bed farthest from the door. She saw the ugly black gas masks hanging on the backs of their chairs. And in the corner behind the card table were the tanks she'd seen on Happy's back when the terrorists seized the ship. She might not live through this ordeal, but at least there was one threat she could eliminate right now.

"What are you sitting on your pretty little

ass for, honey?" Happy said in his Brooklyn accent. "Boys want to see you dance."

"Dance?" she said, smiling sweetly.

She stood up and reached behind her, fussing with her apron strings. "Shouldn't I take all this off first?"

"Yeah, baby. That's a great idea," Happy said. "That's it. Take it off. All of it. Real slow."

"Real slow," she repeated, smiling as she brought the 9mm automatic pistol around where they could all get a good, long look at it.

"Fuck," Paddy said.

"You said it, not me," Fancha said.

She raised the gun, squeezed the trigger, and shot Happy the Baker in the crotch. Giving him just a second to look down at the spreading bloodstain and realize what had just happened to him, she then raised the gun and put one in the middle of his face. A cherry-and-black blemish instantly bloomed on the bridge of his nose, and a piece of his skull about the size of a quarter hit the wall behind him in a spray of red mist.

The other two, terrified, were diving for the floor. She took a step forward so she'd have a clear shot at each of them. She took her time, gripping the pistol out front with two hands the way Stoke had taught her at Gator Guns, aiming carefully, squeezing the trigger gently. She shot each one of the men in the head.

Once, then twice.

She collapsed back onto the bed and pulled out the sat phone. Thank God for speed dial. Her hand was shaking so badly she couldn't have punched more than one button.

"Stoke?"

"Fancha, you okay?"

"Baby, I just killed three people. They were going to . . . rape me, and I just —"

"Aw, honey, I'm so —"

"No, no. Shh. I'm okay. Happy is dead. I shot him. Those gas canisters I told you about are here in his room. I think they're just small enough to go out through the portholes if I can get them open."

"Do it now, okay? I would love to know there is no gas in play when we come aboard."

"Hold on."

She was back on the line a minute later. "Canisters just went overboard," she said. "Gas is gone."

"Great. Now, hostages? Still in one place?"

"Yeah. All in the ballroom, most of them trying to sleep on the floor. Some huddled around the tables. Ten armed guys standing around the perimeter."

"So, ten standing watch over the hostages, ten off duty, maybe sleeping. That's a big help."

"Thanks."

"How long till you get down to the bridge, baby?"

"Ten minutes, if I'm lucky."

"Don't be lucky, be careful. I love you. See you soon."

60

The submarine lay at a depth of 600 feet below the surface, maintaining neutral buoyancy.

In the middle of her control room were two periscopes on a raised platform. One of the periscopes had a surface video camera that sent pictures to monitors throughout the control room and to the captain's quarters. Each monitor now displayed an image of the giant zeppelin hovering five hundred feet above the ocean's surface. Except for the flashing red running lights along her hull and a few lit windows along the center of the fuselage, she was mostly dark, darker even than the black sky behind her.

Directly in front of the two periscopes was the duty station — or the "con" — which is the watch station of the officer of the deck. Tonight, Lieutenant Commander Lawrence Robins had the con. To his right was the fire-control station. Forward, the three bucket seats of the control station, now manned by two enlisted men who operated the diving planes and the rudder, the planesman and the helmsman. In the middle sat the diving officer. To the left of the planesman was the ballast-control panel with two emergency blow handles.

Robins looked aft at the assault party waiting impatiently at the base of the conning tower. He caught the eye of Commander Hawke, who nodded his head once and gave Robins a thumbs-up. The SEAL teams were more than ready. It was go time.

"Blow emergency main ballast tanks," Robins said quietly.

The diving officer reached over and pushed in the two valves simultaneously, then pulled up, triggering the sub's emergency surfacing maneuver. The two valves sent high-pressure air from the air banks flooding into the EMBT, the emergency main ballast tank.

The submarine instantly rocketed straight to the surface like a 6,000-ton torpedo.

Her bow came out, flew out of the water, almost vertically, the hull rising at an impossible angle, before falling back into the dark sea and settling directly beneath the hovering airship.

Two enlisted men, Ensigns Blair and Mansfield, raced up the ladder first. It was their job to open the main hatch in the sub's "sail" or conning tower. As the SEALs crowded forward to begin their rapid ascent up the ladder, the two crewmen up top now mounted a compressed CO_2 gas-powered harpoon gun atop a swivel base. The base contained an enormously powerful high-speed electric winch. The harpoon gun, used normally in emergency rescue operations, was capable of firing a rubber-coated grapnel hook trailing a thousand feet of steel mesh cable with astounding accuracy.

"Only get one shot at this," Blair said to Mansfield.

"Yeah, I know. I need a frozen rope."

That's what you needed when a foundering vessel was sinking fast in twenty-foot seas, a frozen rope. You needed to put one right on the money, hook a steel bulkhead or something solid, before she slipped under the icy waves with all hands.

Mansfield put his eye to the high-powered scope and looked up the barrel of the harpoon gun. He got the center of the pod's superstructure in his crosshairs. Twin steel beams ran fore and aft on either side of an emergency hatch in the belly of the pod. These perforated steel brackets secured the bridge pod to the fuselage above. He'd be firing directly at the one nearer the hatch. If they were lucky, the thick rubber coating on the grapnel hook would be sufficiently noise-deadening so as not to alert anyone inside the pod.

That was the theory come up with by the

genius brigade in the wardroom, anyway. The two ensigns had their doubts, but it wasn't their job to offer suggestions. It was their job to hook up to the airship and start winching this big four-hundred-foot-long mother right down to the sub.

The terrorists were threatening to throw live hostages out the door if anyone messed with them. Mansfield's mission was to get the airship down to sea level fast enough to take that option off the table.

"Okay," Mansfield said, peering through the scope crosshairs at his target. "Fire!"

Blair yanked the lanyard that fired the harpoon. There was a *whoosh* of expelled gas, and the grapnel hook shot upward toward the underside of the zeppelin, a trail of steel cable beneath. Mansfield kept his right eye glued to the scope.

"Oh, baby," he said, raising his head and smiling at Blair.

"Frozen rope?"

"Fuckin' A, podnuh. Nailed it. Hooked the damn cross beam a foot from the hatch."

Blair pushed the red lever that operated the big winch inside the base of the harpoon. The cable snapped taut as the slack disappeared in a heartbeat, and slowly but surely, the winch began to reel the massive airship down toward the sub's conning tower.

"Outta the way!" one of the first SEALs to emerge through the hatch yelled. The big black guy, a veteran named Stokely Jones who'd come aboard at Bermuda, was on that steel cable and climbing hand over hand up toward the ship faster than either Blair or Mansfield had ever seen a human being move before. Especially one his size and carrying forty pounds of weapons, equipment, and ammunition on his back.

"Something's very wrong here," *Pushkin's* first officer said to his captain, Dimitri Boroskov. He was staring in disbelief at the instruments arrayed on the ship's master control panel.

"What is it?"

"We're losing altitude, sir."

"Don't be absurd. That's impossible," the captain said, his eyes rapidly scanning the console, looking primarily at the internal gas-pressure gauges. The Vortex I had been designed with twin hulls. An outer hull of thin, rip-stop material and a rigid inner hull of microthin titanium, this lightweight metal hull strong enough to survive all but the most catastrophic disasters. Sandwiched between the two hulls was ninety million cubic feet of helium.

The only things that could possibly cause a loss of altitude would be wind shear from a thunderhead or a loss of gas from inside the outer hull. There was no storm activity within fifty miles. And every one of his gauges showed no signs of leakage. The exterior hull pressure readings in all compartments were pegged safely inside the normal range, just where they were supposed to be. No leaks. No wind. It made no sense at all.

"All pressure readings normal," Boroskov said. "Slight wind out of the northeast, two knots gusting to five."

"That may well be, Captain. But look at the altimeter, will you? And the variometer. We are definitely descending."

"I don't believe it. Must be something wrong with the altimeter gauge. It's giving a false reading."

The captain leaned forward and stared out at the black sky and the few stars scattered near the horizon. "We certainly appear to be stationary, at any rate."

"Only because the descent rate is minimal, sir. Look! Four hundred ninety feet above sea level and dropping. We've lost ten feet according to the altimeter! And the rate seems to be increasing!"

"Impossible."

"Should I notify Commander Yurin? He demands to be kept abreast of anything unusual, sir."

"Not yet. We don't want to look foolish, and there might still be a simple explanation. Call engineering first. There must be a leak somewhere. Perhaps the computer systems monitoring the internal pressure gauges are malfunctioning. This could be the problem. Still, we take no chances. Get engineering teams to go over every square inch of this ship's interior. Find that leak, if it exists, and fix it!"

"Aye-aye, sir!" the first officer said, and ran for the ladder, while the captain nervously eyed the outward-looking radar, looking for any enemy incursion into their no-fly zone.

"Sir?" his first officer said a moment later, pausing at the bottom of the ladder and looking up toward the open hatchway.

"What is it now?" said the captain, frantically scanning the altimeter, elevator position indicator, and inclinometer. At eye level was his variometer, which he used to measure the ship's rate of rise or fall. With his left hand, he spun the elevator wheel, trying to detect and correct changes in trim. He was intent on moving the airship forward now, attempting to gain altitude, but he couldn't seem to do either.

He had the oddest sensation of his entire career.

He felt that his ship was *stuck* in midair.

"I believe there is now another problem, Captain," he heard his first officer say behind him. Boroskov looked quickly over his shoulder. What he saw, at first glance, did not appear to be a problem.

He saw a beautiful pair of legs descending the ladder, shapely calves, knees, thighs. At first, he thought the woman might be naked, and then he saw the short black satin skirt, the apron. Finally, the beautiful woman with the dark red hair stepped down from the bottom rung. She was wearing the uniform of the housekeeping staff, but she was not anyone he recognized. She had a gun in her hand. Things were getting so strange. The captain shook his head as if he could clear away this craziness.

"You two speak English?" the dark-skinned woman asked.

"Da, da, da," the captain replied. "Yes, yes, yes, of course."

"Good. I want both of you to remain very quiet. Keep your hands up in the air where I can see them. Good. Now, move toward the hatch."

The two officers did as they were told.

"Now, open the hatch."

"Open it?"

"You heard what I said. Open it!"

The captain made for the hatch, but the first officer had other ideas. He turned, screamed something in Russian at the captain, and lunged for Fancha with both hands outstretched, going for the gun.

There was no time to hesitate. She fired one round, caught him in the knee, and he buckled to the floor, writhing in pain.

The Russian captain, very shaken now, cranked the big stainless-steel wheel around a few times. There was a pop, a hiss of air, and then the hatch cover was shoved upward violently by someone below. The steel edge of the round door caught the captain under the chin, and he, too, went sprawling, bleeding from a deep gash.

Fancha looked down and saw Stokely's smiling face beaming up at her.

"Hey," he said. "Look who's here."

"Oh, baby, oh, baby, oh, baby," she said, reaching down to touch his face.

"Honey, you got to get out of the way. I got about thirty pumped-up killer angels climbing up my tail crazy to come aboard as quickly as possible."

Fancha moved to the rear of the control-room pod and watched an endless stream of heavily armed men in black, who had climbed hand over hand up the steel cable, now come pouring up through the hatch. Stoke had the captain and the first officer off to the side, grilling them aggressively at the point of a gun about the current whereabouts of all of the terrorists, especially the ones who were not to be found in the ballroom.

She saw Alex Hawke poke his handsome head through the hatch and smile at her.

She'd never seen a man look so happy in her life.

"Fancha," he said, grinning at her. "You did it."

61

SEALs don't train with regulation human-silhouette targets. They use small three-by-five index cards taped strategically over the silhouette. To qualify, you had to be able to hit the card with a double tap, two shots in rapid succession, whether you were popping up from below the water or bursting into a hijacked airliner packed with terrified passengers. SEAL instructors don't care how you shoot, one-handed, two-handed, right- or left-handed, doesn't matter, as long as you hit tight, man-killing groups every single time.

The heavy loads the two SEAL platoons were using tonight would knock the terrorists aboard the airship down no matter where they hit them. Head, chest, arm, leg, didn't matter. The terrorists who had hijacked this airship didn't know it yet, but their life expectancies had just dropped to zero.

The assault-and-hostage-rescue group quickly divided itself into two platoons, one on either side of the pod's ladder up to A Deck. Stoke and Harry Brock would take the Alpha Platoon, Stoke commanding. They would search the ship from stem to stern. They'd be looking for any tangos currently off duty, sleeping, or simply hiding and capture or eliminate them. Basically, a door-to-door sweep of the entire airship.

Meanwhile, Hawke and the fourteen men of Bravo Platoon would go directly to the ballroom, take out the Russian tangos guarding the hostages, and secure any other hostages in sickbay or otherwise not found with the main group.

"Listen up," Hawke said, addressing the whole squad. "This, as you gentlemen all damn well know, is a game for thinkers, not shooters. That's always been true, but it is especially true tonight. When we go in with our flashbangs and smoke grenades, we're going to enter a room full of screaming, shell-shocked hostages, many of them elderly and infirm, and perhaps a dozen highly trained Russian terrorists. As you know from the briefing, these guys are very bad news, formerly the death-squad commandos in Chechnya."

"OMON, skipper?"

"Exactly. So, the trick will be *not* shooting. Every round we fire in there will be accounted for. I don't need to tell you we probably have the American vice president's wife in there on the floor. Also her White House security detail. When bullets fly and the fit hits the shan, as it surely will do, these U.S. Secret Service men will immediately cover her body with their own. These men are not, I repeat, *not* attacking the vice president's wife."

"Thanks for the heads-up, skipper," one of the younger SEALs said, laughing.

"Little humor," Hawke smiled.

It was easy as hell to get too tight at the run-up, too tightly wound, and that was the last thing he wanted his squad to be feeling at the moment.

There were a more few chuckles, and Stoke said, "This is serious shit, guys. Any monkey can shoot people. You men know better than anyone what counts right now is the split second when you know to back the hell off. Okay? Listen to the man!"

Hawke, all trace of humor gone, said, "Once the spoon pops on the first smoke and flashbang grenades, you have two-point-seven seconds before the blast. Fingers off the triggers until you aim to kill. Look all the way into the danger zones before turning into the room. When you get inside, key your focus on weapons, not movement. Maintain fields of fire, and for God's sake, don't fuck this up. All right? Everybody ready? You all know where to go, so go, dammit, go!"

He and Stoke stood back and let the teams

race up the ladder to reform in the lounge area at the top.

Stoke had made sure a crewman from the sub would fast-rope up the cable with a bosun's chair and help Fancha back down to the sub, get her to sickbay if necessary. The captain and the first officer were likewise to be removed from the pod and hauled down to the sub for intense interrogation.

At the top of the grand staircase, the hostage-rescue team split into two parties. Stoke took Alpha left down the ship's central corridor, where they would begin a room-by-room search of the entire vessel, every deck, every nook, every cranny.

Hawke and Bravo went right.

Every member of the team had memorized the ship's layout. They knew every crack, turn, and stair, including the ballroom's location and layout on the diagrams. Just two minutes later, Hawke and his assault team were silently checking weapons and gear one last time outside the ballroom's main entrance, just beyond the line of sight of anyone inside.

Hawke looked at the digital timer ticking down on his watch and stepped forward, stopping just short of the door. He had affixed a noise suppressor to his M8 and now held it at eye level, the selector set for a three-round burst. Should an unfriendly step outside the room now, he was dead. He reached into his bag of tricks and pulled out a flashbang. He slowed his breathing. Adrenaline was coursing through his system, just enough to maintain the right edge. In his earpiece, he could hear Stoke breathing.

"Bravo," Hawke said into his tiny lip mike.

"Copy, Bravo," Stoke replied. "Alpha is at yellow. Request compromise authority and permission to move to green." Yellow meant Stoke's squad was at its last position of cover and concealment. That no-man's-land between safe and totally rat-fucked. His team had orders not to engage any enemy until Hawke's primary force had initiated its assault on the ballroom.

"Bravo at green," Hawke told Stoke, cupping a grenade loosely in his left hand. "Stand by, Alpha . . . ten seconds . . ."

He looked at his team, making final eye contact with as many of them as he could. "Remember," he told them one last time, "key on weapons, shoot surgically, think four steps ahead."

The team nodded. Hawke saw they were ready. It was finally time for everybody to get real busy, hop and pop.

"Alpha, you now have compromise authority to move to green . . ."

He paused a beat. He knew Stoke was moving.

"Five," Hawke said to his team, "four . . . three . . . two . . . one . . ."

Hawke heaved the first of many stun grenades through the ballroom door. Next, the smoke grenades were tossed inside.

Craaack!

A hundred and eighty decibels of distraction preceded Hawke, who leaned into the smoke and noise and violence as his team stormed into the ballroom behind him.

Bullets from the OMON troops ringing the room full of hostages instantly zipped over their heads with loud, supersonic retorts. Huge sonic explosions rocked the ballroom as the team charged through the hot zone. They were sidestepping wailing hostages as they lobbed more flashbangs and smokes ahead of them and expertly executing terrorists as they encountered them, head shots, torsos, whatever shots they could take. Surgical, like the man said.

The return enemy fire was wild and sporadic as panic and confusion spread. But not all of it. The Russian OMON forces had clearly been training for an attempted hostage rescue, just as Yurin had told Stokely under duress.

Hawke had seen two or three of his guys go down, wounded or dead. A lot of lead was still flying. He was shocked to see a few hostages struggling to their feet, two old men reaching down to help their wives get off the floor. They all held hands and, stumbling blindly through the smoke, tried to make

721

their way toward a door with a lighted exit sign.

They hadn't gone six feet when all four of them were brutally executed by two OMON guys guarding the exit door. Hawke saw the wanton murder, dropped to a knee, sighted his M8, and unloaded on one of the two Russians, rounds to his head that would sever the connection between brain and spinal cord. He looked for the other one, but he'd disappeared into the smoke toward the stage.

Hawke decided to follow. Murder got you the death penalty in this room. But suddenly, he was taking fire from above. Where? He whirled around. There were two tiny window openings in the wall above the stage, and he saw the glint of a muzzle protruding from one of them. It looked like a projection booth. Fire from above was lethal. He grabbed a stun grenade from his bag and pitched it through the second window. The resulting explosion of sound and the smoke pouring out had neutralized the shooter, at least temporarily.

62

"Locked door, skipper," Harry Brock said to Stoke. Harry put his ear to the door. "Noise inside. Sounds like TV."

Alpha Platoon had already cleared one entire deck, killing two tango sentries and three more sleeping inside some kind of dorm room. They had just mounted the stairs to the promenade deck. Pricey real estate from the looks of it. Suites and shit like that. Lots of gold fixtures and silk-covered sofas out in the hallway.

"Blow it, Harry," Stoke said.

"Breacher up!" Brock said, and a lanky young Iowan named Harry Beecher stepped past them to the door. Beecher the Breacher, he was called. He was carrying a sawed-off, pistol-gripped 12-gauge Remington shotgun loaded with two specially designed Hatton rounds. He also had a .45 in a cross-draw holster strapped across his chest and a bagful of flashbangs.

Stoke signaled for the rest of the squad to

proceed ahead, clear the rest of the corridor. He calculated the three of them had enough firepower for this one room. The rest of his team moved on, clearing room after room, as sporadic automatic-weapons fire echoed all through the corridor.

Stoke called it, and Beecher put the gun to the lock.

Boom-boom!

Beecher had chipped out the dead bolt, and Stoke kicked the door open, went in low, half a step, and turned to his left.

"Hostage left!" he yelled as Beecher and Brock moved inside.

He instantly recognized Vice President Tom McCloskey's wife from her pictures in the papers and on TV. Bonnie McCloskey sat in a chair, her hands cuffed in her lap as two wild-eyed OMON bully boys on either side held guns to her head. She looked exhausted and beat to hell, but she smiled angelically at Stoke, sweetly, as if he'd just dropped in for tea. For a terrified hostage, few sights are more welcome than a beautiful Old Glory patch on somebody's shoulder, coming through the door.

To the right, two more Russkie tangos were just coming up off the couch where they'd been watching *Black Sunday* on a plasma. Harry Brock, still moving forward at a crouch, dropped the one on the right with a three-round burst to the chest. Beecher had pulled his pistol and took out the guy on the left with one round to the forehead, a big .45mm ouchie that would never ever get all better.

"Drop your guns!" Stoke shouted at the two men still holding guns to the vice president's wife's head. Catching his mistake, he screamed it again in phonetic Russian, swinging the barrel of his M8 rapidly back and forth from one bad guy to the other as he moved forward, just aching to pull the trigger.

"Get the fuck down!" he yelled, advancing with his M8 at head level. "Get the fuck away from that hostage! *Now!*"

Brock was now edging his way along the wall behind the bound hostage and her two captors. The Russians were wide-eyed with indecision and fear, knowing that if they shot their captive, they were dead men standing, also knowing that if they turned their guns on the huge black man . . . Stoke's concentration was so intense at that moment that he could actually see their fingers squeezing the triggers as Brock stepped silently forward and shot each man from one foot behind, two split-second double taps that literally took the tops of their heads off.

Stoke launched himself forward, grabbed the hostage under the arms, and got her out of that room in a hurry. Nobody needed to see and smell the kind of carnage that filled that room any longer than they had to. He carried her straight across the hall to an open room they'd previously cleared, sat her gently down on the bed, and quickly sliced the plastic cuffs off with his knife.

"You okay? You need a doctor? We got a medical corpsman with us."

She looked at him blankly, her eyes welling with tears.

He turned and shouted toward the open door, "Harry! Get the corpsman up here, *pronto!*"

"Happening as we speak, boss!" Brock said, sticking his smiling face inside the door.

"No, no, wait," the shaken woman said. "I'm all right. Get your corpsman to help those poor people in the ballroom. Some of them are terribly ill and afraid. Especially the elderly. Please, don't waste any more time on me. I'm fine. Perhaps some water, and if I might just lie down for a moment?"

"Here's water," Brock said, tossing a bottle to Stoke. "I'll dispatch the corpsman to the ballroom right away."

Harry bolted.

"Ma'am, let me help you with that pillow. That man's name is Harry Brock, Mrs. McCloskey. He's a CIA field agent. He's going to see that you get home to Washington safe and sound. There's a Navy plane waiting at Bermuda. I'll have you there in less than an hour."

"So, it's — over?"

"Yes, ma'am, it's just about over."

"Thank you," she said, looking up at Stoke, and then the big tears started rolling, and she collapsed against the pillow. "Thank you so very much."

"You're most welcome," Stoke said, not letting go of her hand.

"Those poor people down there. All that shooting. Can you possibly save them?"

"We are certainly trying, ma'am. We've got the best hostage-rescue team on the planet down there right now. I think it's going to be all right."

Hawke, eyes burning red from flashbang smoke, barely saw the lone tango trying to escape the carnage. It was another muscle-bound brute with close-cropped blond hair, using the smoke screen to try to slip through the curtains at the back of the stage. Hawke caught a bit of profile as the guy disappeared and recognized him instantly. It was the barbarian who'd gunned down the four elderly hostages in cold blood, the very same bastard he'd lost in the smoke a while earlier.

Yeah, this had to be the guy from Miami, all right, the one Stoke had told him all about. An OMON officer named Yurin who'd specialized in killing small children in Chechnya after the carpet-bombing of the Chechen capital at Grozny. In wardroom briefing,

Stoke had referred to him as the baby killer. This was Yurin's operation, Hawke knew, and if you kill the head, you kill the snake. He wiped his stinging eyes, moving rapidly through the smoke toward the stage.

Hawke mounted the stage and pushed through the heavy velvet curtains. It was pitch-black backstage, but he heard gunfire above and saw flashes of light beneath a door at the top of a metal stairway. It had to be the projection booth. Most, if not all, of the Russian operators had been taken out by Bravo by now. But the effect of Yurin's fire on the dance floor below would be murderous: firing into the panic, killing indiscriminately, the elderly people filled with hope now, running madly for the exits, only to be cruelly cut down as they tried to escape.

Hawke mounted the steps three at a time.

The door was slightly ajar, and he kicked it open with his boot. He tried to bring himself to shoot the bastard in the back but just couldn't do it.

"Hey, baby killer!" Hawke shouted, his M8 trained on the Russian's broad back as the OMON commander slammed a fresh mag into his subgun and squeezed the trigger, the explosive chatter deafening in the tiny room.

"What did you say?" the guy said, rapidly pulling away from the little window and bringing his gun around to bear on Hawke.

"I said baby killer. That's you, right?"

Hawke's finger was already applying pressure to the M8's trigger when the Russian looked up into his stone-cold eyes.

"Hawke?"

"That's me," Alex said, and cut him to ribbons with a sustained burst from his very lethal weapon.

63

Washington, D.C.

"Sit down, Tom," the president told his vice president.

The poor man was a walking train wreck, pale and trembling, two days' worth of stubble on his haggard face. He'd been pacing the hallway outside the White House Situation Room for hours, chain-smoking Marlboros and drinking countless pots of coffee. The McCloskey children were upstairs in the Residence, waiting for any word on their mother's fate, trying to console their father whenever he came upstairs to console them.

"Damn it, we should have heard something by now," McCloskey said from the doorway. The big man crossed the room and took his customary seat at the table beside President McAtee. Looking forlornly at the large digital clock on the opposite wall, he added, "The assault commenced nearly an hour ago. It's a blimp, for God's sake. How long can that take?"

He pushed a soggy box of half-eaten pizza away from him, knocking over a water glass.

The president reached over and squeezed his forearm in what was a likely futile effort to reassure his friend.

"Tom, we've got the toughest, most professional team in the world on that airship right now. If anyone can save Bonnie and all those poor people, it's Alex Hawke and the Navy's Team Six boys. You know that as well as I do, Tom."

"You're right. I'm sorry, Mr. President. It's just —"

"Totally understandable is what it is," the president said, rubbing his own fatigue-reddened eyes and nodding at the Joint Chiefs chairman, General Moore. "Charlie, please continue. NATO troop redeployment in Poland, Czechoslovakia, and the Baltics. Where are we on that?"

It was well after midnight, Washington time, an hour later in Bermuda. The wan and drawn faces of the men and women in the room bore mute witness to the unbearable stress the entire White House staff was under. It had been a hellish week.

The boyishly handsome FBI director, Mike Reiter, in particular, looked like unadulterated hell. He looked like a man who was about to give the president of the United States some really, *really* bad news. And in fact, that was precisely why he was there.

Now, less than a week before Christmas, 1600 Pennsylvania Avenue had assumed a bunker mentality. This despite the cheery tree just put up in the Blue Room, the red, green, and gold Christmas decorations throughout the residence, and the huge lighted tree standing on the fresh blanket of snow covering the South Lawn.

There was little cause for cheer this Christmas. A megalomaniacal ruler had seized power in Russia and was threatening world war. A Russian death squad was holding four hundred terrified and exhausted hostages at gunpoint on an airship over the North Atlantic, including, just to spice things up, the lovely wife of his own vice president. Merry bleeping Christmas, Jack McAtee thought, scribbling the three words on his pad and drawing some scraggly holly leaves around them as General Moore wound up his report on NATO redeployment. Moore turned, looked solemnly at Reiter, and spoke to the president.

"Mr. President, Director Reiter is here to give you a report on what the FBI has learned during its ongoing investigation into the recent bombing at Salina. Mike?"

Reiter got to his feet.

"Mr. President, I'm afraid what we've learned at Salina indicates that we confront a threat that is far more serious, far worse than anything we could have ever imagined. The potential exists for a catastrophe of enormous, worldwide magnitude here. I've got a few slides here on PowerPoint, and I'd like to use them to demonstrate what we're —"

"Mr. President?" a naval orderly said, striding rapidly into the room. "Sorry to interrupt, sir. Urgent call for you coming in from Moscow."

"Korsakov." The president scowled, picking up the phone directly in front of him. "Wonder what the crazy bastard is up to now."

Reiter and Moore just looked at each other and shook their heads.

"Yes?" McAtee barked into the phone. "This is the president."

"Ah, Mr. President. Good. Thank you for taking my call. Our negotiations with your embassy personnel have been most unsatisfactory. I have terminated discussions. As you know, we are at an important crossroads in the relationship of our two nations, and cool heads must prevail."

"There is nothing cool-headed about invading sovereign nations and expecting the civilized world to sit back and do nothing, Mr. Korsakov. Listen to me very carefully. You are treading on very dangerous ground. Extraordinarily dangerous ground."

"And do you think that moving ten divisions of NATO troops onto my country's borders is cool-headed? As you know from our last conversation, I am currently trying to negotiate the release of four hundred innocent hostages, including the wife of your Vice President McCloskey. We are at a delicate stage in these negotiations with the Chechen Sunni Muslim terrorists aboard my airship. Your threats will do little to aid these discussions, I assure you."

"Don't insult me further. We both know damn well the terrorists who hijacked that ship are not Chechen Muslims. They are OMON special forces operating explicitly at the Kremlin's direction. And if any harm should befall those poor people, I shall hold you personally responsible."

"Think what you wish," Korsakov said. "Let their blood be on your hands. I wash my own of the matter. But I will tell you this, Mr. President. What happened in Kansas can and will happen elsewhere. I will give you twenty-four hours. In that time, I expect to see NATO and U.S. troop withdrawals, a stand-down of naval forces in the Black Sea, and your own personal guarantee, in writing, that the Western allies will not interfere with my country's desire to reestablish the unity of all Russian citizens within Russia's naturally ordained borders."

"Naturally ordained?" McAtee said. "What the hell does that mean besides illegal? Can you cite some legal precedent for that phrase?"

"This conversation is terminated, President

McAtee. Look at your watch. Unless my demands are met, exactly twenty-four hours from this moment, I will shut off the flow of energy through the Ukraine to Europe. They're having an especially cold December, and it's about to get a lot colder. Twelve hours after that, an unnamed Western city with a population in excess of one million souls will cease to exist. Then we move to five million population twelve hours later, then ten, and so on. Until you decide to be more cooperative. Do we fully understand each other?"

McAtee slammed the phone down.

"Christ," McAtee said. "The man is absolutely insane! He's threatening to shut off the gas pipelines to Europe and blow up the whole damn world one city at a time unless we pull back. Khrushchev was a bully and a thug, but at least Jack Kennedy didn't have a deranged psychopath on his hands. Blow up a city of one million? Five million? How the hell can he do that, Brick? Dirty nukes?"

Kelly looked at the president until the anger had subsided and he was certain of his complete attention. "No, sir. Something far more insidious than dirty nukes. As Mike was saying, the FBI has been looking into how the Russians took out Salina. It's not good news, I'm afraid. In fact, it's extraordinarily bad news. Mike, would you continue?"

"The frightening thing is, sir, these are not

idle threats. For decades, we've all been focused on big bombs, nuclear devices in the ten-to-twenty-megaton range. But Korsakov, over a period of many years, has been using countless millions of small, innocent-appearing devices to basically hardwire the whole world with inordinately powerful small bombs, preposterous as that may sound. At first, we found it hard to believe ourselves. These Zeta machines are —"

"Sorry, Mike. Zeta machines? Help me out here."

"Computers, Mr. President. You probably know them as Wizards. Low-cost Russian computers, designed and built by Korsakov's company, TSAR, that have been sold by the tens of millions everywhere on the planet. And inside every single Zeta is a bomb. Each computer contains eight ounces of a non-nuclear explosive called Hexagon, plus GPS transmitters that continuously broadcast the machine's location. Each one capable of remote detonation. And —"

The president had a stunned look on his face. "How many of these things are out there, did you say? Millions?"

A young female orderly entered the room, mouthing the word *urgent* at the president, and silently handed him a single sheet of paper folded in half. The president quickly read the message while Reiter continued.

He folded the note, placed it under his

water glass, then looked across the room and found Tom McCloskey's desperate eyes. He gave the man a silent thumbs-up and mouthed the words *Bonnie's okay.*

McCloskey dropped his head into his hands, his shoulders heaving.

"Tens of millions of these weapons, Mr. President, in every city and town on the planet. Perhaps hundreds of millions. In homes, schools, office and government buildings, airports, churches, literally everywhere. The Pentagon, for God's sake. Millions and millions of bombs. In every city and country on earth. At the push of a button, Korsakov can take out a city, a country, a continent, a —"

"Good Lord," the president said, sinking back in his chair as the enormity of what he'd just heard began to sink in. All of the blood had drained from his face, and Kelly began to fear he was on the verge of a stroke.

A few moments later, he recovered a bit, leaned forward, and placed both hands on the table.

"He needs to be stopped, Brick. You, too, Mike. Now."

"We're working on that, Mr. President, believe me."

"I want hourly updates. We do whatever it takes. State believes an invasion of Estonia is imminent. If one goddamn Russian soldier plants a foot where it's not supposed to be,

I'm going to Congress. I'm going to ask for an immediate declaration of war on the Russian Federation. I mean, we are going to the *wall,* you understand me? Does everyone in this room understand me?"

"A preemptive strike against Russian cities?" Moore said.

"You're goddamn right, Charlie. That's exactly what I mean."

Heavy silence followed, everyone rearranging pencils and papers as they saw the whole world going up in flames before their very eyes. They understood, all right.

The end of the world was in plain sight.

"That note, Mr. President," an obviously relieved Tom McCloskey said, still unable to tear his eyes away from the folded white paper beneath the president's water glass. "Any more news in there about the hostage situation?"

For the first time in days, the president smiled.

"Yes, there is, Tom. Very good news. Bonnie is safe. Distraught but physically unharmed. At this very moment, she is en route to Bermuda. A Navy plane there is warming up its engines, and she will be on it and headed home to Bethesda in less than an hour. She wishes you and the kids Merry Christmas and can't wait to see you."

"And the rest of the hostages, Mr. President?" McCloskey asked, his eyes shining.

"All of the hostages have been rescued, Tom. The airship itself is now under the control of the U.S. Navy, having been taken in tow by one of our submarines en route to Bermuda. There were some hostage casualties. Minimal, considering the extreme nature of the situation. But still, an intolerable loss of innocent lives."

"Oh," McCloskey said, bowing his head. "Oh, my God. Those poor people. Thank you for that message, Mr. President. I didn't think I could —"

"Tom. I think you should go upstairs to the Residence and tell the children their mother's coming home in time for Christmas."

McCloskey rose unsteadily from his seat and headed for the door.

"Merry Christmas, everyone," the vice president said in a strangled voice as he left the room.

Alone in the Oval Office, snow falling gently beyond the windows, McAtee quietly sat at his desk staring at the phone. He'd done all he could do. If the Russians were determined to have a war, by God, they'd get one. But there was something he was missing here. A critical piece of the Russian puzzle buried deep within his brain years ago, during the Cold War, back in the days when he'd chaired the Senate Arms Committee.

He stared at his phone until his eyes lost

focus. It wouldn't come.

And then it did.

The Brits had once had a mole deep inside the Kremlin. Not a high-level mole but a very effective one, as McAtee remembered. He was military originally, a colonel or perhaps even a general. Then, later, KGB. What the hell was his name? He'd been very helpful during the Korean Airlines incident, and that was the last McAtee had ever heard of him. He'd gone off the screen. But if he was still alive, and still an insider . . .

He picked up the phone and called Sir David Trulove's home number. It was almost seven in the morning, U.K. time. Surely he'd be up and about, even though it was Sunday.

"Hello?" said a sleepy voice at the other end.

"David, it's Jack McAtee."

"Good morning."

"You've heard the good news about the airship?"

"Yes. I received a call from Bermuda a few moments ago. The sub and all of the survivors are en route there now. Good show, I daresay. My heartfelt congratulations."

"I want to thank you for Red Banner's leadership on that one. Your man Alex Hawke did one hell of a job. Especially considering the fact that no one on earth had ever done anything like it before. And this woman — what is her name? The passenger who managed to get the hatch open for our boys?"

"Fancha is the name I was given by my chief of station. Not one of the passengers, apparently, a shipboard entertainer."

"That's it. Must be quite an amazing woman. Took enormous courage to do what she did. Well done all around."

"Mr. President, I think the lion's share of credit has to go to your young SEAL teams. Magnificent job, from what I understand. Very few casualties at our end. If transoceanic airships are the coming thing, and they may well be, we now have a textbook scenario for any future hostage crisis."

"David, I called about another urgent matter. Now that we've taken the airship out of play, I'm determined to remove these damn Zeta machines from the table as well. You're aware of these things I assume?"

"Indeed, I am. The FBI shared all of that information with MI-5, MI-6, and New Scotland Yard during the night. Tens of millions of bombs, all connected? It's frankly unbelievable but apparently quite true. This new Kremlin fellow is absolutely mad. My chaps are hard at it as we speak. It's a bloody nightmare, all right, but there has to be some way to take out those things."

"I've been sitting here thinking about that. We have to assume Korsakov, or someone close to him, has to have some kind of detonator. A nuclear football, for want of a better term. Agree?"

"I certainly do. A unified way to trigger countless small bombs simultaneously. Like Salina but on a grander scale."

"Exactly. So, we need to find and neutralize that damn detonator before Korsakov or someone else can use it. He gave us twenty-four hours before he takes out a Western city of one million souls."

"Good God. Well, best luck on that. So far, we're absolutely stumped around here. I've got a crisis team on this specifically as well. We just have to crack it, that's all there is to it."

"David, bear with me a moment. You had an asset inside the Kremlin during the eighties. I can't remember his name, but —"

"Stefanovich Halter? A don at Cambridge?"

"No, no. I know Professor Halter. This man I'm thinking of was ex-military. KGB. Tough, smart, Teutonic bastard, a German-Russian, almost neo-Nazi, as I recall, but if you threw enough money at him, he'd play ball. Helped us with that Korean airliner they shot down, the one that strayed into Soviet airspace. I dealt with him directly through the CIA. Greedy bastard, but he delivered the goods."

"Sounds like most of the chaps Ivan Korsakov surrounds himself with. You're looking for someone extremely close to the Tsar, I take it. A trusted confidant of long standing."

"Exactly."

"I see where you're going with this. Good thought. I'll get on this immediately. See if we can't sort out your man. Determine if he's still alive, and if so, if he's any kind of key player in the Tsar's new regime."

"How quickly can you get back to me, David?"

"As you will remember, we had more than a few KGB doubles on MI-6 books for a while way back when. We had numbered accounts for them in Zurich or Geneva, some offshore in the Caymans and elsewhere. Shouldn't take me too long to get someone onto this, see if there are still some active accounts on the books."

"One minute sounds good to me."

"We'll do our best. I warn you, though, we haven't used these fellows since the collapse of the Soviet Union in 1991. As I say, I'm not even sure if any of them are still alive. Red Banner's charge is to rebuild the old Moscow network. Just begun scratching the surface there, I'm afraid."

"Is there anyone at all on your side who could find out quickly? Every second counts from here on in."

"Stefan Halter might actually recall the fellow you're after. He's deep cover in Moscow right now, but he's spent time in Bermuda recently, briefing Hawke and Red Banner on dormant Moscow assets. I'll ring him post haste."

"Do that. Sir David, I don't need to stress how vitally important this is. I need a reliable asset deep inside the Kremlin, and I need him now. Someone who can help us get close enough to Korsakov to neutralize his goddamn worldwide web of death machines. The CIA says Korsakov's private airship arrives in Stockholm in twelve hours. He shows up at the Stockholm Concert Hall two hours later to accept his Nobel. I'd like your Red Banner boys on him the second he lands. Got any ideas? Hawke would be ideal."

"Alex Hawke? May need a bit of a rest-up after Energetika and this Bermuda operation, I'm afraid."

"No time for rest-ups, David. I'd appreciate it if you could get your man Hawke on the next thing smoking to Stockholm. That's where Korsakov is headed, and that's where we need him. We'll provide transportation. Agreed?"

"I'll ring him now."

"And David, tell your Mr. Hawke one thing directly from the American president's lips to his ears, will you, please?"

"Certainly."

"Everything is riding on this. Everything."

"Got it. I'll ring you back as soon as I have something definite on your Kremlin question. Cheerio."

Cheerio?

Did they still say that over there?

64

Kungsholm, Sweden

The tiny village of Kungsholm was roughly one hour by car from the center of Stockholm. As it was nearly buried within a deep, dark wood, Hawke had found it rather difficult to locate. The limbs of gnarled old trees on either side of the lane were laden with freshly fallen December snow and threw long black arms across the scene. The quaint cottages glimpsed now and then on either side of the narrow thoroughfare seemed supernaturally quiet.

No movement, save a delicate mist wafting across the road and into the thrusting, yearning tangle of the woodland fringe. Perfect stillness. It was as if some evil wizard had recently waved his wand above all the rooftops, sprinkling fairy dust that put the village's few inhabitants to sleep for an eternity.

Hawke motored slowly through the town. Smoke curled from a few chimneys, rising through spindly black tree limbs sharply etched against the rose-gold afternoon sky. But these few wispy smoke trails were the sole signs of human life. On the outskirts of town, he had seen three magnificent reindeer staring at him from the safety of the woods, frozen in place, nostrils quivering, their huge black eyes glistening.

Hawke was shivering behind the wheel of an ancient Saab in which both the heater and the windscreen wipers were woefully inadequate. Despite this deliberately inconspicuous vehicle, he'd somehow picked up a tail leaving the airport, a blacked-out late-model Audi. After a bit of cat and mouse in the narrow cobbled lanes of the Gamla Stan, Stockholm's Old Town, he'd finally managed to lose them, whoever they were. Russian secret police, he supposed, the Tsar's men. Korsakov would no doubt have his Third Department operatives watching the airports and rail stations.

Having made it safely out of Stockholm and driving south through the Swedish countryside to Kungsholm, he was now looking for any road signs not completely frosted over with snow. He was struggling a bit with the map unfolded on his knee. He wasn't fluent in Swedish, and the damn thing was no help at all.

He was not yet prepared to admit that he was lost, but he was considering getting out his mobile and calling Stefan Halter, his contact, when he finally saw the snow-filled lane he was probably meant to take. He put the wheel hard over and skidded into it, careening harmlessly off the snowbanks on either side. The trees above him intersected to form a long dark tunnel snaking through the wood.

Stefan would be waiting for him at the end of this lane. An Interpol safe house here in Kungsholm had been chosen for Hawke's rendezvous with the Russian double agent Halter had identified for the White House. All he knew was that the agent, whose name Hawke had not been told, was a man President McAtee had dealt with in the past and that Hawke's meeting with him had apparently been specifically ordered by the president.

Hawke's brief on this new mission had been straightforward enough:

Get to Kungsholm, Sweden, as fast as he possibly could without attracting undue attention. Find Halter.

The simple two-story farmhouse appeared through his frosted windscreen. It was built of roughhewn stone and had a sharply pitched roof of slate and two large chimneys at either end made of brick. It had a storybook quality, Hawke thought, which seemed to be the norm in this neck of the woods.

He parked the Saab next to a battered Mercedes sedan in a small yard just outside the entryway, climbed out, and rapped thrice, then twice, on the heavy wooden door, just as he'd been instructed.

The Russian mole, Dr. Stefanovich Halter, just as tweedy and natty as Hawke remembered him from Bermuda, pulled the door open. The smell of wood smoke inside was pleasant, and the weary British spy was pleased to come in from the cold.

"Alex," Halter said, wasting no time on amenities, "prepare yourself."

"Tell me, Stefan."

"The man you're about to meet is General Kuragin, the head of the Third Department, the Tsar's private secret police. He's waiting at a table in the kitchen. He's a bit tight, I'm afraid."

"Nikolai Kuragin?" Hawke said.

"Indeed. Know him?"

"I met him briefly at the winter palace. He's the Tsar's oldest and closest friend, is he not?"

"Well, let's just say the general's loyalty has never been above reproach and leave it at that."

"Drunk, is he?"

"Not yet, but he's working on it."

"Take the bottle away."

"Good cop, bad cop, as you Yanks say. I'm the good one. Listen, he's got the Beta detonator with him. It's one of only two in existence. It's manacled permanently to his left wrist. He bloody sleeps with the damn thing."

"Beta detonator? What the hell does it detonate?"

"Everything."

"What do you mean, everything?"

"The whole bloody world, basically."

"You're not serious."

"I'm deadly serious, Alex. Look, there's no time to explain now, but Korsakov has basically hardwired the whole world with explosives inside computers. Zeta machines."

"The Wizards? I own one."

"Yes. Sounds far-fetched, I know, but it's not. It's bloody reality. Witness the demise of Salina, Kansas."

"You said two detonators. Where is the other one?"

"Always with the Tsar. Kuragin's is the failsafe backup in case something untoward should happen to Korsakov."

"Is our general feeling cooperative?"

"He will be when he learns how much we're prepared to pay for the Beta detonator."

"Am I doing the negotiating?" Hawke asked.

"We'll double-team him. He wouldn't have agreed to come here if he weren't for sale, that I can promise you."

"What's our ceiling?"

"Fifty million U.S. dollars. But we'll start the bidding at twenty. I've already transferred that amount to his account in Geneva."

"I knew I'd gone into the wrong business," Hawke said with a wry smile. "The kitchen is back this way, I assume?"

"Lord Hawke, welcome," General Kuragin said, getting somewhat shakily to his feet and extending his hand. "We met briefly under slightly grander circumstances a week ago in the country. The Tsar's winter palace."

"Indeed we did, general," Hawke said, shaking the Russian's skeletal hand and taking a seat at the old butcher-block table. The man's splendid black uniform, heavy, deep-set dark eyes, and pale yellow skin gave him an uncanny resemblance to Himmler, if Hawke's mental picture of the old Nazi was accurate. Halter joined them at the table, and Kuragin ceremoniously filled the glasses at each man's seat from a half-empty carafe of vodka. Kuragin spoke first, and what he said brought Hawke upright in his chair.

"I understand you spent some time sharing a cell with my old friend at Energetika, Lord Hawke."

"Putin is your friend? But you helped overthrow him."

"Things in Russia are not always what they seem. There are wheels within wheels, Lord Hawke, believe me."

"Oh, I believe you, general. Absolutely Byzantine."

The general nodded, a fleeting smile on his lips. He'd actually taken the word as a compliment. Then he covered Hawke's hand with his own, patting it as one would a child's. The bony fingers were trembling, cold as ice.

"Putin was most impressed in his appraisal of you. In fact, it was Putin himself who insisted I meet with you today."

"Really? Why?"

"Why do you think? Surely he brought you into his confidence. Made his future plans known to you that night in his wretched cell."

"He did, indeed," Hawke said, replaying bits of the long conversation in his mind.

"And?"

"Eliminate the Tsar and return to power," Hawke said slowly, sitting back in his chair. This entire Russian affair was suddenly clicking into place like the encryption rotors inside an Enigma machine.

A riddle wrapped in a mystery inside an enigma, Churchill had said of Russia, and truer words were never spoken. Hawke sat back, sipped his vodka, and studied the man.

General Kuragin was the one secretly protecting Putin inside the prison. And it was Kuragin who would orchestrate Putin's return to power once the Tsar was safely out of the way. And it was Kuragin who would emerge from this latest coup even more powerful than from the last two or three.

Yes, it was all quite clear now. He'd finally found him. The man MI-6 had long ago dubbed the Third Man, the unseen power behind the Kremlin throne.

It was never Ivan Korsakov, as Hawke had gradually come to believe.

It was General Nikolai Kuragin.

Palace intrigue was a noble tradition in ancient Russia, and Hawke had managed to get himself tangled up in this bloody intrigue without even knowing it. He'd come to Russia suffused with confidence, ready to practice his craft, to spy on them, only to learn that he was merely a tiny pawn on their great board. And the Third Man, the grandest chess master of them all, had been using him all along.

Using the pawn to take out the king?

Kuragin smiled, his eyes like black slits behind the thick lenses, and Hawke had the disconcerting sensation that the man had been reading his thoughts.

"It was you, wasn't it, general? You had me arrested and thrown into Energetika Prison for a bloody *job interview!*" Hawke said.

"Hmm. Let's say I may have put the notion into the Tsar's head. Of course, Korsakov had no idea you would live long enough to speak privately with our beloved former prime minister. No, Ivan the Terrible assumed you'd be impaled shortly after your arrival inside those forbidding black walls."

"Ivan the Terrible," Hawke said, smiling at the wily old spy. "Surprising you, of all people, would call him that. Your dear friend."

"He's a fucking monster," Kuragin said with sudden ferocity. "Impaling his enemies by the thousands is child's play for him. Bringing about the total destruction of my beloved homeland by incurring America's nuclear wrath is much more difficult. And yet that is precisely what he is about to do."

"Unless you stop him."

"Unless *you* stop him, Lord Hawke. I can never be seen as having anything to do with this, this . . . whatever you intend to do, for obvious reasons. I believe the current American expression is plausible deniability. I intend to have very plausible deniability, I assure you. Excruciatingly plausible."

Hawke glanced at Halter, wondering how much he already knew of all this. Had Stefanovich Halter traveled all the way to Bermuda to take Hawke's measure for Kuragin? It was surely possible they'd been planning a role for him even then. But Halter was giving nothing away. Men who'd spent their lives playing both sides of the scrimmage line were good at that kind of thing, else they paid in blood.

"I think perhaps we understand each other, general," Hawke said, making his decision even as he said the words, raising his glass. Putin was far from perfect, but he was vastly preferable to the vainglorious psychopath who represented the status quo.

The pawn now saw the whole board as if from above and found he was more than willing to make the next move.

"To world peace," Kuragin said, raising his own glass.

"To world peace," the other two echoed, and then all three of them downed their drinks in a single draught.

"General," Hawke said, glancing at his watch, "tell me more about your lovely bracelet and the object attached to it."

"Certainly," Kuragin said, pushing the detonator closer to Hawke. "What do you wish to know?"

"How does it work, for starters?" Hawke asked, picking it up and turning it over in his hands. He eyed the detonator carefully, contemplating the enormous power of it. It was simply a smaller version of the brain-shaped Zeta computer but without the brain-stem stalk to support it. Polished to a mirror finish. Quite heavy, with a hairline crack around the exterior, where it opened.

"The two extant detonators, called Beta machines, are connected by Bluetooth and other sophisticated wireless servers to every Zeta machine on the planet. I can easily program this Beta to blow up a single Zeta or, say, a hundred million of them. Individually or simultaneously. Only at the Tsar's command, of course."

"You actually can blow up the whole world with this thing," Hawke said, eyeing Halter again. "Right here. Right now."

"Basically, yes, I can, but I won't. I am not insane. Not yet, anyway. The Tsar, on the other hand, would be perfectly happy to do so if someone on the other side either miscalculates or underestimates and gets in his way."

"Amazing," Hawke said, placing the Beta machine carefully on the table. He took the carafe from where it stood in front of Kuragin, poured himself a fresh drink, and looked at the two men with something akin to admiration.

Hawke said, "You don't stockpile bombs or spend billions on reactors, delivery systems, nuclear subs, ICBMs. No, you distribute your bombs among your enemies! Better yet, you make a fortune by *selling* your enemies the seeds of their own destruction. Millions of them over a period of years. Such a simple, ingenious way to gather the fate of the world into one's own hands."

"Thank you," General Kuragin said.

"This was *your* idea?" Hawke said, astonished. He'd naturally assumed the mad genius had been Ivan Korsakov.

"Yes, I'm to blame for this madness, I'm afraid. The military strategy of seeding the bombs, at any rate. Korsakov was the scientific genius behind designing and creating the actual Zeta machine. My grievous error was in letting my military strategy for Russian dominance fall into the wrong hands."

"The Tsar's."

"Of course. I should have seen this coming. I did not. Now, I will pay for my mistake and correct it at a single stroke."

"Still, the Zeta-network idea is brilliant in its simplicity," Hawke said. "I'll give you that much."

"Simplicity is a cornerstone of genius. Tell me, Lord Hawke, have you ever heard anyone exclaim, 'I love this idea. It's so damn complicated!' "

Hawke smiled. Here he was, sharing a bottle with a man who'd hatched an evil scheme for world domination, and he found he rather liked him.

"General," Halter said, "you were telling me earlier that each of the two Beta detonators also contains Hexagon explosives, correct? Like the explosives inside the Zeta computers."

"Yes, but each Beta is packed with twice the explosive power. This one can explode the one in the Tsar's possession, and vice versa."

"Why?" Hawke asked.

"In case one or the other ever fell into the wrong hands, of course. The Tsar wanted to be able to eliminate that person instantly.

He's not comfortable sharing such power."

"Except with you."

Kuragin nodded his head, "Except with me, the only man on earth he trusts."

Hawke ignored the implicit irony in this and said, "You're saying you could use it now, to kill the Tsar?"

"I could. There is a code, known only to me. I enter it, arm this machine, press Detonate, and it will instantly explode the other Beta. If the Tsar is anywhere within, say, a radius of five hundred yards, he dies. But I never murder people, Lord Hawke. I have people murdered. It's why I'm still alive."

"The Tsar presumably has the Beta with him at all times?" Hawke asked.

"Of course. His nuclear football. Chained to the wrist of his bodyguard, named Kuba, a highly trained assassin who doubles as his driver. Kuba is never more than a few hundred yards away from his lord and master."

Kuragin pulled a pack of cigarettes from his inside pocket, extracted one, and lit it with a paper match. The same brand Putin smoked, Hawke noticed, Sobranie Black Russians from the Ukraine.

Hawke pushed his chair back from the table and smiled at the general.

"General Kuragin, when was the last time you checked your account in Geneva?"

"I don't really know. Some months ago, I suppose."

"And what was the balance at the time?"

"Five million, I believe. American dollars."

Hawke pulled his sat phone from his jacket pocket and placed it on the table in front of the Russian.

"You might want to give your Swiss bankers a call, general. Just to confirm your current balance. According to Dr. Halter, it should now be twenty-five million."

"Twenty million dollars to save the whole world? It hardly seems enough," Kuragin said, gazing at them from beneath his heavily lidded eyes.

"Shall we say thirty million?"

"Say it and find out."

"Thirty million."

"Not enough."

"All right. We are prepared to pay you forty million dollars for that machine, General Kuragin. And the code that goes with it, of course. Effective immediately. Dr. Halter will call the bank in Geneva with wiring instructions for an additional twenty million dollars."

"Can you say fifty?"

Hawke glanced at Halter, who nodded his head. Stefan had held the sat phone to his ear, speaking French to an anonymous banker in Geneva as the negotiation progressed.

"Fifty million dollars," Hawke said. "Final offer."

"I accept."

Halter spoke a few more words into the phone, handed it to Kuragin, and said, "This gentleman will confirm that an additional thirty million dollars has been electronically placed in your account, general."

"This is Kuragin. My account number is 4413789-A. May I have my balance, please? I see. Well, thank you very much. *Au revoir, monsieur, et merci.*"

He handed the phone back to Halter and pulled a gold pen from inside his uniform jacket.

"Here, I'll write the code down for you inside this matchbook cover. Now, I must ask you both to leave the room. But first, please bring me some clean towels and a large bowl of ice. Also, that meat cleaver hanging by the stove, if you'd be so kind. It looks reasonably sharp."

Hawke and Halter looked at each other, stunned, as the Cambridge don pocketed the matchbook with the detonator code printed inside.

"Surely you're not planning to do anything foolish, general."

"On the contrary. If it appears in any way that I have given up this damn thing voluntarily, I won't last five minutes. Every KGB agent in the world will be lining up to assassinate me."

"Wait," Hawke said. "I'm sure we can get that damn bracelet off with a hacksaw. We'll think of some way to make it look as if you were abducted, and then —"

"No. I appreciate what you're trying to do, but I've been drinking vodka all day in anticipation of what's coming, and I'm damn well ready to do it. It is the only way for me to survive this, I promise you. Even the most cynical Russian would never believe a man capable of doing such a thing to himself!" He laughed at his own notion and filled his glass to the brim.

"You'll have to explain giving up the code, general," Hawke said.

"A moment of weakness? A butcher has a meat cleaver poised above your left hand, and he asks you for a number. Few among us could resist the temptation to give it to him, wouldn't you agree?"

Hawke and Dr. Halter rose from the table and brought him the items he'd requested. Hawke couldn't resist running his index finger along the edge of the heavy cleaver's blade. Sharp as a razor, it instantly produced a thin line of bright red blood on the pad of his fingertip.

"Please leave me alone until it's over and done," Kuragin said. "When you return, you can bind me to this table in a convincing fashion. There is a length of heavy rope beneath my chair. Then call the emergency medical ambulance. And then you must leave at once. Understood? And never tell a living soul what has happened here. Never."

"Yes," Hawke said, holding the swinging kitchen door open for Dr. Halter. "We understand perfectly."

The two men walked out into the adjacent living room and sat in the two wooden chairs facing the fire. Neither spoke for a few long minutes.

"He's finishing the vodka," Hawke finally said, gazing into the flames, "then he'll do it."

"Do it? You don't actually think he'll go through with this insanity, do you?" Halter said, an incredulous look in his eyes. "No one has that kind of courage. No one."

"We shall soon see, won't we?"

A moment later, a horrendous *thunk* was followed by a howl of animal agony that pierced Hawke's soul. He leaped from his chair and raced into the kitchen.

Kuragin had done it.

Bright red blood spattered the white stucco wall beside the kitchen table. The bloody left hand, still twitching, was completely severed from the forearm by the blade of the meat cleaver, now buried at least an inch deep into the wooden table. The general had pitched forward in his chair when he passed out, his forehead resting on the table. He wasn't making a sound. Shock had already set in, and the man was clearly unconscious, blood spurting wildly from the grievous wound at the end of his arm.

Hawke quickly wrapped the man's bloody stump in a tightly wound towel and plunged it into the bowl of ice, while Halter collected the blood-spattered Beta detonator that had fallen to the floor. That done, Halter picked up the kitchen phone and rang for an ambulance, giving the address of the farmhouse, saying only that a man had been found grievously injured and was losing a lot of blood. A doctor should come as quickly as humanly possible. He hung up without giving his name.

"What time is the Tsar accepting his award tonight?" Hawke asked, as they carefully lifted the general's body and placed him faceup on the table. Hawke used the heavy hemp rope the general had placed beneath his chair to bind the man in a position required for an amputation. It looked real enough, he decided, stepping back to inspect his efforts. As if a man had been bound and relieved of his hand with a meat cleaver. It might work.

"The banquet is at seven, I believe," Halter said. "Why?"

"I plan to be there," Hawke said. "I want to make sure his Imperial Majesty, the new Tsar of all Russia, gets the rousing welcome he so richly deserves."

"Alex, there's something you should know

right now. Korsakov is threatening to destroy an unspecified Western city with a population of one million if the NATO troops just deployed in Eastern Europe are not pulled back from the borders. He phoned the White House and gave President McAtee twenty-four hours to demonstrate his willingness to back off whilst he regained his lost territories."

"When was this?"

"Sixteen hours ago."

"So, we've got to move very quickly."

"I'd say that's an understatement of a huge order of magnitude."

"Get into the bloody car, then, man! You've got the code? The matchbook?"

"Yes. In my waistcoat pocket."

"A bunch of random numbers, from the look of it. Mean anything to you, professor?" Hawke turned the key, praying the damn car would turn over. Now that the sun had dropped behind the forest, the temperature had plummeted. The highway back to Stockholm would be treacherous.

"One-seven-ought-seven-one-nine-one-eight. Seventeen July, nineteen hundred and eighteen. The exact date of the night Commandant Yurokovsky and his Chekists herded the Romanovs down into the cellar of the house in Ekaterinberg and murdered Tsar Nicholas II, the Empress Katherine, the heir, their four daughters, and the servants."

"Why would Korsakov choose that date, do you suppose?" Hawke asked. The motor caught on the second try, and he grabbed first gear, racing out of the farmhouse yard, the old Saab whining in its traces.

"It was the last night of the Tsars, Alex. Perhaps he fancies himself as the dawn of a new era, wouldn't you suppose?"

"Yeah, I suppose he does," Hawke said, accelerating up the snowy lane, careening once more off the snowbanks lining the road. He drove with ferocity. But in his mind was a perfectly composed picture of his beautiful Anastasia when last he'd seen her. They'd not spoken in days. Tonight, she would be with her father in Stockholm as he accepted his Nobel Prize from the king of Sweden. Somehow, he'd find her. She'd invited him, after all.

Sooner or, he hoped, later, the Tsar would learn that the second detonator had been forcibly taken from Kuragin and fallen into enemy hands. When he did, Hawke knew Korsakov would instantly trigger the thing and detonate it, not caring which enemy had it or where they were.

Which made the timing of everything to come a bit more interesting. He and his new friend Dr. Halter were literally babysitting a live bomb.

Someone would be first to push the button. And someone else would be first to die.

Hawke, his mind racing, knew he'd have to find some way to take the Tsar out when he was alone, or at least get him out in the open. He couldn't, wouldn't, accept any collateral damage. He could not conscience the death of innocents.

Such as the woman he loved.

Or, and here his heart paused a beat, their unborn child.

65

Stockholm

The Nobel Prize banquet ceremony is held each year at the Stadshuset in Stockholm. Even a monarch's coronation cannot rival the Nobel celebration in terms of pure grandeur and epic scale. The massive Stadshuset complex, with its three-hundred-fifty-foot tower at one corner, is built in the Swedish Romantic style. It stands on the banks of the Riddarfjarden, a freshwater lake in the heart of Stockholm. Tonight, Sweden's beautiful State House was ablaze with light.

Alex Hawke, shivering as he climbed out of the Saab's passenger seat, thought it looked like a great medieval fortress, but Professor Halter had informed him that it was built in 1923.

"Are you sure you're not going to freeze to death out here?" he asked the professor. Halter would remain in the car while Hawke went inside. Halter was dressed for Russian winter, wearing an *ushanka,* the Russian trapper's fur cap with ear flaps, and a full-length bearskin coat. Sitting behind the wheel, his brow furrowed in concentration, he resembled some great bear, fiddling with the silvery Beta detonator on his lap, making sure he'd know how to use it when the time came.

"I'll be fine. But try to hurry this up, will you?" he said. "It is frightfully cold, and we're rapidly running out of time. He intends to destroy the first city on his agenda in a little less than two hours."

"I'll be twenty minutes," Hawke said, glancing at his watch. "Thirty max. Keep your eye on that entry door, and please keep the engine running. When he comes out, he will likely be in a hurry. You see his car and driver over there, the liveried chap standing beside the heavily armored Maybach? He'll head for that, straightaway."

"How the hell do you know that's his car?"

"I'm a British spy, professor. Besides, it's got Russian plates. Moscow. Now, try to stay awake. Maybe turn the heat down."

"What heat?"

Hawke smiled, shut the passenger door, and raced across the snowy car park to join the party inside. He felt his mobile vibrating in his trouser pocket. Anastasia? He'd rung her cell phone from his room while he was shaving; perhaps she was returning the call. No time to find out now. He'd just have to call her later. He'd not spoken to her since they'd kissed good-bye when he boarded the Navy fighter at Ramstein. But since then, he'd been maintaining a fairly active schedule. With any luck, he'd see her tonight. But whether or not they'd have time alone, he had no idea.

He knew he had roughly two hours to get the Tsar out into the open, in the countryside, preferably, somewhere where he could take him out without endangering anyone else. Two hours was enough time, perhaps, but there was a slight complication. He had no idea how he was going to accomplish this objective. Ah, well, he'd think of something.

First things first, he thought, showing his beautifully engraved invitation to the security chaps at the entrance. He'd need to smoke Korsakov out of the massive crowd inside the banquet hall. Find a way to force him outside in the open. And do it rather quickly. That would be the trick.

The Nobel guest list included some 1,300 dignitaries from around the world. This closely guarded A List included the Nobel laureates and their families, their majesties the king and queen of Sweden, and the entire royal family, plus various European heads of state and a smattering of celebrities and bigwigs. The dinner was always held in a magnificent space called the Blue Hall, and Hawke hurried there now, the inkling of a workable idea just forming in his mind.

He was late. He and Halter had pushed the

ancient Saab to the limit on the icy roads returning north to Stockholm, and he'd barely arrived with time enough to race up to his room at the Grand Hotel, shower and shave, and don his white tie and tails. With some help from Sir David Trulove, Hawke had managed to get his last-minute invitation courtesy of the British ambassador to Sweden.

When he arrived inside the venue, he was first surprised to find that the famous Blue Hall was not blue at all. The architect had originally planned to paint the great hall blue but changed his mind when he saw the beauty of the handmade red bricks. The name, however, stuck.

The gala dinner was just beginning as Hawke straightened the white piqué tie at his neck and made his way along a great gallery overlooking the guests still being seated in the vast hall below. Thirteen hundred people, with all that chatter and tinkling china and silverware, made for quite a din. And then there were the trumpets.

Vast numbers of trumpeters in period costume lined the gallery balustrade and both sides of the grand staircase leading to the floor below. Their gleaming brass horns were as long as Amazonian blowguns. They sounded an impressive fanfare before each of the few remaining laureates and dignitaries was announced, everyone pausing regally at the top of the staircase, waiting to hear their names called before descending.

There was a stern chap in court regalia with a great ornamental staff, and just after the fanfare and before someone's name was announced, he'd bang the staff down on the marble step, making a fine noise that got everyone's attention.

Hawke joined this august line of Nobel geniuses, wondering if he'd get a whack of the staff and a fanfare. He certainly hoped so. He'd never had a fanfare before.

At the foot of the staircase, a temporary stage had been built. At the center of this flower-bedecked podium was a gleaming mahogany lectern, where an elderly white-haired gentleman, the presumed head of the Nobel Prize Committee, was introducing the winners and assorted Swedish big shots as they made their way down the broad marble stairs.

There were television cameras everywhere, and Hawke knew the annual ceremony was being beamed around the world to an audience of millions.

A vast worldwide audience only made his germ of an idea all the more appealing.

Perpendicular to the podium was a massively long dining table that stretched the entire length of the huge hall. This brilliantly laid table was reserved for the laureates and their immediate families and, of course, the king and queen, their daughter, and the royal family. Here at this table, one would naturally suppose, he would spy his favorite Tsar. The man's car was outside. Was he inside? He had to be.

Hawke stepped out of line a moment and, ducking between two trumpeters, leaned out over the balustrade to peer at the crowd below. Spread beneath him was an undulating sea of women in beautiful gowns and sparkling jewelry with gentlemen resplendent in white-tie evening attire, all lit in the warm glow of countless candles. He pulled a cigarette-thin but powerful Zeiss monocular from inside his black cutaway and scanned the guests seated at the royal table from one end to the other, then back up the opposite side.

Halfway down, on the far side of the table, he saw Anastasia, exquisite in a diamond tiara. She was seated beside her father, who wore a great red sash across his chest and many jeweled decorations. Tsar Ivan was speaking expansively to someone across the table, and his daughter was listening, a smile on her lips. He zoomed in on her lovely face. He wasn't so sure about that smile. It looked brave, pasted on. His poor darling.

He was desperate to speak with her. Would she have her mobile at a gala like this? Perhaps not, but worth a try.

He pulled out his own, saw his message

light flashing, and punched in her number, watching her through the monocular as he heard it ringing at the other end. *Yes!* She reached down to pick up her evening bag and was about to open it, when her father grabbed her wrist, squeezing it cruelly by the look on her face. *Bastard.*

She returned the bag to the floor and pasted the smile back on her face. He waited for the tone and then spoke.

"Darling, I pray you get this soon. I'm here at the banquet. If you look up at the balcony between the trumpet players, you'll see me smiling down at you. Listen carefully, this is vitally important. I can't explain now, but it's imperative that you get away from your father. As quickly as possible! It's extremely dangerous to be anywhere near him. I wish I could explain more, but I beg you, make any excuse, say you're ill and have to use the loo, anything, but run at the first opportunity! I love you. We'll be together soon, and I will explain everything."

He shoved the thing back into his pocket. Well, at least it was almost over. Somehow, they'd both survive this night. And when it was over — no time for that now.

The line was moving quickly, nearing the end, and he stepped back to take his place. The important fellow in front of him was introduced and proceeded down the steps, his wife at his side, her diamond necklace and earrings sparkling in the spotlights. Hawke took his place alone at the head of the staircase and waited, as the spotlights found him.

The staff came down with a great thump, and then the trumpets sounded a rising series of triumphal notes. A clarion voice rang out, "Your royal majesties, ladies and gentlemen, may I present Lord Alexander Hawke!"

He couldn't imagine how the British ambassador had pulled that one off, but he was delighted. The fanfare still ringing in his ears, he put his hands in his trouser pockets and descended the wide steps in a somewhat jaunty fashion, affecting — unsuccessfully, he imagined — a kind of Fred Astaire nonchalance. He wished he could see Anastasia's face at this moment, as this little performance was meant for her. And her father, of course. He'd have paid a pretty penny to see that face right now.

The Nobel Committee chairman was at the podium, standing next to the old fellow introducing this year's winners in Physiology or Medicine. As he spoke, the honorees were making their way from their seats at the royal table back up to the lectern for a short acceptance speech. Along with his invitation, there'd been a copy of the evening's program in his hotel room, and Alex had carefully studied the order of presentation he'd taped to the bathroom mirror while he dressed.

After Medicine, he knew, came Physics, the Tsar's prize.

Showtime.

Instead of proceeding to one of the many hundreds of round guest tables on either side of the lengthy royal one, Hawke remained discreetly on the podium, standing politely to one side with a group of officials as the four winners for Medicine made their brief remarks.

The Nobel chairman thanked the winners as they left the stage and then said, "And now, your royal majesties, the prize for Physics. I'd like to welcome Sir George Roderick Llewellyn of the British Royal Academy to the podium to present this year's winner."

Hawke walked toward the elderly chairman, who glanced once, then twice, over his shoulder, covering the microphone with his hand so he couldn't be heard by the huge audience.

"You're not Sir George," he whispered as Hawke drew near.

"Sorry, no, I'm not at all, am I? Poor old fellow took ill, I'm afraid to say. I'm his replacement. Alex Hawke, British Embassy. How do you do?"

The lovely old gent, a bit flustered, shook his hand and walked away from the lectern, muttering something angrily in Swedish. He clearly wasn't accustomed to last-minute changes in schedules on this night of nights.

Hawke adjusted the microphone upward to suit his height and looked out over the enormous crowd.

"Before I begin, I'd like to say hello to a few familiar faces I see in the audience this evening. These wonderful and brave people are all survivors of the horrendous hostage crisis aboard the airship *Pushkin.* Welcome, ladies and gentlemen. I'm glad you're all here tonight! Would you stand, please, so that we can acknowledge your presence?"

The crowd erupted into cheers and applause as the rescued laureates and their families got to their feet, many of them with smiles of gratitude for the handsome Englishman who stood at the podium.

"The Nobel Prize for Physics," Hawke said in a loud, clear voice, "is presented this year for outstanding achievement in the field of black matter. Black holes, things in the universe so dense that no radiation, no light, can escape. You can't see it, but you know it's there. Your royal majesties, ladies and gentlemen, the man we all honor here tonight is no stranger to dark matter. As he makes his way up here to the podium, let me tell you a little bit about this murderous and truly evil human being."

The room went dead silent save the sharp intake of a thousand breaths at once. There was suddenly a good deal of murmuring and hand wringing on the podium. This new speaker was clearly deviating from the well-rehearsed script they all held in their hands. There was no mention of "murder" or "evil" in their copies.

"In addition to his brilliant scientific achievements, Russia's new Tsar builds prisons. Like the one called Energetika, built, ingeniously, on top of a radioactive nuclear-waste site on a small island off St. Petersburg. Here the Tsar has restored the ancient practice of impalement. For those of you unfamiliar with this medieval torture, the victim is stripped naked and placed on a sharpened stake. The tip of the stake is inserted into the rectum and gradually pierces the body's internal organs until —"

Someone, a woman at the royal table, Hawke thought, screamed loudly. She was thrown bodily from her chair as the new Tsar of Russia tried to force his way through the crowd to the stage. A spotlight was immediately swung his way, and Hawke could see the demonic rage in his eyes all the way from his perch on the podium.

"Sorry for the commotion," Hawke continued. "As I was saying, the wooden stake perforates the perineum or the rectum itself and takes perhaps a week to kill the victim as it travels upward through the body and —"

"Stop him!" the Tsar howled, clambering over chairs and shoving aside anyone who got in his way, including the very furious

King Carl XVI Gustaf of Sweden, in his desperate efforts to gain the stage and get at Alex Hawke's throat, shouting all the while, "Someone stop this fucking madman!"

"Sorry for these beastly interruptions," Hawke said, continuing with his conversational tone despite the shouted threats and the imminent arrival of the enraged Tsar at the podium.

"In addition to the marvels of impalement, let me touch briefly on our honoree's invention of the Zeta computer. Hailed as a godsend in Third World countries, the Zeta computers are actually powerful bombs, used just last week to destroy an entire American town. But the Americans are not our honoree's only target. No, he has shipped countless millions of these cleverly disguised bombs all over the world, creating a worldwide web of death, which he is even now using to threaten his political enemies, forcing them to stand by and watch as his Russian storm troopers sweep into Eastern European countries, the Baltics, East Ukraine, and other sovereign nations in an effort to reclaim these lands for Russia and —"

Hawke stood his ground as Korsakov clambered up onto the podium and headed straight for the lectern. The man was literally snarling, stringy loops of saliva flying from his open mouth as he crossed the wide stage. Hawke smiled and calmly continued, as if nothing were out of the ordinary.

"Under this self-proclaimed Tsar, the New Russia will become like the old Soviet Union. A cynical tyranny, a cruel and heartless state, no rule of law, trampling on basic rights and human dignity, expansionist by creed, and — oh, here's our honoree now — I'd like you all to welcome —"

Korsakov reached out, ripped the microphone from the lectern, and flung it to the floor in a fury.

"I will kill you for this!" he said in a low growl, going for Hawke's throat with his outstretched hands.

Hawke, still behind the lectern, thought a physical brawl at the Nobel podium would be a bit unseemly, so he pulled the small Walther PPK automatic from his shoulder holster and shoved the muzzle deep under the Tsar's ribs, aiming straight for the heart.

"No, sire, I will kill you," Hawke said in a low voice. "Here. *Now.* Or we can step outside and settle this matter like gentlemen. Which do you prefer, you murderous bastard?"

He now shoved the Walther up under the Tsar's chin, grabbed him by the lapel, and yanked him closer. He was aware of security men edging toward the lectern.

"I will do it," Hawke said. "Believe me."

"He's got a gun!" one of the Nobel officials shouted, and the members of the Nobel Committee still on the podium either dove off the stage into the crowd or raced up the staircase between the bewildered trumpeters.

The Tsar looked into Hawke's icy blue eyes. The Russian was breathing heavily through flared nostrils, his pupils dilated, his nose only inches away from the hated Englishman's. He spat full into Hawke's face. Then he turned and leaped from the podium onto the royal table, sending china and crystal crashing to the stone floor.

"You will have cause to regret that, sir," Hawke said to his retreating back. The man was storming the length of the tabletop, slashing flaming candelabras aside with his hands and kicking great urns and tureens of hot soup out of his path toward the main exit at the far end of the table.

Hawke holstered his Walther, pulled his white handkerchief from the breast pocket of his cutaway, and wiped the Tsar's saliva from his face. Various security men seemed to be making their way toward him, so he simply dove into the hysterical crowd and resurfaced a hundred yards away, melting into a seething mass of identically dressed men heading for the exits.

There was utter panic and pandemonium in the hall.

He was afraid he'd quite ruined the entire evening.

But after all, some things just couldn't be helped.

66

The Maybach roared out of the car park on two wheels as Hawke raced up to the Saab. Halter was sitting in the passenger seat with the engine running and the driver's door open. Hawke jumped behind the wheel and fastened his safety belt. Engaging first gear, he slammed the accelerator to the floor, popped the clutch, and fishtailed out into the Avenue Hantverkargatan, taking a right turn just as the Maybach had done. He was hoping for a glimpse of taillights, but the Tsar's big black automobile had already crossed the large bridge and disappeared.

"You did it!" Halter said. "You bloody well flushed him out!"

"Yeah."

"Before or after his moment of glory?"

"I'd say what his moment lacked in glory was more than compensated for by drama."

Halter smiled. "Good work."

"Damn it," Hawke said, slamming the wheel with his closed fist. "He's going to be tough to catch, much less keep up with. A real automobile would have come in handy tonight."

"Relax, Alex. I know where he's going," Halter said, holding onto the dashboard with one hand, cradling the Beta detonator in his lap with the other.

"You do?"

"Yes. I heard him shout at his driver as he was getting into the car. 'Morto!' That's an island out in the Stockholm Archipelago. The Tsar has a summer house there, the only house on the island. It used to belong to King Carl XIV Johan. Built in 1818."

"How the hell do you know that?"

"I'm a professor of history at Cambridge University."

"Stefan, please tell me that he was alone when he came out."

"No. His daughter Anastasia was with him."

"Damn it! I told her to run!"

"You spoke with her?"

"No. I left a message on her mobile. Did she seem a willing passenger?"

"Hardly. She was screaming obscenities, trying to escape from her father, who was holding her by the wrist. Korsakov and his gorilla of a driver were trying to force her into the backseat. It looked as if she banged her head pretty badly on the roof. She slumped to the ground, and they stuffed her into the rear seat. The driver, by the way, had the Tsar's Beta detonator manacled to his wrist. We're good to go."

Hawke, while relieved that Anastasia had obviously gotten his message, knew what Halter had to be thinking.

The doomsday clock was ticking, but they still had sufficient time to get away from the civilian population. They could do this as soon as they reached a stretch of deserted road beyond the outskirts of Stockholm. Blow the crazy bastard straight to hell with the Beta detonator up there in the Maybach's front seat.

Because both men knew that in little more than one hour, the Tsar intended to murder at least a million innocent people with the push of a button on that machine. Sir David Trulove had informed Halter that Washington would retaliate immediately. At this very moment, there were twelve U.S. Navy Ohio-class submarines on high alert in the Baltic, the Barents Sea, and the North Pacific. Each sub was carrying twenty-two Trident II nuclear missiles bearing up to eight multiple warheads, up to 3.8 megatons apiece.

MI-6 had recently determined that Russia's early-warning radar system was vulnerable. A single British or American nuclear missile detonated high in the atmosphere would blind all of the early-warning radars below, rendering them unable to monitor subsequent launches. Russia, seeing a launch, would then be faced with a terrible decision. Wait and see if a Trident missile explodes and blinds its radars, or launch a retaliatory strike immediately. Halter, like Sir David and the man in the White House, had no doubt which way Russia's new leader would respond.

World War III.

Downshifting and sliding around a turn, Hawke felt as if his head were full of angry bees. What the hell was he going to do? His duty was clear, but his heart was a formidable foe. He loved that woman, deeply. She was carrying his child. He had to find a way to save her, even as he averted a world catastrophe by killing her father. He'd find a way. He had to.

"Bastard," Hawke said, the horsepower-challenged rattletrap going airborne as he crested the bridge at full speed. The streets of Stockholm were patched with black ice, and unlike his adversary, he didn't have four-wheel drive. Catching the Maybach was going to require some ingenuity.

"Which way to this Morto? I still don't see the bloody Maybach. Are you sure he didn't turn off on a side street somewhere here in the Gamla Stan?"

"There's only one road to the sea, Alex. He'll be on it, don't worry."

"As long as you say so, professor."

Halter had turned the dim yellow map light on and held the Swedish map across his knees. Unlike Hawke, he didn't seem to have any trouble reading it.

"We head due east on this road along the fjord. Route 222, called the Varmodoleden. We follow the mainland coast all the way out to the Baltic Sea. There are literally thousands of islands of various sizes east of here. Most of them with a few houses or villas. Eventually, we'll come to this little town of Dalaro right on the Baltic proper. I see some dotted lines here. Looks as if there's a ferry service from there out to Morto."

"Good. We take him out at the ferry."

"We can't chance it. Look at the map. I think we can take him out right here. This stretch of road coming up in a few miles is wooded on both sides. No houses for a few miles in any direction."

"We can't take him out in the car, Stefan. Not now."

"Of course we can. We have to, Alex, for God's sake! What are you thinking? Korsakov's men could have found Kuragin by now, put the whole thing together! If so, this thing in my bloody lap blows at any second!"

"I need to get him alone, that's all. I'm sorry."

"Alone?"

Halter looked at him, speechless. Then he understood. The daughter. Of course. Hawke was involved with the Tsar's daughter. It must have happened in Bermuda. And he had recently been with her at the winter palace. Holy mother of hell, that was a complication he'd not even dreamed of. Well, he had the Beta in his hands. If worst came to worst, he'd just —

"We'll do this at the ferry, Stefan. It's the only way. I'll get Anastasia out of that car somehow. Don't worry about how. As soon as she and I are clear, do it. You got that? We don't touch the father until the daughter is safely outside the kill radius."

"Alex, you're not thinking. What if he beats us to the ferry? Then what?"

"He won't."

"Alex, listen to me. You, of all people, must know you can't let your personal feelings enter into a situation of this magnitude. I'm sorry about the girl. It's obvious you have feelings for her. But if I see us running out of time, I will act. I am going to take him out, no matter what. You understand that, don't you?"

"Hang on," Hawke said, ignoring the question and accelerating out of a turn. "I'm going to drive as fast as I possibly can without killing us. How much time have we got until he starts blowing up the planet?"

"An hour and ten minutes."

"Should be enough."

"It has to be enough. Please listen to me. If I see it's not, I'm going to take this man out, Alex. It's my sworn duty to do so. As it is yours, I might remind you. I know you've got a gun. You can try to stop me. But I swear to you, I will gladly die pushing this button. Understand?"

Hawke ignored him.

"Aren't there any bloody shortcuts to the ferry?" he asked.

"No."

"Bloody hell," Hawke said, braking and fishtailing through another turn. Luckily, most of the local constabulary was busy providing security at the Stadshuset tonight.

Hawke's driving that night was either inspired or insane, depending on your point of view. He somehow kept the car out of the icy fjord, remained mostly on the road, at any rate, his eyes always a hundred yards ahead, willing the vehicle to go where it was pointed.

He fished his mobile out of his pocket and speed-dialed Asia. *Answer, answer, answer,* he prayed, but all he got was a machine and a beep tone.

"Hey, it's me. Look, I'm right behind you. I'm coming for you. When you get to the Morto ferry, you'll have to stop. That's when you run, okay? Just jump out and run as fast as you can. I'll find you. I love you. Don't worry. It's going to be all right."

Occasionally, he'd look sideways at Halter. The professor's eyes were always straight ahead. He had the Beta in his lap, programmed with the code, his finger on the trigger. Hawke knew that if Halter should feel the Saab leaving the road, headed for the trees or into the inky waters of the fjord on their left, he'd instantly push the button, no doubt about it. He'd see an enormous flash of light on the road far up ahead, flames climbing into the night sky, an explosion vaporizing the Tsar of Russia and his daughter, Anastasia.

And so Hawke drove furiously on, waiting, praying to see a blinking brake light on the road ahead. Something, anything that would prove he was gaining ground on the Maybach and the woman he loved.

But he never did.

67

Hawke skidded to a stop at the top of the hill next to a sign for Dalaro. He'd made it there in less than half an hour, nearly going off the road dozens of times, never once catching a glimpse of the bloody black Maybach. Now he was praying Halter had been right about the Tsar's destination. If he wasn't —

"This is it," Hawke said, putting on the emergency brake and climbing out of the car. "Now, where's that ferry?"

Halter got out, too, moving to the front of the car, the Beta in his hands, gleaming in the light of the headlamps. "There," he said after a few moments of peering at the tiny village at the bottom of the hill.

"Where?"

"Down there to your left. Bottom of that little road leading through the woods over there. I saw taillights flash at the edge of the water. It has to be him, Alex. No one else would be going over to the island at this time of night."

"Is the ferry already there?"

"I can't tell. Maybe. Too far away to see."

"Get in."

They sledded rather than drove down the tiny road, the Saab now merely a toboggan, careening through heavy woods of pine and spruce down to the sea. Hawke kept his foot on and off the brakes the entire way, only accelerating when they slowed, not minding at all the fact that he was bashing both sides of the car against the trees on the sides of the narrow road as long as he kept the thing moving forward.

Hawke saw starlit sky ahead and reached down and switched off the headlamps; this was on the slim chance that the Tsar had glimpsed them racing along the fjord in their efforts to catch him.

If Hawke was driving them right into a trap, he'd like his arrival to be a surprise. And besides, even in the forest, there was enough moonlight reflecting off snow to see by.

Suddenly, they were out of the woods, the icy road dipping right down to the black water.

Five hundred yards below, he finally saw the Maybach's big red brake lights flash.

The mammoth limousine was pulling slowly out onto the tiny ferry, large enough for only two vehicles. A crewman in dark coveralls was motioning the driver forward, all the way to the bow rail. Inside the yellow glow of the small pilothouse window, Hawke saw the ferryboat skipper's black silhouette, even noticing the pipe he held clenched in his teeth. Amazing the things your mind took in at times like this.

"This might be tight," he said to Halter as they careened toward the ferry. "Can you swim?"

"Hurry, for God's sake, they're about to pull away!"

It would be a close thing.

Hawke leaned on his horn, tinny but loud, and flashed his headlamps as he floored the Saab. He accelerated the rest of the way down the steep hill, watching the lone crewman heaving the first of the lines ashore. Hawke was still thinking he just might make it aboard, even if it had to be on the fly, but then he saw the Tsar fling open his door, step out onto the deck, and scream something at the bewildered crewman.

The ferryman clearly wasn't going to wait, and now all lines were cast off, and the fluorescent red-and-white-striped gate with the blinking red warning light was descending. Suddenly, the ferry was pulling away, a puff of smoke from its stack, steaming toward the black shape of Morto in the distance.

"Damn it!" Hawke cried, hitting the brakes, sliding into a spin, yanking up on the emergency brake, and stopping on a patch of dry pavement barely in time to avoid going down the ramp and into the icy waters of the fjord.

He climbed out of the miserable Saab and stood watching the little ferry make its way across the choppy waters toward Morto Island.

He'd lost her.

"Let's go!" Halter said, climbing out of the car with the Beta machine tucked safely under his arm. Hawke breathed a sigh of relief. For whatever reason, Halter had decided to play this out to the end, give Hawke until the last possible moment before ending this.

"Where?"

"I saw a house with a dock out on the end of that point. Where there's a dock, there might well be a boat."

"How much time?" Hawke cried, following Halter across the slippery algal rocks that lined the shore.

"Forty minutes! We might still save her, Alex. We'll try, anyway."

As logic or fate or luck would have it, there was a boat.

A beautiful wooden runabout, maybe twenty-five feet long. She looked fast enough, Hawke thought, racing down the dock toward her. She looked well maintained, probably with a big inboard Volvo engine. They could make it over to Morto in a hurry.

"Check the helm for ignition and keys," Hawke shouted to Halter. Hawke leaped aboard at the stern and opened the engine-hatch cover as the professor jumped down into the cockpit.

"No luck!" Halter cried.

"Never mind, I've got it," Hawke said, two bared wires in his hands. Suddenly, the big 300-horsepower engine roared to life. And just as suddenly, it conked out.

"What's wrong, Alex?"

"I don't know. Felt as if it wasn't getting any fuel."

"Fuel shutoff valve?"

"Yeah, but where is the bloody thing on these engines is the problem. I'm looking."

"Alex, we have perhaps thirty-five minutes until the beginning of the end of the world. Find it quickly, would you, please?"

Hawke muttered something obscene as his head disappeared below the hatchway. Halter stood in the cockpit, watching helplessly as the ferry bearing Korsakov moved ever nearer to the long dock emerging from the heavily wooded island, a low-lying black silhouette on the horizon.

"Cast off all of the lines except the stern," he heard Hawke's muffled voice behind him say. "Just in case I find the damn valve. Wait, is this it? Yes? No, damn it!"

Five minutes later, the big Volvo rumbled to life again, and Hawke came up through the engine-room hatch in a hurry. He un-cleated the stern line and jumped down to join Halter in the cockpit, grabbing the wheel and shoving the throttle forward. The sleek mahogany runabout surged forward, throwing a wide white wake to either side.

Five minutes later, they were ghosting up to a rocky beach with the motor shut down. Hawke hopped off the bow with the anchor in his hand, waded ashore, and wedged the hook between two large boulders. Then he hauled the boat in closer to shore and called out to Halter, "Are you coming?"

"Can't you get it in any closer?"

The man was sitting on the stern with his legs dangling over the side, cradling the Beta machine in both hands.

Hawke was about to tell him to be careful, when the windshield of the runabout exploded into a million pieces. He whirled in the direction of the gunfire. A guard with a German shepherd at the end of a leash was running toward them, shouting something in Russian. He extended his arm again, aiming his submachine gun at Halter on the run. Hawke pulled the Walther from his holster, drew a quick bead, and shot the man once in the head.

Halter was splashing ashore, holding the detonator above his head, as Alex bent over the dead body.

"What the hell are you doing?" Halter said.

"Looking for a radio. See if he called us in."

"And?"

"Nothing. No radio. Good. Here, take his gun. Bizon Two. Excellent weapon. Know how to use it?"

"Of course."

"Good. I hope the sound of those shots didn't carry up the face of that rock. Here are a couple of extra mags of ammunition. Let's move. I saw the house from the water. It stands right at the top of this granite cliff. But I think I saw a path up through the woods around that point. We'd better hurry. Time?"

"Nineteen minutes," Halter said, worry plain on his face.

"Let's go."

"God, this is close."

"I hope God's watching this channel," Hawke said, sprinting down the beach and up into the woods at a dead run. His mind was racing, too. Find Anastasia, find a way, any way at all, to get her away from her crazed father before he and Halter killed the man. Five-hundred-yard kill radius? Is that what Kuragin had said about the Beta's destructive range? He'd do it somehow, get her outside that circle of death.

But he was fast running out of time.

And Halter still had his finger on the trigger.

68

Hawke was first to reach the clearing at the top of the granite cliff. And first to see why the Tsar had been in such a hurry to get to the island of Morto.

By Tsarist standards, the house itself was nothing extraordinary. It was a four-story Swedish Baroque mansion, standing in a wide snowfield, pale yellow in the moonlight. The interesting thing was not the old mansion but the silver airship hovering just a hundred yards above a steel mooring mast on the rooftop. The ship was descending, coming in to dock. The same ship Hawke and Anastasia had flown to Moscow.

Handling lines were even now being tossed down from the bow to a crew waiting on the roof. Red navigation lights fore and aft were blinking, and there was a massive Soviet red star on the after part of the fuselage. On the flank, the word *Tsar* in huge red letters was illuminated. Korsakov was in a hurry to get out of Sweden and back to Fortress Russia, it seemed.

The rooftop was well lit. Hawke whipped out his monocular. He could see a number of sharpshooters and armed guards in addition to the ground crew now handling more tether lines as they were tossed down to the roof. At least the damn thing hadn't already taken off with Anastasia aboard. No, she was still somewhere inside that house. There was still a chance.

He'd find a way inside. Get her out of that house. And then —

"Crikey," Halter said, slightly out of breath, joining him at the edge of the woods. "A bit steep, that."

Hawke was too busy calculating the odds to reply. There was open ground all the way around this side of the house. It was perhaps a hundred yards to the covered entranceway at the front door. But he could circle around through the woods. Maybe the house was closer to the tree line around the back. He pulled the Walther from its holster, checked that there was a full mag and a round in the chamber. It wasn't much of a weapon against sharpshooters with SDV sniper rifles. But then, what the hell were you going to do? Life was seldom perfect.

"Time?" Hawke asked.

"Fifteen."

"A bloody lifetime," Hawke said. "I'm going inside that house and bring her out."

"That's insanity! It's wide-open ground for at least a hundred yards on all four sides of the house. Bloody suicide with those sharp-shooters up there, Alex. Use your head, man!"

But Halter saw a look in the man's cold blue eyes that told him any argument was a waste of precious time. He slipped out of his fur coat, spread it out on the snow, and placed the machine carefully on top of it. With practiced fingers, he knelt on the bearskin, opened the Beta, and booted it up. Then he flipped an illuminated red toggle, arming the unit.

"Do what you have to do, Stefan. I'd do the same in your shoes. But I'm going inside that house now. I'll get her out. Or I won't. If I'm not back in ten minutes, with or without Anastasia, blow the whole damn house down. Kill the madman and everyone else inside. A million lives are at stake. It doesn't matter who dies in there to prevent that."

"Alex, listen, it's bloody *over.* I'm sorry about your friend in there. But you can't help her now. You won't get twenty feet across that open ground. They've got night-vision equip-ment. I can't even give you covering fire with the Bizon, because they'd take me out before I triggered the detonator. Christ, just wait until he boards. We'll take him out when the ship's over the fjord. I'm just sorry as hell, but that's the end of it."

"I have no choice, Stefan. I'd rather die out

there in the snow than live the rest of my life
knowing I didn't try to save her. All right?
You understand that?"

"I guess I do, Alex, God help me."

"Good enough. Give 'em hell when the
time comes. Cheers, mate."

"Cheers."

"Here goes nothing," Hawke said with a
smile, and then he was on his feet and running across the impossibly broad expanse of
moonlit snow, head down, arms and legs
pumping, the covered entryway to house only
sixty or so yards away now . . .

He almost made it.

Shots rang out, three or four bursts of
them, heavy automatic-weapons fire from the
roof. There were little geysers of snow erupting all around the running and spinning
Englishman. He dodged and darted, keeping
his head down, sprinting like a madman,
desperately zigzagging for the safety of the
entryway.

The first round caught Hawke in the right
shoulder and spun him completely around.
Halter, watching his new friend from just
inside the tree line, found the shocking sight
of his red-black blood spraying voluminously
over the white snow horrifying. But Hawke
managed somehow to keep his feet beneath
him and keep moving toward the house.
Another round caught him in the left thigh,
and he spun again, his left knee barely graz-

ing the snow before he rose again and limped forward, dragging his wounded leg through the crusty snow.

Halter watched him raise the little Walther and fire at the men above who were killing him, even as yet another and another round struck him, and he collapsed to the ground. Hawke lay there, motionless, gazing up at the stars, small snow geysers erupting all around him, some missing, some of them no doubt finding their target. Halter checked his watch and looked down at the machine.

Then his eyes returned to his comrade, alone out on the snow, gravely wounded, surely dying.

He looked at his watch. Eleven minutes. Was that time enough to run out there and try to drag Hawke back to the safety of the woods? And still take out the Tsar before he used his own Beta machine to kill a million people? Maybe just enough time. But he could be shot down himself, of course, die trying to save this brave man. A man who would so willingly, so *cheerfully,* sacrifice his own life to save the woman he loved.

It would be a death well worth dying, he thought, trying to save the life of a man as noble as this one. Yes, he could comfortably live, or die, with that.

Or he could sit safely in the woods as Hawke died, bled to death out there on the snow, knowing that by staying put, he was perhaps saving the lives of a million souls. It was what Hawke had wanted him to do. What he'd told him to do, in fact. But if he did that, was he any more worthy than the monster they'd both vowed to kill? If he wasn't willing at least to *try* to save Hawke's life, what made him one iota better than his avowed enemy?

Bugger all, he thought, seeing Hawke's inert body twitch as another round struck home. He might actually succeed, after all, he told himself. Save Hawke and still pull the Beta trigger in time.

It would be a very close thing.

Professor Stefanovich Halter had a decision to make.

Hawke was alive, for the moment, anyway. But he knew he was not far from death. Blood was pumping out of him from too many places. A gentle snow had begun to fall. He closed his eyes. The snowflakes felt like butterfly wings grazing his cheeks. He knew he'd failed. But he also knew he'd tried. And so it would end. He'd done his duty. There was nothing left to think or say. It was, finally, over.

The screams from the third-floor bedroom could be heard throughout the house. The elderly Swedish servants paused and looked at each other, shook their heads, and went on about their duties. They were long accustomed to these horrible cries.

Every summer, they would come to Morto, the widowed count, his beautiful daughter, and the twin boys. And over the course of every summer, since her childhood, the father had found reason to beat his daughter. Beat her when he was angry. Or depressed. Or had swilled too much vodka after supper. Beat her and whipped her so badly that sometimes the doctor had to be fetched from the mainland.

One night, when the poor child was only ten or eleven, Dr. Lundvig had come out of Anastasia's room with sadness in his eyes and softly closed the door. Waiting for him in the darkened hallway, he had found Katerina Arnborg, the head housekeeper. He confided that he'd seen evidence of other kinds of abuse. He whispered to her that it was so vile that perhaps the police should be notified.

But Katerina had been terrified of the count's wrath, and so she had never told a living soul. The old doctor had never come back to Morto Island. He'd died a month or so later, drowned in a boating accident out on the fjord in the middle of the night. An unsolved mystery to this day.

The next doctor they'd had was a Russian from Stalingrad, and he never said anything to anyone when he emerged from the child's room.

Katerina now stood on the stairway landing below Anastasia's bedroom, listening to the two of them up there as he caned her mercilessly. She still hated herself for her cowardice, not saying anything all these years, and now it was far, far too late for that.

She'd never seen the count so drunk as when he'd arrived home from the Nobel ceremony. He was raging at his daughter as he dragged her up the stairs behind him. Suddenly, the screams coming from the child's bedroom were even louder.

And inside the bedroom, "Get away from me, you bastard! No more. I'm a grown woman! Not your little whipping girl who cowers before the great —"

"Traitor! You think I don't know what's going on? I told you to rid yourself of that bastard child growing inside you. And did you listen? No! No! And . . . no!"

"I *hate* you! Do you understand that? I've always hated you! Even your own sons despise you for the monster you are! You have no idea how much we all laugh at your stupid arrogance, your perverted —"

"Silence! You knew what he was going to do tonight. You planned it together, didn't you? Humiliate me before the whole world. You are a traitor, Anastasia. To me, and to all of Russia. You don't deserve to live."

"It's not true. As much as I've learned to loathe you, I'd never conspire against you. I love Russia too much, God help me."

"Get up! Get on the bed. And then —"

"Never! If you think that is ever, *ever* going to happen again, you are truly mad. You'll have to kill me if that's what you want. I know you're angry with him, for what he did to you tonight, but I love him and I'm going to marry him and have his child!"

"In hell, perhaps."

"You should see yourself now, standing there. The mighty Tsar. Beating his pregnant daughter. How majestic! How brave and noble he is! How —"

From outside, the unmistakable sound of gunfire. Heavy automatic weapons. The Tsar smiled as he looked toward the window, Anastasia's small bedroom repeatedly lit with bright flashes from the rooftop above. He dropped the cane and moved to the window.

"Silence, daughter! You think he's coming for you? Your great hero arrived to save you, is he? Come here and have a look!"

"Please. Just go. Leave me alone."

"The spy is dead, Anastasia. Do you hear me? Dead."

"What are you saying?"

"I knew he was coming here for me. Following me, this arrogant British spy. And I was ready for him. Don't you want to see him? Your dead lover? Get up and see for yourself!"

He seized her arm and dragged her bodily

over to the window, took her face in his violently shaking hand and pressed it against the windowpane, forcing her to look down into the snow-covered gardens.

He lay faceup in the snow, his arms flung wide. There was blood everywhere, on his body, on the snow around him, spreading black in the moonlight. He was still, and the snow was falling on his face. It was true. Alex was gone.

"Oh. Oh, my God, you've murdered him, you madman, the only human being I've ever loved!"

"Get some clothes on. We're leaving for St. Petersburg. The doctor will come for you in two minutes. He'll give you something to calm you down. I have some important business to attend to during the crossing. Soon the people who humiliated me tonight will feel the pain. Tonight begins the end of the West and the glorious triumph of Mother Russia. And you, my little traitor, will be a witness to history."

The door slammed, and the monster, too, was gone.

69

Halter burst out of the woods at a full run. He had the automatic rifle at his shoulder and was firing up at the clearly silhouetted snipers on the roof. He had the element of surprise and, with his weapon on full auto and at this range, even moving, his fire suppression was instantly effective and deadly. He saw two snipers pitch forward and plummet four floors to the snowy ground below. The deaths of two comrades caused a sudden, if momentary, cessation of fire from above. Heads disappeared beneath the parapet.

His wholly unexpected appearance and the Bizon's vicious firepower gave him a few precious seconds to reach his fallen comrade. Hawke lay on his back in a spreading pool of blood-soaked snow. He was conscious and breathing, Halter saw, quick shallow breaths, but he was grievously wounded in any number of places and losing a lot of blood. Another second or two out here, and they'd both be dead.

"Give me a hand here, will you, old sport?" Hawke gasped, his voice hoarse with pain.

Halter couldn't carry him, but he got an arm under him, and Hawke made use of his one good leg, getting to his feet with a rush of pure adrenaline. The two men moved surprisingly swiftly toward the woods. Halter was deceptively strong, and Hawke was hobbling but determinedly keeping up with him as best he could. They were totally exposed, and both men fully expected to die before they reached the tree line.

Suddenly, more sporadic fire erupted from the roof, rounds thunking into the ground all around them as they struggled toward the safety of the tree line barely twenty yards away.

Halter paused, turned, and unleashed another lethal burst of heavy fire with the Bizon on full auto, great thumping rounds that blasted chunks of cement from the parapet and either killed or wounded at least some of those still trying to bring them down. Hawke was still on his feet, using Halter for support, and he emptied the Walther's magazine at the remaining guards visible on the rooftop. Two more pitched forward into space, and under this final bit of covering fire, the two men were able to dive into the relative safety of the thick woods.

■ ■ ■ ■

They quickly found the bearskin in the small clearing, and Halter gently lowered Hawke to the ground. Rounds were still striking the trees around and above them, whistling and cracking in the branches, sending showers of freshly fallen snow down on the two men. Halter took a moment to examine the worst of Hawke's wounds.

"You'll live if you're lucky," Stefan told Hawke. He'd ripped his own shirt into strips and was applying tourniquets to the gravest injuries, pressing a folded piece of his white shirt into the very worst of them, the shoulder. The thigh and the rest of his injuries were flesh wounds, superficial. "That should do it. You'll be all right, at least until we can get you to a doctor."

"Goes without saying," Hawke murmured. He knew it was standard procedure to tell a dying man he was going to be perfectly all right.

"Just hold this compress on with your left hand, press it deeply into the shoulder wound. Now, where's that damn Zeiss scope of yours?" Hawke managed to pat the outside of his jacket, and Halter pulled the thing from the inside pocket.

"Time?" Hawke asked weakly.

"Three minutes. A bloody eternity, eh?"

Halter held the scope to his eye and peered up at the rooftop. The lights had been extinguished. But in the moonlight, he saw the Tsar running at a low crouch for the airship's bow entry stairway, surrounded by his cordon of security forces. He could see the liveried Maybach driver's cap, the big fellow named Kuba cradling the Beta machine attached to his wrist, two steps behind Korsakov as they mounted the steps and disappeared inside the hull.

A second later, two more men emerged from inside the house, bearing a stretcher. He couldn't make out any faces, but there was clearly a woman on the stretcher. He saw an arm fall limply, only to dangle over the side as she was lifted up inside the ship. Drugged, no doubt. He saw the sleeve of the full-length white ermine coat she'd been wearing at the Nobel ceremony and knew without a doubt it was the Tsar's daughter, Anastasia, on that stretcher.

"What's happening?" Hawke whispered.

"He's getting aboard. He'll be aloft in a few seconds."

"Is he — alone?"

"No, Alex. I'm sorry. She's traveling with him."

"Give me that bloody machine," Hawke said, his voice weak but grim.

"Alex, no. I'll do it. It's better if I do it."

Halter had the detonator in his hands now,

808

his forefinger poised on the illuminated red trigger button. Hawke had lost a lot of blood. His mind might not be clear. Halter eyed him carefully. Could he, even in this very last moment, try to save the woman he loved? It was not at all beyond the realm of possibility.

The great silver airship separated from the mooring mast and quickly rose twenty feet above the rooftop before commencing a slow turn to the east. She'd probably be headed out over the Baltic, across tiny Estonia, making her Russian landfall at St. Petersburg.

Halter, transfixed, watched the ship sail directly over him, clearly visible from the small clearing where he and Hawke remained on the bearskin.

"I *want* to do it, Stefan," Hawke said, his voice stronger now, perhaps, but full of strain and heartbreak. "It's my responsibility. The president ordered me to take this man out. It's my duty."

"Nonsense. I'm going to detonate, Alex. Ship's out over open water now. No danger of any fiery wreckage falling on the houses below. Can't wait a minute longer."

Hawke managed to sit up, his hands bloody from the gunshot wounds, his whole body shaking terribly. He held out both hands to Halter, his eyes following the endless passage of the airship.

"Please?" Hawke said.

"Why? Why must you do it?"

"I don't think I could ever forgive you, or me, if I sat here and watched you do it. But I might be able to forgive myself one day. I might. Because it's my *duty*, Stefan."

Halter handed him the detonator, helping him hold it, because Hawke's hands were shaking so badly and slippery with his own blood.

They could still see the majestic airship plainly through the bare treetops of the forest. She had sailed out over the fjord, her powerful motors helped by the prevailing winds. She was lovely to see, a gleaming silver arrow in the full moonlight. Her winking red lights reflected on the surface of the water below as she sailed away, bound for the opposite shore.

"What are you waiting for, Alex?"

"Nothing," he said, his voice already dead, moving his finger to the trigger.

Hawke wasn't thinking of Korsakov or the evil that madman intended to wreak upon the world as the final minutes and seconds wound down.

He was thinking only of his beloved Anastasia as he rested his finger on the blinking red button that would end her life.

How she'd looked emerging from the water that sunny afternoon on Bermuda so long ago. How grand and full of life she'd been racing the sleigh across the snowy Russian landscape, the reins of the troika in her hands, shouting commands at her chargers. And the warm, perfumed nearness of her in the darkened box at the Bolshoi, that moment when she'd leaned over and whispered those words, telling him he was going to be a father.

He hadn't saved her, hadn't saved either of them, had he?

He had loved her so.

His finger moved of its own accord and pushed the button.

It began with a crack in the sky. The sound of the explosion was unimaginable, as if atoms were splitting. A great thunder rolled through the forest, a shockwave bending the trees in its path. The world was suddenly illuminated with false daylight, a supernova of blinding orange, and the high branches of the trees above Hawke's head stood in stark relief, like skeletal images in an X-ray.

He leaned forward and saw the *Tsar* erupt into flames, first at the bow and then racing along the fuselage toward the stern. He heard loud cracking noises, probably massive internal bracing wires snapping inside. The thin fabric skin of the outer hull, supposedly flame-retardant and self-extinguishing, was soon hanging in tattered bits from the skeleton of the frame, some of it already consumed by the fiery blast. Burning fuel spewing upward from the top of the ship was causing low pressure inside, allowing atmospheric pressure to collapse the hull into itself.

There was another muffled detonation and a resounding thud as the *Tsar*'s back broke. He saw the great ship crack in half, and the rapid expulsion of gas made the little remaining skin at the stern begin to deflate. Flames were still climbing four or five hundred feet into the air.

No one could have survived that, Hawke thought. Burning bodies and huge chunks of flaming superstructure were falling into the fjord when he finally looked away. He closed his eyes and lay back against the bearskin.

"Listen," Stefan said, bending over him. "You've lost a lot of blood, dear boy, and I've got to get you to a doctor as quickly as possible. Dalaro's large enough to have at least an emergency trauma center. I think the fastest thing is to take the speedboat back to the town dock. Have an ambulance meet us there."

"Let's go," Hawke murmured, raising his head to look at Halter, his voice very weak, beginning to go.

"Alex, there's no way you can make it through the woods all the way back to the boat. I'm going to get the boat and bring it around to this part of the island. Then we'll get you down the trail somehow. Just lie here and rest. I'll be back in ten minutes."

"Thank you for . . . for . . ." Hawke whispered. He wanted to thank the man for saving his life but couldn't summon the strength. He let his head fall back against the bearskin, listening to the crunch of snow as Halter quickly made his way down through the woods to the water. He looked up into the whirl of falling snowflakes, trying to focus on just one. Focus. He needed focus.

The president. Had to call the president. Tell him the threat had been blown away. He still had his phone? Where? He patted himself down, feeling all of his pockets.

After a few moments, he dug his hand inside his blood-soaked trouser pocket and pulled out his mobile. He wiped some of the blood away from the keypad with his sleeve and held the thing unsteadily right in front of his face. He needed to call the president. Now. Tell him the Tsar was dead. That the immediate danger was over. The Beta, the football, gone. His message light was blinking. Maybe the president had called him. Yes. That's what had happened.

He punched the code to get his messages.

He held the phone to his ear.

"Alex? Darling? It's me. Oh, I do wish you'd pick up one of these times. We haven't spoken in so long, and I've so much to tell you. First of all, I love you with all my heart. Madly, deeply, truly. But you already know that, of course. And now, the news. I saw a doctor here in Stock-

holm this morning, a baby doctor, you know, and he did a sonogram. We have a beautiful healthy baby on the way, darling. And they can even tell the sex! Do you want to know? Now? Or should I wait and tell you in person later tonight when I see you at the ceremony? Oh, I've been so torn about it all day. What to do, what to do? Oh, I do have to tell you, I must, or I'll just burst. Ready? It's a boy, Alex. I'm going to have your son, darling! Isn't that the most wonderful news in the world? I love you so very much. I can't wait to see you tonight. I do hope you're still coming. I love you, Alex Hawke. We have our whole wonderful lives in front of us, darling. I'm so happy. Good-bye."

Hawke heard the guard dogs first. The guards themselves were right behind them. Flashlight beams crisscrossed wildly over his head as they all crashed through the woods toward him, shouting furious directions in Russian. He rolled over and grabbed the Bizon, shoved in a fresh magazine, and racked the slide. He waited until he could see the eyes of the snarling dogs tearing through the woods right toward him, and then he started firing at everything that moved, his eyes blurred with tears.

EPILOGUE

The treasure hunter had been down too long; the air in his lungs was nearly exhausted. He'd been diving the wreck most of the day. Free diving, without tanks, since the wreck lay in fairly shallow water, only down about twenty feet or so. Besides, he'd never much cared for canned air. The water was pellucid this time of day, and shafts of sunlight streaked down through the blue, dappling the sand and coral.

The wreck, what was left of it, was lying on its side, surrounded by tunnels and small caves, home to parrotfish and grouper, all of them come out to dine. They hovered nearby, hoping for any delicious morsels, worms or tiny crustaceans, that might float their way in the clouds of sand stirred up by his digging.

There are more than three hundred fifty documented wrecks ringing the island of Bermuda, and he'd visited a few, the *Hermes,* the *Iristo,* and the *Mary Celestia.* This one was undocumented and not much prized by tourists or historians, but there was treasure here, there had to be. He'd begun the exploration earlier in the day, with high hopes and great enthusiasm.

But he was tired now, early hopes had faded, and this would be his last dive. He thought he saw something, a brief glimmer, but a school of bright blue-and-yellow surgeonfish fluttered by his mask, obscuring his view. When he looked again, nothing. A fluke of light, perhaps, that's all it had been.

Moments earlier, kicking his way along the hull, he'd been keenly aware of a rather large barracuda. The fish, sleek as a blade, was hanging motionless, staring at him with one white-rimmed black eye, his jaw agape and filled with ragged, needle-sharp teeth. Barracudas always gave him the creeps, and he was relieved when the big fellow moved on.

His lungs burning for air, the diver willed himself to stay down longer. There was one area at the bow he'd not yet searched, and he was just pushing along the bottom in that direction when he saw a flash, something protruding from the sand, out of the corner of his eye. Feeling a tingle of excitement, he pushed off the bottom and swam to his right.

The treasure he sought was partially hidden. The only reason he'd spied it at all was a random streak of sunlight. It lay beneath a long, thick timber, half buried in sand. He shot his hand forward toward the glitter, and his fingers closed around it.

He kicked hard for the surface, lungs afire.

A few seconds later, his clenched fist broke the surface. His head followed, and he pushed his dive mask back on his forehead. Grinning widely, he raised his balled fist aloft in triumph. After many long hours of free-diving the wreck, by God, he'd bloody well got his treasure.

He looked around, eyes squinting in the fiery afternoon sun. His small sloop, *Gin Fizz,* was bobbing at anchor fifty yards away. He swam for her, deep, powerful strokes through the chop, the treasure still clenched in his tight fist. When he reached his boat, he kicked his flippers and hauled himself aboard at the stern.

The wind had freshened considerably and was filling in from the southwest. He hauled down on the halyard raising his mainsail, and a few moments later, the *Gin Fizz* had her lee'ard rail down, her course set north-nor'east for St. George's Harbor. He saw Nonsuch Island off his port beam and shortly thereafter a tall white tower with a broad red band, St. David's Light. The sky was darkening to the west, and he tapped the glass on his cockpit-mounted barometer. The needle dropped quickly to 29.5. In the distance, high, thin cirrus clouds crept across the sky.

At Gunner Bay, the first fat drops of rain

struck him in the face. Although he couldn't have told you why, he made a decision. Rather than put into St. George's Harbor and head for the yard on the southern tip of Ordnance Island, where the *Gin* would undergo some much-needed work on her old gasoline engine, he would continue on around the eastern tip of St. George's. His Norton was parked at the town docks, so he had no worries about getting home later, even after dark.

Half an hour on, he'd sailed through two short, blinding rain squalls, and another black mass of cloud was moving in from the southwest. He deliberated something inside himself for a moment and then reached into the lazerette and pulled out a cork-stoppered bottle of Gosling's black rum. Keeping one hand on the tiller, the mainsheet wound tightly round his wrist, he plucked out the cork with his teeth and took a healthy swig. It was almost five o'clock, and anyway, what the hell?

As his old chum Harry Brock was wont to say, "Any poor bastard who doesn't drink, when he wakes up, he knows that's the best he's going to feel all day."

After his recovery, the first two months of which had been spent at a private hospital outside Stockholm, he'd headed back to Bermuda and Teakettle Cottage. He simply couldn't face another cold, wet spring in London.

The sea and the sunshine had gradually worked their way back inside his bones, if not his heart. For a while, he actually thought he'd gotten everything back to plumb, level, and square. But an odd thing had happened. He couldn't sleep. He'd wake up suddenly at all hours of the night, sit straight up in bed, drenched in sweat, panting, a flaming orange glow imprinted on his retinas. He'd try to go back to sleep, lie there for an hour or more, but it was useless.

He'd pad out to the bar, have a seat, and pour himself a stiff one. Sometimes one, sometimes two, sometimes more. And then, somnolent at last, he'd go back to his bed, sometimes sleeping until dawn. But sometimes not. The odd thing was, he'd grown rather fond of his insomnia. Sitting alone at his carved monkey-wood bar, some scratchy old Cole Porter disc on the Victrola, drinking rum in the dark, all of the ghosts banished to the dark corners and recesses above the rafters.

A few mornings, Pelham would find him, head down on the bar, snoring loudly, an empty bottle standing guard over him. And once or twice lately, he was pained to admit, Pelham had found him sprawled on the floor.

He was sailing nor'west now, around the eastern tip of Bermuda, coming up on Tobacco Bay. And beyond that pretty little bay, he thought, taking another swig, easing the *Gin*'s mainsheet, was another pretty lagoon called Half Moon Bay. It was well hidden, tucked inside the mangroves that ringed the island called Powder Hill.

He tied the *Gin* up at the dock and walked ashore in the hard rain, bottle to hand.

Looking up at her house, he noticed that the pink bougainvillea on the upstairs verandah was badly in need of a good pruning. And the front door was hanging open, swinging back and forth in the strong wind, the rain gusting inside. The wooden shutters, faded and peeling, were banging in the breeze.

He entered the dark house and closed the door behind him. He climbed the familiar stairs like a sleepwalker, surprised to find himself standing inside her shadowy studio, listening to the rain beat a steady tattoo on the tin roof.

He let his eyes grow accustomed to the square, high-ceilinged room — the easels, paint pots, and stacked canvases, the fan-shaped wicker chaise that looked like an emperor's throne. He felt lightheaded and collapsed into the nearest chair, a deeply upholstered one facing the fireplace. It was getting very dark in the studio now; the sun was low. He found a match and lit a small oil lantern on the table. It threw a flickering light on the walls.

After a moment, he looked up at the painting hanging over the mantel and heard a voice.

I've always reserved that spot for the man I love. That's my father.

Anastasia had spoken to him. Yes. She'd been sitting over there on a blue stool, working at her easel, just before she'd dematerialized.

But it wasn't her father in the gilded frame.

No, it was his portrait hanging there.

Stretched out naked, on the fan-shaped chaise, in the light of a golden afternoon.

He sat and stared at the portrait for a while. It was a good enough likeness, he supposed, this fellow in the wicker chaise, but it wasn't at all him. No, the man in the portrait was someone else. He had light in his eyes, blood pumping in his veins, a pulse quickening beneath the skin.

The man up there was alive and in love.

He got up, thinking he'd take the painting down and shove it into the stone fireplace, smelling of old damp wood. Toss the lantern in on top of it.

Watch it burn.

Standing at the hearth, the lantern in his hand, he saw that there was already a burned painting in the fireplace. He saw a charred bit of heavy gilt frame, a whole corner of it. He knelt down and pulled it out, removed what was left of the painting, out onto the hearthstone.

The frame and canvas hadn't burned completely. A charred bit of her father's handsome face was still staring out at the world, his hand holding the reins of the fierce white stallion, looking every bit the great hero.

Ivan the Conqueror.

He blew out the lantern and returned to the *Gin*.

The rain had let up. He could sail back to St. George's, pick up his motorcycle, and still be at Shadowlands in time for dinner.

"Alex Hawke, you're positively drenched," Lady Diana Mars said, ushering him into the library, where his friend Ambrose sat before the fire. Congreve got to his feet and opened his arms, embracing Hawke.

"Darling, get him a sweater or something, would you, please?" he asked Diana. "He'll catch his death in those wet clothes."

"Certainly, darling," she said, and hurried from the room to fetch something for him.

"Sit down, Alex, close to the fire. Drink?"

"I've already had enough, thank you," Hawke said, taking the chair next to Congreve's.

"You know, I've been meaning to talk to you about that. Diana and I are both a little concerned about your drinking and —"

Hawke smiled. "Please, Ambrose, not now.

I want this to be a happy night. I've even brought you something, you see. Something for you to give to Diana."

"Really? What on earth?"

Hawke dug deep into his pocket and pulled out the treasure he'd found buried beneath the sea.

"What is it, Alex?"

"Have a look," he said, placing it in Ambrose's hand.

"It's Mother's ring!"

"It is, isn't it?"

"How on earth did you ever find it?"

"It was easy enough. I knew where to look."

"My God, Alex. I never thought I'd see it again. I cannot possibly thank you enough. You know, I'm going to give it to her tonight. I've waited too long as it is."

"Yes, you have. Don't wait a moment longer."

"Are you quite all right?"

"Splendid."

"Look at the firelight reflected in the stone. It is lovely, isn't it, Alex?"

"It is."

"A diamond is forever, as they say."

"Yes. Forever. I think I should be going. I just wanted you to have the ring." He got to his feet.

"Not staying for dinner? We're counting on you."

"Another time. I think tonight is for you

and Diana, Ambrose. Three's a crowd when a man is giving a woman a diamond ring. Represents eternity, you know. Serious business."

Congreve walked Alex through the house and out to the porte-cochere, where he'd parked his motorcycle.

"I can't tell you what this means to me, Alex. And to Diana. You've made us both so very happy."

"See you soon, I hope," Hawke said, climbing aboard the Norton and firing it up.

He rode out of the light and into the darkness of the trees, rain dripping from the heavy leaves.

He stopped at the coast road, debating which way to turn.

Left was home.

Right was someplace hot, smoky, and loud, where a man could drink in peace.

A diamond is forever, he said aloud, his words lost in the wind as he whipped his machine hard to the right, roaring along the coast beside the moonlit gun-metal sea, twisting the throttle hard, accelerating brutally up the hill.

No.

Nothing is forever.

Nothing.

ABOUT THE AUTHOR

Ted Bell is the former chairman of the board and worldwide creative director of Young & Rubicam, one of the largest advertising agencies in the world. He is the *New York Times* bestselling author of *Hawke, Assassin, Pirate, Spy,* and *Nick of Time* and makes his home in Palm Beach, Florida.

The employees of Thorndike Press hope you have enjoyed this Large Print book. All our Thorndike and Wheeler Large Print titles are designed for easy reading, and all our books are made to last. Other Thorndike Press Large Print books are available at your library, through selected bookstores, or directly from us.

For information about titles, please call:

(800) 223-1244

or visit our Web site at:

http://gale.cengage.com/thorndike

To share your comments, please write:

Publisher
Thorndike Press
295 Kennedy Memorial Drive
Waterville, ME 04901